ELEMENTAL CONVERGENCE

Books by Autumn Green

Aris Magica Series
(in reading order)
The Keepers of Aris
Elemental Convergence

ELEMENTAL CONVERGENCE

AUTUMN GREEN

Searching Souls-Kansas City, MO

The choices you make decide the future you will live;
So fight.

Prologue

Her eyes were red.

Cryis's breath hitched. He'd seen them like this before plenty of times, but the way Jay stared straight ahead was different as if she had just awoken from a long dream. The cabin grew silent now that her screams had stopped.

Cryis remembered what had happened just hours earlier—there had been so much blood. Ami had been tending to Taybeith's wounds when everything went wrong, Lyid had been resting nearby, and Riley and Dylan had yet to return from when they departed the cabin that morning. Then Jay had suddenly been drawn into her Soul World to face Aturdokht while the Demon inside Taybeith reawakened, and chaos ensued.

From the window across the room, the light sprinkled the bed, creating a spotlight on Jay. Cryis glanced behind him at Ami. She was slumped over Taybeith, and her hands were shaking, along with the serum she still held. The ends of her blonde hair were streaked in blood. Cryis wasn't sure if it belonged to her or Taybeith.

Taybeith was out cold underneath her. His black hair sprawled across his face, and his clothes were torn in various places. The needle from the syringe was still stuck in his neck. On the floor beside him, Lyid was leaning against the bed. He looked worse for wear, but his bulbous orb eyes stared ahead past Cryis in fear.

Cryis turned back to Jay. Slowly, he lifted his hands from her shoulder and scooted towards the end of the bed. Jay's long white hair was soaked in blood from the wound in her stomach. The purple veins that had been coming from under her skin had stopped pulsating and had faded back inside of her like a virus. With a wave of her hand, Cryis watched as Jay sealed the injury, turning it into a healed pink scar. Cryis's breath hitched; Jay was incredibly calm.

Behind him, Ami struggled to pull the syringe out of Taybeith's neck. Once she did, she re-hooked it to the tranquilizer and laid the tube on the bed beside Taybeith's unconscious body. Bruises covered her hands from where she had fought against him. Ami pushed her hair back behind her ears and looked over at Cryis with a worried expression. Cryis held out his hand, motioning for her to stop moving. He looked over at Jay. He could feel that something was wrong as her attention shifted from him to Ami.

"Princess," Cryis said cautiously, using the nickname he'd reserved for every Ancient. Jay turned her gaze back to him. Her eyes looked empty as if she didn't recognize any of them. She stared at him for what felt like a long time before Cryis could see life come back into her irises. The red in her eyes was ablaze with a sudden fire.

"You." Jay cruelly said. Her voice didn't sound like her own, but a voice Cryis would recognize anywhere. Her voice was cold and alluring, pulling him in.

Cryis felt his heart clench inside his chest.

Aturdokht. He thought alarmed.

In an instant, Jay moved from the top of the bed and was upon Cryis. Her hand grasped his mouth shut while the other went to his neck. She slammed him back into the post of the bunk bed. Cryis felt magic surging from Jay's hand into his skin, where they met. The power she held embolized his entire body from fighting back. A growing burning sensation worked its way from the outside in; his vision began to blur, and his mind started to grow blank at the smell of burning flesh. Cryis could barely see as Ami and Lyid approached Jay from behind.

No. Cryis thought, trying to warn them, but the way Jay held onto him, he couldn't speak.

Jay smiled wickedly down at him.

Cryis struggled under her grasp. The burning sensation spread from his face down his neck to the rest of his body. He began to feel it in his chest, quickly spreading to his heart. He felt as if he would burst.

Cryis watched as fire erupted out of Jay's opposite hand, sending both Ami and Lyid flying into the nearest wall. Neither one of them got back up.

Jay let go of Cryis. She looked drained, but only for a moment, and not long enough for Cryis to regain his composure. She grabbed his face in her hands again. Cryis felt the burning sensation once more as it scorched his skin. He let out a muffled, agonizing scream.

"You've always been quite the problem." Jay scoffed, Aturdokht's voice overlapping hers.

Cryis lifted his heavy arms and grabbed hold of both her wrists. He tried to pry her hands away, but her grip on his face only dug deeper. Jay's expression seemed to be satisfied with his struggle.

Cryis managed to move her hand just enough to speak. "Fight it." He said in one breath.

Jay chuckled, "Enough of your meddlesome nature. It ends today," she promised.

Cryis squeezed her wrists tighter, and using the little energy he had left, he began to pull. The burning feeling in his chest grew, setting itself apart from the pain he felt from Aturdokht's magic. Jay screamed, releasing Cryis, and he dropped to the floor, barely conscious. She held her hands to her chest, backing away from him. Cryis looked at her through weary eyes, and the last thing he saw was blue butterflies followed by gold tendrils between himself and Jay.

Chapter One

Cryis had been reliving the same memory every night, and the nightmare didn't end, whether he was asleep or awake.

"Damn." Cryis groaned. He slowly opened his eyes and was met with the concrete ceiling above him.

After losing Jay, when Cryis had first awakened, it had been to a burning cabin. He'd done his best to get Ami, Lyid, Taybeith, and himself to safety, but the fire had already consumed the safe house, leaving everyone suffering from injuries. Thankfully, Dylan and Riley never returned from their adventure that morning, and Cryis could only hope now that they were still safe.

With the Headmaster—sometimes called the Professor—and Doctor Herron still missing, Cryis called upon the only person he knew who could provide the medical help his friends needed without arousing suspicion from the Aris Magica Council and its Hunters about what had transpired. He knew it'd only be a matter of time until the council found out that Aturdokht had returned and had taken Jay as her vessel.

Despite knowing the deception Taybeith was capable of, Cryis's main priority was ensuring Ami, Lyid, and Taybeith survived. Back at the cabin, the Demon inside of Taybeith had nearly killed them, but it had also almost killed Taybeith as well, and Cryis couldn't leave him to die. Little did he know his quick thinking would land him in a human prison facility monitored by the CIA.

Cryis woke to find himself still in that very same jail cell. He wasn't sure how much time had passed but guessed it had been a few weeks at least, judging by the color of his burn marks. He didn't even know how the others were fairing, but he trusted they were being taken care of.

The cell he was in had no bars or windows, just a solitary box with a single locked door. Cryis had taken the liberty to brighten up the room by drawing a window beside his bed above the thousand tally marks inmates before him had scratched into the concrete. He had yet to add to the wall; he wasn't that desperate. He was still banking he wouldn't be in here for much longer. The room had one grotesque toilet pressed in the far corner, one shattered mirror hanging above the sink, and a shambled cot pushed up against the wall.

Cryis sat up from his bed and brought his knees to his chest, and his head fell between them. He couldn't get the image of Jay's red eyes out of his mind. To make matters worse, he kept feeling a presence in his thoughts ever since that night. It never spoke, but it was there consistently torturing him with the same dream.

Cryis stumbled out of bed and shuffled to the sink across the room. It only took him four steps to reach it. He turned on the water, which sputtered at first before falling at a steady stream. It didn't matter how long he ran the water—it would still be cold.

Cryis splashed some of the water on his face before turning it off. He looked up, meeting the gaze of his reflection in the broken mirror. The tips of his white hair were damp, pressed against his forehead, while the rest of his hair fell to his shoulders. It had grown over the past couple of weeks. His face was gaunt, his cheekbones sharp, and his skin ghostly pale, covered in small bruises and burn marks that had yet to fully heal. He'd been keeping himself malnourished since being brought here, making it difficult for his body to regenerate. He wasn't sure if he had no appetite for the food the guards brought him or if he was punishing himself for losing the one thing that mattered to him. He had no energy to pull from. Even an Immortal had their limits.

When Cryis had first arrived at the prison, he'd been unrecognizable. Both of his eyes had suffered, leaving him blind. His skin had been completely burned from the neck up. However, the next day, most of it was gone. It freaked a lot of the guards out, except for one agent, Luke Kanon.

Before arriving at the prison, Cryis had reached out to his contact, Vastille, but had been handed over to Agent Luke Kanon instead. Although Cryis had a long history with Vastille, he hadn't spoken to him in years, so Cryis wasn't shocked by the negligence. Cryis was aware that Vastille was an Aris Magician, and even though Kanon knew of their world, that fact had remained a secret.

Over the past few weeks, Cryis had come to tolerate Kanon, even though, generally, Cryis wasn't very fond of human company. From Cryis's experience with humans, their self-preservation always came first. Yet, Kanon had shown his determination to get Cryis and the others back on their feet and help put an end to the war between Aturdokht, even if his ways were ambiguous at times.

Cryis understood the necessity for Kanon to keep Aris Magica a secret from the other guards while still providing them the security they needed while they recovered. But he wasn't thrilled to be a prisoner until further notice.

Cryis gripped the sides of the sink, causing his knuckles to turn white. He continued to stare at himself in the mirror. Something inside him had broken free that day at the cabin. Ever since he fought against Jay, Cryis could feel a growing restless power within him. He recalled the blue butterflies he'd seen. Together the magic had formed a barrier between Jay and him that had saved his life. He remembered the fury he'd seen in Jay's eyes because of it. Cryis couldn't blame her, the magic both frightened and angered him. And ever since that day, Cryis's eyes had turned from their natural blue to a red, mimicking Jay's. He glared at his reflection. Just another reminder of his failure.

Cryis took a deep breath before pulling away from the sink. He backed against the wall in between the toilet and his cot. He knew what time it was; the guards were never late when it came to pestering him. Soon after, Cryis heard the familiar sound of footsteps and the jingle of keys approaching his cell.

Right on time. Cryis thought.

Cryis's stomach tightened from hunger, the next time he was offered food, he'd take it. He heard faint voices on the other side of the door.

The door swung open. Cryis stayed where he was, glued to the wall. One man walked in dressed in the standard navy blue guard uniform. The guard's hat was pushed low over his head, hiding every part of his face except for his angular chin. The guard kept his gaze to the ground. Beneath the cap, Cryis caught the familiar glimpse of buzzed orange hair. He'd been the most recent guard that had been assigned to tend to Cryis's injuries. Due to the timely precedent nature of his healing, Kanon had taken precautions to make sure it stayed mostly unnoticed by frequently switching the guards on Cryis's rotation. Cryis had only met him one other time, and he ignored any conversation the guard had attempted, wiping it from memory. The only thing that stood out to Cryis was his orange hair because it reminded him of a cat's fur. The guard pulled out a pair of silver handcuffs and began to approach Cryis.

Cryis was surprised to see the guard here without his first aid kit, the usual one with the handcuffs had been middle-aged and grumpy. Cryis shrugged. It didn't matter who took him to questioning; they were all the same.

Cryis held out his hands, putting his wrists together. He hated this part, every time, the guard would put them on too tight, and Cryis would have the worst time healing the rings they left around his skin. He assumed it was because Agent Kanon had yet to inform them that he wasn't the ruthless criminal they all were made to believe. Most humans didn't know about the existence of Aris Magicians. Cryis took comfort in knowing that hadn't changed; it meant Aturdokht had yet to make her move.

"That won't be necessary, I hope," Agent Kanon said, playing the role perfectly.

A tall black man walked through the door, stepping in front of the guard. As usual, the agent was dressed in a sharp black suit with a white undershirt. Cryis could tell by the fabric that his clothes were expensive and cared for. Kanon's hair was shaved as well, and his beard was freshly lined, sporting flecks of gray.

Cryis smirked, surprised to see Kanon this early in his rounds. Usually, he didn't get a visit from the agent until late afternoon, and lately, it was rarely a pleasant one, both parties left equally frustrated. Kanon dismissed the guard, who made sure to close the door behind him on his way out, leaving them alone.

Cryis let out a slow cat-calling whistle, "Agent Kanon, recruiting kind of young these days." He gestured to the door where the guard no doubt stood waiting on the other side. This time, Cryis had taken notice that the guard was much younger than the other guards he'd been assigned to.

"Please, call me Luke. After all, you've earned it." Kanon stepped closer to Cryis, closing the distance between them. "My hope is that we have become very close friends these past few weeks."

Cryis scoffed, slouching against the wall. "I'm honored, Luke."

Kanon smirked, annoying Cryis. All he wanted to do was cross the room and wipe that smug look off Kanon's face. Cryis hated being looked down on, especially by a child. He had walked the Earth far more times than Kanon could imagine.

Cryis took in a shaky breath, then another and another, until he felt calm again. "So, how long do you plan to keep me here?"

For the past week, he'd asked Kanon this question every day. He suspected by now the others were still undergoing treatment, if their injuries had been half as bad as the ones Cryis had sustained, they wouldn't be going anywhere for a while. But Cryis could no longer wait on them; he had to act soon if he hoped to have any chance of stopping Jay before Aturdokht could do any harm to anyone through her.

Cryis had known Aturdokht's plan for a long time. She wanted to throw the human world into disarray. In the past, Aturdokht had always had a vendetta to get rid of the humans, calling them a virus that plagued and misguided Aris Magicians. After she was finished with them, she would go for the council to take control of Aris Magica from the inside out.

The last time, Aturdokht had nearly completed her mission, only to be sealed by the previous Ancient before she could lay waste to the entirety of humanity. Instead, her acts had been covered up by fire season. Cryis knew, with her new-found body, she could easily achieve this, especially since the humans had no idea how to deal with magic they didn't even know existed. On top of all that, Aturdokht was cunning, she had more patience than Cryis had ever given her credit for. He hated to admit it, but he wasn't sure what she was capable of this time around.

Cryis sighed, not giving Kanon a chance to answer, "Look, I'm grateful for the help you've given me. You've helped me get back up on my feet and concealed our identities, but I can't stay here forever."

"You mean I've held up my end of the deal," Kanon said grimly.

Cryis drew his lips in a tight line. When Cryis had first arrived and asked about Vastille, Kanon had told him that he was taking a personal vacation and that he would oversee handling the case. Cryis had been wary at first, but even though human, Kanon had great knowledge of Aris Magicians, Aris Magica, the Headmaster, Jay, and the prophecy. The last one had caught Cryis's attention; very few knew of the prophecy. Better yet, the Headmaster trusted Kanon. It was the only reason Cryis had entrusted himself and the others to Kanon in the first place. But lately, something had changed within the man, and Cryis couldn't quite put his finger on it. After living as long as he had, he'd learned to be a good judge of character.

Still, Kanon was right; he had held up his side of the deal. He'd kept them all safe and hidden from Aturdokht and her forces. Kanon had explained under the guise of criminals, most of the guards stationed here wouldn't ask many questions. This helped the agent maintain control.

Kanon had promised the CIA was at his disposal in locating Jay. All Cryis had to do was help him find the Headmaster and Dylan. According to Kanon's sources, their safety was as crucial as finding Jay. Cryis knew he was right on that too. The Headmaster was an ally of the CIA from what Cryis had gathered, but Dylan was a direct connection to Jay and a weakness to Aturdokht. If given the chance, he knew Aturdokht wouldn't hesitate to get rid of the kid.

"And like I tell you every day, I have no idea where he is." Cryis paused. "Why? Has something outside changed?" Cryis saw a nerve twitch in Kanon's procured smile.

"It's not what you think," Kanon said, losing his smile. "From the stories Doctor Herron told me, I expected a sea of fire and magical beings to descend, but there's been absolutely nothing." He had finally closed the distance between

Cryis and him. "It's quite..." he paused before continuing, searching for the right words, "Disappointing."

Cryis quirked an eyebrow. *Disappointing?*

He didn't realize that word was even in Kanon's vocabulary. Usually, the man was keen on factual optimism that valued the safety of humanity.

What's changed? Cryis wondered anxiously.

He'd had a lot of time to think while recovering in prison. He knew things were different this time, with Jay being the last reincarnation of the Ancient. But, in the past, Aturdokht had never tried to take the Ancient as her vessel. He'd known Aturdokht since the beginning when she was still Mirama, a quiet village girl coming into her powers as a Witch. He'd even befriended her along with Emilia, the first Ancient. During their time of friendship, Cryis never thought Aturdokht had been patient, yet time and time again, she proved him wrong. To pull off what she had, embodying Jay, had taken time. Leaving Cryis to wonder what else she was capable of now. Still, it was hard for Cryis to believe that she suddenly was this much wiser now, he still sometimes saw her as that hopeful young girl—his friend.

Kanon narrowed his stare. "Regardless, you and your friends still pose a danger to society alone, even without this prophesied Witch. Which the Headmaster assured me was being handled." He leaned into Cryis so that they were nearly nose to nose. "This is what I get for trusting the fate of the world to a bunch of kids." Cryis rolled his eyes, taking offense. Kanon took a deep breath, putting a single step between them. "Try to understand from my point of view; my sole goal is to ensure the safety of the citizens of this country. I can't do that without some answers. You may not know where the boy and the Headmaster are now, but you know where they went."

Cryis frowned, why was Kanon so adamant about finding these two? He understood, but at the same time, he had assumed the CIA agent would also be searching for Jay just as hard, but he hadn't mentioned any update on finding her in the past week. Not like before.

The quiet presence inside his thoughts stirred, causing Cryis to grow alert. Kanon had given him no reason to distrust him, yet Cryis couldn't bring himself to tell the agent the truth. Although unsure of where Dylan had been heading, he was certain he knew where the Headmaster went.

"Where's Ami, Taybeith, and Lyid? I'd like to see them." Cryis asked instead, something inside him was prompting him to ask.

Cryis barely knew the kids, but as a favor to the Headmaster, he continued to keep their best interest in mind. Even if they had died because of their injuries, Cryis still wanted to know their whereabouts. It was his job as an Immortal to reap their souls and guide them to the next part of life. He closed his hands into fists, thinking the thought that they were gone from this world angered him. If he hadn't failed, they wouldn't be as involved as they were. Nonetheless, he needed to know what had happened to them.

"They're fine." Kanon stated flatly. He thought for a moment before adding. "Their injuries were far worse than yours, so they've been moved and kept in the ICU." A slow, audacious smile crept on his lips, sending a chill down Cryis's spine.

Cryis held his breath for a moment, what Kanon said made sense; their injuries could have been easily far worse than his, but for some reason, he didn't believe him.

"You'll get your answers once I get mine," Kanon finished.

Cryis groaned, annoyed. He pinched the bridge of his nose, looking away from Kanon. He shook his head, Cryis could see the stress written all over Kanon's face despite his curled smile. Kanon retraced his steps back to the door. He rested his hand on the knob. "It's imperative that we work together to put an end to this war before it's begun."

"Don't you think I know that...more than anyone," Cryis said defeatedly. Cryis pushed away the uncertain thoughts he had towards Kanon. The agent was right, and the more Cryis worked against Kanon, the worse it made things for everyone. He sighed, "The Headmaster left to take the other students into Aris Magica. My guess is he's still there, no doubt the council would let him leave as easily as he came."

But not without answers first, Cryis thought to himself.

The council took threats to Aris Magica seriously, even going as far as to start wars within the human world to cover up threats to the safety of Magicians.

"The council," Kanon muttered under his breath. Cryis quirked an eyebrow, not quite sure if he heard him correctly. Kanon cleared his throat, speaking louder. "So, he is safe, excellent news. This is indeed a start."

Cryis instantly regretted telling him even that, "So…"

Before Cryis could finish his thought, Kanon interrupted, "There's still the matter of the boy." He turned back to face Cryis, but his hand still rested on the doorknob.

"I'm sorry, but I really don't know where he is." Cryis said.

"I see…" Kanon nodded his head in acceptance, although his voice said otherwise. "In any regard, there is one other thing I'd like to address with you. In an effort to stay on equal footing with the threat at hand, I sent a task force to retrieve Doctor Herron's notes conducted on the serum. We were able to deduce some of her work noted on the original owner, Doctor Steuben's creation of it. I believe we humans cannot rely on the unknown protection of Aris Magica forever. Therefore, as a contingency, we should have our own way of protecting ourselves from—" His eyes lingered on Cryis with distaste, "your kind."

"What does that have to do with me?" Cryis asked.

"Everything, so I am told. At least by my lead scientist." Kanon impatiently tapped his foot. "Aris Magicians have a different notion of DNA sequence that can be extracted from the blood and altered to create a cure of a sort or a weapon, much like that serum that Jay and Dylan came for a couple of weeks ago. But apparently, the blood of an Immortal has a long-lasting effect." Kanon grimaced, "At the time, I didn't realize what I had in my possession had been so valuable."

When Kanon blinked, Cryis saw Kanon's brown eyes glass over to black. Cryis rubbed his own eyes, meeting Kanon's gaze again, but his eyes were his usual brown. Had Cryis imaged it? He hadn't been getting much sleep lately. Cryis stared for a moment longer, but Kanon's eyes never changed.

Cryis took a slow, deep breath in and out.

"And now what," Cryis asked, "You want to create your own? In the wrong hands, Luke, that could be dangerous. I'm sorry, but I can't assist you in creating that. The first one was as much of a mistake as this one."

When the Headmaster had first told Cryis of the serum's existence, it felt like an excellent solution to stripping Aturdokht of her powers for good, but after seeing Ami use it on Taybeith, he had his reservations. The boy had looked more dead than alive. Some part of him still hoped Aturdokht...no Mirama, could be saved. Plus, he knew Jay and Dylan had risked a lot to get such a weapon out of the hands of humans, he wouldn't be a part of putting it back in their grasp.

"It seems we are at a crossroads." Kanon said. Kanon turned towards the door again, when he spoke, he didn't bother to look back at Cryis. "You've given me no other option then." Kanon closed the door behind him, leaving Cryis alone, but not for long.

A few moments later, the door opened again, and four identically dressed guards marched in. Cryis instantly recognized one of them as his usual escort. He never cared enough to ask for his name, but he was the heavier-set man with a bushy mustache and a grumpy attitude. The closest guard whipped out a baton that cracked with electricity. Cryis pressed himself against the wall, with nowhere to run.

Cryis held up his hands in surrender, "Is this honestly necessary?" He glared at Kanon, who had returned, standing in the doorway. Cryis never resisted any request of them before, knowing it was just for show since Kanon had everyone believing he was a dangerous criminal.

"Turn around." The heavier guard commanded.

Cryis obeyed, facing the wall. If Cryis were at even half of his strength, he could have easily overpowered the guards and broken out of this prison. But with his body as weak as it was, one hit from the taser baton would knock him out instantly, and it would take days for him to recover on top of his already injured body.

Cryis felt the cool metal handcuffs snap over his wrists. "Easy." He warned.

"Shut your mouth." The same guard snapped, shoving Cryis forward. The other three guards followed Cryis closely on either side of him, creating a human box.

The five of them stopped in front of Kanon. "Take him to the basement," Kanon said. "Kazimir has set up shop there."

One of the guards shoved Cryis forward again, "Move, parasite."

Cryis grimaced as he passed Kanon. He wondered what horrendous story the agent must have told his men for them to willingly treat him this way. Perhaps the grueling murderer who found a way to live forever. Cryis chuckled to himself; it wouldn't be far from wrong. After all, living as long as he had, one was bound to bloody their hands eventually.

The guards led Cryis out the door and down a series of halls. Each hallway looked the same; each withheld a single metal door across a long wall. The lower they traveled, the more often the doors became. Cryis suspected each floor went by the level of crime. The worse ones were confined alone, much like him, while for the others, cell doors became replaced by bars, but the cells were empty. Cryis wondered why. Perhaps Kanon had designed a prison specifically for Aris Magicians.

The prison was unlike any normal prison Cryis had been in, lacking the normal cellmates and most likely located in a desolate place. Cryis had been unconscious when they brought him in, so he had no idea where they were located. Although, he doubted Kanon had enough time to transfer him out of the state of Oregon.

Cryis had only known him for a couple of weeks but easily discovered Kanon's distrust toward his kind, all because he couldn't understand that there were those more powerful than the human race. So, it wasn't unlikely that Kanon had found the means to create a separate confinement specifically for Aris Magicians, at the very least to keep them a secret for national security.

Cryis was more disappointed in himself for trusting the word of a human. He should have known it was only a matter of time before Kanon used Cryis and his friends for his benefit. Another serum would ensure the safety of humans but put innocent Aris Magicians at risk. Cryis knew deep down that Kanon saw all

Aris Magicians as a threat, and not just Aturdokht and the ones that followed her.

But still, something felt off about the situation. Cryis wasn't sure if it was the voice within him leaning him towards these thoughts or just his distrust of humans seeping through.

From the day Cryis had met Agent Kanon, he'd been a diplomatic man but not impatient. Yet, nearly every day, Kanon pressed Cryis for more information regarding finding Dylan and the Headmaster. Beforehand, although concerned for their safety, he'd stressed helping Cryis in finding Jay and putting an end to it all before things got out of hand and any humans got hurt. But now, it seemed his focus had shifted, but why?

The presence in Cryis thickened, consuming him with that question. He had a bad feeling, but Cryis knew he had no choice but to adhere to Kanon's request until he got to the bottom of it.

Chapter Two

Jay's long fingers tapped against the wood carving of the armrest. Beneath the red dress she wore, she had crossed her legs, also tapping the heel of her shoe into the base of the chair, or throne as Aturdokht liked to call it. Her patience was dwindling. Aturdokht had been so close to gaining another piece of the puzzle she'd been constructing, only to let it slip right through her fingers. She hadn't intended to come across another Elemental so soon.

The heavy doors across the room slid open, grating against the marble floor. Phagos walked in, the hatred Jay had once felt for him had turned into admiration. Underneath the dim light, his dark purple fur appeared almost black, while his horns caught a tiny glimpse of the light above them. He was dragging with him another desperate human. Their feeble expression brought satisfaction to her lips.

As he approached, Jay found herself saying, "Welcome back Phagos."

"My queen," Phagos said. He tossed the human's body forward. They scrambled forward, falling onto their knees. "I've brought you another one for your experiment."

Phagos had done an excellent job collecting humans and Magicians on her behalf without raising any attention from the Aris Magica council or human authorities. Most of their collection was built on people neither side would miss: runaways, criminals, and recluses alike. Jay frowned, taking in the frail form of the human at her feet. Magic coursed through her left hand as natural as breathing, and she used it to keep the person on their knees, kneeling. Since she'd bonded with Aturdokht, magic had come so much easier than before, even though it wasn't Jay controlling it but Aturdokht, Jay felt every moment of its power. "This one looks weaker than the last one you brought me."

Phagos grinned, "Not everyone will be as strong-willed as that Hybrid we captured."

Jay grimaced, disappointed, but only for a moment. "Speaking of, how is he?"

Phagos's grin widened, "The progress he's made is outstanding. I think he'll be ready to go within the next couple of days."

"Wonderful." Jay clasped her hands in her lap, "Even the council won't be able to stop what's coming." Hatred bubbled inside her, making it difficult for Jay to continue staying conscious within her mind.

"There is one more thing my queen," Phagos gleamed, "We found the Wizard."

No, Jay found herself thinking, but the thought was immediately squashed as Aturdokht's voice overpowered her again. "Wonderful. Who will go? Send someone with competence—"

"I'll retrieve him myself." Jay bristled but allowed Phagos's interruption to slide. "It will be faster this way."

"Very well. If the experiment is finished by that time, send some of them with you. I'd like to see how they do in the field." Jay finished. Phagos's grin turned into a snarl, but he didn't disagree. "And how is *my Wizard* recovering?" She asked, referring to Taybeith, the young man she'd retrieved a couple of days ago. Aturdokht had high hopes for him.

"He's awake, and he sent me to deliver a message."

"Oh." Jay leaned forward; he had been such a good informant for her before at the Institute, so she had no doubt his words would not bring happiness to her ears.

"The Immortal you search for is being held at that prison as well."

Once again, it had been so close. Her fingers curled, her nails digging into the wood. Fire rose along the walls around her. Still, her face maintained a perfect image of elegance and control. "Tell Kazimir to bring him to me."

Chapter Three

The pain was too much, startling Dylan from his sleep. It shot across his chest over the scar embedded in his skin, the one he had received from Aturdokht a few weeks ago. It was followed by an ache that traveled down his whole body. He awoke with a hand fisting the shirt above his heart, while the other hand with his trident scar held onto the bed sheets beneath him.

When he first opened his eyes, the world around him was blurry. He could barely make out the room around him or the clothes he wore. He stretched out his feet, relying on his other senses to help him. He felt a soft wool-like texture ahead of him; a blanket sat in a crumbled pile at the foot of his bed.

He craned his neck, seeing a shadow of movement to his right. A blurred person came into view, followed by the form of another. Dylan squinted his eyes at them, unable to see through the thick haze blocking his sight.

The pain in his chest expanded like a balloon. Dylan's forehead was drenched in sweat, and he was having trouble catching his breath. A stale smell overtook the room as the walls around him felt like they were closing in. Dylan felt smaller by the second. With every breath he took, his vision grew cloudy until, eventually, the darkness swallowed him.

A second passed before delicate, cool hands pressed against his rib cage, the pain growing, then fading, then growing again before an icy coolness enveloped him. His eyelids fluttered but were too heavy to open to see who was healing him. Despite his hysteria, Dylan had no trouble recognizing the gentle pull of magic.

A barrier of sounds broke into his mind as the fog slightly lifted. There was a steady beeping followed by the sound of pacing footsteps before Dylan's mind was able to settle on the sound of the two voices talking in gentle whispers before him.

A sigh filled with exhaustion before the voice of a girl spoke. "He had another attack."

Dylan felt a third hand press against his forehead, soothing his hair against his skin. Confusion crept at the edges of his mind; he was sure the voice had belonged to a girl, but the hand on his forehead was massive and weathered.

The hand fell away as the second voice spoke. "He'll be okay; it will just take some time." The second voice reassured. Dylan knew that voice, he'd heard it for years. It was the Headmaster.

It didn't make sense, how was the Headmaster here? Where was here? Dylan's thoughts felt so muddled he could barely make sense of them. Now and then, he'd get a glimpse of a girl wearing a white dress or a sword rushing towards him, but everything was jumbled together. Despite the healing he felt coursing through his body, his head ached from trying to recall any memories.

"We just had to be sure that..." The girl's last few words were drowned out by another series of noises Dylan picked up on.

Beside him, the beeping had stopped and was replaced by a revving hum of a machine. Another soothing yet icy coolness filled his body as the last of his panic resided, allowing him to take a full breath. His heartbeat slowed, and the hands from earlier slipped away.

"After today, I'll release his mind." There was a pause before she continued. Her voice seemed strained against her words. "It'll feel like a dream for a moment, but it'll all come back to him quickly and painfully. Are you sure you want me to stop?"

"He just needs rest." The Headmaster said. "You did what you thought was best; no one can fault you for that. But I implore you to tell him the truth when you're ready."

Finally, Dylan managed to blink open his eyes. It took him a second to break through the barrier of blurriness before he was left staring at...leaves.

"That's it. Deep breath in, deep breath out." The girl instructed. Dylan's hand fell from his chest to his side.

Dylan turned, facing a girl shrouded in light and staring down at him. For a minute, he mistook her for Jay, his eyes widening, and his heart skipped a beat, only for a moment. His vision cleared, giving him a full view of the girl before him. She had dark-rooted hair that was woven into blue-green braids, and she didn't look much older than he was. It wasn't her.

"Everything is going to be just fine." The stranger assured him. Dylan's eyes began to feel heavy once again as the warmth from his chest faded and darkness overtook him. "I promise."

Chapter Four

Dylan groaned, squeezing the bridge of his nose. For a moment, he had thought he had heard the Headmaster's voice, but that was impossible, Dylan reminded himself. After the attack on the Institute, the Headmaster left them to get the other students to safety. Dylan groaned a second time, he felt like crap and strung up on a series of drugs. He hadn't yet opened his eyes because he couldn't bring himself to. An elation of soreness spread throughout his muscles, but just as quickly, it subsided. Dylan felt as if he hadn't moved, slept, or eaten for a few days or more. In times like these, he missed Faith and her healing magic, whoever had healed him had done a sloppy job.

A lump grew in the back of Dylan's throat upon thinking of Faith's name. Dylan felt a tear fall from his eyes and roll down his chin. She was gone, and so were many others. His memories came back to him in broken pieces, events of the battle at the Institute came rushing back to him. Faith had been a nurse at his boarding school until she and so many others died in the fight against Aturdokht's forces, causing them to relocate to the safe house hidden deep within the forest. Dylan sighed, lifting a hand over his head. So much had happened in such a short time.

The room was quiet, the exception being the steady beeping coming from somewhere behind him.

It's too quiet. Dylan thought to himself.

He hadn't remembered the safe house being that way. Where was everybody? Dylan quickly sat up, his eyes flying open, blood rushing to his head and causing a spell of dizziness that turned the room. Dylan grabbed his head until the room stopped spinning.

Slowly, this time, Dylan surveyed his surroundings. His vision went out of focus but returned to normal in a matter of seconds after a few quick blinks. The leaves he had been met with before belonged to a long-potted plant that created a canopy over the bed. Dylan had been lying on a small, uneven, woven cot. A makeshift curtain from a patterned sheet hung from one side of the ceiling to the other, blocking him from seeing the rest of the room. The walls were woven with straw, just like his bed. Fresh light came in from the window on the opposite side of his part of the room.

The sun barely grazed the bottom of his bed and the floor beneath it. Dylan moved to get out of bed and paused. He looked down, finding his arm connected to an IV. He traced the IV back to the machine beside his bed that was hooked up to a secondary machine, revealing the source of the beeping. He'd seen the machinery plenty of times in hospitals to know that it was different from a human heart monitor and IV pump. Instead, the machine was filtered with magic, and instead of reading his heart rate, it read the levels of magic inside him. It wasn't a high number since being a Hybrid meant he didn't carry magic in the same way other breeds did, but it was within range: 70/340. Magic levels were much like a human's blood pressure; each breed displayed a different quota, but as long as they were within range, it could provide clarity on an Aris Magician's health.

He wasn't sure if he should remove it or not, but he also didn't feel comfortable just sitting here and waiting. Dylan looked down at the blanket covering him. It was a mint color that resembled the plant's leaves. He craned his neck towards the window. From where the bed was, he had a good view of the world outside.

Dylan peered out of the window to see a dozen dome-shaped huts forming a neighborhood. Each one was built with a low roof woven together by the same dark twig. The walls of the huts looked like they were made of a mixture of what resembled stone and clay, gently smoothed to form the base of each hut. From the huts, he could see there was also an archway covered with a bridge of flowers at each entrance.

The closest hut also had a stone pathway that looped around the side, disappearing into the gardens that lined either side of each outer wall. Dylan racked his brain, trying to think of any place in Oregon that matched what he was seeing, but he came up empty-handed. Even from the room, he could tell that the surface of the ground outside was flatter than he was used to.

Up above, Dylan saw a group of Fairies fly past, their wings a blur as they fluttered at incredible speed behind them. His mouth dropped open. He was still in Aris Magica. He leaned forward to get a better look at them, but the IV in his arm stopped him. Where the hell had Riley brought him?

"Riley!" Dylan shouted. But there was no answer. Dylan frowned. Even though his memories were a puzzle, he knew the last person he'd been with was Riley.

More of his memories began to resurface as if trying to piece together the puzzle. He remembered leaving the safe house early in the morning with Riley. They had just wanted to check out the road where Dylan had first met Aturdokht before stumbling into a trap. Phagos had been waiting for them, and Jay had shown up to help. Phagos had drawn his sword, but Jay had taken the attack intended for Riley and then nothing. Everything after was blank. It felt like something wasn't quite right, as if the memories he was trying to piece together were just splinters of a false reality.

"Ugh..." Dylan groaned as his head began to throb again.

He leaned his head back against the wall behind the bed and massaged the bridge of his nose. His head continued to pound even harder as Dylan pushed himself to remember more, but he was only met with a hazy blur of images. It was gone, his memory, well, not gone, but fragmented. Dylan took in five deep breaths, allowing for the headache to pass, but it didn't. His body felt weaker than it was, even with the injuries he'd sustained. He closed his eyes, letting his mind wander to the questions he'd been avoiding asking himself. Dylan gritted his teeth as the pain in his head returned.

The awakening. Jay…

The thought of her name sent his heart spiraling as fast as his mind was spinning. Dylan couldn't get the image of Phagos driving his sword through her stomach before everything went black again, repeating itself in a cycle. He clutched his heart, the pain from his head spreading.

Dylan slumped forward into the bed. His eyes darted back and forth between the bed and the machine, the rates of his magic spiking. He squeezed his eyes shut, focusing solely on his breathing. He repressed the memories he'd seen, focusing only on the steady sound the machine had to offer, finding a way to ground himself.

Slowly, Dylan's heart calmed, and the pain subsided from his head. He pushed every thought and uncertainty he had into a box deep in his mind. He could worry about Jay and the others after he figured out what was going on and where exactly he was.

"Riley?" Dylan repeated, his voice lacking as much strength as it had before. Still nothing. But the uneasy feeling Dylan felt came from what he'd just experienced. He'd never felt like that before, out of control of his emotions.

"What was that?" Dylan whispered breathlessly, rubbing his chest.

He looked straight ahead, staring at a spot on the wall where it met the ceiling. Had he just experienced a panic attack? Dylan sucked in a shaking breath before letting his hand fall to his side again. He looked down to find that same hand trembling. He covered his other hand with it. He had to find Riley, Jay…somebody.

Dylan went to remove the IV in his hands, but before he could, the curtain across the room slid open. His eyes widened in shock, seeing the girl with blue-green braids slip inside. When she spun around, her surprise reflected his.

"You're awake?" Her shock was quickly masked by indifference. "How are you feeling?"

Dylan looked from her to the empty room. "Is Riley there?" Dylan asked, uncertain.

"Riley?" The girl asked, feigning ignorance or confusion, Dylan couldn't tell. She still had one hand on the curtain. "Perhaps you should lie down." Even though it was a request, it felt like an order.

He couldn't help but notice how beautiful the girl was. She was tall, maybe even a bit taller than he was, and her body held an athletic shape to it. Her eyes were dark and foxlike. On either corner of her eyes, there was a faint blue swirled design that reached for her hairline, at first, it looked like makeup, but the more Dylan stared, he began to realize it was a tattoo. She wore a blue wrap that only covered her chest. The sleeves were made of leather wrapped around her forearms to her elbows. Her pants covered her navel but stopped mid-thigh as brown armor-pocketed flaps hung from either side of her hips. Beneath them were two hidden daggers on one side and a retractable spear on the other hip. Dylan suspected she used magic to conceal the spears' true size. Sheaves in her boots hid even more daggers. Dylan's fingers twitched, begging to get his hands on one of her daggers. They were his favorite weapon, and he missed his own.

Dylan found himself pulling the blanket to his chest. He was only in a thin paper shirt with no pants. Suddenly, he felt uncomfortable. He cleared his throat. "Where the hell am I?"

The girl sighed. "I..." She rethought her words. "Fairy District." She stated. "I'll go get the Headmaster; he wanted to know once you've awakened."

Dylan's eyes widened. The Headmaster was here, so he hadn't imagined it. Relief flooded through him, knowing that the answers he sought were so close. Perhaps the others had been relocated here as well. Maybe Jay had been as well.

Dylan watched as the girl before him tensed. Her grip on the curtains turned her knuckles white. He hadn't realized he'd said that out loud, but the girl's reaction to Jay's name unsettled him.

"How's your head?" The girl asked.

Dylan lifted his hand to his head, catching a glimpse of the trident scar on the inside of his left wrist. "It's fi—" His voice caught in his throat as another searing pain filled his head and shot down his spine as more memories rose to the surface. A woman wearing a black cloak was holding out a hand to him. "Aturdokht..." Dylan said breathlessly, gritting his teeth.

"Shit." The girl cursed, dashing toward him. "I'm sorry about this, but if I don't return them all to you now, you'll break." She placed a hand over Dylan's forehead. When he met her gaze through his tears, he saw guilt flash in her eyes. "I'm truly sorry about this."

Chapter Five

Cryis was led to an elevator at the end of the hall after taking so many stairs to get to it. The guards ushered him inside and pressed *b*. Cryis closed his eyes for the ride down. The light that came from the elevator's ceiling was too bright to handle. His cell had little to no light. The only bulb hanging from the ceiling was dimmed, anything brighter, and it took Cryis's eyes a while to adjust.

The elevator finally stopped, reaching its destination. Cryis was surprised to find the basement level of the complex so small compared to the levels above. It wasn't even the length of one of the hallways. Right as they exited the elevator, there was a door. They walked through the door, only to be immediately met by another.

Cryis found himself staring at the back of a room that could only be a few square feet. In the center of the room was a table with two chairs on opposite ends. On the far back wall was another table with test tubes and an assortment of medical equipment. In front of the chair closest to him were handcuffs attached to a chain coming out of the table. At the base of the chair was another set of cuffs coming out of the floor. To the left of them was a huge double-sided mirror. Cryis knew that the other side held more guards watching him.

"I don't want any funny business out of you." The guard said. Not recognizing the voice, Cryis looked over at the guard and found it to be the young man from earlier.

Cryis tilted his head curiously, finally getting a better look at the guard. Cryis was right to think the guard was still a kid no older than eighteen or nineteen. The guard's face was clean-shaven, and the bridge of his nose looked like it had been broken before, but what stood out the most to Cryis was the guard's eyes. They were a deep fuchsia. Cryis blinked, thinking he'd seen them wrong.

The guard must have noticed; he quickly lowered his hat, further hiding his eyes. "You—" Cryis's voice trailed off, he recognized those eyes.

Cryis used to know someone with the same kind of eyes. He tried to think of the person, but a pain struck through his mind, throbbing behind his eyes. Cryis looked away, panting breathless from the sudden attack.

What the hell, he thought. That was a first; he couldn't remember a thing.

The other three guards pulled Cryis from his daze, forcing him to sit down in the chair. They removed the cuffs from his hands and placed them into the handcuffs attached to the table. They locked his ankles in the chain on the ground. Cryis kept his eyes strained on the young man as he slowly walked away back towards the door.

Cryis had seen it correctly, the boy's eyes were indeed an unnatural color. A very rare color he'd never known a human to have. And only one Aris Magician. Cryis saw a dark face hovering over him with the same eyes before the memory quickly faded as the headache began to start back up. Cryis still couldn't quite remember; it had been so long, but they were the last eyes he'd seen right before becoming an Immortal.

"Wait...you." Cryis wasn't even sure what he wanted to say.

Cryis couldn't exactly tell this boy where he'd seen those eyes before. Even if Kanon had told them magic existed, it was still a lot to comprehend that people could live forever. Plus, Cryis had been alive for so long, memories from his life before becoming an Immortal had faded a long time ago or had become too skewed to tell the truth from reality. Cryis shook his head; he could be wrong about the boy's eyes.

"Whatcha lookin' at moron?" The heavier guard teased. He thumped Cryis in the back of the head. "Eyes forward."

Cryis wiped his bewildered expression from his face. He sighed, deciding to let it go, but kept his attention on the younger guard. "Could I maybe get a hamburger before all this begins, I'm starving." Cryis leaned back in his chair, making the chains attached to his wrists rattle. "Preferably grass-fed. I'm turning over a new leaf." He taunted.

The young guard smirked, amused. The older guard glared at him and then turned to Cryis, saying, "It's your own fault for never eating the food we bring you." He huffed, "I'm not sure why Agent Kanon even requires us to bring food to a criminal like you anyway." The guard's arrogant smile widened. "If it were up to me, I'd let you starve, but you do a good job doing that yourself. Makes my job a lot easier."

Cryis rattled the chains as he held his hands out in a shocked expression, "Oh really? So, these chains are just an added peace of mind for the weak guy?"

The guard's smile vanished quickly, replaced by anger. "Why you!" He grabbed Cryis by the collar of his shirt. Cryis chuckled. The guard pulled back his arm, ready to throw a punch. Before any contact was made, the younger guard grabbed hold of the older guard's elbow, stopping him.

"Wait!" The boy shouted. He looked back at Cryis nervously. Under the pale light, the boy's eyes became more electrifying. A pain shot through Cryis's head again as a weighted sense of familiarity came over him from the guard's gaze.

A man with dark skin like coal and long white dreads appeared in Cryis's mind. The man had scars all over him, running up his arms and face. As quickly as he appeared, he disappeared, leaving Cryis riddled with questions.

"What was that?" Cryis mumbled. Nothing like that had happened before.

The guard sighed, leaning down to talk to Cryis. "Look, I don't know what you did to get yourself brought here but trust me when I say, just give Agent Kanon what he wants. He's not the man you want as your enemy."

"So, I heard." Cryis said, gritting his teeth. The headache began to subside again. Cryis noticed the older guard scowling at them both from the corner. "What's your name kid?" Cryis said to the younger guard.

The guard snorted, "Kid? Maybe I should've let Harold punch you."

Cryis grinned at the guard's joke.

"It's Arthur."

Cryis nodded his head slowly; the name didn't suit the guard. "Huh, I once knew a king by that name." Cryis said, implying that the name belonged to righteous leaders and not followers.

"What?" Arthur asked, confused.

"Come on, let's go!" Harold, the older guard, grunted. He headed back towards the door, followed by the other two guards.

"Wait," Cryis said in a hushed voice. "Let me let you in on a little secret, Arthur," Cryis said, leaning as far over to him as he could before the boy left. Cryis wanted to be sure Kanon had truly kept the existence of Aris Magicians a secret. Arthur stopped hesitantly. "I'm immortal." The shock Cryis had expected to see on Arthur's face wasn't there, so Cryis continued. "Whatever anyone tries to do to me will roll off me like water." Cryis relaxed back in his chair, his chains rattling as he did. "I won't help Kanon with this."

Arthur laughed, surprising Cryis. His laugh was enjoyable to listen to, sounding like chimes on a bell. "Got to say, that's the first time I've heard that one."

Arthur patted a hand on Cryis's shoulder, "Relax, you're not responsible for finding the cure for cancer, the doctor just needs blood and skin samples from you. We get it from all the inmates."

Cryis's faint smile turned to a frown. *Cancer?*

Cryis resisted the urge to laugh, so that's what Kanon had told the others that he was aiding in creating a cure for cancer. How charitable of him. At least Kanon had kept his word on keeping Aris Magicians' existence a secret.

"Before you ask me about your rights, Agent Kanon said you signed a consent form to get a reduction off your sentence." Cryis tuned the kid out; he was a chatty one. Arthur met Cryis's gaze with curiosity. "What even are you in here for—" Arthur abruptly stopped, clearing his throat. His eyes focused forward.

Cryis knew from Arthur's expression that a superior had arrived, but he was more concerned with how Kanon was hiding the fact that magic existed from everyone after Cryis had displayed acts of healing numerous times upon his arrival. He was grateful indeed, but despite all of that, magic should have been revealed to the humans by now. Aturdokht would have used its chaos to easily distract Aris Magica while she conquered the human world.

Cryis's eyes widened with a glimmer of hope; perhaps Jay had somehow managed to hold off Aturdokht from taking complete control over her soul. Cryis shook his head, clasping his hands together. Was that even possible, Cryis had witnessed it with his own eyes, Jay hadn't been strong enough to resist Aturdokht. But then he'd underestimated an Ancient once before; he couldn't make that same mistake twice with Jay.

"I'm at a loss." Cryis admitted aloud.

"Well, so am I." An unfamiliar and chilling voice chuckled.

Cryis sat up straighter in his chair, suddenly attentive. Every hair on his body stood on edge. Cryis had assumed Kanon was the person who had entered the room, but the man who now sat across from him proved differently. Cryis felt a danger to the man, although he suspected he was only human.

The man looked nothing like a scientist at all. He was dressed in a solid black suit and tie as if he were dressed for a funeral. The man's shoulders stuck out like daggers under the suit, and his skin was paler than Cryis's with a blue hue to it. A ghastly scar cut through the man's left eye, leaving the man blinded on one side. The scar traveled into his bald head. He held Cryis in a cold stare with his single soulless eye.

"Hello." The man's voice curled Cryis's toes. When the man smiled, his mouth fell into a *v* shape. "I'll be damned, the agent was telling the truth. He'd found one."

Cryis couldn't smell anything off about the man in front of him. Every Aris Magician had a faint scent that an Immortal could pick up on telling their ties to Aris Magica. The man before him had none, making him a regular human, yet Cryis still felt an alluring pull of something that resembled magic coming from him. Cryis didn't fear much, but something told him people should fear the man across from him. The man was death itself.

The scientist leaned forward, causing Cryis to lean away from him. The room felt smaller than it already was. "A damn Immortal. Rare indeed." The stranger cackled callously.

So, he knows about me. Cryis was careful to hide his emotions from the man. *But why did Luke tell him the truth?*

"You're the one I've been looking for." Cryis craned his neck to watch as the man circled the table to the back table behind him. Something about the way the man spoke set Cryis's nerves on edge. "Well," the scientist paused, "not you specifically, but your kind."

The man picked up a syringe in one hand and a needle in the other before returning to face Cryis. "I'm sure Luke briefed you on his version of what is to happen."

"You're trying to recreate the serum and use it as a weapon." Cryis responded curtly.

"Now, why on earth would I bring that vile thing back." The man scoffed, stopping behind Cryis's chair. "Plus," he leaned down and whispered into Cryis's ear. "It wouldn't work on the likes of you Immortal." The man grinned. He rested his hands on Cryis's shoulders, giving him a tight squeeze. He let go, standing to full height. "No, no, I have something else in store for you, something I can only achieve with the blood of an Immortal."

Cryis arched an eyebrow, confused. Had Kanon lied? "Get to the point." Cryis growled, growing impatient.

A cold, clammy hand found its way to the back of Cryis's neck. His head was slammed into the table. Cryis's ears filled with a piercing ring as his vision was covered in black spots. A pain like no other split through his head.

The man dug the syringe into Cryis's neck. A cool liquid spread through his body, burning his insides like fire before the feeling quickly turned to ice. "It's a sedative." The man said deadpanned.

He released Cryis's neck, pulling the needle back. "Just in case things go astray."

Cryis felt a blanket of darkness beginning to fill his head. He blinked it off, fighting the effect of the medicine. He tried his best to sit up but instead only managed to slump back into his chair. The man gently patted Cryis on the cheek. "You're going to help me create something that will ensure the safety of us all." Cryis shook his head, unable to hear the man well.

The feeling inside him rose in a panic, causing Cryis to grow nauseous against his own emotions.

"Who knew human bodies could be so fun." The man bemused as he grabbed onto Cryis's arm. He turned over his arm, exposing the inside of his wrist.

"What?" Cryis said groggily.

Human? Bodies?

A thought was pushed forward in his mind, one he should've realized much sooner. The familiar tug of magic coming from the man was indistinguishable. Cryis's eyes widened.

Soul possession, Cryis thought desperately.

The door across the room opened a second time, directing Cryis's attention to it. Kanon stepped inside quickly, closing the door behind him. Cryis's gaze turned to meet Kanon's, but he avoided his stare. Cryis's heart accelerated, he had to warn the agent.

"Have you gotten what you needed Kazimir?" Kanon asked.

Kazimir?

Cryis felt a tinge of familiarity from that name, his heart skipped a beat, he knew that name, but it didn't belong to a human. The fog from before was already starting to lift, his body's natural healing process burning through the sedative.

"Just about Luke." Kazimir crooned.

Kazimir tapped the veins inside Cryis's arm until he found the one he was looking for. He stuck a needle inside. Cryis helplessly watched as it began to fill up with his blood. He glanced at Kazimir's eyes, seeing an insatiable hunger in them as he stared in Kanon's direction.

"Good." Kanon said approvingly, clapping his hands together. "If we plan to stand a chance against what's ahead, we'll need that cure."

"Of course." Kazimir agreed, but Cryis could hear the lie in his voice.

Kazimir looked over at Cryis and grinned. Cryis narrowed his gaze, putting the pieces together, he'd met Kazimir before, decades ago, before Demons had been exiled across Aris Magica, Kazimir was known for soul possessing humans. Kazimir was one of Aturdokht's best Demons and brightest minds. He wasn't a strategist, but he'd been infamous for experimenting with his magic on humans and Magicians. As far as he knew, though, Aturdokht didn't know his whereabouts. So, what was he doing here, and why did he need an Immortal's blood?

Cryis wasn't sure how a Demon had made its way into Kanon's facility, but he knew he couldn't let it leave no matter what. Not with his blood.

Kazimir removed the needle from Cryis's arm, the syringe attached now filled with dark red blood. He held it up to the light. "She will be pleased." He whispered only low enough for Cryis to hear.

Cryis mustered all his strength to break through the final relapse of the sedative. He lunged at Kazimir with both hands, forgetting the chains on his wrists. Kazimir jumped up out of reach in one swift movement. His movements were like those of a tiger, the main body of the Demon form he possessed.

"Woah, Cryis!" Kanon shouted, alarmed. "It's over. Calm yourself."

"These damn chains!" Cryis cursed.

Cryis pushed himself out of the chair. He twisted his body and used his feet to kick the chair up and towards Kazimir. But Kanon was there intercepting the furniture before it even got close to the man. He set the chair down with force and stomped over to Cryis, but Cryis paid him no attention. Instead, he was focused on Kazimir, who had set the vile of blood on the back table and had picked up another syringe.

In a blink of an eye, the Demon was standing behind Kanon.

"Cryis, you're overreacting, this i—" Kanon's words came to a halt as his eyes rolled into the back of his head. Kazimir had knocked him out from behind. Cryis watched helplessly as the man went down, slumping over the table before him.

"What gave me away?" Kazimir asked curiously. Cryis regained some of his composure, glaring at Kazimir. "No matter, Immortal, I've gotten what I came for."

"And what was that? What is Aturdokht planning?" Cryis growled, holding back his anger just long enough to get an answer.

"You'll find out soon enough." In one quick movement, faster than Cryis could see, Kazimir struck him with the needle.

Once again, Cryis could feel himself slowly drifting away as his body couldn't keep pace with his healing. "I'll...kill...you..." Cryis struggled to say.

Kazimir wickedly grinned. "You've said that before."

Chapter Six

"He can hardly walk, sir." Cryis heard Arthur say.

Cryis's mind was in a dark haze, leaving him barely aware of anything happening around him. He felt himself being moved, as well as the feeling of familiar hands on his body.

"It's his fault, Kazimir had to keep him sedated." Cryis overheard Kanon mumble.

Cryis moaned. His body felt as if it had been dragged through nails. Perhaps it had. Arthur had a grip on Cryis's arm on one side, supporting his body upright, while Kanon held the other. Between the two of them, they were the only ones keeping Cryis from collapsing.

"Put him in his cell," Kanon ordered. "And bring him something to eat." He sounded disgusted.

"Can I attend to his injuries, sir?" Arthur asked. Cryis felt his arm on Arthur's side grip tighter.

"He'll be fine," Kanon said. "Just leave him and report back to your post. Am I understood?"

"Yes, sir." Arthur said begrudgingly.

Cryis heard a door opening before he was dragged inside his room and laid down on his bed. The last thing he heard was Arthur's receding footsteps before darkness overtook him.

The next couple of hours were a blur. Cryis continued to fade in and out. He wasn't sure what Kazimir had given him, but it left his body feeling much weaker than before. He recalled being fed some food to aid in his accelerated healing, but he couldn't distinguish dream from reality. At one point, Cryis thought he saw a man with dark skin and fuchsia eyes standing over him. The man's body resembled a spirit, allowing Cryis to see directly through him. The man smiled faintly before disappearing. His spirit seemed to float inside of Cryis. Cryis felt too exhausted to figure out if what he'd seen was real or not. He was hardly aware of his surroundings, spending most of his time asleep in his cell.

Everything hurt like hell. Cryis lifted his hand and ran it over his face. He finally found the energy to open his eyes and sit up from his bed. He stopped, hearing Arthur's sudden voice at his bedside.

"I'm not supposed to be doing this; I could get reprimanded for helping you." Arthur rambled under his breath. "But during your outburst, you re-opened your burn scab." With a single tug, Arthur secured the bandage over Cryis's left hand.

Cryis looked over to find his right hand wrapped in white bandages. But unlike his left hand, blood had already soaked right through it. His burns from the explosion had yet to fully heal. He'd only managed to get back the first layer of skin recently. Cryis examined his arms, at least the bruising was almost gone.

"Oh, you're up." Arthur sounded relieved, only for it to be followed by dis-appointment. "And you've bled through again." He groaned, digging through the first aid kit at his knees. He was kneeling beside Cryis's cot. "Didn't I just redo this one?" He said to himself.

Cryis sat up, letting his hand fall to his side. He looked around, noticing he was back in his cell. He swung his legs over the side of his bed so that he faced Arthur.

Arthur began to protest, "What are you—just stop it."

Cryis caught himself staring at the objects in Arthur's hands. In one hand, Arthur held a pair of scissors and in the other a small white tube. A first aid kit sat on the floor between them.

"What are you doing here?" Cryis asked curiously.

It was so strange to see medical supplies before him. He hadn't needed such things in a very long time. Even when his injuries were at their worst, in a matter of minutes, they would heal. Arthur looked just as surprised as Cryis felt.

"Your eyes...they're—" Arthur leaned in towards him.

Cryis blushed but then looked away, annoyed. "Red." He finished for Arthur. "Yeah, I know," Cryis looked for a quick excuse, "it's a hereditary problem." He lied. He touched his hand to his hair, alarmed, nearly forgetting about the oddity of his hair color. "Oh, and this—it's dyed." He lied again. Arthur hadn't believed him with the truth the last time Cryis had told him, and the last thing Cryis wanted to do was freak the kid out further.

"What, no." Arthur said, disregarding Cryis. "Healed!" He beamed. "Already? It's only been a few hours." Arthur glanced at the tube in his hand. "This must be some powerful antibiotic ointment."

Cryis couldn't help himself and began to laugh, really laugh, finding Arthur's response almost adorable. His laughter was harsh and raspy, coming out of his throat. But he was amazed at how humans could create logical explanations to understand what they couldn't comprehend.

Arthur didn't find it as amusing. Instead, he busied himself with reading the antibiotic's label. Cryis noticed he was without his hat. Arthur's entire head had been buzzed, not just the back. Cryis wondered if he should do the same to his hair; it had gotten a lot longer, and he hated it. It meant that more time had passed, moving on without him.

Cryis met Arthur's eyes. Arthur reminded Cryis of an alley cat, the way his eyes seemed to pierce his own. Cryis couldn't help but find Arthur beautiful. Instinctively, Cryis reached out his hand with the sudden urge to pet Arthur's head.

He was surprised when Arthur grabbed his hand. "Here, give me this." He pulled Cryis's hand closer to him.

Cryis held his breath, masking his embarrassment as heat rushed to his face. "What's wrong?" Cryis's voice squeaked.

"Nothing. It's…" Arthur sighed, "I should go ahead and stop the bleeding again on this one."

"Oh," Cryis relaxed. He smiled to himself, already feeling the injury on his hand closing. The cat would be out of the bag soon enough. "Seriously though, I wouldn't bother." Cryis wondered why he had gone to the trouble to lie to Arthur in the first place, but something about the boy made him nervous.

Arthur ignored Cryis and cut through the bandage, setting it aside on the floor.

"Remember when I told you I was…" Cryis hesitated, "Immortal?"

"Kanon said you smacked your head pretty good." Arthur mumbled while unraveling the tape that had been underneath the bandage. "You should apologize to him, by the way, he said you attacked him too."

"I wasn't joking about that." Cryis confessed, disregarding what Arthur had said but still catching the lie Kazimir had crafted. Cryis hadn't been the one who attacked Kanon.

Arthur snorted, "When pigs fly—what the hell!" He exclaimed.

The burn that had been on Cryis's hand was gone as if it never existed. There wasn't even a scar left behind on his skin. Cryis felt stronger than before, the food he'd been fed had helped him retain his energy, allowing him to recover at a faster rate than he had been for weeks.

Cryis turned his hand over, flexing and stretching his muscles. "See, I told you."

Arthur grabbed Cryis by the hand again and pulled him closer. Cryis was forced forward, nearly falling off the bed. Arthur turned Cryis's hand over on his own, his eyes wide and curious.

"But how? Why?" Arthur exclaimed. He stared at Cryis curiously. "Are the others healed?"

Without waiting for Cryis's permission, Arthur began cutting away all his bandages. The wounds around his neck and other hand were both healed as well. Arthur brushed his fingers along Cryis's neck, where some of the worst burn marks had been. His touch sent a tantalizing chill down Cryis's spine. He found himself wanting more of it.

"I can't believe this." Arthur whispered, amazed. He pulled away from Cryis and fell back on his hands.

Cryis nodded in agreement. "Most can't." His eyebrows furrowed as a thought began to form, "What did Kanon tell you about me exactly?" Cryis asked, trying to understand.

Arthur shook his hand, shocked. "Wait, Agent Kanon knows?" Cryis nodded in response. Arthur sighed. "Not much, just that you lot were dangerous criminals, your degree of criminal activity was classified, but I just assumed the worst." Arthur explained. "He said you liked to play mind tricks, making us see things that aren't there." Arthur stopped and thought for a moment before continuing, "But that was real, wasn't it?"

Cryis smiled sadly, "We usually do a better job at staying hidden from humans. To protect ourselves, but also to not draw unwanted attention."

"You're talking about yourself as if you're not...human?" Arthur said, but it came out sounding more like a question.

"I know. In a way, I'm not." Cryis stopped himself from explaining more.

"So, the others," Arthur gulped, "are like you?" Cryis nodded again. "How are you so calm right now?" He asked nervously.

"I could ask you the same thing." Cryis said. Arthur's reaction was far from what Cryis had imagined it to be. He'd never seriously told a human about his immortality before, let alone shown them.

"I'm just trying to wrap my head around this." Arthur confessed, speaking slowly. "And the others are just like you?"

Cryis hesitated, unsure how much he should tell him, but he needed an ally to get out of here. "I'm the only Immortal, but the others have their own forms of magic." He looked down at Arthur, alarmed. Arthur looked as if he would pass out any second. "You good kid? You're sweating."

Arthur wiped the sweat from his brow, "Yep, just processing." He took a couple of deep breaths. "And the people Agent Kanon is searching for, I'm assuming they're like you all," Arthur nearly laughed as he said the word, "magic."

Cryis nodded again. His heart ached thinking of Jay and the others. "I'm doing my best to protect her, but I don't know where she is…where anyone is. I wasn't lying about that." Cryis confessed. "Listen, Arthur," Cryis said slowly, "it isn't safe here anymore for us, I need…" He retracted his statement, he couldn't leave the others, not while Kazimir was here. "We need to leave."

Arthur suddenly stood up. "I think I should go speak to Agent Kanon." He let out a deep sigh. "This sounds like something he should know."

Cryis glared at Arthur. "Haven't you been listening to a word I'm saying?" He said harshly. Cryis couldn't trust Kanon anymore; he was beginning to think the film he'd seen over Kanon's eyes hadn't been his imagination, especially if Kazimir was here. "This place isn't safe if I don't get out of here now, Aris Magica—"

"Aris Magica?" Arthur asked, confused.

Cryis stood up, making himself nose-to-nose with Arthur. Arthur backed away nervously, tripping over the first aid kit. Cryis groaned, grabbing hold of Arthur's arm to stop him from falling. As he did, the world around them seemed to stop. All Cryis could see was Arthur. He took this moment to study the boy before him. He noticed the freckles that lightly dusted the bridge of his nose, as well as the tiny flecks of blue that swam in his fuschia irises. Cryis knew immediately that he could stare into his eyes all day. Getting lost in the sea of Arthur's gaze. He watched as Arthur's face turned red. Cryis blinked, suddenly embarrassed himself. He'd been so distracted by his own thoughts he hadn't realized he'd been staring for so long. He looked away, ashamed, he shouldn't involve Arthur in his problems.

Cryis spoke softer this time, "There's nothing more you can do to help me any further than you already have." He gestured to the first aid kit.

"But you just said you're in danger." Arthur protested.

Cryis could tell the kid was pure of heart, and he admired the kid's tenacity but not his stubbornness. It would get Arthur into a lot of trouble. Cryis pinched the bridge of his nose. "No. Just trust me." Cryis pleaded. "Kanon," Cryis thought back to Kanon's sudden adamance on recreating a cure, he wondered if Kazimir was using Kanon's fear against him or if he'd managed to possess his soul's desire along with the human body he hid in. It wasn't uncommon for a Demon to use such magic as well. "He can't be trusted right now, and somebody like you isn't enough to stop him." Cryis said coldly. He didn't want to hurt Arthur's feelings, but if it protected him and the others he cared for, Cryis would do anything.

"But you'll die." Arthur said, even though the phrase sounded awkward coming out of his mouth.

Cryis smiled sadly, "I can't die, remember? Immortality doesn't have a time limit." He lied.

Every Immortal had a purpose, soul reaping, and then a secondary purpose only known to themselves. Once that purpose was completed, then the Immortal could finally rest, passing the burden onto another unfortunate soul. Cryis had thought his secondary purpose was to guide the Ancient until she finally defeated Aturdokht, but he'd failed. Plus, he didn't feel any closer to death when he met Jay, the last Ancient reincarnation.

"You sure about that?" Arthur challenged.

Cryis narrowed his gaze, surprised the kid could see through his bluff. Cryis had seen it happen once when an Immortal had lost their ability and passed it to another, although the memory was hazy. Once again, Cryis saw a flash of the man with fuchsia eyes like Arthur standing over him, but this time, Cryis was lying in the snow, blood dripping on his face from the man. The memory quickly vanished again. Cryis pinched the bridge of his nose in frustration.

Perhaps Arthur had a point. Lately, Cryis was taking a lot longer to heal, even the smallest of cuts. Cryis had assumed it was because he was malnourished, but maybe it was because he didn't want to face the truth.

"Arthur." Cryis began. He needed him to understand.

"What?" Arthur stuck up his nose in defiance.

Cryis looked him in the eyes, "The world will end if—" Cryis gasped, stumbling back away from Arthur. The man from his dreams appeared, overlapping Arthur's body.

The man stepped toward him, as did Arthur, to try to stop him from falling, but Cryis snatched his arm away and fell onto the bed instead. His head pounded, and his eyes began to water from the sudden pain.

"Hey? Are you okay?" The man spoke concerned; his voice still sounded like Arthur's.

No. Cryis thought. *You can't be.* He closed his eyes.

Cryis knew the man before him from a lost memory of his past. It had something to do with his immortality. The man and the memory had begun to appear in Cryis's mind the moment he met Arthur. Cryis dreaded what it could mean. Arthur's words about his immortality having a limit echoed in his mind. Was Arthur meant to replace him?

Cryis could feel his heart sink to his stomach. He took another deep breath, followed by another, trying to calm himself. He could barely hear Arthur's worried voice above him. Cryis slowly opened his eyes, and instead of the man staring down at him, it was just Arthur.

Cryis set his gaze on Arthur. *I must be losing my mind*, he thought.

"I'm fine." Cryis sat up, then stood patting himself off as he did.

"Are you?" Arthur challenged. Cryis could see the concern evident in his gaze as he assessed him.

Cryis took another, slow deep breath, tearing his gaze quickly from Arthur's before he got lost in the sea of his eyes once again. He was fine. He had to be.

"As I was saying, the world will end if I—"

"Dammit." Arthur said, glancing behind him.

"Excuse me?" Cryis said, but then he heard the familiar jingle of keys from across the room on the other side of the door to his cell.

Cryis hesitantly glanced at Arthur, who had gone into salute formation. Cryis tried to shake the feeling of guilt off him, but the image of the man and Arthur as one wouldn't leave him. Cryis wasn't sure whether his speculations were correct or if he should keep his distance from the boy or keep him close. The last thing Cryis wanted was to be right. He wouldn't wish immortality on anyone. Cryis walked over to the wall, putting his hands above his head.

Cryis turned to the door, expecting to see Kanon walk through it, but that wasn't who it was. His eyes went wide, and his mouth dropped, taken aback. "Vastille."

Vastille stood in the doorway. He was dressed in a sharp black suit paired with black dress shoes. An American flag pin was pinned to his left chest on the outside of his suit jacket. He blended in, looking like any other agent. His skin was a dark bronze, his bald head shining with oil. He wore double-shaded sunglasses even though they were indoors.

Cryis stared at him, surprised. It had been nearly two and a half decades since he'd last seen him. At the time, Vastille had been a scrawny high schooler. Cryis had met him shortly after the accident that left Vastille blind in one eye, awakening his connection to Aris Magica. His Hybrid gene had been activated, taking over and giving Vastille his sight back. His metallic eye allowed him to control electromagnetic waves in every system.

Cryis had also met Vastille in the lowest part of his life when he was in the process of being vetted to become a CIA officer. Being immortal wasn't enough to fill the void of loneliness he felt when losing a close relationship. Vastille had opened Cryis's heart again, and Cryis would be forever grateful to him.

"You've gotten bigger." Cryis grinned. "Much bigger, like an ox." The jokes didn't stop there, though, as Cryis continued, "Probably couldn't tell the difference between you and it." He snorted, gesturing to Vastille's muscles. Cryis commented on his sunglasses, "Still using that trick I taught you. What happened to those purple ones I gave you?"

Vastille didn't smile at any of Cryis's jokes. "The darker the tint, the better. The other ones I threw away, couldn't stand the sight of them." Towards the end of his sentence, a faint smile formed on his lips.

Cryis fell out laughing, this time, it was much smoother than the one he'd let out with Arthur earlier. "Of course, you couldn't. What took you so long to visit me?" Cryis asked, even though part of him was afraid of Vastille's answer.

Vastille relaxed a bit more. He moved further into the cell. But his expression remained quizzical. "Once I found out Luke was holding an Immortal, I thought it was the girl."

"You know Jay?" Cryis asked but remembered Jay had been detained by the CIA agents not too long ago. Cryis just hadn't known Vastille had been Kanon's partner. "Wait. You didn't know I was here?" Vastille nodded in confirmation. After the explosion, Cryis had sent the message to him. "But I contacted you…" Cryis said, now uncertain.

"You contacted the line I share with Luke. I changed my personal number," Vastille said.

Cryis sighed, he didn't blame Vastille for being less enthusiastic about their reunion. After all, Cryis had left on bad terms with Vastille. He had left a note thanking Vastille for giving him hope again before disappearing from his life forever. Cryis rubbed the back of his neck, brushing his hair aside. "Look, Vastille—"

"Cryis?" A familiar high-rung voice asked from behind Vastille.

Vastille stepped aside, allowing Ami to pass by. She wore an orange jumpsuit. Her blonde hair had grown as well, falling past her shoulders to the middle of her back. Her skin had lost its color and was still riddled with bruises but no burns, and she looked somewhat healthy. Despite Kanon's earlier claim of being in the ICU, it was clear she wasn't as badly off as he had led Cryis to believe. Although, the sparkle of hope Cryis had once seen in her blue eyes was barely visible. Still, Cryis was excited to see her. A huge smile spread across his face.

Ami ran to Cryis, throwing herself on him in a hug, shocking him. Before the series of events that led them to this moment, Cryis had barely known Ami. She had been a student at the Institute who knew Dylan and Jay. However, considering what the two of them had been through together in the cabin, Cryis felt a comforting connection to her as well and welcomed her embrace. If not for the wall behind Cryis, they both would have fallen to the floor with the force of Ami's leap.

"Thank God!" Ami cried. She buried her head into Cryis's chest.

Cryis gently patted her head. He smiled; tears were brought to his eyes. He hugged her back even tighter and buried his head in her shoulder. He could feel her tears wetting his shirt. "It's good to see you too."

Vastille cleared his throat. "Um...at ease." He said, finally noticing Arthur. "This isn't the Army, son."

Cryis had nearly forgotten Arthur was still in the room. He'd been so silent, making himself invisible.

"Agent Vastille," Arthur began, "What are you doing? How do you know these prisoners?"

Cryis felt his heart skip a beat, the last thing he wanted was for the others to mistake Arthur. He was on their side, but Cryis could see in Ami's gaze and Vastille's stance them contemplating what to do with the guard.

Cryis cut Arthur off, "We have to go."

Cryis still held Ami in his arms. Part of him was afraid she would vanish before his eyes like a dream if he let her go. He was terrified he'd imagined them. Maybe he was still lying on the cot while Arthur treated his burns.

"We know, that's why we're breaking you out." Vastille said, his voice devoid of any sarcasm.

"No, you don't understand!" Cryis said at the same time Arthur exclaimed, "What?" The two of them looked at each other.

"What's wrong?" Ami asked, pulling back slightly to look into Cryis's eyes.

"This place isn't safe anymore." Cryis said. "I ran into a Demon earlier pretending to help Kanon recreate the serum. I don't think Kanon is aware, but I think Kazimir is manipulating his desires. The Demon, it's one of Aturdokht's."

"A Demon?" Ami asked.

Vastille turned to Arthur, then back to Cryis. Cryis nodded his head, vouching for Arthur. "He's on our side. I trust him, end of the story." He said.

Vastille arched an eyebrow but didn't question Cryis or Arthur further. "Okay."

Arthur gawked at Vastille in disbelief. "Agent Vastille, he's like, eighteen, barely older than me, and you're taking orders from him?"

"Eh," Cryis surmised, "I wouldn't call it orders, That's a bit of a stretch."

Vastille smirked, "If I'm right, you'd be about 6,718 years old now." Vastille said to Cryis.

"Woah." Cryis said, impressed. "You kept track."

Vastille tapped his glasses, "In a way."

"So..." Arthur interjected, "you're going to break him out...of a secret base...just like that?" He asked slowly. "What about Agent Kanon?"

Ami released Cryis and faced Arthur. She glared up at him, "You ask way too many questions. You're either with us or against us."

Arthur hesitated and looked at Cryis. Cryis sighed, he felt responsible for this kid now that he'd dragged him into his mess. Although he still wasn't sure if he should keep his distance or not, Cryis knew the others wouldn't trust Arthur to stay behind, so Cryis had to convince him to come with them.

"Look, kid," Cryis began, "earlier, you sounded like you were ready to burn this place to the ground to protect my rights." Cryis recalled. "Well, here is your chance." Cryis still saw uncertainty in Arthur's eyes. Cryis walked over to Arthur's side and placed a hand on Arthur's shoulder. "If we don't get out of here now, many people—innocent people—will die in the near future. So just this once, please turn a blind eye."

Arthur lowered his gaze to the floor. Cryis watched as his fists balled at his side, scrunching the fabric of his pants.

"Yeah, about that," Vastille explained. Cryis turned to Vastille. Vastille rubbed the top of his head. Even with shades on, it wasn't hard to see the stress on his face.

"Come on, we're running out of time! Guard rotations change every fifteen minutes," Ami interrupted before Vastille could finish. She stood by the door, poking her head into the hall and then back into the room, beckoning for the rest of them to hurry.

"I'll tell you later." Vastille said, the way he said it unsettled Cryis, creating a knot in his stomach.

"I can't do that..." Arthur's voice trailed off, but Cryis understood. He knew how honest of a kid Arthur was based on the short conversations he'd had with him. Cryis was aware he was asking too much.

Cryis sadly smiled and gave Arthur a pat on his shoulder before passing by him. The decision was Arthur's alone to make, and either way, Cryis and his friends would suffer the consequences of his actions.

Cryis reached the door, but before he passed through it, he looked to the other side of the hall and then back into the room as if he had forgotten something. The only person in the hall was Ami, who waited impatiently for them.

"Something wrong?" Vastille asked from behind Cryis.

Cryis blocked the door. "Where's Lyid and Taybeith?"

No one answered him. Ami stepped back into the room. Her frustration was replaced with anguish. She wouldn't meet Cryis's gaze when she spoke. "Lyid..." Ami's voice was shaking. "Lyid didn't make it. The fire, he protected me from the worst of it." She took in a shaky breath, "Agent Kanon did all he could, but his wounds were too great."

Cryis sucked in a shaking breath. He opened his mouth to say something, anything on behalf of their fallen friend, but nothing came to mind. He had only known Lyid for a day.

"And his body?" Cryis asked, but Ami was already shaking her head. She didn't know.

Cryis felt a bitterness form in his mouth, as a reaper, it was his job to escort his soul to the next part of his journey, and once again, he had failed. He closed his eyes, taking in a long breath as he did.

"And Taybeith," Ami said his name with much disgust. An unsettling tension fell into the air. "He broke out a couple of days ago."

"How?" Cryis asked, opening his eyes again. He recalled Ami using the serum's entirety to strip Taybeith of his powers. He was a Tekhne; his powers were like Vastille's, except his connection to the technological waves ran throughout his entire body and not just through his eye. But a full dosage of the serum should have stripped any Aris Magician of their ability.

Vastille elaborated, "The cameras were only able to pull up fragments of the video. The film was blurry and hard to make out. The only thing I could see were red eyes and a swarm of fire."

Cryis's breath hitched. Out of the corner of his eyes, he could see Arthur looking at him, Cryis knew he was considering Cryis's own red eyes.

Ami shook her head, "The only other person we know with red eyes is..."

"Jay." Cryis finished. Even saying her name aloud brought a taste of despair to his tongue that sunk, adding to the growing knot in his stomach. "We need to find Dylan." Cryis said, thinking back to his conversation with Kanon, if he was right, then Aturdokht was looking for him too. The two of them had been inseparable. Nonetheless, Dylan would at least be able to draw Jay and Aturdokht out of hiding. He felt bad about leaving the Demon to his vices, but Cryis knew he had to find Dylan before Aturdokht did.

"We *need* to go." Ami begged, "Please."

She was right. They had already taken too much time discussing when they should have been escaping. Vastille pulled out two guns from the fold of his suit's inside pockets. He passed one to Cryis and the other to Ami. He pulled out a third from his belt. Vastille led the three of them through the door, Cryis bringing up the rear.

"W-wait!" Arthur cried.

Cryis stopped in his tracks. Ami and Vastille continued cautiously down the hall towards the elevator. Cryis didn't bother to turn around.

"I'm coming with you." Arthur said from behind him.

Cryis paused at the door. He wasn't sure whether or not to be relieved by Arthur's decision or terrified. He still didn't know what his vision from earlier had meant, seeing the man with Arthur's eyes standing over him. But Cryis knew there was no time to worry about it now. Arthur had decided on his own.

"Okay." Cryis said, unable to bring himself to say more than that.

Cryis and Arthur came up behind the others. Vastille and Ami were crouching at the end of the corner of a plain gray hall.

"What's the holdup?" Cryis asked, kneeling beside them. As he did, he noticed Ami was barefoot like himself. It didn't seem to bother her, so he said nothing.

"I put the upcoming camera on a loop to buy us some time, but we still have a problem." Vastille gestured to the camera in the corner of the ceiling above them. He released the safety on his gun, ready to fire if it came down to it.

Cryis peered around the corner of the wall, seeing a single guard still patrolling the path right before the elevators. "Oh."

Arthur made his way to the front of the group. He glanced around the corner; the guard's back was still to them. "The stairwell to his left would be better." He mumbled.

Cryis agreed. With the elevator, they risked running into someone a lot faster than the stairs. But the problem of the guard remained as he blocked both exits. The lone guard held a water bottle that smacked against his leg with every step he took.

"Let me handle this." Arthur offered. He didn't wait for their approval as he stepped from around the corner, removing his hat from his back pocket and putting it on.

"Arthur, get back here!" Cryis reached for him, but it was too late.

The guard turned at the sound of Arthur's footsteps. "Hey there, you the replacement?" The guard asked with a heavy Southern accent. The guard and Arthur weren't too far away for Cryis to eavesdrop on their conversation.

"Ah, yeah." Arthur said. He kept his head towards the ground, avoiding eye contact. Cryis assumed Arthur wasn't a very convincing liar.

"Maaan, I tell ya, Agent Kanon's been running us 'round like a pack of dogs. What in hell is so special about Prisoners AC12 and BF14 anyways?" The guard offered Arthur his water bottle. "I even got transferred all the way out west for this shit."

Arthur took it from him, unscrewing the cap. He sniffed the bottle, "Vodka."

Cryis turned to Ami and whispered, "Gross." He wasn't the biggest fan of alcohol, even if the occasion called for it.

"What else would it be? I've been here since six yesterday, pulling a double. If ya expect me not to drink, then your ass is as dumb as chicken shit."

Arthur tossed the bottle back. "I've got it from here."

"That was surprisingly easy." Vastille whispered. Cryis and Ami nodded, watching Arthur in action.

"Sure do." The guard waved the bottle over his head in a spiral motion as he began to walk off.

"He's coming this way." Ami whispered, grabbing Cryis's arm. Cryis watched as Arthur trailed closely behind the guard. "What is he thinking?" Ami asked.

Cryis shook his head; he had no idea, but in three seconds, Cryis watched Arthur knock the guard out from behind by hitting him in the neck. The guard went down fast. Arthur caught him and dragged the guard's body closer to the wall. He propped the guard up in a slumped position, sitting the water bottle in his hand.

"Well, it looks like he has things under control after all." Cryis smirked. He'd underestimated the boy. "Come on," Cryis gestured for the others to follow him toward Arthur.

Cryis approached Arthur, grinning ear to ear. "What?" Arthur asked, offended, "I did what I thought was necessary."

Cryis chuckled, shaking his head as he continued past Arthur. Vastille patted the boy on his shoulder. "Good work, kid."

"Thanks." Arthur mumbled. As Ami passed by him, Arthur stepped into her path. Before she could say anything, Arthur raised a pair of boots between them. He had removed the guard's shoes. Cryis felt a tinge of jealousy as he watched them.

"For you." Arthur said, forcing them into Ami's hands. "It's the middle of January outside, and yeah...um..." Arthur rambled. He looked away as his voice trailed off and fell into an awkward chuckle. He cleared his throat before walking after Cryis, leaving Ami standing alone.

Cryis glanced at Arthur teasingly, "What about my shoes, huh?" Cryis grinned, wiggling his toes as he walked.

Arthur pulled his hat down over his face, embarrassed. "Oh, shut up, I'll get yours next, don't worry."

Chapter Seven

Dylan's eyes widened as Phagos's sword drove into Jay's chest. Life seemed to drain from her face. Phagos smiled wickedly, his snout curling up, revealing his sharp teeth. His red eyes gleamed with satisfaction as he vanished before their eyes. Dylan screamed Jay's name, running to her. She had fallen before Riley. He tried to catch her, but he could barely support himself. His hands phased through her body.

"What's going to happen?" Riley grimaced over Jay's body. Dylan finally reached them both, standing over them.

"I thought you said you couldn't be touched?" Dylan asked, seeing the pain contorted on her face.

"By the living. Phagos was in spirit form too, so his soul can harm mine," Jay began to explain. The color drained from Dylan's face at her words. He noticed her breathing grow labored as she continued to speak, "Physically, I'm fine. Just make it back home safely." As she pulled the sword from her body, she began to quickly fade.

"You shouldn't have done that, kid," Riley said barely above a whisper.

Dylan looked over at Riley; his head was tucked into his chest, and he couldn't tell if the man was crying or not.

Dylan looked back at Jay. He reached out a hand intending to touch her, but the look of alarm on her face stopped him just before she vanished. Instead, he reached *for the sword she'd just removed. It was incredibly heavy in his hands as he lifted it over his head and spun.*

Just in time as Phagos reappeared, snapping his teeth over the blade. The force of Phagos's strength sent Dylan down on one knee. He could feel dark magic resounding from the sword's blade and into its hilt, threatening to shatter Dylan's wrist. Phagos pushed harder against the sword, biting down. Any more, and he would break it.

"Feel the sword!" Riley instructed. Even in the face of danger, he still acted like a professor. "Feel what it wants!"

Dylan's gift was mastery of weaponry. Any weapon in his hands he knew how to use—it listened to him. Weapons had just as much of a personality as a human. Riley had taught him that. Dylan could feel the magic at the sword's core, begging to use him. All he had to do was allow it. Allow his pain and hurt to run free.

Dylan pushed back, staring into Phagos's eyes as he did. At first, all he saw was his parents' death, followed by Phagos nearly taking Jay away from him. He let the pain consume him and flow into the sword.

The vines surrounding the hilt lifted and grabbed onto his wrist and shoulders, supporting him. They helped him stand. Dylan felt Phagos being pushed back as his grip on the blade loosened. His eyes appeared shocked at Dylan being able to wield the full strength of his weapon.

Dylan screamed, tearing the sword free and cutting through Phagos's snout. Blood dripped from the sword's blade.

"Attaboy." Riley said, gripping his side.

Dylan looked back at him. Riley was quickly losing consciousness; Dylan could tell by the look on his face. He started to go to him, but the sword yanked him to the right, blocking Phagos's claw from attacking Dylan. Dylan looked down at the sword, astonished. No other weapon had acted on its own in his hands before. It was almost as if the sword had become an extension of him.

Phagos glared at him, reeling with disgust. A ghastly scar cut directly between his eyes and his snout from where Dylan had cut him moments before. Phagos vanished, then reappeared behind Riley. He picked up Riley's sword before Riley could and charged at Dylan.

Dylan parried, only for Phagos to swipe at his feet. He fell to the ground, his ankles cut. Phagos used Riley's sword to hold down the sword in Dylan's hands. He stood over Dylan and brandished his claws.

"Such a disappointment. Even after all this time, you're still not strong enough." He sneered.

Dylan struggled to free his sword hand, but the sword wouldn't budge. Phagos slashed his claw down, tearing through skin and bone across Dylan's arms and chest. A terrifying scream split through Dylan's throat. He found the courage to look down and saw his chest was in shreds. The edges of his vision began to darken. He was quickly losing consciousness. Dylan could faintly hear Riley's cries from behind them, even see him struggle to his feet. Dylan turned back to Phagos. Phagos wickedly smiled as he attacked Dylan again, hitting the same spot. His claws dug into his skin and...

Dylan screamed; his screams quickly turned into quick, breathless pants as he awoke in a sweat. His memories finally pieced themselves back together, feeling more like a nightmare.

Phagos had nearly killed him; he could have killed him, but he didn't. Phagos had left both him and Riley for dead, destroying the pocket dimension as he vanished. He barely remembered Riley grabbing onto him before he passed out.

Dylan felt a heavy weight in his soul as Phagos's last words haunted his mind. *He wasn't strong enough.*

Dylan became infuriated that he had to hear those words from the enemy. The next time they met, he'd prove him wrong.

Dylan looked up at the ceiling to find himself still in the same room. The Fairy District of Aris Magica. He sighed, not sure to be annoyed or relieved.

Dylan touched his sore muscles and found himself thinking about the healer from earlier. He suspected she was a Fairy. When she had touched him, he felt a tinge of familiarity of healing magic, but also something else he was unfamiliar with. What had that girl done to him? Whatever it had been, his memories were back, and the headache was gone.

"Wow, you took your time, kid."

At the sound of the familiar voice, Dylan craned his neck, finding Doctor Herron sitting in a wooden chair in the corner of the room. The chair hadn't been there before, from what he remembered about the room.

Doctor Herron's wild red hair clung damply to her neck, and although she had changed from the last time he'd seen her to jeans and a green undershirt, she still wore a long white lab coat. "Can you believe how hard it is to find a smoke here, this is why I avoid coming back to Aris Magica." She grimaced.

Upon seeing her, so many emotions flooded through his mind: relief, uncertainty, panic, even happiness. "Y-you're here? How?" Dylan's words tumbled out as he sat up to face her.

She shrugged, "Yeah, kid, here I am." There was a new exhaustion to her voice. "The Headmaster sent me to check up on you."

For a moment, Dylan's gaze moved towards the curtain, hearing hushed voices whispering on the other side. Doctor Herron didn't seem fazed, so Dylan ignored them for now.

"He's here too." Dylan said, not startled by the news since the girl had told him as much before.

Dylan couldn't help but wonder if the Headmaster was with Riley. He also wondered how badly Riley was hurt. To him, Riley had always been invincible, so the thought of him injured nearly terrified him.

Doctor Herron gestured to the bed, "You mind?"

Dylan's frown deepened. "How'd I get here?"

Doctor Herron scooted the chair across the hardwood floor closer to the bed. She kicked up her feet, her white sneakers resting on the corner of the mattress.

She rubbed a hand through her damp hair. "The Headmaster can explain when he gets back, but as for how you got here, kid, you can thank Riley for that."

"Riley!" Dylan's eyes brightened, and he leaned forward, bringing his hands between his legs. He was no longer hooked to the machine, allowing him the autonomy to move more freely than before. "Is he hurt?"

Doctor Herron shook her head. "I don't know, kid." Her expression turned grim. "After bringing you to us, he went back for Jay."

Relief settled into Dylan's chest, at least the two of them were together. "Where are they now?" Concern still withered inside him like a virus.

"We don't know. We haven't heard from him since." Her fingers fidgeted at her side, leaving Dylan to wonder if it was a nervous tick she had when she couldn't smoke.

A lump formed in the back of Dylan's throat. *She was okay*, he thought to himself. *They both were.* He had to believe it.

Doctor Herron lowered her feet, slapping her hands on her knees. "Look, kid, I see the questions written on your face, and I don't have any answers. It would be better if..." Her voice trailed off as the voices right outside the curtain began to grow louder, and an argument ensued.

"We can't keep him here!" A deep voice Dylan didn't recognize said. "He's not even one of us. He belongs in the other world."

"He's a Hybrid. He's just as much like the rest of us, and you know it! Regardless, we can't abandon him either." It was the girl's voice from before.

Dylan looked at Doctor Herron, who let out a heavy sigh. It took all his strength to get out of bed. When he did, he noticed his clothes had been changed for him.

Dylan looked down at the ground, staring at his feet. He blinked. Instead of the paper gown from before, he was wearing thick socks and a silly tunic. The material was soft and silky, the color of the top and pants was a dark purple lined with a gold trim. Dylan met Doctor Herron's gaze. She was fighting a laugh. He rolled his eyes at her.

Dylan rolled his shirt up, stopping just above his heart, and peered down at his chest. The scar lines from before were gone. Someone had completed healing him. He traced a hand down his scar-free arms. He wondered who had done it, as well as who had stripped him naked twice to put him in new clothes.

"She did pretty good." Doctor Herron said approvingly while sitting up straighter to see Dylan's chest.

The word *she* did not escape Dylan's notice. His mind thought back to the girl he'd met earlier, causing him to blush and become embarrassed. He slowly lowered his shirt, self-conscious that someone had seen him without it.

Dylan rounded the bed, heading for the curtain. When he passed Doctor Herron, she stuck out her leg, stopping him from getting closer to the curtain.

He mouthed down at her, "What?"

She wrinkled her nose at him in response but didn't let him pass.

Still, Dylan was close enough now to lean towards the curtain, careful not to press on it.

"This is just great." The second voice complained.

"Crisis, Kai!" The girl shouted in a hushed voice. "You haven't been around him, not like I have. He's not a danger to us."

"He might not be, but she is!"

"He's the key to finding her! Are you really going to let that bit of information slip through our fingers? Or what is this really about? His status? Grow up, Kai."

"Hybrids might as well be humans." The boy, Kai, sneered. "And what, Sy, you found this out in a matter of days you spent picking through his mind!" Kai boasted. "You're just as ridiculous as Arden." Dylan heard footsteps receding.

Arden?

Dylan looked back at Doctor Herron, but she didn't seem interested in the conversation outside. Still, the name seemed familiar, but Dylan couldn't place why.

"No, you don't get to walk away from me!" The girl shouted. Her footsteps retreated as well.

Dylan shuffled his feet across the ground, moving to the other side of the curtain. "Just hear him out, okay?" She begged. "Arden said he'd be able to help turn the tide in this war."

"Arden." Kai snorted. "Because all of a sudden, we trust Arden, another outsider." There was a long pause between the two. "Look," Kai finally said, breaking the silence. "Because of the two of you and your foolishness, the council is now fully involved. So, we need to be careful with how we proceed."

"This might be our chance," she huffed. "My chance! To prove that we're not all alike. I trust Arden, and he has good reason to believe that boy is the key."

Kai snorted, "Is that why you—"

"Alright, enough of this shit." Doctor Herron stood up and marched to the curtain. She yanked it back. The boy and girl on the other side were startled, as was Dylan, by the sudden reveal. "You have an audience."

The girl was still in the same clothes she'd been in earlier, giving Dylan the impression that much time hadn't passed between the last time he'd seen her.

On the other hand, Kai had the opposite appearance. Although he resembled the girl in features and height, his hair was a fiery red, twisted in short dreads. He was shorter than Dylan but more built when it came to muscle. They both shared the same dark eyes, but unlike the girl, he didn't bear the tattoos next to them.

Kai wore a similar outfit to hers. His tank top was a strong red with leather bands around his wrists. The shirt stopped just before his stomach, making sure to showcase his abs beneath. His pants went all the way down to his ankles and tucked into his boots. Strapped to his back was a thin rapier sword and two curved axes that hung from his waist between two similar leather flaps. On his left arm was a tattoo of a ring of fire that wrapped around his bicep like a band. The girl had one as well, peeking up from underneath her collarbone. It looked like a thorny vine that snakes up her neck and behind her hair.

The boy, Kai, was the first to recover. "Great, now I have to deal with the deranged Oracle too."

"You're no walk in the park either, kid," Doctor Herron said back. Kai smirked. He handed her a parchment that had been tucked under his arm. Doctor Herron stepped forward and took it carefully, reading it. "Looks like I've been summoned." She glanced back at Dylan with a sad smile. "Sorry I couldn't answer all your questions, kid. These two will be able to help."

Dylan stifled a snort; she hadn't even given him much of a chance to ask any. But still, he had been glad to see her.

From her pocket, the doctor pulled out a small grey crystal. Dylan had seen something like it before—a similar one that was kept in the Headmaster's office on his bookshelf at the Institute. She turned it over in her hand and then pointed it between the three of them.

"Play nice." Doctor Herron said as she pointed the crystal directly at the girl and Kai. "Answer any questions he might have." Without giving anyone a chance to respond, she squeezed the crystal, and in a flash of light, she was gone.

Dylan took a deep breath, facing the two before him. He had gathered a bit of information from their conversation, and it made sense. If he was in Aris Magica, then there was nothing stopping him from enlisting the council's help in stopping Aturdokht and finding the others. He didn't doubt for a second that Riley had taken Jay and gone into hiding. It was the only explanation for no one knowing their whereabouts. But the council knew everything. If Dylan could raise an army of his own, then Jay wouldn't have to risk her life fighting Aturdokht alone. Dylan was still convinced Jay couldn't do it by herself. It's what made her different from the other Ancients that came before her, she wasn't alone, nor did she have to be. The council had to know that.

"I can help." Dylan said from where he stood. No one responded. "But I need some questions answered first." He had to know what had happened—what *was* happening.

"For starters, my name is Silo." She gestured her thumb to Kai. "My brother, Kasid. You can call him Kai for short."

Dylan extended his hand to Kai. "Dylan."

Kai stared at Dylan's hand and scowled. "You don't belong here." He said.

"Kai." Silo slapped her brother across the arm. He didn't even flinch. She turned back to Dylan. "I'm sorry for his attitude."

"No, no, he's right." Dylan agreed even though he glowered at Kai. "Trust me, it's not like I asked to be here." Dylan took a step towards him. "But I am, so if you don't mind," he took another step until he was staring down at Kai, nose to nose. "I'd like to talk to someone who at least looks like they're in charge."

Kai smirked arrogantly, "Careful now."

Silo stepped in between her brother and Dylan, diffusing the tension. Dylan noticed two thin slits in between her shoulders that looked almost like scars but no wings.

"Okay, fine, what do you want to know?" Silo asked.

"Did you heal me?" Dylan found himself asking. He wasn't sure why it had bothered him so much, but he had to know. He'd only ever been healed by Jay or Faith, and since Jay wasn't a Fairy, healing could take a toll on the user accessing that kind of Old Magic. However, Jay had found a workaround by allowing other objects, such as plants, to bear the burden.

"Yes, I did." She opened her mouth as if she wanted to say more, but then she closed it. She hesitated for a second before asking, "How's your head?"

Dylan smiled, "Better, thanks to you, I'm guessing."

She shrugged, "I'm only asking because we had to mess with it in a way...you, uh, had a really bad concussion."

Dylan nodded in understanding; he'd had a concussion before, and the similarities were there. Plus, he had no reason to doubt her.

"Thank you." He said, grateful she'd taken the time to heal both his old and new injuries. Silo met his gaze with a small smile, followed by a quick nod.

Dylan took a deep breath; it was time to ask the hard questions. "What does this Arden want with me?"

Silo began, "He said you were the key to finding the chosen one who's supposed to destroy Aturdokht."

"Some chosen she turned out to be," Kai mumbled.

Dylan glared at Kai. It took everything in him not to punch Kai. "She's trying her best," he said in Jay's defense. "How do you two even know about Aturdokht?" Dylan asked curiously. He remembered Cryis mentioning that she wasn't someone who was widely known within Aris Magica. Had that been a lie?

"Tried." Silo mumbled.

Dylan furrowed his eyebrows again, wondering what she had meant by that.

Silo let out an exasperated sigh before continuing, "Arden again. Three months ago, he learned about a prophecy entailing details about some ancient evil and an Ancient who'd save us from destruction. No one believed him, of course, but so far, everything he's read has come to fruition. When he brought his findings to the council, of course, they already knew about this evil and its destiny." She added with disdain.

There was that name again, Dylan thought.

"What did you mean by 'tried'?" Dylan asked, unable to get her snide comment about Jay out of his mind.

He couldn't care less how the rest of Aris Magica found out about Aturdokht; his priority was Jay. But she was safe; she was with Riley. He'd gotten her to safety…right?

"The girl made herself a vessel for the damn Witch." Kai explained.

Dylan stumbled back, shocked.

What?

His heart caught in his throat, and the world around him froze.

*Jay was…she was…*he couldn't even bring himself to say it.

And what about Riley? Doctor Herron had said he went back for Jay. If he didn't make it in time, then where was he?

Silo reached out a hand grabbing his wrist to steady him from falling back. The world suddenly became out of focus as Dylan's head began to spin, and his breathing began to accelerate. Aturdokht had taken over Jay's body. If that was the case, then everyone back at the cabin—Dylan felt tears rise in his throat. Ami, Lyid, Cryis, even Taybeith were… the lump in his throat expanded, stealing his breath away. He choked back the last word.

Dylan couldn't see any future where Aturdokht had let them live. Although Cryis couldn't die, he was sure she'd keep him in a place where he would suffer. Dylan felt his knees give out as he sank to the floor, taking Silo with him. She grabbed his arms, pulling him into her.

"Easy." She whispered, gently patting Dylan's back. She started taking deep breaths in and out.

Dylan could feel the way she was breathing and tried to mimic it through his panic. He grabbed her and began to cry into her shoulder. He felt an odd sense of comfort being so close to her. Perhaps because she had been the one taking care of him the past couple of days despite the circumstances that surrounded it, Dylan squeezed her tight. Once again, he'd lost the people closest to him. If only he hadn't left the cabin that morning, then maybe they'd all still be alive, and this whole thing would have been over already.

"That's why after you were brought back into Aris Magica," Kai started to explain, continuing on as if nothing had happened. "Arden wanted us to find you. We didn't have to look far; the old man, your Headmaster, basically brought you to the council's doorstep. Arden believed there was a chance that you'd be the first thing Aturdokht went looking for."

Dylan peered up at Kai. Kai tapped the inside of his wrist, pointing to Dylan's. Dylan turned over his hand and saw the marking for the Infinity Staff on his wrist.

"To get rid of you and that."

Dylan's hold on Silo loosened. "But I can't call the staff without Jay, so I'm not much of a threat," he said defeatedly.

"Well, the council disagrees," Kai said. He sighed before offering more of an explanation, "It's your bond with the girl."

"Jay?" Silo asked. She pulled away from Dylan, meeting his eyes.

"She's the chosen one you refer to," Dylan whispered.

Dylan suddenly became embarrassed by how close they were and put more distance between him and Silo. He rose to his feet. Silo did the same, backing up toward her brother, who gave her a weird stare. Dylan cleared his throat, but his eyes still stung from his tears. Kai's words gave Dylan a glimmer of hope.

"Maybe Aturdokht doesn't have full control over Jay's body, and there's still a chance to save her?" With each word he spoke, the spark of hope widened in his chest despite his voice sounding weak.

Kai scrunched his nose in thought but was already shaking his head no. Silo shrugged, uncertain. "That would explain why she hasn't made a move against the human world or ours." Silo contemplated.

Dylan nodded, his spirits lifting even further. He suddenly felt silly for crying as he had. But he couldn't fathom losing Jay—not again. When she'd been taken by the CIA a week ago, he'd nearly lost his mind. He wouldn't lose her again.

"But," Silo began sounding doubtful, "we could be wrong."

Dylan shook his head in disagreement; he had a strong feeling about this. Why else would Arden and the council be seeking him? He could save Jay—he would, no matter what.

"Okay, but how do you even expect to find this girl?" Kai challenged.

"Same way you would have found me if the Headmaster hadn't beaten you to it. It must not have been easy."

"It wouldn't have been." Kai snarked, arching an eyebrow.

"That could work." Silo piqued. "But Dylan," she stepped closer to him once again, looking him in the eyes. Dylan arched an eyebrow; her gaze had changed to a hard resolve. "It's only right for you to know that my brother and I have been given orders to kill Aturdokht on sight, even if Jay gets caught in the crossfire."

Dylan started at her, baffled. Who were these two to have such orders given to them? From what he'd suspected, they were both only Fairies. As quickly as his shock came, his expression darkened. He wouldn't let it come to that, not if he could reason with the council.

"I won't let that happen."

"Dylan," Silo said pitifully, "you have no idea what she's capable of. What we were shown that is to come."

"I don't care," Dylan said defiantly.

Silo glanced behind her at the clock on the wall. It read half past two. "We still have some time before the council is ready for us. Let's go see Arden," She spoke.

"Ready for us?" Dylan asked.

"They sent word a couple of hours ago wanting to see you once your..." Silo once again struggled for the right words, "healing was finished."

"Oh, you were serious about letting him go through with his plan," Kai said.

"Yes, maybe if he saw what we did, he'll reconsider," Silo explained.

"I won't," Dylan sniped.

Kai rolled his eyes, turning to Silo, "Arden! Are you serious!" He exaggerated.

"Hey!" Dylan shouted over Kai. Kai rounded on Dylan and pushed him against the wall behind him. Pictures above them jiggled against the wall.

"Listen deumage, for a Magician, this is a very delicate situation. The council has never gotten involved in the affairs of the Ancient and the Witch because they've never had to. But," he shoved Dylan again, readjusting his grip, "this time, the chosen is too weak! They find you and bring you here, and you want to throw it all away for a rescue mission! If we fail, then *more* than just the human world and Aris Magica will be lost! Do you want that much blood on your hands?"

Dylan brought his arms up and slammed them hard over Kai's, breaking his grip. He calmed himself, making sure not to match Kai's frustration. They had a right to be scared and angry, but neither one of them knew Jay as he did. The resilience she possessed. If Aturdokht had yet to strike, it wasn't of her own volition but Jay's persistence to keep her back as long as she could.

"No one ever asked you to get involved," Dylan said quietly. "I don't care if it's you, the council, a Demon, a Faery, or even Aturdokht herself."

Out of the corner of his eyes, he saw Silo flinch at his words. Faeries and Fairies shared the same pronunciation, but they were complete opposites of each other. Fairies were good, pure, beautiful magic. Faeries were evil, dark creatures that messed with a person's mind and dreams. They had been banished alongside Demons after the Aris Magica war against humans.

"I will stop anyone who tries to get in my way of saving Jay." Dylan warned. Kai went to shove him again, but a gust of wind blew him back, pressing him against the opposite wall.

"Enough!" Silo growled. "Stop acting like children." She lowered her arms, and the wind ceased.

Dylan looked over at her, rather impressed. The only advanced magic he'd seen from a Fairy was healing magic, even though they were capable of much more. They could also use natural elements, just like Witches.

"Now," Silo sighed. "Clearly, we have different agendas, but it doesn't mean we can't work together, at least up until the end." She walked over to the dresser across the room and pulled out a pair of clothes and boots. She tossed it to Dylan. "Try to blend."

Dylan pulled the hooded shirt over his head. The hoodie masked the shirt he already wore. The material was black and cotton. With his silk pants, Dylan thought he must look ridiculous. "Um, you don't happen to own any jeans, do you?"

Kai snorted. "None that you can fit into."

Dylan sighed and began lacing up his boots. Once ready, the three of them exited the hut onto a cobblestone road. Dylan looked around, amazed. It was almost as if they had gone back in time.

Surrounding them were similar huts enclosed by trees. Despite the cobblestone path and huts, everything else was green, as if spring had come early. Flowers lined the path ahead of them, weaving in and out of the huts. All the trees were in full bloom, and the grass was the brightest green he'd ever seen. Dylan glanced over at Silo.

"Home sweet home." She smiled.

Dylan heard a buzzing noise above them, and he looked up to see Fairies flying past. Dylan also noticed traffic signals suspended in the air as well. The Fairies' wings looked like two twigs with seven giant leaves in each one, as if bred directly from a tree.

"Welcome to the Fairy District," Silo said.

"Are we…" Dylan hesitantly pointed to the sky.

Silo looked away, her expression darkening but staying unreadable. "No."

Dylan sighed, relieved. He wasn't sure how he felt about flying. Kai slapped him on the back and laughed. "Why, afraid of heights?"

"Falling from them, yes. And I don't trust that you'll catch me." Dylan smiled uneasily.

He peered at Silo, "Where are your wings anyway. I noticed you and your brother don't have them…out?" He said, unsure of how to phrase the question.

"Having your wings out, tucked, displayed, whatever," Silo began with a slight annoyance to her voice, "depends on preference. There are ways to hide wings with magic entirely. So even though you can't see them, they're always there." Her hand reached for her spine, and she rubbed the spot nearest her shoulder blade, her fingers grazing along her tattoo as she did.

Kai led the way through the huts. Dylan noticed that they stuck out like a sore thumb. Nearly everyone in the Fairy District was either flying or had their wings out. They'd only passed a couple of grounded people like themselves who strolled along the path. Dylan could tell that the Magicians they passed walking weren't Fairies just by how heavily they were dressed. There was no room for their wings to expand.

Dylan glanced ahead to find a group of kids playing with a spiral cloud of magic. They were kicking it back and forth. Dylan smiled sadly; he recalled playing magic ball with his roommates when he was around their age. It seemed so long ago now.

"Fairy District." Dylan said to himself.

"Yeah, how much did your fancy textbooks teach you about Aris?" Kai asked.

"Probably a lot more than I paid attention to," Dylan admitted.

He wasn't the biggest fan of reading or studying. He spent most of his time skipping classes and training instead. "I know Aris Magica is made up of many pocket dimensions, and there are twelve regions across the world, but the US has the governing force."

"The council," Silo corrected. "But impressive," Silo added.

"Sy, don't encourage him, we learned all of that in kindergarten." Kai huffed, kicking some dirt off the path.

Dylan rolled his eyes. "There are three regions located in the US alone. But I couldn't tell you where they start or end."

"Most can't," Silo said. "But yes, inside this region, we're separated by Districts: Fairy," she waved to the area around them, "Wizard and Witches City, because they always have to one-up everyone else," she teased, pointing off to the west, "and Purist." She listed the third on her finger.

Dylan didn't bother asking about Demon and Faery District, knowing it didn't exist, but even still there were still two breeds missing. "What about Hybrids and Immortals?"

Silo sighed, "Hybrids tend to live in the human world since they can pass the easiest for them. And Immortals, well, they roam between the two."

As they neared the edge of town, Dylan began to see tall buildings with leaves that seemed to be growing out of them. If it weren't for the lights coming from some of the building's windows, he would have thought they were abandoned. He could also hear cars. Silo pointed to a sign up ahead notched in the dirt, then straight past it to Fairy District's Downtown. After that, she pointed to the left to Wizard and Witches City. Dylan glanced left and saw towering glass skyscrapers sticking up above the trees. He could see sparks of magic in the air signal some of the busyness of the area.

"Wow," Dylan said in amazement. It was easy to forget how beautiful pocket dimensions were, if Dylan had only been human, he'd never know of the world that existed right before him.

"Is this really your first time this deep within Aris Magica?" Silo asked, walking back to stand beside him.

Dylan looked over at her and nodded his head. "I guess I just never truly saw myself as part of this world," he said. He smiled sadly. "For Jay and me, we were always so concerned with keeping to ourselves, I honestly, for a long time, didn't see a future for us in either world."

"Sounds like you never gave both a chance." She said, staring at the horizon. A smile spread across her face. She grabbed hold of Dylan's wrist, "Come on!" She began to pull him in the opposite direction, back towards Fairy District.

"Oh no, where the hell are you going?" Kai shouted from up ahead. He tossed a thumb behind him towards the forest. "Arden is this way!"

Silo stuck her tongue out at him, "We still have plenty of time to see Arden and make it to the council on time." She let go of Dylan's wrist and faced her brother. "Are you really going to deprive an Aris Magician of their culture?" She challenged.

Kai looked flabbergasted. His mouth hung open, and his eyes bugged out at her. He stumbled for words, "W-w-what!" He let out a long and loud groan. "Fine! But only one hour. Deal?"

Silo turned to Dylan with a wide grin on her face. "Deal." She held out her hand for Dylan to take. "Follow me."

Chapter Eight

Silo had led Dylan and Kai to the heart of Fairy District. When they'd entered the central street, Dylan had to take a step back in awe. Unlike the hutted neighborhood he'd traveled through earlier, this side of Fairy District was much more modern.

The roads were a reflective color as if they had been freshly rained on, but there wasn't a single puddle in sight. Shops ranging from bakeries to clothing stores to Fairy flight wear lined either side of the street, decorated in dazzling lights and colorful awnings. On every corner, potted trees wove in and out between the shops.

At the center of the street was a statue of a large tree that looked as if it were growing from the ground. On top of it sat a statue of a Fairy on her knees, holding a single flower in one hand while the other was stretched to the sky. Her wings were grandiose and coated in stained glass paint that reflected a multitude of colors onto the ground when the sun glistened through it. In the sky, more Fairies flew past, while the streets were filled with both Fairies and other Magician breeds alike.

Dylan focused on a group of four Fairies as they perused the shops on the corner. They were all dressed in elegant, bright dresses that stopped just before their knees. Their wings were each tucked neatly along their spines. While a couple of them carried shopping bags in their hands, one of them was holding a brightly blended drink. One of them stopped and pointed at a mannequin in the window, leaving the others to laugh and giggle before they decided to go into the store.

Dylan couldn't help but smile sadly. Jay immediately came to mind, and he wondered if they had been born differently, could that have been them one day? He wanted to come back and explore this part of themselves together. He remembered all the times he'd stopped her from trying to find out who she was, and he regretted it. Maybe if he hadn't, then they could have worked toward finding peace in themselves, but...

No one can run from their destiny, he thought sourly.

However, if he had been more open, then maybe she would be with him right now, and they'd be exploring Aris Magica together.

"Beautiful, isn't it?" Silo asked from beside him, pulling him back to reality.

He turned to look at her, finding that she was already staring at him. He smiled, "I had no idea this place existed."

He wondered how many, if any, of the people around him knew of Aturdokht's return. Judging by how carefree everyone looked, he doubted it. Part of it angered him, how could the council hide such a great evil from everyone? If Aturdokht decided to act, everything here—everyone—would be gone. It terrified him.

Kai snorted. "What, you thought all of Aris Magica was some rural, ancient place?" Kai said, half joking.

"Well, yes." Dylan said without any sarcasm.

He hadn't given Aris Magica much thought, as much as he had been a part of the world, there was still a disconnect to it. He had never planned to know more about it than he had to, but now, with war looming on the horizon, he felt regretful.

"Oh, there it is, plus the line's not that long either!" Silo nearly shouted.

Before Dylan could make sense of what Silo had seen, she grabbed hold of Dylan's wrist again and led him down the sidewalk on the left. He didn't resist and smiled as he followed her. Behind him, he heard Kai sigh before his footsteps could be heard as well.

Silo led them to a bakery on the far corner of the street. Dylan could smell an aroma of sweetness in the air before they even got to the front door. On the outside of the building, a sign read *A Witches Brew*. Below was a window sticker of a Witch's silhouette pointing a finger at animated breads, cupcakes, and cakes.

The line was already out the door. Silo stopped just short of it and pointed at the window. Dylan noticed she hadn't let go of his wrist yet, but it didn't bother him. He turned and followed her gaze, peering through the glass. Inside were freshly baked bread, desserts, and cakes lined neatly in a display for passing customers. His mouth watered as he spotted a small square cake with layers of white frosting, topped with four strawberries buried into the bread.

Silo pressed her free hand to the glass, obviously eying the same cake. She and Dylan exchanged a mouthwatering glance. As if in agreement, they both broke into another smile.

"Split it?" Silo asked.

"I was thinking the same thing."

Before Kai could think to stop them, they ran for the line and claimed their spot. It wasn't until then that Silo had dropped her hand from his wrist, offering a quick apology as she did.

"I didn't mind," Dylan said in response.

She scrunched her nose at him, Dylan couldn't help but find her reaction cute. "I have a feeling you're just being polite."

Dylan laughed, genuinely laughed. It was the first time he had in a while. "Believe it or not, I can be just as touchy of a person too." He instantly regretted his words. His face flushed red.

Touchy? Really? He cursed himself internally.

When Silo laughed in response, Dylan relaxed a bit, but his embarrassment didn't go away. Silo glanced past Dylan and rolled her eyes. He turned and saw Kai standing behind him, looking more than annoyed at the two of them.

"What?" She asked.

"I didn't say anything," he said.

"You don't have to! It's written on your face."

Kai rolled his eyes. "The more time we spend here, the less time you have with your little friend Arden. And do you even have the money for this place?"

"No, but you do!" Silo smirked. "Arden can wait an hour longer. Plus, Dylan hasn't eaten."

Kai threw up his hands, "Whatever! Do what you want. From his back pocket, he pulled out a small leather coin pouch and tossed it to Silo. "I'm going to go check out the newest Fairy Flight issue. I'll meet you under Nivea once you're done." He cast Dylan an icy glare before stalking in the direction of the statue.

"What's his deal?" Dylan asked once Kai was out of earshot. The line moved, allowing them both to take a couple of steps forward.

Silo shrugged. "He's always grumpy, birth defect."

Dylan suppressed a smile. "No, I meant with Arden."

A dark shadow fell across Silo's features. "Oh," she said barely above a whisper. She turned away from Dylan and stared inside the shop. "Outcasts have to stick together."

Dylan frowned, wondering what she meant, but he knew better than to ask. Instead, he asked, "What's Nivea?"

Silo looked back at him, her expression lightening with relief, Dylan found himself growing happy because of it.

"Nivea is a person, not a what." She pointed at the gigantic statue towering over the entire place. "She was the Fairy who helped legalize Flight across all of Aris Magica. Fairy Flight used to only be restricted to Fairy District unless you had probable cause to do so. She fought for both Fairies and Faeries alike."

Before the Aris Magica wars, Fairies and Faeries lived in tandem with each other. The only way to truly tell them apart was by the shape of their wings. Fairy wings resembled tree branches full of life, whereas Faery wings seemed to hold a decaying essence to them.

Silo wore a proud smile as she continued. "She didn't care about the prejudices surrounding Faeries at the time and tried her best to stand up for what was right, and I respect that about her."

Dylan had stopped staring at the statue and was now staring at Silo. He could tell how much admiration she had for the Fairy. "She sounds brave." Dylan found himself saying.

Dylan had his own preconceptions about Faeries, especially after meeting Aturdokht. Although he could understand why some Magicians decided to align with her, he couldn't condone what they had done under her rule.

Faeries were weavers. Back at the Institute, he learned about how they would transform memories within people's minds, making them crazy or pushing dark thoughts into their dreams.

The influence they had over humans and Magicians terrified him. He wasn't surprised to learn that they had sided with Aturdokht after he learned about her, too. However, perhaps it was wrong for him to lump all Faeries together, especially since he'd never met one.

"She was," Silo said tightly, her smile had disappeared.

They waited the rest of the time in silence. The line had moved fast, and before they knew it, they had ordered and returned outside the building with their cake. The inside of the bakery had been too packed to even find space to eat. Instead, they decided to wait to eat their cake until they made it to the statue.

When they arrived, Dylan noticed they weren't alone. There were dozens of people posing for pictures with the great Nivea, while others were lying in the grass surrounding the statue, indulging in picnics. The one thing they all had in common was they were all couples.

Dylan looked around for Kai, but clearly, they had beat him to the meeting spot. When Dylan turned back to Silo, she was holding out a baby plastic fork to him. He smiled, slightly nervous, and took it. They ended up sitting where the concrete met the grass. They took turns taking small bites from the tiny cake. A burst of flavor exploded in Dylan's mouth with every bite he took. He had to admit that this may be the best cake he had ever tasted.

As if reading his mind, Silo broke the silence between them and asked, "How is it?"

Dylan still had a mouthful in his cheeks. He vigorously nodded his head. "Reawygood!" He tried to say, but the words blended.

Silo covered her mouth with the back of her hand and laughed. Dylan swallowed. "Thank you," he said.

"For what?" Silo asked nervously.

"For this." He gestured to the cake. "And for showing me this," He waved his free hand all around them. "Without you, I wouldn't have known any of this. I'm grateful to you for it."

"If I knew it would be this easy to win you over, I would have brought over a cake sooner." She grinned before taking the last bite for herself. She waved it in the air between them.

"Hey!" Dylan laughed, leaning towards the cake, as he did, his hand slipped in the grass, causing him to fall forward.

Silo gasped, falling back as well. She held the cake bite high into the air, but before she could use her other hand to break their fall, Dylan wrapped an arm around her, using his hand to stop them from hitting the ground. When he lifted his head, his face was inches from hers. His wide eyes met hers—they were as big as a dear in headlights.

"Sorry," he said breathlessly. His eyes wandered down to her lips. He could see the bit of frosting she had stuck to her top lip. He was so close now he could kiss her. Dylan swallowed the thought as quickly as it came.

Behind them, Kai cleared his throat. "You two finished?"

Dylan instinctively dropped his arm, and Silo fell back into the grass. The last bit of cake fell from the fork in her hand. Dylan winced, "I'm so—"

Silo held out a hand to him, "No, no, it's fine." She scooted back from underneath him and stood to her feet. She brushed the grass from her leathers and offered a hand to Dylan. He embarrassingly took it.

Once to his feet, Dylan and Silo turned to face Kai. He was already shaking his head. "I don't even want to know." He turned on his heels, waving a hand over his shoulder. "Follow me."

Kai led them through the remainder of the street, through shops and people, all the while rambling about his disappointment in this season's flight-wear. Dylan couldn't focus on a single word he was saying. He stared at the ground as they walked, tangled in his thoughts.

His mind kept traveling back to how close he'd been to almost kissing Silo. He wasn't even sure he wanted to kiss her. Sure, he found her attractive, but so much of what she did reminded him of Jay. Jay, who he'd kissed only a couple of days ago. Who he cherished more than anything else in this world, a single sharing of cake couldn't change that. Wouldn't change that.

"As I was saying!" Kai shouted, cutting through Dylan's thoughts. Dylan finally looked up, only to find that they had made it back onto the forest trail.

"No one cares," Silo said. She was a few steps ahead of them both. She came to a stop a couple of steps later. "This way." She pointed to the thicker part of the forest leading to the right. "Shortcut."

Kai's shoulders dropped as he took the lead leaving Dylan and Silo to follow close behind.

The further they walked into the forest, the more disoriented the trees became. They started to take on an unnatural geometric form. They created a twisted canopy of shade from the sun above. The ground became uneven, sloping into rolling hills.

"This place is weird." Dylan mumbled.

Silo giggled. "Only to an outsider like you." Dylan let out a small breath of relief. At least things back at the statue hadn't made things weird between them.

Kai shuddered. "Nope, the newbie's right, this place always gives me the creeps." Kai made a gagging face. "I'm going to scout ahead." He broke away from the group, running up the next hill. His sword and axes clanged together with every step.

Silo laughed again, shaking her head at her brother's dismissal. "Nervous?" She asked, turning to Dylan.

Dylan watched as Kai came to a stop at the top of the hill. Dylan tore his gaze away from Kai and placed it on Silo. "No." Dylan answered without hesitation.

"Good. You shouldn't be. Despite what everyone says, Arden's not bad."

The two walked in silence as they started up the hill. Kai was still waiting at the top of it, and once they reached him, he fell back in step with them.

"Who is he anyway?" Dylan asked.

Silo and Kai both stopped in their tracks. "You're kidding, right?" Kai said with a bodacious laugh. Silo slapped him on the arm.

"Arden Stone," Silo said.

Dylan's eyes grew big. "Arden Stone, as in a descendant of Sylvester Stone."

Dylan watched as Kai drew a symbol in the air of an *S* with a hooked line through it. Arden belonged to the house of Stone. A powerful Wizarding house that had been the first to create pocket dimensions. Sylvester was the Mad Wizard, who had been stripped of his magic.

Dylan opened his mouth to say something, but the only words he could muster were, "You've got to be kidding me."

Dylan could only imagine what people said about Arden Stone. Sylvester had gone from a beloved Magician to a lunatic Demon lover. His cursed reputation lingered with every passing relative, branding them with the mark of Stone, letting others know a traitor runs through their blood.

"He's the one that had us watching out for you in the first place, on account of some Oracle and the council's permission, of course." Silo said the council's name spitefully. Dylan suspected she held the council in low regard.

An Oracle, Dylan thought.

As rare as Oracles were, he'd heard of two now, he recalled Doctor Herron. "I thought Arden was an Echo."

Silo laughed, "Yes, he is, but he does have a friend or two that he occasionally borrows powers from."

Dylan stared at her, bemused.

Is it possible for a breed to obtain another breed's power?

Arden was just as curious and experimental as Sylvester had been.

Silo continued, "Arden can kind of see into the future, you know, but also the past, except for him, he already knows which future you will choose. In contrast, an Oracle can only speculate. He saw you coming the moment fate decided your place in this world. But he's very selective." She rushed out, "So don't ask him any questions about your future, alright?" She warned. From how she talked about him, Dylan could see that Silo admired him.

Silo slowed to a stop. Dylan looked over at her, noticing she was no longer with him. He stopped, glancing back, seeing her a few feet behind. She was nervously twisting one of her braids around her finger. Dylan retraced his steps, coming up beside her. "What is it?"

"I never got the chance to apologize for," she pointed to his head. "Your headache wasn't an accident. I messed with your memories. If Aturdokht used your bond to find you before you were healed, I wanted to make it as difficult as possible. Arden said we couldn't let Aturdokht find you, not in that state."

Dylan held her gaze a little longer before saying anything. Her foxlike eyes reminded him of Jay's in the way Silo looked up at him sincerely. He could tell she was truly sorry.

"I didn't know Fairies could do that." Dylan found himself saying.

Her eyes widened, "We can't!" She rushed out. "I, uh, gave you a tonic through the IV." She nearly shouted the last word.

Dylan laughed. "It's alright, I accept your apology."

The only way to physically use that kind of magic was to be a Faery. He knew as much as anyone that they had been banished and sealed away.

"But," there was one thing Dylan didn't fully understand, "how could Aturdokht find me?" He clenched his fist, "She's only ever been after Jay."

"Well, as your Headmaster explained to me, you and Jay have come to share a bond that ties you in prophecy." She pointed to the trident scar on the inside of his wrist. "I guess he was worried it could be used to find one another, especially with a high magic grip. But I guess we were worried for nothing." Silo admitted.

Dylan shook his head; the Headmaster wouldn't make an inference like that unless he had probable cause. Dylan trusted him, so despite the violation he felt from his memories being meddled with, he understood.

"Your Headmaster is a wise person. Kind, too." Silo smiled. Dylan looked over at her inquisitively. "We spent some time together when you first arrived here. He saw right through me." She shared a secretive smile with herself. Dylan silently arched an eyebrow, staring at her as she did.

Dylan opened his mouth to ask her what she meant, but Kai's booming voice stopped him. "If you're done flirting with my sister!" Kai yelled from the top of the next hill.

Dylan jumped, his hand dropping to his side. He glanced up at Kai, annoyed. Dylan sputtered for a response, but Kai beat him to it once again.

"We're here! Get a move on!" He waved his hands above his head a little too manically.

Silo and Dylan ran up the hill after Kai, once they joined him at the top, Dylan nudged Kai in the rib. He whispered, "I wasn't flirting."

Kai rolled his eyes and whispered back. "Does it look like I actually care? No need to convince me."

"I already have a girl...friend." Dylan said but knew he didn't sound as persuasive as he hoped.

Dylan thought of Jay, but he wasn't sure exactly what they were anymore. On the eve of the battle, they'd shared a kiss, but they didn't have time to talk about what that meant for them. Dylan gently touched his lips, smiling to himself, remembering her body close to his.

Beside him, Kai shuddered. "Gross."

Dylan rolled his eyes and looked below. It was an empty clearing within the forest, but Dylan could feel the tantalizing thrill of magic below. He began to trek down the hill with the others. Once at the bottom, Dylan waved his hands through the residue of magic floating in the air. The magic shifted again, and tiny flakes of spatial magic appeared before him, moving together toward the center of the clearing.

The magic began to form into the silhouette of a person before hardening and falling away like dead skin in a pile of dust. Arden stood in the remains of the magic. His skin was a sun-kissed brown, and his eyes pointed at the end like a cat's. A long golden braid was tucked inside the collar of his tunic. On his right cheek, he had an intricate tattoo of a fancy double *S* with the tails branching off into twisting designs across his face. It resembled the Aris Magica emblem.

Dylan's eyes widened. Magic never ceased to amaze him. He continued to walk ahead of the others towards the man.

"Arden Stone," Dylan said. He glanced behind Arden, noticing the distortion of space. The trees looked blurry, as if a thin veil were covering the space between them. Dylan wondered what Arden was hiding.

Arden shook the dust from the robes he now wore. "In the flesh, darling." Arden grinned.

"You know who I am?" He said to Arden.

Arden chuckled before replying, "I know everyone in this godforsaken region."

Dylan stopped before Arden. "Then you know what I've been through?"

"No." Arden held up his hand, which now had a soft white glow to it.

Arden flicked his fingers, and the light seeped off the tips and danced in the air, turning into the silhouette of two women. They both started to attack each other engaged in a fierce battle.

"I know what you've lost and how to find it. If that's what you want." One of the silhouettes swallowed the other, and the light turned black before turning into ashes. Dylan gasped, staring wide-eyed at the illusion that had represented Aturdokht and Jay.

His stomach dropped at the sight of it. "How?"

"I find information and follow the streams of past and present to its destination. And the information that has made its way to me tells me that hope still exists. But before, you're needed here to set the stage and handle more pressing matters before finding the girl." Arden held out the palm of his hand towards Dylan. Dylan stared at it, confused as to what Arden wanted. Arden grinned slyly, "Information isn't free. Think of me as a mercenary of sorts."

"Arden, enough with the games. Just tell him what he wants to know," Silo said.

Arden shrugged. "I just did. It's not my fault you didn't understand." He pouted. "Anyway, it's not up to me as you know. The council will decide the boy's next move." Arden leaned into Dylan and whispered, "The council's very political these days and watchful. All fuss and no fun."

Kai crossed his arms. "I told the both of you that this would be a waste of time. We should have just gone straight to the council."

Silo glared at Kai before turning to Arden. "You said he could help. *You* told me to bring him here so that *you* could give him the answers he sought."

"I told you to bring him here so that I can get a good look at him, you silly girl." Arden glanced at Dylan and smirked. "And I have."

Silo groaned, frustrated.

Dylan tried to work out the riddle of words Arden had thrown at him. "Why am I needed here? What about finding Jay?" He had to get back to her.

"The Ancient," Arden quirked. "Oh, you'll see her eventually. Your paths, no matter how far you stray, will always cross. But Aris," he waved his hand around, "will soon be in disarray because of the Ancient's actions."

He swayed closer, resting a hand on Dylan's shoulder. Dylan couldn't help but take a whiff of Arden. He smelled like a decaying plant. Dylan scrunched his nose and tried to hold his breath. Dylan could smell Arden's family curse on him.

"The council is the say all and see all of Aris Magica. And they say and see that Jay is a threat who must pay for the atrocities Aturdokht has committed in past lives as well as this life."

"But they've never cared before," Dylan said.

"Because there was nothing for them to care about with a competent reincarnation behind the wheels." Arden said. Dylan gritted his teeth from saying anything.

"But the point is!" Arden shouted. "You've experienced what the council fears firsthand. You can convince those naysayers. With the council on your side, even if an all-out war ensues, at least you'd have the trust backing of the most powerful Magicians of our time."

"Here we go," Kai mumbled.

Arden ignored him, turning both himself and Dylan away from Kai. His robe whacked Dylan in the process.

"Arden's been trying to grab at the council since birth. It's what the Stone family does. I told you we can't trust him." Kai said from behind them.

"Kai, shut it." Silo snapped. She walked over to where Arden and Dylan stood. "Arden, please," she begged. "You told me he would be the key in helping us stop Aturdokht."

"We can stop her after Jay's separated from her. Then she can use the Infinity Staff."

Silo bowed her head, "Dylan, please not now."

"The Infinity Staff, what an intriguing power." Arden hummed.

Dylan gave him a confused look, "How much do you know about the staff's power?" He knew Jay and himself had only scratched the surface when they both called it.

"In the past, the Ancient alone has been able to call it forth. It's strange, isn't it, that it suddenly takes two." Arden said with a slow smile.

Before Dylan had a chance to process what Arden had said, the ground around him began to shake. Arden began to walk away from them.

"Visit the council. They should be ready for you now. They'll fill you in on the rest." Arden began walking back towards the way he appeared, where the pile of dust remained. The ashes of magic picked themselves up, forming a door.

"Arden!" Silo shouted, trying to chase after him, but Kai stopped her. His wings sprouted from his back, resembling firelit leaves. He flapped them, holding her back.

"Toodles. Don't worry, we'll meet again." Arden winked before stepping through the door, as he did, his magic vanished in the blink of an eye.

"Dammit." Silo cursed. "He gets in these moods where he's just so difficult and useless."

Silo pulled free of Kai's arms. Kai retracted his wings and glanced over at Dylan. Silo pushed past them both and walked to the nearest tree, and kicked it, letting out her anger. Dylan watched, knowing exactly what it felt like to feel betrayed by someone you trust.

"Sy, calm down!" Kai shouted over to her. "What did you expect?" He followed up.

"I expected him to cooperate," Silo said, defeated.

Kai scoffed. "Your optimism is rubbing off on her." He scowled at Dylan. "Given his track record, Sy, he comes from a long line of traitors."

"I thought..." Silo faltered, glancing at Dylan. She sighed and looked away. "Never mind," she said, dropping it.

But Kai didn't let it go as easily, "You want to be a hero so badly, don't you? And for what?" Silo flinched at his words. "What did you think? You'd bring him, and then the three of us would ride off into the sunset and take down the greatest evil this world has seen in centuries? Please don't tell me you're that naïve!" Kai yelled.

Kai shot a glare at Dylan and then stalked over to Silo. He grabbed her by the arm and pulled her close. He continued their conversation in a low voice, too quiet for Dylan to make out. All he could see was the crushing disappointment written on Silo's face growing, and it bothered him.

Dylan rubbed the back of his neck as he watched the two argue. He wasn't sure if he had any right to step in. Dylan could see himself in Kai, always trying to protect Jay when he was the one that was inhibiting her from being herself. Looking at Kai now, Dylan wondered if he'd been this stifling as well. He sighed, unable to take it any longer.

"Okay," he walked over to them and tore them apart. "Enough you two." He looked at Kai and then at Silo. "We made a mistake about Arden; it's not the end of the world. And just because he didn't tell us exactly what we wanted doesn't make him a traitor or Silo wrong."

He looked at Silo and smiled softly, he thought he saw a sparkling twinkle in her eyes as she smiled, but when he looked again, it wasn't there. "Let's just go to the council before we lose our minds." He turned to Kai. "Okay?"

"Fine." Kai tore away from them both. He looked over at Dylan. "Just know you asked for this."

<h1 style="text-align:center">Chapter Nine</h1>

The world outside was no kinder than the one Cryis had left behind. The night sky was covered with dark, ominous clouds. A storm brewed, and the mist of falling snow was caught in the fierce winds. Cryis could feel the shrill of winter eating away at his skin through his thin prison uniform. His feet shifted uncomfortably in the worn leather boots that Arthur had found. The air felt like it was getting colder by the second.

The team was crouched behind a tall metal box that buzzed with electricity against the building. The shadow cast from the moon above provided the perfect cover for them.

Cryis calculated the distance from their position to the gate across the field. It was at least a good 800 meters off. Maybe seven to twelve guards stood watch, patrolling in the snow—not to mention the ones stationed in the two towers on either end of the gate. To them, Cryis and Ami were still criminals. No matter how they went about it, their escape would look like a breakout.

Cryis looked behind them at the building they'd just left. They had been kept in a heavily guarded compound. The compound sat on a hill that sloped into a snowy field. The building was a windowless concrete box surrounded by metal poles with wires strung from one roof to the other.

Metal pillars shot up from the ground in a pathway towards the gate. The gate was attached to a wired electrical fence that stretched around the entirety of the field. Cryis could see two concrete towers on either end of the fence and two more standing tall behind the compound. Out of the corner of his eyes, he saw a truck flash its lights as it drove up a winding pathway toward the back of the building.

The only reason they'd made it this far had been because of Vastille's eye. If he hadn't been controlling the electromagnetic current of the prison's security system, then they would have been quickly caught by the guards.

The fence ahead hummed with the sound of electricity. Cryis leaned up against the wall of the building, peering out from the shadows at the guards walking the field. Each one was loaded with a rifle or pistol attached to a holster on their hip. The fence was the least of their worries. If they were spotted, their biggest problem would be avoiding getting shot. Cryis glanced at his group, doubting their ability to maneuver bullets.

"What's your plan?" Arthur whispered through fierce shivers. Vastille and Arthur were the best dressed of them all and still showed signs of freezing in this weather.

Cryis nudged Vastille. He had noticed the cameras on every corner of the building leading up towards the gate. Their little heads swiveled back and forth, looking for signs of danger. Vastille nodded, "Already on it. I've taken care of the cameras and shut down the siren. So, unless one of the guards makes it back inside, reinforcements shouldn't be a problem."

"What about the fence?" Cryis asked.

Vastille removed his sunglasses, revealing his eyes for the first time. One was a hazel, while the other was made of metallic gold. At the moment, it was glowing while Vastille stared straight ahead at the main gate.

"You're one of them, too?" Arthur exclaimed.

Vastille grimaced, "Yes." He put his sunglasses back on. "It's out of my reach; I can't feel the electromagnetic wave I need from here to control it."

"Damn." Cryis cursed. "What do you need us to do? We need that gate open."

"Cover me and get me close. I'm going to have to be practically touching it to shut something that big down."

"Okay," Cryis whispered. "Arthur, you're with me."

"W-w-what?" Arthur stuttered. Vastille passed him a second gun and gestured to the one Arthur already had on his hip.

"You and Cryis take out the men on the ground. If they reach the compound, it's game over for us. Our chances are already slim as it is." Vastille explained. Before moving ahead, he hesitated, turning back to the group. "Try not to kill them if you can."

"What about me?" Ami asked.

"What about you?" Arthur slowly asked in return.

Cryis recognized the determination he saw on Ami's face; it reflected what he felt. "You think you have enough energy to take out the watchers in the towers?"

Ami smirked, "I've made a full recovery. Don't worry about a thing!"

Cryis couldn't help but grin back at her, "'Atta girl." He rose to his full height, towering over the others still crouching in the snow. "We don't have all night, so let's get moving."

The team split. Ami and Vastille ran left, staying low and out of sight, using the metal pillars across the field as cover. Cryis and Arthur ran straight down the middle of the field toward the group of guards.

"Hey!" One of the guards shouted, drawing her gun.

Cryis grabbed his gun, turning off the safety. He had opted for a gun over his scythe. He wasn't strong enough to wield his weapon's magic just yet. If he tried, he'd be face-first in the snow after a couple of swings. He kept his scythe hidden in a small-paired pocket dimension only accessible to him.

The guard came at Cryis fast, but he was faster, raising his gun and putting the guard down seconds later. He tried his best not to go for a kill shot, but still, something where the guard wouldn't be getting up anytime soon. The sound of gunshots alerted the other guards of their location. A group of them began advancing on all sides.

"Shit!" Arthur shouted.

Cryis could see some of the guards trying to use their radios, but each of them failed to connect with anyone inside the building. Vastille had cut their line, rerouting their connection from a distance.

"Comms down." A guard shouted. "Advance on me!"

In a matter of seconds, Arthur and Cryis would be surrounded. Arthur fired his gun, dropping two more guards. Cryis backed up into Arthur, their bodies back-to-back as they dropped a couple more guards to the ground.

Cryis pushed Arthur to the ground as one of the men sent a round of bullets flying in their direction. The bullets flew right through Cryis's arm, protecting Arthur's head. Cryis raised his gun with his opposite hand and fired, but his gun clicked, not expelling any bullets.

"Shit!" Cryis said.

Cryis looked down at his arm punctured with holes, blood pooled from his arm onto his hand, dripping into the snow. Arthur stood up and pushed Cryis down, he leaned over his back and fired off his gun, hitting a man between the eyes.

"For the record, this was a terrible plan!" Arthur shouted over the gunfire.

Another round of bullets went off around them. Arthur grabbed Cryis's uninjured arm and pulled him to his feet. Arthur aimlessly fired bullets as he and Cryis ran to the nearest pillar.

"We're taking a lot of heat! And I think I saw some of the other guards peel off and go after the others." Arthur said once they'd reached the safety of the pillar.

Cryis removed the case on his gun, "I'm out." He tossed his gun aside and ripped the bottom of his shirt. He took the loose material and tied it around his bleeding arm.

Arthur removed his case as well, checking his gun. "I only have a couple of rounds left."

"Dammit."

"What do we do now?" Arthur asked, slumping against the pillar. Another bullet ricocheted off the metal, causing him to flinch.

"How many are there?" Cryis asked.

Arthur peered around the pillar. He fired off two shots before returning into hiding. A bullet nearly grazed his arm. "Three now."

Cryis heard the familiar sound of a blade cutting through the air before he saw it. He barely had time to push Arthur out of the way before the blade cut through Cryis's skin and bone, causing him to fall on all fours. Blood spurted from a gash on Cryis's back where the axe had cut him.

In the distance, Cryis thought he heard Ami shout his name, but he couldn't hear past the pain he felt. Arthur scrambled to him only to be stopped short by the three guards still firing at them. Instead, tailored boots reached Cryis first, stopping right before him.

"Get up." Kazimir cooed. "My queen is looking for you, you know. Had I realized it earlier, I wouldn't have sent you off with my puppet." Cryis peered up at Kazimir. Bloodlust reflected in his voice and eyes.

"Cryis!" Agent Kanon shouted, approaching from the next pillar over. His eyes were glazed with a black film, Cryis had been right; he was being controlled.

Cryis cried out, digging his fingers into the snow. His scream turned into fast, rageful breaths. He pushed himself up, fighting through the pain. He stood up, facing Kazimir. The man smiled at him, satisfied. He clutched his axe in his hands, waiting for Cryis to hone his weapon. Cryis glared, wanting nothing more than to wipe the smug look off Kazimir's cold, callous face.

"*Jevit.*" Cryis shouted, using every last strength he could muster. His scythe appeared and fell into his hands. Its black onyx blade wrapped around his body.

Cryis coughed up more blood, his insides burned; withdrawing the scythe had nearly exerted him. Cryis dragged the scythe through the snow before swinging it up in a beautiful arc aimed toward Kanon.

Kanon drew his gun, but Cryis was faster, the tip of his scythe cutting through Kanon's soul, expelling part of Kazimir's Demon from his body. Cryis ensured his blade didn't cut flesh as Kanon's eyes returned to normal before the man passed out.

"Well, aren't you clever?" Kazimir grimaced, gripping his chest, as part of his soul reunited inside him.

Cryis turned his scythe on Kazimir. Kazimir brought his axe up, blocking the scythe's blade. Cryis's attack lacked its usual power. Normally, a regular weapon wouldn't stand a chance against *Jevit.* Cryis channeled his magic through it, enhancing the blade's strength and usage. Kazimir frowned, a look of disappointment passing over his face.

Cryis stumbled back; he wasn't surprised to see his attack had failed. Kazimir barely allowed him a chance to breathe before he swung the axe at Cryis again.

Cryis spun his scythe, deflecting every hit from Kazimir. Each time the metal connected, a sharp vibration was sent shooting from the staff into Cryis's hands. He could feel the full force behind each of Kazimir's swings.

Out of the corner of Cryis's eyes, he saw Ami knock out two of the remaining guards on Arthur. She pulled Arthur to his feet and further away from Cryis's battle. Cryis could see Arthur trying to resist, but Ami was just as resilient.

"What are you watching?" Kazimir brought his axe down harder again and again like a maniac, taking advantage of the distraction. His laugh echoed inside Cryis's ears.

There was no pattern to his attacks. Cryis blocked Kazimir again, only for Kazimir to kick out his leg, knocking Cryis in his gut. Cryis dropped his scythe down in time to block it.

Kazimir swung his axe again, slicing Cryis's chest as he did. Cryis was unable to bring his scythe up fast enough to block. Kazimir pulled back his axe and licked the blood from the blade.

Cryis had to find a way to get Kazimir to come out of the human body. Otherwise, Cryis couldn't truly touch him. The Demon is Kazimir was too deeply hidden within his soul for Cryis to expel it as easily as he did with Kanon, who was only being controlled through his mind.

Cryis grabbed his chest with his free hand, trying to hold his body together. The wound on his back and arm had yet to heal, and now he was bleeding from his front as well. If it wasn't for the support of his weapon, Cryis would have fallen to his knees.

He leaned against the staff of his scythe; it was becoming harder for him to focus on anything other than the pain he felt.

"What do you even get out of this?" Cryis panted breathlessly.

Kazimir smirked. He rushed at Cryis again. Cryis raised his scythe. "The satisfaction of conducting my experiments." Instead of using his axe to attack, Kazimir kicked up snow, blinding Cryis.

Experiments?

The thought caught Cryis off guard. He felt a punch to his stomach that sent him to his knees.

Cryis dropped his scythe and looked down. A bullet hole punctured his shirt and already bleeding chest. Darkness clouded his vision. He peered up at Kazimir to see him holding a pistol he'd been hiding away. It was aimed at Cryis. How'd he not notice it until now?

"No..." Cryis said weakly.

"Don't worry, my queen wants you alive for now." Kazimir shed the human body, revealing the Demon's true form. Its body was that of a tiger standing on its hind legs, while its head was that of a ram. Its two horns curled out, casting a shadow over Cryis's body. The Demon lifted its axe to deliver another blow.

Cryis felt his body burning from the inside out. Suddenly, everything around felt as if it were happening in slow motion. Kazimir lifted its axe and swung it through the air.

No, Cryis thought he wasn't done yet.

Cryis looked past Kazimir at the gate ahead.

I have to make it.

Cryis felt a burst of energy explode inside him, stopping more blood from leaving his body. He'd felt a similar energy once before back in the cabin when facing Jay.

A blue energy cast around him as Cryis grabbed his scythe, swinging it faster than Kazimir could its axe. The scythe cut cleanly through Kazimir's arm as well as shattering its axe. The Demon's arm fell to its feet, its hand still wrapped around the hilt of the axe as it hit the snow.

Kazimir howled, trying to stop the blood with its other hand. The pain brought Kazimir to its knees. The Demon looked up at Cryis through Kazimir's good eye, with tears glossing its gaze. Cryis's eyes were glowing gold.

Cryis stood over Kazimir, taking in rigid breaths. It would be so easy to just end him now. Cryis gripped *Jevit* tighter. He slowly began to raise it into the air, but the pulse of an electric wave passed over him as the gate was shut down.

Cryis looked up and saw the others hightailing it to the fence. He grimaced and then looked down at Kazimir. The shell of his body was already withering away after losing too much blood. Soon, the Demon inside him would be dead as well. He was unable to read Kazimir's expression as the Demon through him stared back at him.

Cryis sighed and tapped his scythe's staff twice into the ground. It disappeared in his hands. Cryis felt the darkness of exhaustion return as the power that helped him vanished along with the scythe. The blood that had stopped flowing from his injuries resumed, causing Cryis to stagger.

"How?" Kanon's voice broke through the air.

Cryis looked over his shoulder at Kanon, who had regained consciousness. The man was stunned, staring at Kazimir's demonized body as it withered away into nothingness. Cryis had destroyed it, or whatever was inside him had.

Cryis glanced back towards the fence, seeing the others had made it. He turned back to Kanon, searching for an explanation, but Kanon seemed to quickly grasp the situation.

Kanon shook his head, "Go."

Cryis looked away from him and began to run towards the open fence. Heat singed his hair as he passed through the gate in the nick of time before Vastille released his control over its electromagnetic wave.

Ami clutched a hand over her mouth upon seeing Cryis. Vastille and Arthur were both speechless and staring at him. Arthur opened his mouth to say something as Cryis looked over at him but closed it.

Cryis grinned at Arthur, "See...that wasn't hard...at all..." Cryis collapsed.

Chapter Ten

*R*iley. Jay said his name repeatedly, wishing she could just say it out loud and let him know that she was right there. She hated what she was doing to him. Even though it was Aturdokht pulling the strings, it was still her body—her face everyone saw.

She looked down at the table he was strapped to. His eyes were closed, but the pain remained. His skin had taken on a greenish-yellow hue that overlapped with the purple tint of his veins. He had begun to grow ridges that protruded from his forehead, not quite horns yet. She grimaced. He looked so strong, yet weak all at once, and it terrified her. She had never known him to be weak, and even associating him with the word broke her further. After Aturdokht had taken over her body and blown up the safe house, she tried to escape into the forest. That's when she met Riley. He had been on the brink of death himself, yet still found the strength to come back for her. Except it was too late. Jay had already been defeated by Aturdokht, and Riley unknowingly walked right into a trap.

Jay ran her hand over his bald head. She could feel Aturdokht's pride ringing through her. Unlike her connection with Emilia, the first Ancient that she was a reincarnation of, Jay couldn't directly hear Aturdokht's thoughts; instead, she could feel her emotions. Jay missed being able to hear Emilia through the connection she shared with her past self.

Jay surveyed the room at the mix of Magicians and humans she had come to collect. The experiments were going well, but they could be better. The Elemental that Aturdokht had in her possession wasn't much help when it came to boosting a Demon's power, but still, they'd managed to make progress.

"It won't be long now."

Riley stirred, his eyes fluttering open. For a moment, he looked at peace before the pain rushed back in. His gray eyes were bloodshot, and his face was contorted.

"Jay." He said, his voice laced with exhaustion.

"You're awake." She smiled without any sympathy in her voice.

Riley tried to lift his head but only made it a few inches before he fell back onto the table, unable to support himself.

"You're okay, kiddo." He sounded almost relieved, but the look on his face was one of terror. He was frightened of her.

Riley, I'm here. Jay cried out.

Aturdokht narrowed her gaze. She leaned forward until she was only a whisper away from Riley's ear. "Jay is gone." She took delight in seeing Riley's eyes close in indignation but not defeat. Jay had come to realize that Aturdokht liked it more when her experiments fought. "You will be my prize and his downfall."

"I know you can fight this." Riley croaked, each breath more labored than the next.

No.

Jay screamed, but her voice was drowned out by Aturdokht's willpower as she straightened.

Aturdokht glanced over her shoulder to the back of the room at a crow-like Demon with long talons and the body of a human. "Increase his dosage." The Demon nodded in compliance. Jay turned back to Riley. "Hold onto that pain." The Demon walked over and handed Aturdokht a bulging syringe filled with a glowing liquid.

Riley met Jay's gaze, but there wasn't any fear in his eyes this time. It didn't make it easier. Jay grabbed Riley by the chin and tilted his neck to the side.

Forgive me.

Jay stuck the needle into his neck, draining its contents.

Chapter Eleven

She's coming. You must use its power to stop her.

Cryis gasped. His eyes shot open to the darkness of an open sky. A familiar voice had awoken him.

Jay?

There was no response in return. Cryis wondered if he had imagined it.

Cryis tried to sit up, but the pain brought him back down.

"Easy there." Arthur said from across the fire. He sat beside Ami, dressing a bullet wound around her arm. Luckily, it had been a clean shot through.

Cryis worked through the pain until he could turn onto his side and prop himself up on his elbow. The slab of the wood he sat on dug into his skin. Even with the small motion, his entire body screamed in agony.

"What happened?" Cryis half grunted, half moaned. "Where are we now?" He looked around. He couldn't see past the thicket of trees surrounding them in their small clearing.

Only three of them sat around a crackling fire. Its flames danced yellow, red, and orange under the cloudy sky. Ami and Arthur sat across from him, leaning against a fallen tree.

Now that they were out of the compound, Cryis could think more clearly. He could hear the woodland creatures hidden in the shadows of the forest, as well as the creatures of Aris Magica. He knew they were nearby, using the darkness of night as cover. Although most Aris Magicians preferred to hide within the pocket dimensions, some still enjoyed being among humans, although at a distance.

Cryis noticed the mountains peeking up over the trees along the horizon. He recognized the mountain line; they were near Mount Rainier, about 100 miles north of Portland, but only a pocket dimension away from Wizard and Witches City in Aris Magica. The entrance into their district was hidden behind a makeshift waterfall hidden deep within the forest.

As convenient as pocket dimensions were, they were by no means close to one another. Aris Magica was spread out all over the entire world, with each pocket dimension spread out an equal distance from their human world's location. The only exception was at the council's building, which had access to every pocket dimension within their region for easy access for Hunters and clearance personnel. Although there were means of faster travel within Aris Magica, like portal magic and pocket dimension crystals, no one here had the skills needed to control a portal, and Cryis didn't have a crystal on him. Not that it would be of any help either, as the crystals only had pre-destined uses designated by the council, which he always tried to avoid.

Given the close distance, Cryis thought they could escape to Wizard and Witches City, regroup, rest, gather supplies, and then begin their search for Dylan. Aris Magica would have more resources that benefited them than the human world had to offer.

Cryis looked over at Ami; the Witches would be able to give her a healing tonic to help with her injuries. Cryis sighed, looking down at his injuries that had yet to heal. They would also be able to give him one to help speed up his healing process. He just had to convince the others that it was the best move—Cryis stopped himself.

He had told Kanon that the Headmaster was in Aris Magica; it hadn't seemed like a problem then, but after knowing he'd been under Kazimir's hold, perhaps Aris Magica wasn't the best move right now. Cryis didn't know for sure, but the last thing they needed was another fight between Aturdokht's forces, let alone with the Witch herself. The voice from earlier echoed in Cryis's mind, stopping his thoughts again.

You must use its power to stop her.

Cryis frowned in an attempt to push the thought away once again. They didn't have much time if they wanted to find Dylan before it was too late or figure out what the voice had meant by *it*. As much as Cryis wanted to find Jay, he couldn't do anything to help her now. He had to accept that.

Cryis dug his fingernails into his thigh. *I failed, remember?* He thought, pushing it towards the voice clouding his head.

Cryis looked around at the others and noticed that Vastille was missing. "Vastille?" Cryis didn't see him anywhere in the clearing.

"He went to go get more firewood." Cryis noticed Arthur watched him with caution, or was it curiosity?

Cryis knew why. He'd taken quite the beating during his fight with Kazimir. He knew Arthur was still hesitant to believe in Cryis's immortality. Even though he was hurt now, in a couple of hours, he'd be as good as new. Pain suddenly shot through Cryis's chest, rattling his entire body.

"What the hell?" Cryis cursed, leaning back onto his slab of wood. He removed his shirt with difficulty. It had become damp and sticky from his blood.

Cryis was covered in bandages that wrapped around his chest and his torso. The bandages were makeshift from a blue material. Cryis glanced over at Arthur, just now noticing his uniform top to be missing, revealing his plain white shirt underneath.

"You've bled through again." Ami sighed.

She was right. Cryis was soaked on his backside and slowly starting to be on his front. Arthur hurried over to Cryis's side. He attempted to help Cryis sit up, but Cryis shook his head in protest. "It's fine, it'll heal, remember." But Cryis didn't sound confident. Considering how much time had already passed since they'd escaped from the prison, his injuries still shouldn't be this bad. Cryis couldn't even feel his body's healing process starting.

"I know you're immortal," Arthur exasperated, "but I just want to check your progress. And hey, maybe it'll already be healed like last time." He said with a lighter voice. Cryis gave him a sad smile.

"I doubt it," Ami mumbled from across the fire. Arthur glared at her, and she rolled her eyes. "I don't think you will be." She said louder this time. "Vastille looked you over because his eye was twitching out, and he picked up on something inside of you."

What? That's ludicrous. Cryis thought, but he must have said it out loud because Ami answered him.

"No," she retorted. "He detected an emag currency inside of you." She sighed, "I was never good at science." Ami waved away the air in front of her as if she were wiping clean a slate. "However, Vastille thinks it came from the bullet that the Demon shot you with. And that bullet is still wedged deep inside of you. It keeps sending out pulses." She patted her bullet wound. "Maybe the electric currency is what's keeping you from healing."

"That shouldn't affect me," Cryis said, frustrated, but then he thought about it.

Perhaps Ami was on to something, and his body sensed the danger of the bullet ceasing his healing. If his body did heal, then the bullet would be stuck inside of him until he had a chance to get it removed. He could always do it himself.

Cryis lifted his arms so that Arthur could adjust the bandages. "How deep is it?'

"Too deep to dig out without the proper tools," Arthur said as if reading Cryis's mind.

"Just because you're immortal doesn't mean you're invincible," Ami stated.

Cryis frowned. Arthur dropped his bandages to the ground, turning the snow an ugly red. Something about seeing something so pure suddenly disturbed Cryis.

"That was the last of that," Arthur said. He touched Cryis's stomach with cold hands, his fingers grazing closely near the bullet wound. "At least this is almost healed." He mumbled, referring to the gash across his chest where

Kazimir's axe had injured him. The wound wasn't as wide as it had been before. "I can stitch it up later once I have the proper tools."

Cryis's skin shivered under Arthur's touch. He glanced up at him. Arthur was smiling but sadly. Cryis noticed his hair was flecked with tiny pieces of snow, while his face had become a rosy pink from the cold.

When Arthur spoke, Cryis could see clouds of his air before him. "He didn't bleed as much as we thought." Arthur dropped his hand and glanced over his shoulder at Ami.

Ami didn't return his smile. "Even if I'm wrong, Cryis," Ami continued, ignoring Arthur's statement, "you've taken a lot of damage mentally and physically over these past couple of weeks, Arthur told me that you hadn't been eating."

Cryis shot a glare at Arthur as if that had been their little secret.

"I saw it on a report given to me before I became your guard." Arthur bashfully rushed out.

"So that's reason enough why your body has stopped healing...for the time being." Ami finished.

"How was it before?" Arthur asked curiously. He looked to Cryis for a response, but he was glaring at the blood in the snow.

"Before, I'd seen him get cut by a piece of paper and seconds later gone like nothing ever happened, without a drop of blood spilling," Ami smirked.

"Impressive if all paper cuts bled." Arthur challenged. Cryis snorted as Ami rolled her eyes.

"Speaking of before," Ami continued after she flipped Arthur off, "what was that back there?"

"What was what?" Cryis mumbled, but he was sure he had a pretty good idea of what she was talking about.

"I thought I dreamt it...back in the cabin, but from a distance, tonight, it looked like a sea of butterflies were swarming you until they became this blue light with gold trails of magic interwoven together. I thought all Immortals channeled magic through their conduits, but...that came out of you. I didn't know you could use magic like that." Ami explained.

"I can't." Cryis said curtly.

Ami hadn't been wrong about Immortals. He and others like him couldn't use magic freely except for their healing and reaper abilities, but the reaping magic was all used through *Jevit*, a weapon that channeled magic.

Cryis wasn't sure where that power inside of him had surged from, but both times, he had felt something trying to breach the surface from the depths of his soul. Almost like this feeling had awoken and needed to break free. It was too difficult of a feeling to put into words for Ami to understand, so Cryis said nothing. Instead, he continued to stare at the tainted snow and ponder the voice's words once more.

Had the voice been referring to that power when it spoke of *it*? Cryis had a strong premonition that it was. But how did the voice expect him to use this new power within himself? Cryis didn't even know how to control it, let alone where it came from.

"Okay." Ami huffed, annoyed at Cryis's lack of explanation.

Arthur cleared his throat and stood to his feet. As he did, he kicked the ground, covering up the snow tainted with blood. Cryis looked up, meeting Arthur's gaze again, and his chest tightened.

"We have to move now." Vastille walked out of the shadows of the trees behind Ami.

Ami jumped, her uninjured hand fluttering over her heart. "You scared me!" She cried, turning to face him.

"Where's the wood?" Arthur cleared his throat again, breaking eye contact with Cryis and moving closer to the dimming fire.

Vastille removed his suit jacket and tossed it to Cryis, who sat shirtless on the slab of wood. "It's best if we don't stay in one place for too long. Especially after that Demon you just fought. If it was one of hers, I'm sure it's only a matter of time until she knows it's dead too."

"Well, where do you expect us to go? We're not exactly fit to travel." Ami gestured to herself and to Cryis, who had sustained the most injuries. "We've got no leads on Dyl, and gods know where the Headmaster or Riley is. We should just hide for the time being."

Cryis kept the Headmaster's whereabouts to himself; he didn't need another thing to put them off track.

"You're right." Vastille agreed, shocking Cryis. It was almost as if he was admitting defeat.

Ami gave him a shocked look as well, "I...know." She sputtered.

"We need a place to lay low." Vastille clarified. "Frankly, the four of us won't make it through tomorrow in this state."

Cryis wondered if Vastille knew about the pocket dimension nearby that would lead them into Wizard and Witches City. He prepared himself to find a way to convince them otherwise.

Arthur let out a sigh of relief. "You have a little more confidence than I do. I was betting we'd barely survive the next four hours in this weather." He confessed.

"That's why we need to move tonight. I know a place we can regroup that's not too far from here. It'll have supplies you need, and I know for sure it's off anyone's radar." Vastille said.

Shit, Cryis thought.

He was sure Vastille would lead them into Aris Magica, but they didn't have the time.

"No," he said aloud. Cryis stared into the fire, watching as some of the flames faltered, yet the wood continued to burn. Even if he couldn't convince them, they had to at least know where he stood. "I'm not coming."

"No one's asking you to. I'm telling you." Vastille corrected, looking at the others, daring one to refute him.

"You don't get it," Cryis began, "every second we waste not looking for Dylan, Jay gets sucked further into darkness. She's depending on me to pull her out!" Cryis stopped himself, a heavy silence following between him and the rest of the group.

Ever since Cryis had met the first Ancient, Emilia Prestain, he had never failed to make sure her destiny came true, and Aturdokht was sealed away. Cryis sighed, so this was about finding Jay, after all. As much as he tried to accept his loss of her, he couldn't. If he didn't rescue Jay, this generation's Ancient, then he'd have to admit to himself that he had failed, and that scared him the most. He had promised Emilia that he would never leave her side. He had to find her.

"I can't waste any more time."

"Oh, for heaven's sake." Ami sighed. "It's Jay we're talking about, and for all the years I have known her, she has never been the dependent type, and neither has Dylan. We'll find him, both of them. Trust me, wherever he is, she's never too far away. Possessed or not," Ami added crudely. "So just think for a moment, Cryis—"

"I am thinking!" Cryis yelled at her, causing Ami to flinch. He sighed, realizing what he had done. "I still hear a voice calling to me. I know it sounds impossible, but I've always been able to hear the Ancient. And I know this voice belongs to her, and I can't just ignore it."

"Cryis..." Ami said softly; she hesitated, "I want to believe you, but you know as well as I do that it could just as easily be Aturdokht. She's in her body now and no doubt in her thoughts." She pleaded. Cryis knew she was trying to get him to understand how naïve he was being, but he didn't care.

"Look, we get one shot at bringing her back. If we go now, we are just throwing away what little chance we have left. Please, let's get help first." Ami continued.

Cryis knew she was right, but he couldn't shake the feeling that they were wasting time.

"Why don't you try retracing your steps?" Arthur suggested. "Maybe your friends left a hint of where they were going?"

They all looked at him, each showing a different emotion: Ami intrigued, Vastille doubtful, and Cryis was unsure what he felt.

"I've read your files," Arthur began uneasily, "I know about the trauma you all suffered." Arthur paused for a moment, looking across the fire at Ami and then turning to face Cryis. "What happened, if you don't mind me asking? Apparently, the files only told half-truths."

Cryis looked away.

"The last thing I remember was a bright light and then magic coming from Cryis before waking up days later in a jail cell," Ami confessed.

"Cryis?" Arthur prompted.

"I remember everything." Cryis said barely above a whisper. He didn't feel like reliving the nightmare that haunted his dreams.

"That must have been the explosion." Arthur assumed. "Police were sent to your location because a couple hiking in the forest said they saw smoke. You guys were taken to the nearest hospital before Agent Kanon detained you. The hospital didn't know what else to do since you weren't in their system," Arthur explained. "But what if the CIA missed something while combing over the wreckage—something only you guys would gather?"

"Arthur, just stop, please." Cryis said.

He knew the boy was only trying to help, but there was nothing left for the CIA to miss. Plus, it had all been a cover story to get enough police to his location to get everyone to safety, and even that had failed. Lyid hadn't survived. Guilt racked at Cryis's heart, latching on like a leech.

"Cryis," Vastille said, looking over at him, "it's your decision. What do you want us to do?"

Cryis knew Arthur was trying his best to help, but going back to the cabin would take days out of their time. Plus, Aturdokht had destroyed the pocket dimension, so it's not as if Aris Magica could be accessed from there; they couldn't risk a dead end. Cryis looked around, meeting everyone's gaze. He held Ami's gaze the longest. He knew what she wanted from him. He looked away. He still hadn't changed his mind.

"Take us to your safe house," Cryis began and saw an instant relief fall across Ami's face. "We regroup, but then we follow Jay's voice."

Ami rose to her feet. The relief she had moments before was gone. "And if it's a trap?" She asked with a glare.

"Then," Cryis contemplated, "we'll deal with it when we get there."

Chapter Twelve

Before the sun was fully up, Vastille and Arthur had managed to erase any existence of them ever camping in the clearing. Arthur had done what he could for both Ami and Cryis, but he needed more equipment than he carried.

The snow had begun falling again, but not nearly as bad as it could have been. Vastille led them deeper into the woods, Cryis was relieved to find it in the opposite direction of the pocket dimension. He noticed the trees were different from the ones he had encountered on the way to the Institute. Instead of tall, sparse trees with frozen limbs, the trees in Mount Rainier's Forest were thick and full of leaves covered in a beautiful, glazed frost.

Cryis looked closely at one of the branches and noticed the frost held tiny footprints embedded in the ice. He smiled to himself, recognizing them. He assumed it belonged to a Fairy. Fairies could shrink themselves into the size of beings no bigger than a dime. Cryis wouldn't be surprised if some were watching them now.

They began to walk along an upward slope that seemed to last forever. No matter how much any of them pestered Vastille about where they were heading, he'd huff, "You'll see when we get there."

The sun had reached its peak in the sky by the time they had finally reached the top of the hill. The ground was covered in a perfect layer of snow, untouched by human footprints or animals. They stood at the top of the hill on a ring of a wide circle that sloped inward into a steep bowl. Inside the bowl were more trees, the tops of them rustled as a flock of birds flew into the air.

Cryis wrapped his arm around Ami's shoulder and leaned most of his weight onto her; she wrapped her arm around his waist. Arthur, Vastille, and Ami had taken turns supporting him while he slowly healed.

Cryis was already starting to feel much better from when they first started their trek, but he still had a long way to go. The bleeding had finally stopped, but Arthur still believed after the bullet's removal that Cryis would need stitches, at least for the deep cuts along his back and chest.

"We've made it," Vastille said proudly.

Cryis followed Vastille's line of sight, he took a half step forward as he did and suddenly felt the wave of magic that surrounded the inside of the bowl below. Cryis recognized it instantly as a pocket dimension. Hidden well within the trees was a cabin. The cabin almost reminded him of the one at the Institute, but much larger. It had the same log wood build, but it was much more elongated than the boxy safe house. The cabin below also seemed to be about two or three stories. The roof and chimney were made of stone, and smoke flew above the trees, disappearing high into the air. It wasn't abandoned.

"Come on." Vastille ushered them and headed down the hill.

Arthur glanced at Cryis and Ami nervously and confused. Vastille had practically half slid, half stumbled down the hill, and he was in the best of shape of all of them.

Ami waved Arthur away, "I got it," she said with a small smile. Arthur nodded, following Vastille even less gracefully down the hill. "If we stick to their tracks, we should be fine." Cryis looked at the deep footprints the two men had left behind.

"You know," Ami turned her head towards Cryis. The way they stood caused her to have to slightly tilt her head so that she could meet his gaze when she spoke. "You could be a tad bit more grateful. Vastille and Arthur did save us after all," she said, as opinionated as ever, Cryis thought.

Cryis resisted the urge to roll his eyes; he knew Ami was only trying to help. Cryis hadn't said a word to anyone since they'd begun their long trek up the hill.

Even when Arthur had tried to make small talk with him, Cryis had remained mostly silent. His mind was too consumed with thoughts of the voice he'd heard. Even now, it continued to linger in the back of his mind.

Instead, he said, "I am grateful, it's impatience that's more my problem...I would like to think." Cryis smirked at Ami.

She did roll her eyes. "Come on." Ami grunted, putting a step down towards Vastille's footprints, which were the biggest. After a couple of failed attempts to move Cryis with her, she said, "It would just be easier to slide, right?"

Cryis chuckled. "As if you're going to give me a choice."

Ami laughed, knowing it was true. She let go of Cryis and called upon her mist. It was a light pink. The mist often reflected the caster's emotions. It enveloped Cryis, turning into two huge hands as it did. As the mist passed over his skin, Cryis felt a warm tingle of joy from it that echoed Ami's emotions. The hands gently sat Cryis down on the ground and then gave him a guided shove down the hill.

Cryis went sliding at an incredible speed. He flew right past Arthur and Vastille. The end of the hill sloped off into flatter ground, slowing his momentum as he continued to slide right past the trees and into the cabin. The mist around him returned, yanking him back right before he slammed into the cabin's doorsteps.

Cryis panted, breathless and shocked, as if he thought he'd seen his life flash before his eyes. The experience reminded him why he hated sledding.

"Sorry!" Ami shouted from above.

"Careful!" Arthur shouted, coming up behind Cryis. He helped Cryis to his feet. "Otherwise, you'll need more than stitches." Arthur looked back at Vastille. "This it?" Cryis noticed the confusion written on Arthur's face but paid little attention to it.

Cryis looked over at Vastille as well, "Does someone live here?" He doubted Vastille had prepared the cabin for them before coming to their rescue.

In one breath, Vastille answered, "Yes, although I haven't seen her in a long time."

"Her?" Cryis thought aloud.

"Wow," Arthur said, stumbling back. His eyes grew wide, and he looked back at Cryis before looking back at the cabin.

Cryis frowned, unsure why his reaction had been so dramatic. Cryis looked back at the cabin. There wasn't anything grand about it. Cryis stopped himself and chuckled; he had almost forgotten that Arthur was human. He couldn't see into the pocket dimension like the rest of them could, even once entering inside it. The only way a human could see inside was if the user of the pocket dimension extended the invitation. Arthur had only seen an empty clearing until Vastille granted him access.

Vastille walked past Cryis and Arthur, climbing up the four steps that led to the door. He sighed, stopping at the top step and staring down at the end of the porch. It was an open deck, at the end of one side were pots filled with dirt, and on the other end was a swinging chair tied to the ceiling of the porch.

Cryis wondered what was going through Vastille's head. He continued to the door. The door was a smoother wood than the rest of the house. It had a huge bronze knocker in the shape of a wolf with its mouth open. Vastille raised it, intending to knock, but stopped short right before doing so. After a moment of hesitation, he was able to bring himself to knock.

Cryis, along with the others, stood in anticipation, waiting to see who would answer the door. A few minutes seemed to pass before Cryis heard light shuffling from the other side of it, followed by the sound of a lock turning. Cryis released a breath he hadn't realized he'd been holding. A small girl holding the barrel of a shotgun down at them stood in the doorway. She tried her best to look fierce but failed miserably.

The girl was no older than twelve or thirteen. Her skin was the same dark bronze color as Vastille's, and her hair was thick and black like fig roots. Her eyes were big and doe-like while also curious. The first person she saw was Vastille. She looked him up and down, slowly lowering the gun. Her fingers relaxed off its trigger.

"Daddy." She said in the softest voice. Her words filled with disbelief as tears were brought to her eyes.

Cryis watched Vastille's entire body shake with a single breath.

"I'm home," Vastille replied softly. He gestured to the gun. "Do you even know how to use that thing?"

In an instant, the little girl was in Vastille's arms. Beside Cryis, Ami gasped, one hand coming up to her mouth, catching her tears that had fallen, the other holding onto the suit jacket Cryis wore. Cryis found himself staring at the two with an overwhelming feeling of mixed emotions.

Arthur leaned into Cryis so that no one else could hear. "He has a kid?"

Cryis and the others sat in a warm oak wood-built room. They sat around an oval table with a chandelier hanging directly above their heads, lighting the room. In the corner of the room was a built-in fireplace that took up the whole back wall. It was cackling fiercely with fire that heated the entire room.

There were many pictures on the fireplace of the girl as a baby, but no pictures of them together. Cryis noticed the couches they all sat on seemed almost new as if never used. The leather had yet to be creased, until now as he and the others found a seat.

The floor was covered in wood as well, with a large woven colorful rug of oranges, blues, and greens that covered the center. The living room was the first room they'd entered after walking straight through the door. If Cryis looked up, he could see a railing hiding the second floor from them and a set of stairs that led to it.

Cryis sat shirtless on the single couch. He was leaning forward so that his face pressed into the cool surface of the table. He was working his way through heavy breaths. Arthur stood over him, doing his best to stitch the final wound along Cryis's back. Arthur had already managed to remove the bullet from beneath Cryis's skin.

"In my basic training days, I trained as a medic." Arthur snipped off the last bit of thread.

He stood back and admired his work. Cryis wasn't surprised to learn that Arthur had spent time in the military. Still, he found himself wanting to know more about his life.

"Okay, not bad. Only one more section to do." Arthur said brightly.

"Make it quick." Cryis groaned. Cryis turned his head to the other side. He was met with a view of the girl, Eliza, holding out a glass to him. The contents inside were clear.

"Here," Eliza said. "Daddy says it'll help with the pain."

"Thanks, Liza," Cryis grunted. He took the cup from her and briefly sat up so that he could down the drink. The contents inside were strong and sour. "Ugh," Cryis gagged, pulling the cup from his face. It had tasted bitter. "What is that?" He coughed. Cryis was unfamiliar with the tonics of the human world, as he preferred Aris Magica's elixirs instead.

Eliza shrugged. She sat down in the seat across from him. She continued to stare at him. "Why is your hair white?" She asked curiously.

"Uh..." Cryis began at a loss for words.

"It's vodka." Vastille laughed as he walked into the room carrying a tray of meat, cheese, fruit, and crackers. "Eliza honey, his hair color was a personal choice."

Eliza looked to Cryis for confirmation, Cryis nodded with a nervous smile. She seemed satisfied with his answer. He got the feeling Vastille had yet to tell his daughter about Aris Magica and her possible connection to it. Cryis assumed it was because she hadn't manifested any Aris Magica gifts yet.

"It's not much," Vastille said, setting the tray on the table. "But it beats the lack of food you were getting."

"No, this is perfect." Ami said as she came from over by the fireplace and took a seat on the double couch to the right of Cryis. She reached across the table, grabbing an apple slice.

Cryis took another swig from his glass. The taste never got better. "Argh, geez, Arthur." Cryis slammed a hand on the table. Arthur sutured the last stitch before cutting the end of the string.

"Yeah, my bad." Arthur apologized. He had pulled a little too hard on the last stitch. "But," he took a step back, admiring the rest of his work. "That should do it."

Cryis reached his hand behind him to feel his back; the movement caused him to moan. His fingers brushed lightly over the ribbed stitch lines. He returned his hand to his side, slowly sitting upright. The front and back of his body, where the stitches were, felt stiff and rigid. Cryis gently leaned back into the couch. He felt so limited; it was an unnatural feeling for him.

"Thank you." Cryis mumbled.

Eliza offered Cryis a shirt she had been holding in her other hand.

"Thanks," he said, taking it from her. Carefully, he pulled it over his head in a slow motion. The shirt was a plain red color that matched his eyes. He was more surprised Eliza hadn't asked about them yet after her curiosity about his hair.

"Careful. Don't overdo it, or we'll have to redo the whole process." Arthur warned.

"How long until I can do a simple task like put a shirt on?" Cryis asked, annoyed.

"Um…well, normally a couple of days… maybe weeks, but with your progressive healing, probably a couple hours. I'm not sure." Arthur explained, stumped.

"We don't have a couple of days."

"Daddy said you guys can stay here until you recover. We have two extra rooms upstairs." Eliza said. She turned to Ami, beaming with excitement, "Ami, you can share a room with me. I've never had a sister before, so it'll be kind of nice to experience it."

"I don't mind. I've only had boring brothers, so I'll play the role of big sis." Ami said at the same time Cryis proclaimed, "That's great and all, but we'll be gone before sunrise tomorrow." Out of the corner of his eyes, he saw Ami cast him a glare.

Eliza heard him over Ami, and her face fell. She looked over at her dad. Vastille still wore his sunglasses, but everyone in the room could still feel his expression of guilt.

"You're leaving again." She stated sternly.

Vastille looked away, unable to look his daughter in the eyes. The room grew quiet, filled with an uneasy tension. Cryis looked between Eliza and Vastille, wondering about their history.

How long had Vastille been away from his daughter? Where was her mother?

Cryis sat down his empty glass. "No, just us," he said to Eliza.

Cryis felt everyone staring at him, but his only concern at the moment was the girl. He watched as her eyes lit with a spark of hope.

Cryis turned to Vastille. "Your priority is here. You've done enough."

For a moment, Vastille was speechless. Cryis gave him the faintest smile; it was the least he could do for Vastille, giving him a chance to be free of Aris Magica, if only for a little while, after abandoning him many years ago.

"Thank you," Vastille finally said. "But I also can't allow you to leave in the condition you're in." Vastille stepped closer to Cryis. He held up three fingers on his left hand. "Three days. Wait three days, if you do, you're free to go, if not, I'm coming with you." Vastille bargained.

That bastard. Cryis thought.

Cryis groaned, leaning back into the couch. He should have known Vastille would've come up with something like this. He looked around the room, making the mistake of locking eyes with Eliza, who wore a confident expression as if she knew he would reluctantly agree.

Cryis sighed, ruffling his hair. "Fine. Three days. That's it," he agreed, seeing Eliza's satisfied smile.

Vastille nodded. "You have my word." Vastille said gratefully.

Cryis turned to Eliza, "So," he said, dragging out the word. "Which room will I be staying in?"

Eliza led Cryis upstairs. She went slow enough for him not to fall behind. She brought him to the closest room near the steps on the right. The hallway ahead of them was open on one side, overlooking the living room from which they had just left. On the right were five doors. Straight ahead, Cryis spotted a mounted deer head nailed to the wall at the end of the hall. He shuddered as he followed Eliza to the first door, avoiding eye contact with the deer.

Before opening the door, Eliza pointed to the closed door two doors down. All the doors had the same wood frame and white trim.

"That one's the bathroom." She looked at Cryis, making sure he understood, and he nodded. Satisfied, she swung open the door before them. "Here you are."

Eliza flicked on the light switch on the wall beside the door. Unlike the rest of the house he had seen, his room was very plain and simple. A single bed with a blue, gray, and orange plaid patterned quilt sat at the center of the room against the back wall. Beside it, on its left, was a tall wooden nightstand. Across from the bed, on the opposite wall, was a doorless closet that was almost empty. A couple of hangers hung from the rack, and boxes were stacked in the far corners on either side, but there were no clothes.

The floor inside the room was devoid of wood and covered in light brown carpet. Above the bed was a four-fanned ceiling fan with a single bulb attached to the center. Opposite of the door was a single window that emitted a bright light from outside the room. Cryis was surprised any light reached the house with how deep it was in the pit.

"Arthur will be in the room next door. Ami, Daddy, and I's room are the last two doors." She tugged the sleeve of Cryis's shirt. "Let me know if there's anything else you need. Like a haircut." She snickered. "I'm pretty good at those."

Cryis frowned and touched the ends of his hair. It was the longest it had ever been. He smiled to himself as he glanced at Eliza. It had been so long since he'd had anyone doting over him. Faces crossed his mind; faces he hadn't seen in a very long time, he'd nearly forgotten them. His mom and his two younger sisters. All three had dark hair like Eliza and loving doe-like green eyes. He couldn't help but think of them now as he stared at her. It had been a long time since he'd last thought of them.

"Okay, bye." Eliza smiled after some time. She left the room. Cryis watched her skip down the hallway and back down the stairs to return to the others.

After she was out of view, Cryis closed the door and flicked off the light. He walked over to the single window and shut the blinds. Cryis tossed himself on the bed, and before he knew it, he found himself closing his eyes as he drifted off into solitary darkness.

The bed he laid on was much softer than his old cot back in the jail cell and in the bunk at the safe house. He grabbed one of the many pillows beneath him and hugged it to his chest. The darkness pulled him further and further in until his body relaxed, and his pain subsided as he fell into a peaceful sleep.

Chapter Thirteen

"This is going to be fun." Kai mumbled under his breath while cracking his knuckles.

The council building had been quite far, located in another pocket dimension. They had exited the forest through a pocket dimension door near where they met Arden. The forest they returned to was bare and frozen from the winter season happening in the human world. After trekking through the snow for half an hour, they finally reached another pocket dimension that put them at the council's doorsteps.

Kai carried a slight pep in his walk as they approached what Dylan presumed to be the council building. Standing tall just a few meters ahead in his path was a skyscraper. It was the only building for miles. It looked less ethereal and more like something that belonged in any human city but was long abandoned.

Dylan wondered if they had taken a wrong turn somewhere. The building was gray, with many dimmed windows that covered every inch of the building except for the first floor. Huge vines hugged the sides of the building, weaving around the structure as if it were the only thing holding the skyscraper upright.

The vines ran into the ground creating twisted humps that bulged from the earth beneath them, weaving around rock-like structures rooted in the ground at every end of each rooted vine. The top of the building disappeared into ominous clouds hanging low in the sky, giving the council an unapproachable atmosphere, but Dylan didn't scare easily.

Still, Dylan could admit that he was nervous. Meeting the members of the council was a rare honor bestowed upon a few. The council members were highly praised Magicians and the most well-kept secret in the world, for no one knew who sat on the council. Rumors were told that they were the last of the lost Mythical Beasts. Others said that no one knew who they were because they were Whispers, a lost breed of Magicians who could erase themselves from existence. Regardless, the council was quite intimidating.

Dylan wasn't sure what to expect, Aris Magica had already been far from what he had assumed it would be. He thought once he set foot in Aris Magica, it would be a community that was leagues behind the human world, but to his surprise, it was thriving and lively.

Dylan scanned the area around him as the three of them walked towards the building's entrance. Unlike the rest of Aris Magica he'd seen, the area was gloomy and seasonless. There were no leaves on the trees, no grass, and just a gray cloudy sky. Dylan couldn't tell if it was night or day.

The ground was covered in black dirt with no path carved out, just bumps from the vines' roots. The crystallized rocks sticking straight up from the ground ranged in all sizes and went on for as far as his eyes could see. Other than the council building, the rocks were the only things in the vicinity, surrounding every inch of the ground.

Dylan stared closer at the rocks, through the rays of colors, he saw a glimpse of green pastures appear, but when he looked again, the crystals' colors turned to a clouded fog. The further he looked, the more the crystalized rocks seemed to lose their natural glow. An entire section alone was shrouded in gray, void of any other color.

"Where is everybody?" Dylan whispered.

After leaving the Fairy District, Dylan hadn't seen a single Magician in sight. His eyes drifted back to the crystals shrouded in darkness.

"Pocket dimensions in their true form," Silo explained. "And that area over there," she pointed to the crystals Dylan stared at, "sealed pocket dimensions. Demons and Faeries, even the Black Gates, abide in them."

Dylan clenched his jaw, suddenly uneasy about the crystals. He had heard of the Black Gates located deep within Aris Magica. These gates withheld the darkest form of magic known to Magicians and humans alike; the darkness was like a plague consuming everything it touched. It was guarded 24/7 by the most powerful Magicians from all over the world. If Aturdokht wanted to quickly rebuild her army and start a war, opening the Black Gates would be the quickest way to do it. Dylan pushed the thought aside.

Surely, even Aturdokht wouldn't be foolish enough to try to take over the Black Gates. No one could control the anger of those trapped inside them. After all, the creatures there had their own personal vendettas.

"You see those over there?" Silo pointed to the rocks that had deep cracks running through them. "Those cracks mean the seals on them have been broken.

Dylan frowned, "How does that happen?"

Silo shrugged, "With the right amount of power, anything is possible."

"Lucky for Aris, it's only been the Demon seals that are cracked and not Faeries...little menaces, a few gave all of them a bad name," Kai mumbled bitterly. Silo looked away as he said Faeries, Dylan thought he saw guilt in her eyes but ignored it.

When they reached the doors to the building, Kai held out his arms, blocking the entrance. "A couple of rules." He glanced back at Dylan. "One, don't speak unless spoken to. Two, do not speak, period. This isn't a bargaining session. You're here to be judged."

"Kai." Silo nagged.

He shrugged. "I'm just looking out for your new boy toy." He smirked, looking between the two.

Both Silo and Dylan glowered at him. "Grow up." Dylan and Silo said in unison. Dylan glanced at her; she did the same. She blushed quickly, looking away. Dylan smiled to himself; he couldn't help but find her embarrassment cute. The thought caused him to look away as well.

"Yeah, whatever." Kai rolled his eyes.

They reached the front doors of the building. The doors were made of glass and covered in dust so thick Dylan couldn't see inside. Kai pushed them open and walked in. Dylan slowly followed with Silo close to his side.

The entire inside was pitch-black, swallowing them in darkness. Dylan felt Silo grab his hand. Her hand was small inside his and softer than he'd expected it to be. He was instantly reminded of Jay; her hands felt the same. Dylan wanted to pull away but couldn't bring himself to.

Silo guided him forward through the darkness. "This way." She whispered.

Dylan took a step forward, then another, until his foot missed solid ground, and the floor seemed to swallow him whole. He gasped, closing his eyes and preparing for anything short of plunging to death. He squeezed Silo's hand tighter.

Seconds later, Dylan felt Silo's other hand against his back. She was gently patting it. Dylan opened one eye to find himself doubled over, but his feet firmly on the ground. He glanced up to find himself still holding onto Silo's hand. He quickly let go. He could hear Kai snickering beside him. Dylan fought the urge to kick Kai's feet out from under him.

"Are you okay?" Silo asked.

Dylan slowly rose to full height, and Silo's hand moved to his arm. He looked at her hand for a moment, remembering it in his, and blushed. He found her gaze. "Fine."

Silo smiled, "I guess I should have warned you, but time and space work differently in the council building. They can make it appear how they want." She sighed, looking off into the distance, "Guess they went with intimidation." Dylan noticed the twinkle from before in her eyes.

"Yep," Dylan said, unable to take his gaze off her.

"Step forward." A harmonious round of gentle voices echoed around them.

Dylan looked around, alarmed. They were now surrounded by white; there was no division between ground and sky, making it seem like the three of them were suspended in the air. In front of them, three circular icons appeared. Without hesitation or shock, both Kai and Silo stepped onto the icon in front of them. After doing so, it was like their bodies went into a trance-like state. Dylan hesitated.

"Why?" Dylan asked, breaking rule one on Kai's list.

The voices were impatient. "Your life and others might very well depend on it."

Dylan stared at the icon with suspicion. Something inside of him told him to run away, but he needed answers. He sighed; he didn't have much to lose. Dylan slowly stepped onto the icon. When he did, an array of colors appeared in his vision. He was no longer suspended in nothingness but rolling green pastures. The sky was a mixture of blues, purples, and pinks of an early sunrise.

At the top of the hill, three veiled women hovered above the ground. Each wore a different color. The one on the right was dressed in a yellow so bright it was hard for Dylan to gaze upon it. The one on the left was dressed in a gentle blue with patterns of ocean waves decorating the hem of her veiled gown. The one in the center wore a dark pink gown; her veil fell past her shoulders like a bride.

Dylan turned to his right and left in search of his companions, but he stood on the opposite side of the pasture alone. "Where are Silo and Kai?"

"We wanted to speak with you and you alone." The three women spoke in harmony.

Dylan felt unsettled standing before them. He wished now more than ever that he had some kind of weapon. He still didn't know what to think of the council, and if the rumors were true about them being Whispers, he wouldn't allow them to erase any part of his memory.

"The boy is uneasy," the three said. "He does not yet trust us."

"Yeah, no kidding." Dylan mumbled.

The three before him were the revered governors of Aris Magica. Dylan looked around, suddenly angry, all this time he and his friends had spent fighting against Aturdokht, and the council had been on a vacation hovering above a field. Dylan looked over at them and glared. Although he didn't know much about them, he knew they possessed unrivaled power.

Why hadn't they helped them and stepped in?

Dylan wondered, the thought threatening to consume his mind as he faced the council.

The voices continued to speak, "We are three, yet we are one. Guarding and governing the laws that uphold Aris Magica." Dylan already knew that much, but the voices kept talking before he had the chance to explain, "We are the passing between worlds."

The Passing.

Dylan recalled all the pocket dimensions he'd seen outside. Every crystal led to another part of Aris Magica, which could also lead to anywhere in the human world. Dylan's eyes grew wide; he had an idea. If he could find out where Jay was, then by a touch of a crystal, he could be back by her side in seconds.

"No." The voices rang out as if reading his mind.

"What?" Dylan asked, startled. He pinched the bridge of his nose. "Then why the hell am I here if it's not to get Jay back?" Dylan threw his head back and stared at the sky.

Dylan didn't care if Aturdokht burned the world, Jay was his priority—she'd always been. Dylan closed his eyes and took a long, deep breath. When he opened his eyes, his brows furrowed. He hadn't meant that. Aturdokht had to be stopped, but at what cost?

Dylan noticed the sky had changed from an early sunrise to the sun high in the sky. He scrunched his brow. Had that much time passed already?

"We cannot interfere with the choices of an Ancient." Dylan tilted his head forward slowly. He knew that. "Until recently." His eyes narrowed as one eyebrow arched inquisitively. "Nor can we value the life of one soul over another, no matter the kind." They paused, letting the air of their words sink in. "Therefore, Jay must face her punishment alone, and if she loses, then she will perish just as Aturdokht will, as prophecy has ordained."

"One soul." Dylan bitterly chuckled. "Just months ago, she was as normal as normal gets for us. Then, out of nowhere, the weight of the world landed on her shoulders." He took a small step forward. "When she needs you the most, you're going to, what, just abandon her? Her *own* people?" Dylan shouted, growing frustrated.

"She failed."

"Failed?" Dylan was beyond words. How could the council be so heartless?

"What did you expect? From the looks of things, you knew a whole lot longer what was coming, and you didn't think to warn any of us!"

It had barely been a month since Dylan and Jay had learned about Aturdokht's existence and about the prophecy ordaining that Jay was to destroy the Witch. She hadn't even been given time to fully wrap her head around her destiny before it had been thrust upon her.

"She never asked for any of this." Dylan swiped the air with his hand to show his frustration.

Arden had told the council about Aturdokht's return, and they were aware of Jay being an Ancient, yet they did nothing because of a law lost in history telling them they couldn't be involved.

"Faith, Ami, Lyid, Cryis..." Dylan choked back tears, listing the names of the people he'd lost. "Taybeith." Dylan let out a shaky breath, "None of them deserved any of it." He let out a dry laugh once more. "But now you still want peace, yet by doing what? Hiding in the shadows for centuries."

The voices did not immediately respond. They stood in silent patience, allowing him to rid himself of his anger. It wasn't enough; their silence led to more infuriation that continued to rise inside Dylan.

He didn't care if the past Ancients wouldn't let the council interfere, Jay was still only a kid. How did they have such faith to leave the weight of both worlds to her?

Dylan clenched his jaw. He had a feeling why Arden had told them to find him. It wasn't just because of his connection to Jay, but maybe he could convince them to break the law.

Even if he managed to find Jay, they still needed help in defeating Aturdokht. He knew well enough that she wasn't hiding in the shadows without a purpose. If he could get the council to act, then at least he could help Jay by giving her an army. Dylan took a deep breath through his nostrils, trying to center himself. He'd accomplish nothing in anger.

"It's true; there are many unjust laws in Aris Magica that must be changed. So that a disaster such as this does not happen," the council explained. "But we never left." Their words seemed regretful. "Through every cycle of Ancient and Aturdokht, we have always been there watching, yearning to help, but never allowed. It's against a law that exceeds us all from the very first Ancient and Aris."

Aris, the creator of Aris Magica? Dylan didn't understand why the first Ancient and Aris made such a pact.

"Then break it," Dylan said calmly. The women before him were some of the strongest Magicians in the world.

"We cannot."

Dylan felt his heart skip a beat. "Why?"

"It is magic older than us all and binding."

"I've been around magic for a long time now, and never once has it been binding. Magic is as strong as the will of the user." Dylan challenged. "If you want to change something, then stop giving these half-assed excuses and change it."

Silence.

The woman stared back at him in silence.

Shit. Dylan cursed.

Dylan had let his anger get the better of him. But he couldn't help it. These women were some of the most powerful Magicians in the entire world, and they were letting a simple law, too old to matter, stop them from considering doing the right thing.

Dylan felt as if he was Jay's last line of defense. He knew she couldn't fight to keep control of herself against Aturdokht and then fight to destroy the Witch, all while also fighting the very people who should be on her side. Even if he had to fight the entire council himself, he wouldn't let any of them lay a finger on her.

"We need time to process," the three said in unison.

"What?" Dylan said, his voice overlapping on top of theirs as they continued to speak.

"For now, this meeting is adjourned."

"No, wait, you can't just—"

In harmony, their hands waved in a circular motion, and both Silo and Kai appeared beside Dylan, but when Dylan looked back to the council, they were gone. Frustration scorched through his body like a flame.

Kai glanced around, confused, "Gosh dang it. Is it over already?" He grumbled.

Dylan let out a heavy sigh that did nothing to quell his anger. He turned to Silo, concern laced in every word he spoke, "Are you hurt? Where have you been?" He stopped himself, feeling his frustration rising again as he realized what he was doing. His protective side had instinctively kicked in.

Silo smiled gently. "In a room living out our secret desires. It was...nice."

Dylan could see the look of longing lingering in Silo's eyes. She glanced up at him, and fear flashed in her eyes.

"I was," she hesitated, "flying," she finished.

She carefully watched for Dylan's reaction, but he didn't see anything weird about what she saw. He offered her an encouraging smile, but Silo's smile disappeared.

Her gaze hardened as she spoke, "What did they tell you?"

"Hey, you know we can't ask that." Kai snapped.

"That they need time to process their laws in place." Dylan said bitterly. "I couldn't sway them on their stance against Jay." He clenched his fists at his side. "But that doesn't mean I'm giving up."

Before any of them could respond, the room changed, and in a flash of light, the three of them were back outside at the entrance to the council building. Dylan lowered his arm that he'd thrown up in defense to block the magic. The sky was still as gloomy as ever, but Dylan still felt as if no time had passed.

"Freaky." Kai shuddered next to Dylan.

Silo pressed a hand to Dylan's shoulder. "Judgement wasn't passed, so they'll call on you again." She didn't sound happy about it, but Dylan didn't care, it meant he still had a chance to convince them.

He turned to face Silo, causing her to drop her hand. He lowered his gaze. He knew what he was about to ask her would be difficult, but Dylan knew he couldn't do this alone.

"Silo." He carefully looked up at her through his thick lashes. "Kai."

"Oh, this'll be good," Kai jeered.

"I know you disagree, but I firmly believe there's a way to save Jay, and I'm going to find it." He could already see the rejection forming in Silo's eyes. "I need your help. Please." His voice carried so much desperation that he felt as if he were begging. Maybe he was.

Before him stood two people who were ordered to kill Jay if given the chance to save the world from Aturdokht's wrath. But he had to hope that their minds could be changed.

Silo opened her mouth to refute him. He met her gaze and hers alone. "If you can't, then please take me to someone who can."

A heavy silence hung between them, filling the air with so much tension Dylan found it hard to breathe. But after another moment's silence, Silo finally spoke. She let out a resigned sigh but held Dylan's gaze.

"She means that much to you, doesn't she?" Her voice carried a sadness to it that Dylan didn't understand.

Dylan nodded. "She does." His voice cracked, reflecting the hurt he'd heard in Silo's voice.

Kai was the one to speak this time. He stepped in between Silo and Dylan. "Fine. But just know we have our reasons for adhering to the council's orders." He crossed his arms over his chest. "So, if your way doesn't work, then just know where our loyalties lie."

"I understand."

"Good." Kai rolled his eyes, slow and exaggerated, before he spoke again, "Now let's go find Arden."

Chapter Fourteen

To Dylan's disappointment, Arden wasn't home, but he left a note as if he had been expecting their arrival. The note said that he would call for them soon—it was written in elaborate handwriting on a paper softer than a cotton ball. With nowhere else to go and nightfall nearing closer, Dylan, Silo, and Kai returned to Silo and Kai's hut within Fairy District.

Dylan hadn't realized how exhausted he was until his body hit the bed. He hadn't even bothered changing out of the clothes he'd been given earlier.

A knock came from the other side of the curtain as if someone tapped on the wall the curtain hung close to. Shortly after, Silo's voice followed, "May I come in?"

Dylan sat up, propping himself up on his elbows. He nodded, then quickly realized that she couldn't see the action. "Yes! Come in," he called back.

The curtain shifted as Silo opened it just enough to slip in. After she did, the curtain fell back into place. However, she didn't immediately move away from the curtain.

Dylan noticed that she had changed from the clothes she had worn earlier. She was now in a thin blue dress that hugged her curves in all the right places. In the moonlight, the tattoos that cornered her eyes seemed to almost glow. Her wings were once again invisible to his eyes, but he knew they were there.

Dylan still didn't understand the magic that concealed them, but he trusted if he needed to know, Silo would tell him.

Dylan sat up a bit straighter. "What's wrong?"

"Oh!" Silo shifted from one bare foot to the other.

After a second more, she began to walk toward him. Once she reached him, she sat down on the corner of his bed.

"I was wondering if you needed another healing session."

Dylan sighed through his nose as he pondered her offer. His muscles were sore, but it wasn't anything he couldn't handle. The bulk of his injuries were nothing more than added scars now, but he looked towards Silo. He wouldn't mind a free healing session, especially one from a Fairy, where he didn't have to worry about a risk being exuded from it.

"Sure, why not." He shrugged.

She inched closer to him, and as she did, Dylan smelled fresh lemons and mint that rolled off her in waves. The moonlight from the window caught on her braids, showing the small glisten they held from being dampened by water. Dylan shrunk away, wishing he'd washed up. Silo closed the space between them, and as she did, their gazes met.

Dylan felt his cheeks warm. She was so close. He felt as if he had to hold his breath to keep from acting on impulse. Slowly, he exhaled, catching another whiff of the tantalizing blend of lemon and mint. It was intoxicating—perfectly citrusy with a subtle sweetness that drew him in deeper. He found his eyes lowering once again to her lips, now glistening with gloss.

Silo cleared her throat, causing his eyes to snap back up to hers. "You'll have to remove your shirt," she whispered.

"Oh, right." Dylan nervously laughed. He pulled at the hem of his shirt and, in one swift movement, brought it up over his head. He held onto it with one hand as the rest draped over the side of the bed.

Silo took in a deep, slightly shaking breath. She lowered her gaze and then placed her hands on his chest. "You might feel a sting before things smooth out."

"I can take it," Dylan said almost breathlessly as her eyes found him again. He swallowed down the growing lump in the back of his throat.

Silo took another deep breath, but her mouth began to form a small smile. "That's what everyone says."

Before Dylan could respond, he felt Silo's hands heat against his skin. A sharp pain shot throughout his chest, expanding like a rapid-fire in his body. It felt similar to the pain he'd felt when Aturdokht had attacked him back in the forest during their first meeting. The magic felt...dark. Dylan winced.

"I'm sorry," Silo apologized. "Just bear with it a little longer."

Slowly, the pain subsided and turned into an icy draft that washed over his body. As quickly as the pain had arrived, it disappeared, and he felt his body healing from the inside out.

"See." Dylan looked over at Silo, beads of sweat had formed on her forehead, and she looked slightly pale. There was a newfound exhaustion in her eyes. "Not that bad."

"Hey..." Concern etched every corner of Dylan's expression.

Dylan reached for her, placing a hand on her shoulder. He gently pushed her away from him, but she didn't budge. He frowned and instead used both hands to grab hold of her wrists before working his way to her hands. She peered up at him as he removed her hands from his chest and held them in his instead. He lowered their hands to the small space on the bed in between them.

"What's wrong?" Dylan asked.

Silo forced a smile, "I'm a new healer, so there's a bit of an adjusting period." As she spoke, her gaze dropped to their hands intertwined together.

Dylan didn't return her smile. He pulled one of his hands away and used it to wipe the sweat from her brow before cupping her face. She leaned into his hand and closed her eyes. He knew she was lying. He tried to search her eyes, but she continued to avoid his gaze.

"If you don't want to talk about it, then we don't have to," Dylan whispered. "But please, don't lie to me."

Silo slightly turned her face letting out a breath that warmed his hand. She looked on the verge of tears. Dylan caressed her face with his thumb, making small circular motions along her jawline. A single hot tear fell onto his pinky. Silo took in another deep breath.

She opened her mouth to speak, but only one word came out, "I—" She closed it, squeezing her eyes tighter. Dylan held onto her hand, offering what comfort he could. She tried again, "I...I just..." She sighed in exasperation.

Dylan quickly glanced her over to see if she was in any pain, but physically, she looked fine. He'd never seen a Fairy have a reaction as taxing as Silo's had been to healing another person. Fairies were the exception to accessing Old Magic to heal without taking a toll. Yet, from what he saw, it had. Perhaps the effect was different for new healers.

He looked back at Silo. She was trying her best to hold it together, but he could tell it was difficult for her. He set his jaw, his muscles tensing. He let go of her hand and withdrew his other hand from her face. She began to open her eyes as he did.

Dylan wrapped his arms around her waist and pulled her into him, embracing her in his arms. She gasped as her chest hit his. Dylan rested his chin into the crevice of her shoulder and closed his eyes. This was the best he could do for her right now; it was the same thing he'd do for Jay when words weren't enough to help.

After a moment, Dylan felt Silo's chin rest on his shoulder as her body relaxed in his arms. They stayed like that for a while until Dylan felt her breathing slow. At one point, her body became lax against his. He angled his head in an attempt to see her face, but he only caught a glimpse.

"Silo?" Dylan whispered. No response came. "Silo." He repeated, but she had passed out from the exhaustion she'd gained from healing him. Slowly he pulled away but made sure Silo stayed in his arms.

He peered down at her to find her sleeping. Her eyes were closed, and there was a peace to her face that hadn't been there before. Her lips were slightly parted, and her shoulders moved up and down with a gentle ease. Dylan laid her on the bed beside him. He leaned over her and pulled the end of the blanket so that it covered most of her body. He grabbed his shirt from his side and used it to wipe the remainder of the sweat from her forehead. When he finished, he dropped the shirt to the floor. He looked down at Silo, happy to still see her face in a form of peace. Even sleeping, he couldn't help but think that she was beautiful. Dylan grabbed the free pillow from behind him and tossed it to the floor He'd sleep on the ground and check up on her in the morning.

Dylan went to move from the bed, but Silo grabbed a hold of his forearm, stopping him. The action reminded him so much of Jay that he froze. His heart skipped a beat, lurching into his stomach. He forced himself to turn around, the movement stiff. Silo was still sleeping. Dylan tried to pry her fingers away without waking her and failed. She hadn't lost her strength.

He gave up. "Okay, you win." He was too tired to fight.

Dylan settled into bed beside her. He sat upright, resting his head against the headboard of the bed. He closed his eyes, trying to clear his mind away from focusing on how he was in bed with another girl who wasn't Jay.

For a moment, he missed the solitude of his room at the Institute. Instead, he thought about his parents and how much he missed them. They had died at the hands of the Demon, Phagos when he was twelve, that was five years ago. He wondered if they were proud of him. It was a thought he'd had many times before, but at least now he could confidently answer it for himself. He knew they would be. They had always taught him to fight for what he thought was right, and he was.

Beside him, Silo's hand fell from his arm to his lap. Without much thought, he grabbed it, locking their fingers together. His eyelids grew heavy with darkness, pulling him further from the surface of his mind until sleep claimed him too. For the first time in a long time, Dylan fell asleep with a smile on his face.

Dylan rolled onto his side and knew it was instantly a mistake. The sun was streaming boldly through the window and directly into his eyes. He groaned, bringing his arm up to shield his face, but his arm felt heavy as if he was dragging something with him.

Dylan's eyes fluttered open, not something, but someone. He came face to face with Silo. She was still sleeping, but her hand was still clasped tightly with his. Dylan's eyes flew wide open, the events of last night flooding into the forefront of his mind. With his free hand, he covered his mouth, stifling a gasp. His heart was galloping in his chest.

Wait. Dylan thought. It's not like he did anything wrong.

Dylan forced his mind and thoughts to calm down. He'd slept in a bed with Jay plenty of times, especially when something was wrong. This was the same thing, he reminded himself. Silo had been on the verge of passing out last night, and it was partially his fault. He recalled how pale she looked after trying to heal him, how he stopped her. He'd done nothing wrong.

Silo's eyes blinked open. At first, she seemed to still be in a daze as she looked at Dylan and then at their hands that were still midway in the air from when Dylan tried to block the sun. She looked back to Dylan, eyes registering.

"Hey." Dylan lopsidedly grinned, masking his nervousness. "Nothing happened." He quickly rushed out to evade any guilting thoughts she might have.

Unlike Dylan, Silo did not minimize her gasp. She ripped her hand from his and pulled the cover up to her chest, scooting away from him.

Dylan took the liberty to sit up in the bed and clasp his hands in his lap. "You looked sick, and then you fell asleep."

"So, you got in bed with me?" Silo squeaked in such a small voice; Dylan almost didn't hear her.

"No!" He nearly shouted, turning to face her. "I tried to sleep on the floor, but you grabbed me. Do you realize how strong your grip is?" He checked his arm. "I'm surprised I don't have a bruise," he teased, trying to lighten the mood.

"Oh no." Silo sat up and pulled her knees to her chest. "Oh no." She repeated with a groan, letting her head fall on her knees.

"Oh no, what?" Dylan asked, growing more nervous by the second. He hadn't done anything wrong. He was repeating the words in his head like a mantra.

Silo peered at him. "I'm sorry," she said without any explanation. When Dylan didn't respond, she continued, fidgeting with her braids as she spoke. "I get a bit handsy in my sleep. I..." She crossed her braids over her face in a diagonal direction. "I get cuddly," she squeaked again.

Dylan stared at her for a moment and then burst into a fit of laughter. How could someone be so cute and so shy all at once?

Silo let go of her braids and frowned, crossing her arms over her chest. "Stop it, don't laugh!"

"No," Dylan placed a hand on his chest, trying to catch his breath between laughs, "I'm sorry it's not funny." He schooled his expression except for the grin that still played on his lips. "It's alright," he said, and he meant it.

Silo let out a breath, relieved. "Well then." She pulled the covers back, swinging her legs off the side of the bed in one single movement. "I should go," she said, dragging out the last word of her sentence.

Dylan cleared his throat. "Yeah, and I should put on a shirt." He smirked.

Silo glanced over her shoulder, reflecting his expression. "Ha hah."

She stood to her feet and walked to the curtain, but before she could pull it open, the curtain flew to the side, revealing Kai. He was dressed in similar clothes to his flight wear from yesterday, but the colors were a bright yellow and brown instead of the red he'd been in before. In one hand, he carried a folded pile of dark clothes.

His eyes went wide. Silo jabbed a finger into his chest. "If you say one word, I will end you." She glared. When she was sure he'd got the message, she dropped her finger and walked around him, closing the curtain behind her as she did. If it had been a door, Dylan knew it would've slammed shut.

Kai's gaze fell on Dylan, his eyes taking into account his bare chest. His eyes settled into a glare. Dylan raised his hands in defense. "I promise it's not like that," he said.

Kai dropped the clothes he was carrying on the floor. "Get dressed. You have a visitor."

Dylan thought what Kai meant to say was that he had a visitor coming because when Dylan left his side of the curtain, the living room area was empty. Kai and Silo had both left to attend undisclosed business.

Dylan looked down at his clothes, tugging on the hooded top. It was similar to what he'd been wearing yesterday, but the material was hemmed with a dark forest green that nearly blended in with the black background. He took a seat in the closest chair near the center of the room. He had barely sat down when a knock came from the other side of the main door.

Dylan got up and walked to it. He hesitated, reaching for the door handle. He wished he'd asked for a weapon, but then he knew Kai and Silo wouldn't leave him alone if they expected danger. Well, he thought this more of Silo than Kai; Kai wouldn't hesitate to. Dylan cracked open the door, and on the other side stood the Headmaster.

"Professor?" Dylan asked, shocked.

Dylan fully opened the door to find a tall old man standing on the other side. His hair was pulled back to the nape of his neck and tucked inside his clothing. He wore a white robe trimmed with a green that matched the one Dylan wore. Dylan caught sight of his pendent necklace hidden in the folds of his robe.

Not much about him had changed from the last time Dylan had seen him. Even though it had only been about a week, Dylan wasn't counting the time he'd spent on the mend since he was half-conscious for most of it. Dylan was happy to see him.

Dylan glanced behind him, expecting to see the doctor at his side. "Where's Doctor Herron?" He asked.

"She is taking care of some preparations on my behalf."

Dylan bit his lip; he wanted to ask more, but another question began to form on his tongue. "Any news on Riley?"

"No." The Headmaster said gravely. "We each have a role to play in this war." The Headmaster stated. "Riley is a capable man, so let's not lose faith in him so easily."

"But shouldn't we be searching for him?" Dylan couldn't help but say. He'd been holding it in, but he was truly worried about Riley. Riley was the closest thing he had to a father. He couldn't lose him too. He'd already lost Jay. His voice broke, "I just need to know if he's okay," he admitted.

The Headmaster's gaze softened, "Trust," he began, "goes a long way." He turned, gesturing to the path behind him. "Walk with me?"

Dylan clenched his jaw but obliged. He closed the door behind him and followed the Headmaster out into the neighborhood. Today wasn't as busy as it had been the day before. He looked for the kids he'd seen yesterday playing magic ball, but they were nowhere in sight.

"I'm sure you have more questions, Dylan," the Headmaster began with a telling gaze. "Please ask them." He led Dylan along the same path he'd initially taken with Silo and Kai. It was easy enough to recognize that he was leading them out of Fairy District. Soon, they would be on the hill that dipped towards Wizard and Witches City. Overhead, Fairies zoomed past, but Dylan ignored them.

He did have questions. A lot of them. But part of him wasn't ready to admit that. "I'm not sure where to start," he said quietly.

"How about we start by filling in the gaps."

Dylan thought for a moment and then asked, "Where are the students you took from the cabin?"

The Headmaster smiled, "They've been taken to a colleague of mine at the school located within Wizard and Witches City."

Dylan nearly tripped over his own feet. There was a school here, this far within Aris Magica. Until now, Dylan had thought that theirs had been the only one nearby. He hadn't considered the thought that there were other Magician schools.

"How come we never played against them in magical ball or any other sport?" He asked with brimming curiosity.

"Ah, my school was created with a different purpose than the rest, with integration back into human society in mind. With the magic we hone to teach you, there just wasn't time for games." The Headmaster answered with sadness in his voice.

"Maybe it's something you should reconsider." Dylan prompted. "I feel like I've learned so much more about Aris Magica than I ever did at school. I think we all deserve to know it for ourselves while also seeking assimilation into human society."

The Headmaster smiled, a twinkle of pride in his eyes as he surveyed Dylan. "Very wise insight indeed, Mr. McCoy."

They reached the top of the hill. The tall skyscrapers from the city below could be seen much clearer than before. The Headmaster turned to face Dylan; he could see the worn years etched into the lines on his face.

"How are you doing?"

The question surprised Dylan. He honestly hadn't had a chance to think about that outside of how his body was feeling.

"I'm fine. I just..." Dylan sighed. "I want to get Jay back, so I spoke with the council."

The Headmaster nodded. "I heard their stance on the matter concerning Ms. Raremore, as well as your stance against it." Dylan stood a little straighter, hearing the pride in the Headmaster's voice, but his confidence was soon deflated as his doubts became present.

"Am I wrong to believe Jay can be saved?"

The Headmaster pondered Dylan's words for a moment. "Not at all. If you believe it is the right thing."

"I do."

"Then that is enough."

Dylan released a breath, relieved.

Silence passed between them, as did time. Dylan allowed himself the space to enjoy the moment. The breeze in the air sifted through his clothes as well as his hair. There was a slight chill in the air. Despite it being winter in Portland, it felt like spring was beginning within this part of Aris Magica.

After all this was over, he wanted to bring Jay here. His chest tightened at the thought of her. He missed her greatly.

"There you are!" Dylan jumped at the unexpected voice of Arden.

Dylan spun around to see Arden clasping his white robes in one hand as he trekked up the hill. He was in a similar fit as the Headmaster's, leaving Dylan to wonder if they'd come from the same place.

"You left me!" Arden shouted, confirming Dylan's suspicions.

"I wanted time alone with my student," the Headmaster said unapologetically.

"How do you two know each other?" Dylan asked.

"Ah yes, while your Headmaster here ran a school on the cusps of humans, I attended the perfectly good school within Wizard and Witches City. We engaged in frequent staff cohorts to make sure our curriculum was more or less aligned," Arden said displeasingly.

"You're a teacher?" Dylan had a hard time believing that.

"Gods no, a keynote speaker. I warn the students what not to do with magic."

"I tried to get him to visit the Institute, but he always declined," the Headmaster added.

"Hmm, yes, and the answer is still no for when you rebuild that heinous school."

The Headmaster chuckled.

"Shall we then?" Arden said, pulling out the powder of sand Dylan had seen him use before. His stomach churched at the thought of portaling again.

"Where are we going?" Dylan asked, turning to the Headmaster, but it was Arden who answered.

"To build your rebuttal."

"When you meet with the council a second time, you must be ready to stake your claim." The Headmaster stated. "The council is a very wise form of magic but also very old, I'm afraid. They respond to fact and proof alone. We are going to the Magnificum Reordum, better known as the Record Hall. It's a library."

"The library, really?" Dylan asked, dreading the idea. Research was Jay's thing, not his.

"Not just any library." The Headmaster proceeded to explain, "It's an extension of the Grand Library, one of the three libraries in Aris Magica, each serving a separate purpose. This library has many halls you can't see with the naked eye. Each one can be traveled to by a door hidden in the far walls past the bookcases. On the outside are grand clocks that are connected to extending branches that can also be activated for use of travel within the library. If anything were to happen to the library, measures are required for the content to protect itself using these grand clocks on the exterior."

"Now, come along. It closes at five, and this will surely take all day," Arden said.

He threw the sand into the grass. Just like before, it swirled together, creating a door within the mist. He opened it and stepped inside. The Headmaster gestured for Dylan to follow.

Dylan took one last longing look at Fairy District before holding his breath and stepping through the portal. It was only once he exited the door on the other side that he released his breath.

Dylan found himself in the heart of a massive library.

The library reminded him so much of the one at the Institute, as if the Headmaster had based it on this one. Above them, on the dome-shaped ceiling, he could see the clocks rooted inside the tree branches that hung on the outside but also the inside. The branches met at the very center of the dome, creating the sigil for Aris Magica, an elaborate S with a diagonal slash through it.

Dylan stared at it in awe, taking in the detail of the design of the clocks—he counted at least twelve. Each clock was crafted differently and varied in shape and size. Most of the clocks were made from a golden metal with intricate designs etched into the side. The hands of the clocks each resembled a different location. Dylan recognized one as the Eiffel Tower. The detail the artist had put into each clock left Dylan in admiration, and even the crevices on the branches where Old Magic was embedded inside of the tree had been carefully placed. It was marvelous.

His gaze returned to the ground. He'd never seen an array of manuscripts and scrolls this massive, making the Institute's library feel small.

"Wow," Dylan said, mesmerized as he continued to look around. "This is breathtaking." He had to admit it; he'd never really liked the library, but he could easily see himself spending hours in this one.

A pang of sadness wrapped around his heart; Jay loved the library. His hands clenched into fists at his side. A fierce determination settled in place. He'd get her back, no matter what.

Seconds later, the Headmaster appeared behind him, and the door fell. But before the sand could scatter across the library's floor, Arden waved his hand in one swooping motion, collecting it back into the little pouch he'd poured it from. He tucked the pouch away in one of the many folds of his robe.

"Come this way." Arden said.

Arden led Dylan and the Headmaster in and out of the many rows of book-shelves until he reached a table directly under the center of the dome. Above them, the roots of the branches collected into one woven knot that held a burning light inside. Dylan sat down at the table but continued to crane his neck as he surveyed the library.

Where was the librarian? He thought.

In fact, there was no one there but them.

"Is it always this empty?" Dylan asked as the Headmaster took the seat to his left. Arden disappeared back into the rows of books.

"Arden reserved the place just for us," the Headmaster said. "Generally, this library is scarce, not many people have the clearance to enter it." He gestured to the many books surrounding them in a wave of rows. "The information here is well-aged and well-protected. Not just anyone can have access to this kind of knowledge. You understand, don't you?" He asked Dylan inquisitively.

Dylan did understand. He could only imagine the history this library held. The answers it concealed to fully knowing all of Aris Magica. He quickly understood that it was a privilege to be here.

Moments later, Arden returned with a stack of books trailing behind him mid-air. They ranged from textbooks to scrolls to pamphlets that careened towards the table. When they reached it, the books lowered themselves gently down, making a neat stack in order of material directly in front of Dylan. Arden took the seat next to the Headmaster, a smug look of satisfaction on his face.

Dylan groaned. *You've got to be kidding.*

He grabbed the first text on top. The binding was fragile but thick. He pulled it down in front of him. The cover was a dark brown that appeared black at some angles. He ran his fingers over the title, feeling the fine ridges of every line. It read: *Article Law of Aris Magica.* Dylan frowned. He looked over at Arden, who winked. He turned back to the book and opened it to the first page to begin reading.

"Would you like some tea?" Arden asked the Headmaster. "Seems like this will take a while."

"Certainly."

Arden half grinned before rubbing his hands together in front of him. When he pulled his hands apart, two glasses materialized in either hand. He sat one cup down in front of the Headmaster and snapped his fingers. The cups were filled to the brim with tea.

The Headmaster smiled approvingly. "I like mine with sugar."

Chapter Fifteen

Dylan had been reading for hours but had no luck. He'd already made it more than halfway through the stack of books, with only the *Article of Law* offering a decent amount of good information, but it wasn't helpful to his case. Instead, it just further proved the council's point. Aris Magica's law must be upheld, and evil must be destroyed. It also didn't mention the forbidden law they spoke of that stopped them from directly getting involved with the Ancient's affairs. He found it odd, but perhaps he'd just missed it. After all, it was a large book, and he'd only skimmed through it.

He looked over at Arden and the Headmaster, who were still indulging in their tea. They'd offered him some, but Dylan had refused. He closed the book he was reading and turned towards them.

"Can I ask you something?" Dylan asked, speaking directly to Arden.

Arden waved in approval for him to go on.

"When we first met, you said that I was the key. What did you mean by that?"

Arden pursed his lips. He reached past the Headmaster and held out his hand. Dylan began to reach for it in response. "Not that one, the other one."

Dylan paused, frowned, and then switched hands to his left. Once he grabbed Arden's hand, Arden turned it over, exposing Dylan's wrist, the one with the trident.

"What purpose do you think you play in this prophecy?"

Dylan's frown deepened, "I…" He opened his mouth to speak, but his voice trailed off.

His role, truthfully, he didn't know. He knew that he wanted to help Jay, but ultimately, it was her job to be the one to stand against Aturdokht, he was just too stubborn to let her do it alone.

"Intriguing, isn't it," Arden whispered.

He was staring at Dylan's wrist, infatuated. Dylan looked over at the Headmaster, who had taken the liberty to begin reading one of the books from Dylan's discarded pile. Dylan met Arden's gaze once more.

"Once you start believing in your magic and ability to wield it, then you'll understand."

Was he talking about the Infinity Staff? Dylan thought.

Impossible; only Jay and him could call it forth together. But there was a knowing look within Arden's eyes. Arden released Dylan's hand and picked up a pamphlet from the pile. Dylan blinked. He hadn't seen that one there a second ago. He pushed it toward Dylan.

"I can't answer what you do not wish to see for yourself."

Dylan examined the pamphlet before him. The title was written in a dead language. The binding on it was fragile, and he felt as if it would crumble in his hands if he were to touch it.

"*Lex vitita,*" Dylan read, knowing that he'd fumbled the pronunciation.

"Forbidden law," the Headmaster said.

Dylan carefully opened the pamphlet; it only looked to be about ten pages long. He read the first line, and his eyes widened.

There is a reason Hunters were created to carry out the Council's bidding; herein lies the account of what the Ancients stole from us.

This was it, what he'd been searching for.

Chapter Sixteen

Cryis opened his eyes to find himself no longer in the bedroom but in a dimly lit corridor. A few torches aligned the stone walls, lighting a path. Cryis glanced above him, coming face to face with a low ceiling.

Something isn't right. Cryis thought.

He couldn't recall how he had arrived at this place, the pain he had felt earlier was gone as well, just like his room. Cryis looked behind him, but he was met with a dead end. The only way out was forward.

This way.

A strange feeling filled Cryis's head, guiding him to move.

Cryis walked ahead, following the empty hall until it gave way to the right. As he turned the corner, the corridor gave way to yet another hall identical to the one he started from, and it, too, was empty.

Hurry. The voice called.

Cryis recognized it as the voice he had been hearing. It reminded him of Jay's voice, but at the same time, he knew it wasn't, yet it was still a voice he had known for many years but couldn't place.

Cryis's walk turned into a sprint as he raced down hall after hall, following a voice that seemed to echo from his mind and off the walls. Whenever he thought he was close, the voice would guide him down another hall.

After what felt like an hour of running, Cryis came to a room. The floor was made of double-paned glass. When he looked down, instead of his reflection looking back at him, someone else awaited below. Cryis fell to his knees, pressing his hands to the glass as shock overwhelmed him.

"Jay!" Cryis breathlessly whispered.

She was just as she had been the last time he had seen her, except the shirt and jeans she'd been wearing were now replaced with a white gown that stopped at her knees and flared around her in a silky wave. Her long, white hair fell over her shoulders and down her back, floating around her in tight curls. Her eyes were closed as if she were dead.

Cryis saw the gentle rise and fall of her chest, reassuring him that she was still alive. She was alive, but she was somehow trapped within the glass. Her body was suspended in thin air as darkness surrounded her.

A soft glow came from her body, making her look almost transparent. Cryis recognized the space she was in; it was her Soul World. He was being shown a window into her soul.

"Jay!" Cryis said louder in disbelief.

He punched his fist against the glass, begging it to break. She couldn't hear him. Cryis punched the glass again, but no matter how much he tried, it wouldn't break.

Cryis tried to call upon the power that had shown itself to him before in times of need. But instead, all he got in return was a burning sensation building in his chest and hands. He hissed, drawing his hands away from the glass.

He waited for his hands to cool down, cradling them to his chest. "I'm not sure if you can hear me," Cryis laid his hands back on the glass, "but don't worry, Princess." Cryis whispered. "I'll find you and get you back to your body. So, keep fighting."

Jay began to fade before his eyes as the mirror began to distort and change into a new image, rippling like water. Cryis stared at it in a panic. "No!" He cried helplessly. "Jay, JAY!" His voice echoed off the walls.

Watch. The voice demanded.

Cryis glared at the mirror as the rippling slowly ceased, and a blurry image of colors became clear. The image steadied, showing a grand room with a high ceiling slowly forming. The walls were gold with black tendrils carved in the form of flames that led straight to a wooden chair sitting at the back center of the room on a tall platform.

The room was elongated like a rectangular box with a marble floor. The floor held a slight gleam to it as if the ceiling had just rained. Two doors were in the back, and one was open, leading into a tunnel. From the angle at which Cryis watched, he couldn't see what was inside the tunnel. The other door was a metal steel door with a turning lock situated directly across from the back wall.

Cryis dug his nails into the palms of his hands; the room looked awfully familiar. He'd been somewhere like it before, back in the early days of fighting Aturdokht when she was still Mirama. She used to work underground in sewers and tunnels, changing them with magic to fit her preference. Hidden away from both Aris Magica and the human world. Cryis smirked to himself; she hadn't changed one bit.

Before Cryis knew what was happening, he felt his soul being pulled into the glass beneath him. His soul left his body as everything around him suddenly went black. He blinked, opening his eyes and finding himself in a new, heavier existence.

Cryis found himself kneeling before the chair that sat at the head of the room, but he wasn't kneeling of his own will. It was as if fear had compelled him to do so.

Cryis could feel an ominous presence before him and behind him. He sneaked a glance behind him. The first thing he saw was the glint of a huge, thick sword with dead vines wrapped around the hilt, leaning against the wall. Beside it, werewolf feet wrapped in dirty strings of cloth. Cryis's eyes traveled upward, taking in the beast. The creature had the body of a wolf with purple and black fur stained with dried blood. His snout was shut but in a constant scowl as he stared past Cryis. His beady red eyes gleamed with an unquenchable thirst for blood. A pendant was wrapped around his neck, half of the silver chain hidden in his fur. It was without a gem, as if the beast were waiting for the perfect stone to fit inside it. Two curled bronze horns came out from either side of his temple, but the color of them was dulled by the dimly lit room. Cryis felt his chest tighten, the Demon before him was Phagos. It had been a while since he'd been so close to him.

The room changed in the blink of an eye, Cryis no longer stood in the tunnel but in an enclosed room. Cryis stood beside Phagos again as he over-looked a man laid out on a gurney table. Cryis followed his gaze and stared back, horrified, recognizing the man.

Riley lay strapped to a table. His face was contorted in pain, and purple veins bulged from every aspect of his skin. He wasn't alone. Numerous humans and Magicians alike decorated tables like the one Riley was on. Next to each of them was a Demon.

Cryis watched in horror as the one beside Riley hovered a hand over his forehead. A hazy, greenish light poured from the palm of the Demon's hand and into Riley's body. The more magic fed into Riley, the fainter the Demon became, as if his soul was being moved elsewhere. Perhaps it was. Cryis had seen soul possession before, but this was another level and with a Magician no less. But how?

Before Cryis could get an answer, a voice from behind him called out.

"Phagos, it's time."

Cryis recognized the voice but couldn't see past Phagos's large figure to see who it was. Suddenly, the world changed again, and Cryis found himself kneeling once more in front of the wooden chair, back inside the room from before.

Cryis's head swiveled forward without his doing so. "Lady Aturdokht," Cryis heard himself speak in a higher voice compared to his mid-deep tone.

A long-drawn sigh came from in front of him. Before him, a wall of fire shot up from the ground, touching the ceiling. It parted like a curtain. Cryis found himself looking up as someone appeared in the chair as the fire fell.

Cryis's eyes followed the fiery red dress that spread out around the platform like a wedding gown. The dress tapered off into a low neckline, revealing more than Cryis cared to see. The sleeves of the dress looked like phoenix feathers that stopped short of her wrist. Her hair had lost most of its curls and had begun to turn black at the roots, fading into its natural white color. Her once blue eyes were now an emerald green with specks of red lining her irises. The makeup she wore was dark and sinister, her eyeliner making her eyes look much sharper than before. And her lips were full and as red as the dress she wore.

Jay.

Cryis knew who she was instantly, even with Aturdokht's hold on her body. It was Jay, but she looked different from the version of her he saw trapped in her Soul World. She was beginning to look more and more like Aturdokht.

Cryis began to panic, and he wondered if what he was being shown was happening in real-time or if he was being shown what was to come. All he wanted to do was run to her, but the body he was inside would not move, the body would barely even hold Jay's gaze for long.

"Why must you continue to disappoint me, Nimbalus?"

Cryis heard himself speak again, this time in an ushered begging voice, "Y-y-yes, your m-m-majesty. Ah! L-l-lady Aturdokht. M-m-my apologies." Cryis cowered before Jay's feet.

Cryis looked at the ground, seeing his reflection in a puddle of water. He was trapped inside a Demon. His face was that of a bird with a sharp-curved beak. His beak was black as if rotted, and his feathers were a sickly yellow. The rest of his body was shaggy with feather-like fur covered by a ragged navy suit and a plaid tie. His feet were talons that stuck out of the shoes he wore. Cryis couldn't feel wings on his back or anything with all the feathers that seemed to weigh him down. He was trapped inside a Vulteron Demon's body. A Demon of prey and a very strong predator in a fight.

"Any news, Phagos, from Kazimir? Has he obtained my Elemental yet?" Jay asked. Although it was still her voice, Jay was beginning to sound more like Aturdokht. Her voice held an allure to it that hadn't originally been there.

Cryis had been right, Kazimir was working with Aturdokht. But why had he needed Cryis' blood?

Elementals. Cryis thought, lingering on the word he'd heard Jay speak.

Cryis knew nothing good could come when those things were involved.

But what could she possibly want with them?

The magic the Elementals held was great but also dangerous and extremely hard to control. Cryis was reminded of his new mysterious power.

It can't be...

"Aside from the location I've already narrowed down, the other one has escaped. And Kazimir is dead." Phagos said from behind Cryis. There was a finality to his tone as he spoke.

Out of the corner of Cryis's gaze, he saw Jay's mouth twitch into a dark frown. "Pity."

Cryis watched as her fingers scraped against the chair's armrests. Aside from Phagos, Kazimir was another Demon who had been with her from the start of the war she raged. He took pride knowing he'd been the one to finally bring him down.

"Did Kazimir at least finish his other task before he died?"

"Yes, we administered the dosage to your favorite test subject." Phagos said triumphantly. The arrogant smile from before returned on Jay's face, sending Cryis's stomach in a spin. "The elixir Kazimir created now seems to have a nice reaction to Demon magic before beginning the experiment."

Aturdokht smiled with pride at Phagos's answer, and the reaction sent a chill down Cryis's spine.

"Would you like me to send a hunting party to the Elemental's last location?" Phagos asked.

"That won't be necessary, I've found it already." She looked straight at Nimbalus, and her smile deepened as if carrying a secret. "And it'll come to me in due time."

Aturdokht fiddled with the amulet around her neck that Cryis hadn't noticed before. It was a tiny red gem. She snatched it off and twirled the gem in her hands before it began to disappear inside of her.

Cryis quickly realized the gem for what it was: an Elemental. She had already obtained one of the three Elementals, and from the conversation he'd heard, she would soon have the other two.

"After all, I have something he wants." Jay whispered, turning the fading gem over in her fingers. A faint glow trickled from it as fire danced along her fingertips.

Cryis was able to feel the heat from where he knelt. The Elemental had made her fire stronger.

Jay rose to her feet, swiping the dress behind her in one swoop, and descended the stairs before him. Cryis followed her with his gaze as she passed by him. Their gazes met for a brief moment, and Cryis could have sworn he saw her smirk at him. She stopped only a few paces behind him, standing in between him and Phagos.

"Taybeith, do come in." She said with a wave of her hand.

Cryis shifted his gaze to the tunnel to see Taybeith enter the room from a mist of dark fog. He uneasily maneuvered his way around Phagos, who was leaning beside the entrance into the tunnel. Phagos lifted his snout in the air and smirked, revealing sharp, jagged teeth.

Taybeith cleared his throat before speaking. "Aturdokht," he said in a low deep voice. Taybeith barely glanced at Cryis, showing little interest in him.

Cryis stared back at him, shocked to see Taybeith in one piece and on his feet. He'd seen the effects of the serum used entirely before, and it left the former Magician crippled for months until he was able to resume daily activities, but Taybeith looked fine.

Taybeith was in his usual black suit. His hair was combed back into a low ponytail at the nape of his neck. Cryis wondered if it was because of the Demon still inside of him. The Institute's nurse, Faith, didn't have time to extract the Demon out of Taybeith before the attack had hit.

"You." Cryis managed to say.

Everyone looked back at Cryis with a surprised expression, except for Jay. Cryis felt Nimbalus's hand rush to his mouth. He didn't stutter this time. Cryis had managed to take the reins of the body, but only for a second.

Jay smirked but ignored Cryis and turned back to Taybeith. "How is our project coming along?"

"The experiments all responded to the Demons well. Soon, none of them will be able to remember a thing, and it'll be ready for distribution to the others," Taybeith explained.

"Fascinating." Jay began as Phagos rolled his eyes clearly in disagreement about the operation. "Oh, lighten up, Phagos," Jay said, noticing as well, "I have much bigger plans for you than petty possessions."

Jay spun around, facing Cryis. She looked directly into his eyes, her smile growing wider as if she wanted to laugh. Cryis felt almost as if she were looking through Nimbalus and directly at him. Jay nodded her head in a greeting. The smile she gave him sent chills down his spine.

She knows. The voice from earlier had returned.

"Take care of our guest." Jay gestured to Nimbalus.

Cryis's eyes widened in fear, feeling the heat of Phagos's flaming sword come down on him. Suddenly, he was ripped free from the host.

Cryis's eyes flew open as he awoke. He was back in his room. The sun no longer shined through the closed blinds, leaving Cryis in the dark. He lay in bed, breathless, sweaty, and tangled up in the covers. He quickly sat up, rerunning through the nightmare he'd just lived, trying to process what he'd been shown. Cryis had been right. Jay was still alive, but she was running out of time, they all were.

Chapter Seventeen

For a moment, Cryis had forgotten where he was. His eyelids were too heavy to open. Not only that, but the world around him also kept spinning, even in darkness. Voices he recognized continued to drift in and out of the hell entrapping him.

"How long has he been like this?" Arthur asked. Cryis opened his eyes to see a blurred version of Arthur standing over him.

Cryis could feel the weight of his mattress sink as Ami sat on the edge of his bed. "He lost a lot of blood before you stitched him, remember? It's probably been a while since he's ever lost this much." There was a small pause before she continued. "Maybe he's rejecting the medicine you gave him?"

"I didn't give him any." Arthur confessed. Cryis felt a warm hand press against his forehead. "Does he have a fever?" Arthur asked.

"No, he's ice cold," Ami said, surprised.

Their voices trailed off again as Cryis felt himself being dragged back into the darkness of his Soul World. His Soul World was a pit of darkness, except there was no end to it. The deeper he went into himself, he found a soft blue beating light that began to grow and grow with each heartbeat. The closer he drifted towards the light, the further away it would pull.

Cryis reached out his hand, attempting to grasp even the faintest touch of it. The light resembled a small floating lantern. Its glow was oddly familiar to the magic he had felt in his times of need. Overwhelming, suffocating, yet beautifully calm.

Familiar fuchsia eyes appeared out of the darkness before quickly vanishing. The small blue light transformed into a tiny blue butterfly, moving its way toward Cryis. A gold trail of magic surrounded the butterfly in a rotating spiral.

Memories Cryis had buried centuries ago began to rush across the panels of his Soul World, and he knew what the light was before it even reached him. The Soul Elemental. One of three Elementals that were magic in its purest form.

"Cryis."

Cryis spun around to find himself face to face with another soul floating within his own. The purple flame grew into a person with dark coal skin and long white dreaded hair. He wore a blazed tunic made of purple fire from his soul. And his eyes were the fuchsia color Cryis had continued to be haunted with.

"You," Cryis whispered.

He knew the man standing in the darkness before him. Upon seeing the man's face, a name he'd long since buried in his memories came rushing back to him. The man before him was Tarquin, who was once known as one of the original four guardians of the Elementals, but also the man who ruined and saved Cryis's life.

"Do you remember me?" Tarquin asked carefully.

Cryis turned away from him and glared at the Elemental hovering nearby before reluctantly shifting his gaze back to Tarquin. Cryis was ashamed to admit that he'd nearly forgotten the man until recently.

"I've come to return the memory I stole." Tarquin placed his hand on Cryis's soul, and he felt a warm rush run throughout his body, igniting his Soul World.

Cryis watched as dreamlike flashes played across the black wall of his Soul World. Cryis saw himself in his human form, lying on the ice of a bare, wasted field. His clothes were rags of cloth torn and drenched in blood. Some of it had been his own, and some of it belonged to others. He'd been jumped by bandits on his way home to his village.

The light was leaving his brown eyes as the puddle of blood grew beneath him; he was dying. Tarquin kneeled before him, but his once fuchsia eyes were instead a startling blue speckled with golden flecks as he stood over Cryis. He tried to speak, but blood splattered his lips and black hair.

The memory was a distant one, long buried in Cryis's mind, much like the rest of his life before he became an Immortal. The boy's hair was much shorter than Cryis's hair was now, and his skin was sun-kissed by the sun from the many hours he had spent out in the fields during the warmer seasons.

Cryis barely recognized himself, and until now, he had no recollection of that day or who he had been. Cryis began to remember his old life, if only he had stayed at home that day with his younger sisters, would he have suffered the fate that was to come next?

"I choose you at your last breath." Tarquin said.

As the memory played out before Cryis, he began to remember who Tarquin had been to him. Along with being a guardian of an Elemental, Tarquin was the town's healer. It wasn't until later that Cryis had come to find out that he was an Aris Magician.

Cryis had known very little about Aris Magicians but knew of their world. At that time, Aris Magica had yet to cut ties with the human world, and all Aris Magician breeds still roamed the Earth freely.

Tarquin's white hair was stained with Cryis's blood as he knelt over his body. Cryis noticed a spear sticking out from Tarquin's chest. Blood pooled down his shirt. Despite being an Immortal, Tarquin had been dying as well.

Tarquin cupped his hands together close to his mouth and blew into his hands while whispering the harnessing words, *"Anima ligature,"* before proceeding to say, "There have always been three keepers of these great forces. One passes while another is reborn. I choose you to take on my mantle of protection."

"Why would you do that?" Cryis whispered, watching the memory play out. He wore a pained expression, knowing the stretch of the burden Tarquin had forcibly given him.

An orb of blue and gold light began to seep into the space between Tarquin's hands from his breath, followed by the man coughing up blood. Cryis noticed Tarquin's gold eyes turn into the electric blue of an Immortal's eyes, the same as Cryis's, as the Elemental's magic left him.

Cryis's eyes widened. For centuries, it had been a mystery where Tarquin had hidden the Soul Elemental, but it had never been lost, he'd never gotten rid of it, as the other guardians had.

"Cryis," Tarquin began, holding the magic above Cryis's dying body. "My dear boy, I pass this burden regretfully to you. The keeper and guide of souls is now your purpose."

Tarquin pushed the orb into Cryis's dying body, and as he did, Tarquin's blue eyes returned to their normal fuchsia color. Cryis took his final breath as a human boy before his body was revived as a Magician.

Cryis's black hair turned snow white, and his skin faded to a pale, lifeless color. The Elemental's power could be seen coursing through his veins until Cryis had fully reawakened with bright blue eyes.

The memory faded to black, leaving Cryis, Tarquin, and the Elemental in darkness once again.

"The Elemental buried inside you has once again awakened," Tarquin began. The air between them had grown exceedingly thick.

Cryis had forgotten how he had become Immortal. He just remembered waking up and suddenly knowing what he had become and what he had to do. Many years had passed before he met the first Ancient, Emilia. He remembered searching long and hard until he had finally found her and knew his purpose was to help her seal Aturdokht and to guide souls to the next life.

Cryis stared at the Elemental. He never knew that he had been one of the beings honored with keeping watch over great magic and that it had been inside him all along.

"But why now?" Cryis said aloud. Any thought in his Soul World seemed to echo off the walls of his mind whether he spoke them aloud or not.

"It's because someone has gone searching for them and has activated one of their powers." Tarquin's soul sighed heavily. "The more you use its power, the less you'll become."

"Lesser," Cryis thought. "You mean…" He hesitated. The Elemental was given to him with his immortality, and now it was taking it away. His time as an Immortal was coming to an end.

Tarquin's soul flickered. "My time is up. My purpose has finally been fulfilled."

Cryis looked at Tarquin with fearful eyes. He wasn't sure if he was ready for it to be over. "But I still have so many questions I—" Cryis stopped himself, seeing Tarquin's sad smile. He was ready.

Tarquin had been around for much longer than Cryis had and had waited for this very moment to meet him again before his soul could truly rest. Cryis knew the feeling, each Immortal bore it. Until their purpose was completed, they would remain tethered to life in one way or another. Knowing that Cryis was unable to resent Tarquin, nor would he be responsible for keeping the Magician bound longer.

"Will you guide me?" Tarquin requested.

Cryis nodded. He called upon *Jevit*. Even inside his Soul World, the scythe appeared once called. The Elemental shone with a great light, much like the aura transcending from his scythe. Cryis took a deep breath and pointed the scythe at Tarquin. The blade wrapped around his body, and Tarquin's soul returned to its soul flame.

Cryis hesitated, staring at the lone flame. Its fire was softly fading. Cryis closed his eyes, knowing what had to be done. "Let your soul be purified and the gates of the heavens open wide," Cryis recited. Tarquin's soul continued to fade from existence. "The rest is up to you."

Cryis felt a great sadness as Tarquin's soul vanished. His scythe disappeared as the Elemental's glow dimmed. The butterfly flapped its wings and continued to hover next to Cryis. He reached out his hand to touch it. This time, the Elemental did not shy away.

Cryis could feel its power calling to him. The more he drew from its power, the lesser he would become. Tarquin's words haunted his mind, but part of Cryis was tired of fighting. The burden he'd carried was becoming too great, and he longed for it to be over, but at the same time, he didn't want life to end just yet.

The Elemental's light grew brighter once more as Cryis's hand drew near. Gold trails of magic began to swarm around him as Arthur's face came into view. He was smiling. He opened his mouth and began to speak, but Cryis couldn't hear the words coming out of his mouth. Cryis's eyes grew wide, knowing why the Elemental was showing him the boy. Arthur would be the next keeper and Cryis's successor as an Immortal.

"No," Cryis said barely above a whisper. The light swarm of magic around him grew more intense, turning red at the corners as if angry. "Enough!" Cryis said defiantly.

Cryis felt himself being pulled from the Elemental and dragged further down into his Soul World until he hit something resembling solid ground. The voice he had heard in his dreams echoed around him. Cryis looked around for a person but couldn't find anyone. Everything around him was still a murky black.

You've spent enough time here. Leave.

"Is this your doing?" Cryis asked furiously. "Show yourself! Why do you continue to hide?"

The fact that you still cannot recognize me proves you aren't ready yet.

"What?" Cryis shouted into the air.

You'll have all the answers you seek in due time.

As if the voice were trying to guide him, a huge oak door appeared out of the darkness. The door had a woman with wings sitting on a lone petal engraved into the wood. Cryis had seen this door before and knew exactly where it was in the heart of a library hidden within Aris Magica. Aris Magica had three well-known libraries, all extensions of the Grand Library: the Record Hall, the Hidden, and the Forbidden. Each provided well-protected knowledge that was linked back to the Grand Library. If one location was destroyed, it would return there.

"Why did you show me that? What about Jay? Take me back to her," Cryis demanded.

The time has come for you to leave.

Out of the darkness, the door faded, replaced by a hand that exploded with light. It grabbed Cryis's soul and ripped him free of his Soul World, expelling him out.

When Cryis came to, he was staring at a ceiling. The lights in the room were off, but the blinds of his window were open, allowing the sun's natural light to brighten the room. Cryis sat up slowly to find Eliza sitting in a chair beside his bed. He was still in Vastille's cabin. For the past couple of days, he'd been drifting in and out of sleep.

Eliza mimicked Cryis's blink of surprise. She leaned forward, resting her elbows on his bed and her chin in her hands. He shifted his gaze to the window behind her, then back at Eliza to find her still staring at him. He looked down to find himself in a fresh shirt and pants. His body felt a lot better too, and he felt fully healed. He reached out his hand and rubbed the back of his neck.

"Did you just die, mister?" Eliza asked.

"Die?" Cryis asked her right back.

Eliza nodded. She leaned back in her chair to explain. "Yes, D-I-E, die."

Cryis arched his eyebrow, slightly withholding his annoyance. "I know how to spell die."

Eliza rolled her eyes and frowned. "Well, I thought because you're really old, you'd also be hard of hearing," she mumbled.

Cryis frowned to himself. *What a brat...*

"I get that a lot." Eliza shrugged. She swung her legs back and forth under the chair, kicking the side of the bed.

Cryis stared at her, stunned. "Did you just read my mind?"

"Yes," Eliza said shyly. She peered up at Cryis with doe-like eyes. "Please don't tell my dad, he'll freak."

"Vastille?" Cryis was still surprised he was the father of an actual child.

"No, John Doe." Eliza stuck out her tongue. "I already know about Aris Magica, my dad thinks pretty loudly. But he's not ready to tell me yet, so I want to respect that."

"You're a wise kid," Cryis complimented.

"Wiser than you," she retorted.

Cryis clicked his tongue, *and not a stranger to sarcasm either*, he pushed the thought to her.

Eliza stood up from her chair. "By the way, you have some weird dreams," she said before she headed for the door. She paused with her hand on the knob. "Oh, and Daddy said to find him out back once you woke up. Bye, old man." She smirked before closing the door behind her.

Cryis pushed the covers to the end of the bed and then pushed his hair behind his ears. "Why am I not surprised she's Aris Magician," Cryis mumbled. "Now I know how Jay felt the first time I spoke in her mind without permission." Cryis shuddered, feeling violated.

Before getting out of bed, Cryis let out a long sigh. He was the keeper of the Soul Elemental, and Arthur was his successor. Cryis didn't know how to feel about it. He wasn't sure if he should be sad that his time as an Immortal was coming to an end or if he should be glad that he finally would have a chance to experience a normal life again. However, Cryis knew one thing: no matter what the Elemental had shown him, this was not a burden he wanted to pass on to Arthur.

Cryis let out one more heavy sigh before getting up from his bed. He walked over to his window and peered through the blinds. Sure enough, there was Vastille out back chopping wood off a stump. Cryis smiled, looking down at him, and then he noticed his reflection in the window. His eyes were no longer red but had returned to their normal blue.

Cryis wandered around to the backside of the cabin, following the deep foot-prints Vastille had already made in the snow. He had borrowed the purple puffy coat from Eliza, but even that wasn't warm enough. Cryis saw Vastille before he had noticed him. Cryis wondered how the man was surviving in just a light windbreaker coat and thin gloves.

"Your daughter is quite the character," Cryis said with a smile as Vastille chopped a piece of wood apart from another.

Vastille threw his axe into the snow and looked up as Cryis approached him. "You're up." He didn't sound surprised but relieved. "Ami said you had a fever."

Cryis frowned. "I feel fine." Much better than he had in weeks. He stopped short of the hefty pile of wood Vastille had created. "But I have some news that I think everyone should hear."

"What is it?" Vastille removed his gloves, stuffing them into his pocket. Cryis noticed he wasn't wearing his glasses as he stared at Cryis, awaiting an answer.

"I know what Aturdokht's next move is, and I know where to go to find out how to get ahead of her."

Chapter Eighteen

"Okay, walk me through it again. What exactly did you see?" Vastille asked as he readjusted the way he sat in his chair. He kicked up his leg, crossing it over his other one. He had changed into jeans and a plaid buttoned-up shirt; it was strange seeing him in anything but his black suit.

Everyone was back in the living room, sitting around the coffee table. Vastille sat in the loveseat while Cryis and Arthur occupied the long couch together. Across the coffee table, Ami sat alone on the other couch. Everyone had changed, like Cryis.

Ami was no longer in the jail jumpsuit but an oversized t-shirt that must have belonged to Vastille and a pair of basketball shorts belonging to Eliza. Her hair had a heavy wave to it after being freshly washed, and her body was scrubbed clean.

Arthur had changed as well; he was small enough to fit into a pair of Eliza's sweatpants and a shirt from Vastille too.

Cryis cleared his throat, facing Vastille, "In my dreams, I heard this voice that led me to Jay. I saw her." Cryis explained while the others listened intently. "Her soul is trapped inside her Soul World, while Aturdokht is planning to collect the Elementals."

Ami scoffed, "Great voices. Really?" as Arthur said, "What are Elementals?"

"You don't know this, but," Cryis turned to Ami, "I used to be able to communicate with Jay telepathically before Aturdokht took over. And if memory serves correctly, Jay should be able to also hear the first Ancient's voice as well, just like the others."

Ami sputtered for a response but didn't have one in return.

"Back at the safe house, after Aturdokht knocked you and Lyid out, she tried to attack me. That strange magic manifested around me and scared her off, I think, but it turns out that power is an Elemental. The Soul Elemental, to be exact."

"So, what...it woke up?" Ami asked, concerned.

"Of course!" Arthur said, catching on quickly. "It may be the reason why you've had trouble healing. That power is feeding off your immortality." Cryis looked at him, surprised by how quickly he was piecing things together.

"But how is this possible? After all these years, you're just now finding out that thing is inside of you?" Ami asked. "Wasn't it lost to history?"

"Because the man that chose me sealed it away and my memories of it."

"Oh..." Her voice trailed off.

"And an Elemental, Arthur," Cryis began, "are sources of power created at the beginning of Aris Magica. Their magic is pure Old Magic. The four leaders during the Aris Magica wars were blessed with protecting the four Elementals: Ignis, Život, Anim, and Chi." Cryis looked around the room and was met with confused stares. "In simpler terms, Heart, Life, Soul, and Energy. Aturdokht has already found the Heart Elemental, and the Soul one is inside of me."

"That leaves two left," Vastille said. "Where are they?"

Cryis shook his head. "The Life Elemental is safe; it's with your Headmaster." He looked at Ami.

"The Professor?" Ami shouted, nearly falling off the couch. "W-what? How? Why did—" She took a deep breath, calming herself, "If you really think about it, it's not that shocking. After all, it's the Headmaster."

"Who?'" Arthur asked.

"The Headmaster at my school." Ami waved him off. "And the last one, please?" Ami asked.

Cryis shrugged. "It was destroyed a long time ago. The last one didn't exist until the others were used. The past keepers came together and created it, and then some say it was destroyed, others lost, but no one really knows."

Cryis thought back; the last person to hold the Energy Elemental had been Selena, and that was centuries ago. After she died, no one knew what she had done to the Elemental. And from the looks of his dreams, Aturdokht wasn't concerned about finding the fourth one either, the original three would be enough.

"Okay, so where does that leave us? If Aturdokht has one, and technically, we have two, we can just use it to defeat her, right?" Ami suggested.

Cryis shook his head again. "No, it's not that simple. The Elementals alone are dangerous and hard enough to control as it is. We can't let them come to-gether. But..." Cryis's voice trailed off as he considered the voice's instructions.

"Go on," Vastille said.

"The voice told me to go to the library between the two worlds," Cryis confessed.

"The Hidden Library?" Vastille clarified.

Cryis nodded his head. "It might have some scrolls or rituals on how to A, get the Soul Elemental out of me or B, awaken Jay."

Aturdokht knew Cryis had the Soul Elemental, but if Cryis could pass the Elemental to Arthur without his immortality, then they could gain the upper hand, stalling Aturdokht, even for a little while longer.

"Shouldn't we be looking for the Headmaster if that's her next target?" Ami interjected.

"He can manage on his own," Cryis said. He knew of her Headmaster's magic and great feats. He was a powerful Wizard and didn't need their help to fend off Aturdokht.

Ami huffed, still in disagreement. "Okay, but the library is a waste of time! When we could go straight where you saw Jay and just free her soul."

"We can't, it's not that simple," Cryis said.

Cryis had sensed it, Aturdokht's magic had grown even stronger since she had obtained the Elemental. They wouldn't stand much of a chance against her—not without the Infinity Staff—but they needed both Jay and Dylan to call it. Plus, there was the second matter of what he had seen. Cryis clenched his jaw to prevent himself from relieving the horrific vision of what he had seen being done to innocent people.

"Something else about your dream is putting you on edge, isn't it?" Arthur asked quietly. Cryis felt the weight of the couch shift as Arthur scooted closer to him.

Having Arthur next to him brought a wave of comfort. Even the way Arthur offered an encouraging smile eased him slightly. But Arthur was right—something else was bothering him. Along with Arthur's watchful gaze, he could feel Vastille and Ami's eyes on him as well. Cryis glanced down at his hand resting on the couch, the other settled in his lap. A moment later, Arthur's hand covered his, and his heart skipped a beat.

Cryis glanced at Arthur and sighed, "While I was there, Aturdokht was talking to Taybeith and Phagos about some experiment and how distribution was almost ready." He hesitated, unsure how to continue, but he knew they deserved to know the truth.

Beside him, Cryis felt Arthur shift, moving his hand from resting on top of his to gently grabbing it. Suddenly, the nervousness he felt wasn't from what he was about to say. Instead, he became acutely aware that Arthur was holding his hand. Cryis took a deep breath, exhaling through his nose, trying to steady his racing heart.

"I saw Riley." Cryis finally found the courage to say. He met eyes only with Ami; she seemed to be holding her breath. "They were feeding a Demon into his body..." Cryis choked on his words, "I think the experiment had something to do with a new form of soul possession." Cryis was still shaken about what he had seen. It was almost as if Aturdokht was trying to merge souls taking a Demon's soul possession to another level.

"I'm sorry, Ami." Cryis added. Soul possession on an Aris Magician was forbidden for a reason, nothing good ever came from it.

Ami took in a tight breath before speaking. "M-my Professor is stronger than you think," she said, her voice faltering slightly.

Cryis noticed the tremor in her tone but decided to say nothing and instead chose to believe her because the alternative was unbearable.

No one said anything. A heavy silence settled over the group as the weight of Cryis's words sank in. The only sound came from the steady ticking of a clock across the room. Absentmindedly, Arthur caressed Cryis's hand with his thumb. Cryis focused on the slow, repetitive motion of Arthur's thumb tracing a half-circle on his skin before starting again. It was comforting. Yet, the comfort was at odds with a growing tension, as if Cryis had forgotten how to breathe. He forced himself to think, trying to process what he had just revealed. The experiments he'd witnessed terrified him, and he wondered what it would mean for the world if Aturdokht succeeded.

"Do you think the Elementals could help us separate Jay from Aturdokht?" Ami asked after some time had passed.

"There are rules and limits to their magic, but maybe," Cryis said, unsure whether giving her hope or not was the right thing to do.

"Okay then." Ami sighed, sinking into the couch.

Eliza walked in, carrying a tray holding five mugs. The mugs smelled of hot chocolate as steam garnished the air. "Dinner is served." She smiled, setting the tray down and picking up one of the mugs.

The warmth of Arthur's hand slipped away, leaving a slow sadness that filled Cryis's heart. Arthur took the mugs and passed them out to the others.

"Thank you." Cryis said as he claimed his cup.

Eliza leaned up against her dad's chair and took a sip of her hot chocolate. "How much longer is this meeting going to last?" She gestured her thumb to Vastille, "We have a movie to watch." Her gaze settled on Cryis, awaiting an answer.

"We're done. He's all yours," Ami said, smiling up at Eliza. Cryis looked at her, confused. They still hadn't agreed on what to do. Ami took a sip from her mug. "We leave for the library at dawn."

Cryis blinked at her, taken aback, but when Ami didn't say anything, he smiled at her, thankful she'd agreed to follow him. She rolled her eyes, taking another sip of her drink, but still smiled back, although it didn't reach her eyes.

Cryis grimaced, knowing her thoughts must be consumed for the safety of her Professor and her friends.

"Um," Arthur raised his hand like a bashful student. "Where is this library?"

"It's hidden in downtown Portland." Ami replied. Arthur subtly nodded his head in understanding. "Vastille, you think we can borrow that truck I saw sitting in your garage?" Ami asked.

"How did you—" Vastille began.

"I got bored and explored a bit earlier." Ami shrugged, taking another sip.

Vastille ran a hand down his face. "Sure, fine." He reluctantly agreed. "Just bring it back without a scratch."

"Men and their cars," Ami mumbled. "I'll drive, so don't even worry."

"No!" Cryis and Arthur both shouted. They looked at each other, Cryis was unable to hold his gaze for long without thinking about the fate he would soon have to bestow on Arthur. Cryis felt his face warm with guilt, and he quickly turned away.

"Arthur should drive," Cryis said.

"Me?" Arthur's voice cracked, pointing to himself.

Ami scoffed, "Whatever." She sat her empty mug back on the tray, already finished. "I'm going to bed. I'll see you all bright and early." She rose from her seat and walked over to Eliza, pulling her into a tight hug. "In case I don't see you again." The two exchanged a gentle smile before Ami walked toward the stairs.

Cryis watched her climb the stairs. "We should all turn in soon." Cryis had a feeling today would be the last time any of them got a peaceful sleep.

Vastille stood and picked Eliza up with him. He turned to Cryis and Arthur, "Anything you need before you leave, let me know, and I'll get it for you. I'll try my best to keep Luke off your tail in the meantime."

"I know you will," Cryis said. "Goodnight."

"We'll be in the den." He smiled at Eliza before the two of them disappeared around the corner.

Arthur got up and began collecting the scattered cups. "Are you done with yours?" He reached for Cryis's.

Cryis looked up uneasily at Arthur as he grabbed his mug from the table. He feared he was right about Arthur being chosen to inherit not only the Soul Elemental but also his immortality as well. He felt the unending feeling to protect him from bearing a burden he had no desire to bear. No one deserved such a cruel fate. If only he hadn't met Arthur, then he wouldn't be wrapped up in any of his misfortune. Cryis instantly felt remorseful for thinking such things.

"You don't have to come, you know. It's not your fight," Cryis said anyway.

Arthur shrugged, "From what I've heard so far about this Aturdokht person, it feels like I have no choice, I'm like the advocate for the human race."

Cryis chuckled. "We've already got two of those."

"Your missing friends, Riley and Dylan?" Arthur asked.

Cryis nodded sadly, then grimaced, thinking of Riley. He hoped Ami was right. As much as he wanted to go look for them, he knew they would only be wasting time. "We'll find them, or they'll find us. I'm sure."

Before it's too late, he thought to himself.

"Good, but in the meantime, I'm not going anywhere," Arthur smiled.

Cryis's heart for a moment skipped a beat as he met Arthur's gaze, and his smile returned, but only for a short while. He felt ashamed, knowing he felt at ease in Arthur's presence while also knowing what fate had in store for him. Cryis wasn't sure what to do. He didn't know if he should tell Arthur the truth or not.

"Get some sleep, I'll see you in the morning," Arthur said. He smiled down at Cryis, affection clear in his eyes. Cryis's heart raced in response, unable to resist the effect. Arthur took the dirty mugs, disappearing into the kitchen before Cryis had a chance to make up his mind.

"Yeah...okay," Cryis whispered to himself.

Dawn came faster than Cryis had expected. The sun had barely broken over the horizon before Ami had come to his room to awaken him. She was dressed in new clothes: jeans and a long-sleeved shirt paired with a winter coat. She passed him a stack of clothes before leaving the room. Cryis found out that Vastille had gone to the store in the middle of the night and had bought them clothes that fit.

Cryis slipped on the jeans and a plain green shirt. While he laced up the brown boots, a quiet knock came from the door across the room. Cryis looked up in time to see Ami slip inside. She was now holding a winter coat in her hands. Her hair was pulled back into a low braid.

"Ready?" She asked as she looked Cryis up and down.

Cryis extended his hands to show her, "Ready."

Ami nodded, looking away from him and nervously around his room. He could tell that something was eating away at her, the same way it had been chipping away at him yesterday.

"What is it?"

She let out a deflated sigh. "It's just I have a bad feeling about this. You said it yourself that Jay's spirit was in some sort of coma. What if Aturdokht is the one that showed you that dream," Ami began, she stared at Cryis with pleading eyes. "It could be a trap."

The thought had crossed Cryis's mind, but he knew deep in his heart that it had somehow been Jay who had called him there. He couldn't explain it in words, but it had been her, he was sure of it. Suddenly, Cryis felt the compelling urge to confide in her.

"Ami," Cryis began slowly, "my time is almost up." He met her gaze with a sadness of his own.

"What?" Ami gawked at him. Her voice was barely above a whisper.

Cryis sadly smiled. "Do you know what it's like to stare death in the face?" Ami looked back at him, confused. He sighed, realizing she didn't understand, so he said it more plainly. "I think Arthur's my replacement."

"For what? The Soul Elemental or your immortality?" Ami asked in a serious tone, but he could already see the solution working its way into her eyes.

"Both," Cryis admitted curtly.

Ami gasped. Cryis watched her process the information before her eyes went wide with understanding. "But he's human—" Ami stopped herself.

They both knew that it didn't matter when an Immortal was chosen. A human could become an Immortal if chosen by either fate or another Immortal. Every Immortal's transformation was different, just like their purpose, although they all shared the responsibility of guiding souls to the next life. They were the only breed, with the exception that it didn't matter if you were an Aris Magician or not.

"My predecessor had the same eyes," Cryis thought aloud. Cryis couldn't deny that he felt very drawn to Arthur, it had been the same with Tarquin. "After he passed his immortality to me, he didn't die right away. I think it's because he was the keeper of an Elemental."

"So what? You think you can pass Arthur the Elemental without your immortality?" Ami said, putting two and two together. She gasped again, "Has it ever been done before? I thought no one could avoid an Immortal's fate?"

Cryis nodded. It hadn't been done before, but that was part of the reason why he wanted to visit the library.

"Aturdokht would never expect to look for the Elemental within a human." He said.

Ami sighed. She looked up at Cryis with worried eyes. Another knock came from the door as Arthur came in. Ami looked over at him with regret in her eyes. Arthur frowned, stepping around her.

"You both ready? The truck is," Arthur said, looking between Cryis and Ami.

Cryis forced a smile and grabbed the bag on the floor next to the bed. "Of course. Let's go."

Arthur shrugged and led the way out of the room. Cryis stopped, panic creating a fist around his heart once again.

He turned to Ami and whispered, "Please don't tell him, not until I know it can be done first."

Ami nodded but wouldn't meet Cryis's heavy stare. Cryis took it as an agreement and stepped aside to let Ami out of the room. Before leaving, Cryis gave one final look at the room he had borrowed. A pain of nostalgia hit him, knowing he wouldn't be coming back. He sighed, closing the door.

Arthur and Ami were both waiting downstairs near the front door by the time Cryis had made it down the steps and into the living room. Vastille was waiting at the front door with them. He carried a duffle bag on his shoulders but was dressed in plaid pajama pants and a white t-shirt as if he'd just crawled out of bed.

"Thank you for everything," Ami said as she hugged Vastille.

"Of course." Vastille held out the duffle bag to Arthur. "As many guns and ammo as I could gather. Also, I checked the police scanners. Luke's tied up with another situation at the moment, but that doesn't mean he doesn't have someone else looking for you, so keep yourselves alert."

Arthur lightly chuckled, taking the duffle bag from him. "We sure do have a lot of enemies, huh?" He began to open the door but stopped. "And the other thing we discussed?"

Vastille grinned, "Don't worry, I rigged the system. You were killed in action."

Arthur looked back at Cryis. "Best to cover our trail as much as we can."

Cryis looked at Vastille, repeating his words from yesterday, "Smart kid."

Vastille turned to Cryis. "Take care of yourself and find Jay. That girl's a fighter; she'll be alright."

"Right," Cryis said, hopeful. Cryis started to walk past Vastille; he opened the door, feeling a blast of cold air bite at his skin. Ami and Arthur walked ahead down the steps. A truck was parked at the foot of the hill. Cryis could only imagine how the ride up the hill would go.

"Vastille." Cryis stopped at the top of the stairs.

Cryis couldn't find it in himself to turn around, if he did, he knew there was a chance Vastille would notice the regret in his eyes. There were a lot of things in life Cryis wished he'd done differently, and his history with Vastille was one of them. But Cryis couldn't leave without letting him know how grateful he was to have met such a man.

"Thank you."

Cryis didn't wait for his response and closed the door behind him. He followed Arthur's footprints to the truck. His boots crushed the snow beneath him as he walked. He let out a shaky breath, seeing it materialize in the air. It was the first time that Cryis was experiencing *last times*. Part of himself felt sad, but there was also a part of him that felt relieved. He'd been waiting for his life to end for so long, and it had finally come.

Cryis reached the truck, opened the back seat, and hopped in. Immediately, he was filled with warmth from the heaters blowing.

Arthur looked back from the driver's seat. "Where to..." His voice trailed off.

Cryis sniffed, feeling a tear fall down his cheek. He looked away, embarrassed, and quickly wiped it away.

"Downtown Portland," he said. "There's a pocket dimension there that can take us directly to the Hidden Library." Cryis looked back at Arthur, but he had already turned forward. Cryis was thankful he didn't ask.

"Okay. Seatbelts everyone." Arthur put the truck into gear, and his knuckles tightened on the wheel. "You're in good hands."

Chapter Nineteen

Dylan had expected his second meeting with the council to happen immediately, with only a day or two passing in between at most, but instead, it had been much longer. He was beginning to lose hope. All this time he'd spent deriving a plan to convince the council to get involved in a way that would help Jay, all the time he'd spent with Arden and the Headmaster studying up on Aris Magica history and laws now felt like such a waste. He'd already missed four days from recovering from his injuries when he'd first arrived, and now he was nearly twelve days behind Jay. He couldn't help but feel that he was too late. On top of it all, there still hadn't been word about Riley's whereabouts. He tried not to dwell on that much, knowing that Riley was one of the most capable men he knew.

"Look alive, deumage!" Kai shouted as he swiped his rapier at Dylan's feet, knocking him to the ground yet again.

Dylan hit the grass hard; the force of the weight pulled him from his thoughts, but instead of getting up and retaliating, he leaned back onto his elbows into the grass beneath him. Where was his head at today?

Dylan gripped the two daggers he held in each hand; he was happy to be holding a weapon again. For the past week, he had been sparring with Kai. Generally, the battlefield was pretty even, but this was the third time Kai had managed to catch him off guard within the hour.

Dylan sighed, leaning his head back to stare up at the sky. The sun was hiding behind a group of white fluffy clouds. Birds in various colors with long feathered wings flew overhead. They were still in Aris Magica, but they'd taken up sparing over the hill looking down to Fairy District. Most Fairies didn't need to venture this far since the next town was in the opposite direction.

A shadow not belonging to himself cast over him as Silo came into view. Her braids were pulled back into one single braid today, and the color she had added to her standard flight wear was lavender. She smiled down at him, flashing him a row of her perfectly straight teeth. He noticed her front two teeth were slightly bigger than the rest, which only made her look even cuter.

Dylan grinned back at her, welcomed by her presence. Silo snickered before reaching down and flicking a piece of grass from his hair and then another from his shoulder. He had taken the liberty of wearing various versions of the hoodie and light pants he'd first been given when he had first arrived. Once again, the fabric of his clothes was black but lined with a deep purple on the hems, now covered in grass.

"Hey, you," he greeted.

"You just going to lie there all day?" Silo asked, tilting her head slightly to one side.

Dylan sighed but kept his smile. "Guess not." He leaned forward, causing Silo to lean back as he rose to his feet. The minute he was up, he turned and faced her.

Behind him, Kai shouted, "Oh good, maybe you can put him on his ass for a change!" His voice grew closer as he approached.

Dylan rolled his eyes but continued to look at Silo. She laughed in response.

Before Kai reached them, Dylan sobered. He lowered his voice so that only Silo could hear, "Any word from the council?"

She lowered her gaze. "No. They haven't sent a missive for you yet." She met his gaze again. "But I'm sure it's coming."

"How much longer?" Dylan asked. "The longer we wait, the more chance Jay has of becoming one with Aturdokht."

Silo glared, but it held no heat. "You mean, the more chance of destruction she can cause."

Dylan scoffed. "As far as we know, Aturdokht hasn't done a single thing to the human world or our world. You're just paranoid like everyone else in this realm."

Silo scowled, taking a step toward him. She jabbed a finger in his chest. "Do you really believe that for twelve days, she hasn't made a single move? Everything I've been told about that Witch counters that."

"That's because the council is terrified of the thought of her." Dylan's voice began to rise. "When, in actuality, they don't know her."

Silo dropped her hands. Dylan glanced at his side, seeing Kai step up beside him out of the corner of his eye. His gaze fell back to Silo. "Are you talking about Aturdokht or Jay?" She sighed, "The sooner you realize they're the same person, the better off we'll all be."

"Both. The council fears them both because they can't control them due to some forsaken law," Dylan said. He confidently tilted his chin. "But I can change that."

Dylan was fully beginning to believe that he was the loophole the council needed. Through him, they could help Jay. All he needed was a chance, even if they weren't willing to give him their support. Once they got Jay back, and she gave her blessing as the Ancient, they could work together with the council to put an end to Aturdokht.

"Damn." Kai slapped a hand on Dylan's shoulder. "Even I'm starting to believe him." He turned to Silo, "But sounds like someone is jealous," He teased as he wriggled his eyebrows.

Silo scoffed, "You're both impossible."

Dylan grinned confidently, "I know."

Dylan met Silo's gaze with a teasing arrogance that made her smile. He liked it when she smiled—it was contagious, even for him. He had started to build a life here, and his connection with Silo had grown naturally. After all, it was because of her that he felt so at ease in this place. Dylan smiled to himself, though he had to admit Kai deserved some of that credit too.

Kai lowered his hand and crossed his arms, "Ew, stop flirting with my sister!" Dylan rolled his eyes, used to Kai's insistent teasing by now. "Alright, let's go again," Kai said, his voice dropping to a serious tone. He pointed his rapier at Silo, "You join in too."

She was in the process of removing the collapsed spear at her waist when she paused, looking straight ahead. Dylan followed her gaze to see Doctor Herron trekking up the hill. Her hair ablaze in the sun's glare. She was dressed in her usual lab coat, wearing jeans and a yellow top underneath.

"This better be good," Kai grumbled, already sheathing his sword.

Dylan tucked away his daggers in his boots and then began walking to meet her halfway. Doctor Herron looked more tired than when he'd last seen her. "What are you doing here?" He asked.

She looked gravely between Dylan, Silo, and Kai. "The council is ready for you. It's time."

Chapter Twenty

The council building was the same as it had been the last time Dylan had arrived, the only difference was his resolve. He wasn't scared anymore but determined to be heard. Dylan looked up to see the low, ominous clouds sitting low in the sky and covering the top half of the building. His gaze shifted back to the door before him, still covered in dust and unlit from the inside. He stepped forward, ready to open the door, but Silo gently grabbed his shoulder. The action caused him to pause.

Looking back at her, he could see the worry swimming in her eyes. "You sure you're ready for this?"

"I am." Dylan offered her a small smile.

Silo let out a breath, some of the tension leaving from her shoulders. She dropped her hand after giving his shoulder a tight squeeze. "Okay then. Good luck." Her mouth twitched into a smile, but an unreadable mask quickly replaced it as Dylan opened the door.

Dylan led the way inside this time, with both Kai and Silo at his side. They were immediately transferred into the familiar white void. Three women veiled in the same bright colors as before, yellow, pink, and blue, stood high above them, each exuding so much magic it made Dylan pause. The sky was different than before, encompassing a sunset sky with a full moon that reflected a dimming light across the rolling hills.

"Welcome," the voices said in unison.

Dylan waited for an apology to follow for making him wait so long to see them, but one never came. He clenched his jaw but tried not to let it bother him. If he'd learned anything from all his research the past couple of days, it was that the council were very proud Magicians.

This time, Dylan didn't wait for the council to state their claim. Judgment would be passed today whether they liked it or not. The moment Silo and Kai disappeared from his side Dylan stepped forward to speak.

The rush of magic coursed through his body, but unlike the last time, the scenery didn't change as he settled onto the circular platform that had been awaiting him. He took a deep breath.

"I know the truth of what happened between you and the Ancient. What she stole." Dylan said. He crossed his arms over his chest, finally feeling as if he could gain some ground.

Dylan had read how the first Ancient, Emilia, had stolen magic from the council to stop them from being involved in her affairs with Aturdokht. She had believed Aturdokht could be saved, while the council had wanted her soul to be destroyed.

"And I know how to get it back." He waited for them to respond before continuing.

The council met his gaze intrigued. "Go on."

"Once Jay is back to herself, she will restore the power she took from you lifetimes ago." He knew it was a risky move, speaking on behalf of Jay, but he knew her, and he knew she didn't have any reason to stop the council from helping her. He knew Jay wouldn't want to do this alone. More than anyone, he knew that she wanted Aturdokht gone as much as he did.

"You speak for the Ancient."

"Yes," Dylan stated, even though it hadn't been a question. "I do."

"Aturdokht is a dangerous threat. We cannot gamble on an empty promise when we have Hunters who are more than capable of putting an end to her now before it is too late."

Dylan furrowed his brow, staring at the ground. They made a good point. But he knew there was a better way to put an end to this war and save Jay. He recalled what he read in *Aris Magica Law*.

"An innocent has every right to stand trial if given the chance." He raised his gaze to them. "Article 1.9 Volume 131. And until then, the council must grant them respite."

"Aturdokht is not innocent."

"But the Ancient is," Dylan countered. "Just because she became a vessel, that does not change. Right now, you have no proof that Jay has committed any heinous acts on behalf of Aturdokht's willpower." He let out a deep breath. His heart squeezed inside his chest, aching, causing Dylan to fist his hands at his side.

Arden's words recalled in his mind: *you're needed here to set the stage.*

Dylan knew what he had to do. Suddenly, the solution seemed so simple that he felt ashamed for not realizing it sooner. But after everything he'd learned in the library, from his experiences in Aris Magica to his time spent with Silo and Kai, it all made sense.

"Look, I know right now you can't help directly and can only assist through others. I know you want to stop Aturdokht and protect the balance of Aris Magica more than anyone, and more than anyone, you three have sacrificed the most." But so had Jay. Even now, she was still risking her life for a world she barely knew. Once this war was over, Dylan vowed to show her the beauty of Aris Magica.

"You can still do that and abide by your laws." He met their gaze with fierce determination. "Use me," Dylan stated with a strong resolve echoing in his voice. He could be the bridge between the conflict the council had always helplessly watched unfold from afar.

The middle-veiled woman in pink stepped forward, speaking alone. Her voice was soft and mothering. When she spoke, Dylan felt a sense of familiarity towards her. "Things are different this time. In the past, it has always been the Ancient reincarnated and the Immortal, but this time, the Ancient was never alone in the beginning and has chosen not to be in the end. You were the unaccounted factor."

Dylan nodded his head. The unaccounted factor neither the first Ancient nor Aris had planned for. He knew this, and it was about time he'd embraced the role.

"There is a problem," the veiled woman said, causing Dylan's heart to plummet. "She had the power to destroy Aturdokht since she is the last reincarnation, but she failed."

That's right, Jay is the last Ancient, Dylan thought in despair. But he still didn't understand why it had to be her.

Dylan sighed, he needed to concentrate on the task at hand. "You've said that, but so what if she didn't make the blood moon? There will always be another opportunity, and I know more than anyone that she can make that happen, but we need her here to do that."

The single veiled woman continued, "Jay has been possessed by Aturdokht. She is now her vessel, complicating things."

Dylan gritted his teeth. "But is Jay..." he searched for the right words, "She's still somehow in there?"

"That remains to be seen," the woman said. "There has never been anyone known to come back from a soul possessing, making your role even more important to help us achieve victory."

Dylan could barely process what she had said. Jay had lost in a way he had never imagined she would. She'd suffered the same fate as Taybeith. Dylan recalled Phagos's sword piercing her. Was that when it happened?

"What if your Hunters fail? Then who will be the line of defense then?" Dylan challenged.

Dylan had to keep trying to make them see reason. No matter how they looked at it, they all needed Jay. He needed her. As the conversation went on, Dylan realized it wasn't just about wanting Jay to defeat Aturdokht—he wanted her safe, more than anything. He needed her like the very air he breathed. She had become a part of him, someone he couldn't imagine a future without. He loved her, more deeply than he thought was possible. His only regret was coming to that realization now.

"We know," the women said, surprising Dylan with their agreement. "That is why we must ask this of you if we are to use you. Before she regains all her power, Aturdokht must be found and destroyed, even if it costs the Ancient her life. Her prophecy must be fulfilled."

Dylan's eyes widened, the cage on his heart squeezed tighter, puncturing holes in it. His breath hitched. "Say that again," he said darkly.

How could they ask that of him? His heart started to race at an untimely speed. No matter what they said, she was still Jay.

"Otherwise, Aris Magica and the human world will be in ruin." The council said.

The center-veiled woman who had stepped forward looked to the other two, and both nodded their heads in unison. The woman in pink lifted her veil, letting it fall from her face and glide down her shoulders.

The sky above changed before his eyes to the night sky, lit with brilliant stars that seemed to cast a spotlight on her alone. Dylan took a step back, overcome with shock. The woman's skin was as dark as the Earth's ground, and her gray hair was twisted in tiny dreads that cascaded down her back.

The woman's face reminded Dylan so much of Jay's, with her round nose, high cheeks, angular chin, and full lips. The woman before him looked as if she hadn't aged a day from the day she disappeared.

"It can't be." Dylan's knees buckled, but he did not fall.

"You have many more questions than you came here with, I'm sure." The woman said slowly and carefully.

"Eradine..." Dylan said, flustered.

"It's Mrs. Era to you." She chuckled, placing a hand on her hip. She still had as much sass to her voice as ever.

"I...how...but you? We thought?" Dylan couldn't find the right words.

Dylan had no idea what to think. He'd always been confused about her and her husband's disappearance, but part of him felt betrayed like Jay had. Although they shared no real relation, he'd once thought of her like family.

There'd been a time when she had been at every birthday, every t-ball game, every major event in his life, even Christmas, until she wasn't anymore. At one point, Dylan had thought of her as a second mom. He remembered grieving her departure, wondering if she was coming back. Eventually, he'd convinced himself that they had died like his own parents, better than accepting the truth that they'd abandoned him just as much as they'd abandoned Jay. And now she was here, alive and smiling, asking him to end her own daughter's life without even trying to save her. The shock he felt moments before faded to despair.

Eradine began to close the distance between them. Dylan tried to make himself move, but he was rooted in place. He wasn't sure if he was trying to run to her or away from her.

"We never left because we wanted to," Eradine said slowly. "We left because we were called." She had finally closed the gap between them and placed her hands on his shoulders.

Dylan noticed they were the same size now. He felt himself shrinking away, but the sincerity and grief in her eyes gave him the courage to stay and face her.

"We had every intention to return, but we knew to keep her safe and you safe, we had to leave."

"So, you knew all along?" Dylan asked weakly, finding his voice.

Eradine nodded. "We knew long before she was born, but when her magic manifested, our suspicions were confirmed. We knew the path we had to take to ensure the path she was meant to walk, albeit knowing it would be difficult and perhaps end in tragedy."

Dylan searched her eyes for any regret but found none. She and her husband were Aris Magicians. Dylan had so many questions. "So, Mr. Raremore, he's—"

"Yes, he's in Aris Magica as well, holding the darkness at bay. It's been restless these days."

Dylan's heart sank further, the Black Gates. Jay's father was there guarding it.

"As much as I'd love to answer all the questions I see in your eyes, I can't. We have more pressing matters to attend to and not a lot of time." Eradine said.

She pulled Dylan into a brief hug. He melted into her, able to hear her heartbeat in his ears. Being in her arms like this made him miss his mother. He'd bottled up his grief from losing her for so long. Tears welled in his eyes before rushing down his cheeks.

Eradine hugged him tighter. She gently patted his back. "There is still hope that Jay may be rescued from this darkness," she whispered.

As quickly as the hug came, she pulled away before Dylan had a chance to respond. "Shhhh." She wiped the tears from Dylan's eyes before the compassion in her eyes was replaced by a cold mask. She stepped away from him. Her body pulled back in line with the others. The veil lifted from her shoulders and fell over her face once more.

Dylan felt the cage on his heart lose its grip. There was still hope, regardless of whether the other council members felt the same. Eradine had given him hope, and that was enough for him. He stared back at her in disbelief. He still couldn't believe she was here before him.

"We recognize the care you hold for the chosen." Eradine's voice blended in with the other two women. "We cannot hold one soul higher than the rest. Aris Magica must be protected, and although we cannot interfere alone, we can through you. The past cannot repeat itself when its cycle can be broken once and for all."

"What do you expect me to do?" Dylan challenged. "Only an Ancient can destroy Aturdokht."

The women all pointed to Dylan. "You hold the power as well. The Infinity Staff rests within you."

"Within us both," Dylan corrected.

"No. It takes both of you to call it, but you are its keeper this time instead of the chosen one. Like we said, you are the unaccounted factor, a loophole."

Dylan's eyes widened. All this time, he'd thought the power was split between them both. "So, there must be a way I can call it, but how?" Dylan mumbled.

He remembered holding the staff in his hands and feeling the endless power it possessed. Maybe enough magic to separate Jay and Aturdokht.

"You have a difficult decision ahead of you. If the chosen fails to break herself free, then you must be the one to stop Aturdokht. No matter the cost."

"I understand," Dylan lied, his voice barely a whisper. He would save Jay no matter what. "But we can't do this alone. If I promise to help you, then you must help me," he bargained.

It didn't matter if he or Jay managed to stop Aturdokht; there would still be the matter of the Demons and Faeries Aturdokht had in her army. They couldn't handle them alone.

"The law states that you cannot meddle in the affairs of Aturdokht, but Demons and Faeries are not the same as she is." Dylan smirked; he wasn't the only one capable of twisting the rules. By asking the council to help him, they weren't directly interfering with Jay's purpose.

The council thought for a moment. "Another loophole, one we've always overlooked in the past." A heavy pause seemed to last in the air for quite a long time before the council responded. "Very well. If you manage to dispel Aturdokht, we will step in and handle the rest. Judgment has—"

"Wait!" Dylan said, stopping them.

Doubts began to cloud his mind. If he failed, then they would be fighting Aturdokht and her army on their own. He still didn't trust the council, but he felt it was right to only ask.

"I challenge you to seek how far you're willing to go to watch the world suffer. If I fail and can't rescue Jay or destroy her, Aturdokht will decimate the world. Will you then still sit idly by watching as the past repeats itself, or will you find the power I know you have to defy the odds and break a binding law? No matter how much power the first Ancient had or Aris, that power was passed to you. You three are the protectors and guides of all magic. You're more powerful than you realize." Dylan said.

"Oh," the voices responded. They seemed to smile, but it was difficult to tell behind their thick veils.

"Oh, what?" Dylan asked, he held his breath, fervently awaiting their answer.

The woman on the right spoke alone. "This boy has much more faith in us than we realized."

The woman on the left followed, "Perhaps you pose another loophole."

The voices returned as one, "Judgment has been passed, and this concludes his trial." Once again, in one harmonious movement, their hands waved, and both Silo and Kai reappeared beside Dylan.

Dylan was relieved to be reunited with them both again. He'd grown to form a close connection with the two despite the heavy *what-ifs* that hung in the air between them.

Dylan turned to Silo, "Was this wait better than the last one?"

She returned his smile, "It was about the same."

Kai groaned, "Speak for yourself, mine was awful," he complained.

Silo smiled gently. "So, how did it go this time?" This time, even Kai leaned in curiously.

"Better," Dylan admitted, even though he still wasn't sure if the council had accepted his offer, at least this time he'd got their attention. "They said that I hold the power to defeat Aturdokht," Dylan said quietly. Silo's smile returned but quickly faded again as Dylan continued. "But I have no idea how to call forth the Infinity Staff without her."

"Dylan." It was Eradine speaking this time.

The other two women had disappeared, as did the room they were in. The four of them were back outside at the entrance to the council building. The sky was still as gloomy as ever, but Dylan still felt as if no time had passed.

"Freaky." Kai shuddered next to Dylan. Dylan finally released the breath he'd been holding.

"There's been another expecting your arrival. Follow me."

Dylan's heart leaped to his throat, wondering who it could be. Had they found Riley? Even the Headmaster hadn't known his whereabouts. Dylan knew better than to get his hopes up, but any news was good news at this point.

Eradine led the way, taking them from the building and towards the crystal rocks. "Welcome to the Passing."

Silo nudged Dylan in the side, getting his attention. He had been so focused on Eradine that he hadn't realized she'd been talking to him. "Hey, did you hear me? I've never heard of one of the council members speaking alone. Do you know her?" She whispered.

"A little," Dylan confessed. Silo gave him a quizzical look with a slight tilt of her head. "Mrs. Eradine, wait up." He ran to catch up with Eradine to avoid more questions from Silo. Dylan fell into a steady pace beside Eradine, slightly breathless from the short jog. "Are you ever going to answer any of my questions?"

Eradine smiled, "I'll answer two of them."

Dylan nodded; it was a start. "What did you mean by you were called?"

"I was called to a higher purpose, just as you were when you went to the Institute and began this journey. Or the call you feel to still protect my daughter." Eradine winked, causing Dylan to blush before he cleared his throat. "She's more capable than you think; don't forget that." Eradine reminded him.

Dylan stopped in his tracks, causing the others to do the same, "How would you know that?" He mumbled. "You left." *Don't forget that,* he thought to himself.

Dylan could feel the others' eyes on him, but all he saw was Eradine's sad stare. "Yes. She'll need time to heal." As she spoke, her eyes shifted past him.

Dylan knew she was no longer speaking to him, but her thoughts were centered on Jay. He averted his gaze to the ground. Maybe he was being too harsh on her. After all, he was glad Eradine was alive at least. Dylan glanced up to see that Eradine began walking ahead once again. He followed her, shuffling his feet in the dirt.

"Oh, and speaking of my daughter," Eradine piqued, the sad stare no longer lingering in her eyes, "How are things going, have you two made it official yet?" Eradine glanced over at Dylan and touched her lips, followed by another wink.

Dylan stumbled and gasped, covering his mouth. *The kiss.* "You know about that!" He whispered embarrassedly. "How?"

Eradine laughed. "Is that your second question?" Dylan began to panic, shaking his head. Eradine gently patted his arm. "I'm teasing." She smiled. "I was born in Aris Magica," she said distantly. "One day, I was destined to take the place of a new generation of protectors. Although I hold much power now, nothing's changed," she said sorrowfully. Dylan got the feeling that she often disagreed with the council's laws. "I must put my duty before my wants. But the two of you grew up to be magnificent Magicians who fight for what they want, and I am so proud of you." She looked at him and smiled, speaking to him as if she'd been watching him ever since the day she left. "And in our place, the two of you have had great mentors that guided your way."

Dylan smiled sadly, thinking of Riley. He could only imagine how he would've handled the council if he'd been there.

He really would've handed it to them.

Dylan laughed to himself thinking of it, but doing so brought forth a wave of sadness. He needed to find him. He looked over at Eradine. He knew she would help him if he asked, but he also didn't want to put her in a compromising position if the rest of the council refused.

Eradine led them through the crystal rocks, weaving in and out of them. Dylan frowned, there was a more pressing question on his mind that had been bothering him. He stared pensively ahead. "The Black Gates," Dylan whispered as if the word was taboo.

"The end of the universe." Eradine stopped before a pocket dimension.

The jagged crystal rock stood as tall as she did, vines wrapped around the base providing the support for it to stand. Inside, the fog lifted, and Dylan caught a glimpse of people walking along a winding pathway headed to a building half hidden by white fluffy clouds.

"At the very end of all magic is darkness. An evil of hatred made from both humans and Magicians."

"Do you think Aturdokht will try to attack it?" Silo asked. Dylan glanced back at her; she'd caught up to them.

"That remains to be seen. She has in the past, but the first and third reincarnations stopped her," Eradine said.

Eradine placed a hand on the crystal. The fog entirely disappeared, and the building in the clouds became clear. It was the Record Hall. Dylan hadn't had the chance to see it from the outside. It was magnificent.

The building was held up by three large pillars. The entire building was made of gold, except for the door, which was a deep shade of blue. The door was massive, taking up more than 1/3 of the library's front wall. The building itself took the shape of half an oval that sat on top of the plate of the three pillars. It was curved on the sides and flat on the bottom. Dylan had never seen anything like it. The image quickly changed to the inside of it.

The ceiling was shaped like a dome with clockwork wiring hanging from the sides of the wall. Interwoven between the spindles of the clocks were thick tree branches that stretched too high to see from the outside of the crystal. The floor was a clear reflective marble, and the bookcases matched it almost as if the floor and shelves were one. Thousands of books were throughout the library for as far as the eye could see.

Silo pointed to one of the tree branches and clocks above. One of the clocks was turning as the branch connected to it had lit up to a silver-blue-white color. "You see that there, a door has been activated."

Dylan watched as the branch's light dimmed as the clock stopped turning. He had a theory on how the travel system of this library worked. From the branch's glow, he could tell that Old Magic ran through its core, cycling into the clocks that controlled the place one traveled to. He wondered if the clocks only accessed present locations or if time was also a factor in how the doors worked.

"*Magnificum Reordum*," Eradine said.

"Great." Kai rolled his eyes, unenthused. "I hate traveling this way. I'd take Arden's portal any day."

Silo shook her head. "I'll let him know you said that." She frowned, staring at the image. "What could be waiting for us in the Record Hall?"

"Here, take this." Eradine pulled out a crystal like the one he'd seen Doctor Herron use earlier: a pocket dimension crystal. "When you've completed your journey, use it to return to the Passing." She handed it to Silo, who then put it in the pouch at her waist.

"This gate will stay open for three hours. Until then, you may come and go as you please. Perhaps you'll find the answers you seek." She looked at Dylan alone. He nodded his head, determined to find a way to call forth the Infinity Staff and rescue Jay. "I will wait here guarding the passage." Silo began to step through, but Eradine stopped her. "As a Hunter, know your duty should he fail."

Silo smiled proudly and nodded, preparing to go again. Dylan looked between the two. "A Hunter?" Dylan darkened. He had read about Hunters in the pamphlet Arden had given him in preparation for meeting with the council. He'd used their creation against them just moments ago. He turned to Silo; she was one of them.

Silo didn't immediately meet his gaze, but Dylan still recognized the guilt in her eyes. She let out a deep sigh, turning to face him. "Aris Magica is broken into levels for its protection. The only access to other parts of Aris is through pocket dimensions, which are spread out among both worlds. Instead of searching those down, the council has linked gateways here," Silo gestured around to the crystals. "They protect us, as do us Hunters." She pointed to herself and Kai. "We do things the council cannot discreetly do themselves. We hunt people who the council decides need protection or need to be judged." Silo paused, taking a deep breath. As she did, her gaze softened when she finally met Dylan's eyes. "I'm sorry I didn't tell you."

Dylan stared at her in disbelief. He knew that much about Hunters already, but what he didn't understand was why Silo hadn't told him until now.

"Three hours isn't forever," Silo said. She went through first, her body shattering into tiny fragments before floating inside the crystal.

Kai groaned, following her. "I hate this part!" His body shattered as his hands touched the crystal going inside as well.

Dylan glanced back at Eradine. His heart caught in his throat with the fear of never seeing her again. "Aunt. Era, you'll still be here when I come back, right?"

She smiled, reflecting the same sorrow in her eyes that were in his. "I'm not going anywhere."

Chapter Twenty-One

Dylan's entire body felt like it was being pulled apart, but the feeling stopped right before he thought every fiber in his body would disconnect. When he came to, his vision was hazy, but he could tell both Kai and Silo stood over him.

Dylan's sight quickly returned, and he found an extended hand stretched out before him. Kai looked down at him, smirking arrogantly. "Next time, try landing on your feet and not your ass, deumage."

Dylan scoffed and slapped Kai's hand away, standing on his own. "What's a deumage?" It wasn't the first time Kai had called him that.

"Nothing good," Silo said, glowering at her brother. Silo sighed, "It's a dirty slang given to Hybrids. You're dead magic."

Dylan frowned, "Dead magic? But a Hybrid's magic is New Magic."

"No, I know your magic is New Magic, but dead magic means defiled, dirty." She glanced at Dylan apologetically. He got the point. He glared at the still smirking Kai.

Dylan brushed himself off and looked around. Although he had been here before, this place still amazed him. They were in one of the many aisles. Bookshelves towered on either side of him. It felt so familiar being surrounded by books again, he'd spent so much time in the Institute's library the prior month that any library started to remind him of home.

"Exactly what are we to find here?" Dylan asked, staring at the books on the shelf on either side of them. None of them seemed helpful. He also recalled Eradine mentioning someone was waiting for him, but Dylan couldn't imagine who he would find or know in a place like this.

"So many questions." Silo sighed with a small laugh. She pointed down the hall. "Let's go there towards the front so we can talk about what the council said to you." She began to walk.

Dylan took a deep breath as he walked, savoring the scent of old books. However, his enjoyment was soon disrupted by the smell of smoke and the sound of hushed voices growing louder as they walked further.

"Must you smoke that heinous cigarette in here? You'll upset the knowledge in the air," a familiar voice complained.

"Professor?" Dylan said. He recognized the voice quickly.

The aisle gave way to a sharp right, but at the end was a square opening connected to another hall of books on the opposite side. Within the opening was a long table surrounded by six chairs. Two chairs were occupied.

Dylan came to a stop at the table's edge. Before him sat the Headmaster and Doctor Herron. He couldn't mask his disappointment at it not being Riley, but he was happy to see the two of them again and so soon. Doctor Herron still wore the same clothes from earlier, but she was without her lab coat. She held a cigarette in one hand and a lighter in the other. She sat with her boots propped up on the chair beside her. The Headmaster looked the same as the last time Dylan had seen him. His gray hair was pulled back away from his face, and the green amulet he wore hung from his neck on a silver chain. He sat behind a small stack of books. The frustration that had ridden his dark brows moments before was replaced by a sudden lapse of joy.

"Oh, you made it," Doctor Herron said. "Good." Her voice lacked the joy Dylan had seen on the Headmaster's face.

"And you found a cigarette," Dylan said coldly.

She held it up to him proudly. "Turns out they're not so hard to find here."

Silo and Kai finally caught up to Dylan, coming to a stop on either side of him. The Headmaster met Dylan's gaze before rising to his feet. He walked over to Dylan in a few short strides and firmly grasped his shoulder. When he spoke, there was a twinkle in his eyes, "Now, before you ask any of the questions I see prying in your eyes, sit." He gestured to the empty chairs. "We have much to discuss."

Dylan took the seat closest to where the Headmaster had been sitting. He noticed the books the Headmaster had pulled out. All of them were about the power of mystical myths. Dylan noticed a staff on the cover of the book on the top of the stack. It resembled the Infinity Staff in a way, but instead of two mantles shooting from the top of the staff, there was only one mimicking half of a heart.

The Headmaster pointed to the other chairs, "Please, all of you sit."

Silo slid into the seat next to Dylan. "Good to see you again, Headmaster," she said, shocking Dylan that she already knew him. Then he recalled how she said the Headmaster had brought him to her. It made sense, especially since, at the time, he needed a healer.

"Likewise."

Kai took the seat on the other side of Silo. "Who's he again?" He whispered.

"He's the Headmaster of my former school in the human world," Dylan explained, overhearing him. However, Dylan had left out that the school had been hidden within a pocket dimension.

"Fascinating," Kai said, leaning forward in his chair, looking intrigued. He followed the Headmaster with his eyes as he sat down. "How'd you manage to hide a school of such grandeur from humans? Couldn't have been easy with the chaos your students' magic brought."

"A story for another time," the Headmaster stated. He turned to the doctor. "This is my colleague, Virginia Herron."

"Yeah, her I've met," Kai smirked.

Doctor Herron raised her lighter in the air. "A pleasure, I'm sure," she said with her deep and raspy voice.

"I wouldn't call it that." Kai laughed.

"I imagine much of today has come as a shock for you, but allow me to get right to the point as I'm afraid we are short on time." The Headmaster paused.

Dylan nodded, remembering they only had three hours before the council expected them back. Still, he wanted to tell the Headmaster about how the meeting had gone. "By the end of today, I will be dead."

Dylan's mouth dropped. He looked at Doctor Herron to correct him, but she wouldn't meet Dylan's gaze. He looked for words to say but fell short. All his questions fell away upon hearing the Headmaster's devastating news.

The Headmaster continued speaking as if nothing happened. Dylan couldn't help but tune him out as he looked down, feeling a hand on his thigh. He looked over at Silo, who was smiling at him. A tear fell from Dylan's eye and onto her hand. He quickly wiped it away, swallowing his feelings of despair. Dylan realized the life he led at the Institute was coming to an end, even after all of this was over, some part of him knew he wouldn't be coming back to the same place where he grew up.

Silo patted him gently, whispering words Dylan couldn't make out under her breath. A soothing feeling encompassed his body, relaxing him. She cast a tranquility spell on him. Everything he'd felt moments before had subsided as a stillness washed over him, bringing him back to reality. He glanced at her as the words the Headmaster spoke suddenly became clear.

"Recently, Doctor Herron had a vision, and at the center of it was Jay holding all three Elementals and the Infinity Staff."

Doctor Herron stubbed her cigarette out on the table, leaving behind a black stain, and pointed toward the Headmaster, "I told Ivan not to return to the cabin that day because his life would be in danger if he did. Nothing good comes from the resurfacing of those bastards."

"Elementals?" Dylan finally brought himself to say.

Silo pulled her hand away and hugged herself. She let out a shaky breath, "Elementals are sacred works of magic that hold the oldest Old Magic inside. They were passed down from the original four guardians, but the fourth one was destroyed ages ago after a single use."

Dylan looked at the Headmaster. He still had much to ask him about the Infinity Staff and its origins. Maybe knowing would help him find a way to call it forth alone, but the mention of the Elementals at play concerned him. Dylan noticed the Headmaster holding the amulet he wore close to his heart.

"Is that one of them?" Dylan asked, finding the courage to meet the Headmaster's gaze.

But, the Headmaster wouldn't meet Dylan's gaze and instead stared forlornly past him. "The Wizard, Morbid. The Castor, Lyid. The Fairy, Aytox. The Immortal, Tarquin. They were the last to unite the Elementals, creating the fourth one given to the Enchantress Serena. The four of them sealed the Black Gates alongside Aris. Although there were still cracks that managed to escape their wrath," the Headmaster explained.

"Cracks?" Dylan thought back to the broken seals on the crystals from before.

"You've seen them before," the Headmaster began. "Aturdokht's ability to wield power over Demons and Faeries. She has one of these Elementals, Heart. It's what makes her fire so strong. And she will be coming for this one as well." His fingers traced the gem's lines, "Life." The Headmaster began to mumble a slur of harnessing words under his breath that Dylan had to listen carefully to in order to make them out, "*Ex vita revirescit, potestate iuro uti fide. Teipsum revela.*" He waved his hand over the amulet; from it, he pulled an orb of energy from its center as wide as the palm of his hand. "Aturdokht is coming for this, but under no circumstance is she to possess all three. And at the moment, neither can Jay, not as she is now, not until their connection is severed."

Dylan's heart fell. Upon hearing the Headmaster's words, Dylan understood why the Headmaster knew his death was coming. Still, it didn't make it any easier for Dylan to digest. He looked at the Headmaster, consumed with grief. Dylan wasn't sure how much more sorrow he could take.

"Old man," Kai said, "I thought you said this lady saw the chosen harboring all three Elementals. Well, which Jay is it?" Kai challenged. "Plus, rumor has it that no one's seen the last Elemental since Tarquin had it."

Doctor Herron shrugged, "Couldn't tell you, runt." Kai groaned profusely.

"Headmaster," Silo said slowly, "if Aturdokht is coming for you, then according to the Oracle's vision, she'll have two. If we find the third one, do you think we could stop her without the Infinity Staff?"

"It's never been done before," the Headmaster said.

"But no one knows where the third one is!" Kai shouted. "Am I invisible or something?"

"Wait," Dylan said. He thought now was a better time than anything to bring up what the council had asked of him. "There might be a way." Everyone's gaze around the table fell on him at the sound of his voice. Dylan released a steady breath before continuing, "The council asked me to intervene on their behalf."

"What?" Doctor Herron said, surprised, her boots falling from the table as she leaned forward. "How?"

"By killing Aturdokht, even if Jay isn't free yet," Dylan paused, looking around at each of them. "With the Infinity Staff," he sighed, "I have the power to pull it out myself and use it."

The Headmaster looked away in frustration. He'd never seen the Headmaster look as disturbed as he did now. "Of course, they would ask this of you."

"Wait, so we don't even need the Elementals? We could've killed the Witch, like, yesterday?" Kai shouted.

"No!" Dylan shouted in defense.

"But Dylan," Silo began.

"No! I won't! I'm going to use it to save her." Dylan looked at Silo with determination in his eyes; she glared at him but didn't argue back. He looked over at the Headmaster, "Can it be done?"

"The Infinity Staff is a strong controlling power; it takes great conviction to wield it, let alone call it. You can't have any unwavering thoughts in your heart," he said. "But as for calling it alone, I have no idea how it can be done." the Headmaster admitted. "Perhaps the Hidden Library will have a clue on both the staff and the third Elemental."

Silo's face lit up, "Of course."

Dylan looked between them, unsettled, "Just how many libraries does this world need?"

"It's one of the sacred three built by Aris himself. It holds his secrets of the world of magic," Silo explained.

"Oh, how could I be so careless not to know that." Dylan rolled his eyes.

Kai pounded his fists together, "So, you're telling us to run away and hide while you die and hand over the Elemental? Why don't we just stop her with the Elemental we do have? To hell with the staff!"

"You can't. Trust me, this is the best way," Doctor Herron said. "No matter the plan, it won't work without the staff, and you will die. That is how it's always been ordained, so hear Ivan out on this one." Dylan caught the despair in her voice as she said the Headmaster's name.

"With my death," the Headmaster put the Elemental's true form back inside the amulet and removed the chain around his neck, "another must shoulder this burden." He tossed the necklace into the air, and it floated instead of dropping.

Dylan watched it, mesmerized. The Elemental began to glide to them. Dylan wondered what one could do with the power of Life if having such magic felt just like holding the Infinity Staff. Dread filled him thinking about it; the staff's power had nearly consumed him, and it felt further away than ever now. The Elemental continued past him, stopping in front of Silo.

"Me?" She shrieked as the amulet fell into her lap.

"Wow, way to go sis. How do you feel?" Kai asked proudly.

"She hasn't even put it on yet," Dylan said, masking his disappointment that the Headmaster hadn't chosen him.

Kai and Dylan stared at Silo, waiting for her to don the necklace, but she never did. She just squeezed the gem in her hands, keeping it firmly in her lap.

Doctor Herron sighed, getting up from her chair. "I'll get started with the portal." She pointed to Kai, "You, come help me. I'll need your magic." Kai shrugged and got up with her.

Dylan, Silo, and the Headmaster sat in silence. Dylan still couldn't fathom that this would be the last time he would see the Headmaster. He wanted to thank him for everything he'd done. If it hadn't been for the Headmaster or Riley, Dylan wouldn't be who he is today. Dylan hated war. It took so much and always left behind so little. He'd lost a great deal already: his parents, his friends, and now his mentors. That's why it was so important for him to get Jay back—he couldn't lose her too.

"Dylan," Silo said, being the first to break the silence. She looked over at him, not continuing until he met her gaze. Dylan could see the determination in her eyes, "Before we leave, you need to know that Kai and I will do anything to ensure the safety of our home. Even if it means killing Jay and forcing you to do it," she said.

"I know." Dylan took in a shaky breath, "But she's a lot stronger than you think," he said. "And before you get the chance, I'll bring her back to us."

Silo pursed her lips in a straight line. Dylan saw a muscle in her jaw tick as she did. "I—" She looked away, "I hope you're right."

Before Dylan had a chance to respond, the ceiling started to shake, and the glass from the clocks' faces rattled, silencing the library. Silo and Dylan both looked up. Another sound exploded outside, shaking the ceiling more. This time, the glass fell, raining down on them, and branches snapped, oozing out Old Magic.

"*Vitrum pulvis*," the Headmaster whispered, turning the glass into dust before it reached them.

Dylan stared at the glass, mesmerized as it turned into tiny, harmless particles. Dylan could feel the Headmaster's magic vibrating through the building. "Incredible," he whispered.

Dylan looked up in time to see a winged talon coming directly for him. Before he had time to react, Kai was there with his rapier, blocking the attack intended for Dylan. The creature pulled back, its wings revealing the face of a vulture coated in sickly-looking feathers. Its beady red eyes looked over Dylan searchingly.

"Idiot," Kai snarled, pushing the Demon off and then driving his rapier through it. "I thought you were a skilled fighter?" He said to Dylan, cleaning off his sword.

Dylan heard a loud screech and then saw another Vulteron appear. He grabbed the chair he'd been sitting at and swung it, knocking the bird out of the sky. He kicked it as it tried to get up. Kai drove his sword into it, finishing it off.

"I am if you'd give me a weapon!" Dylan instantly regretted leaving behind the daggers he'd been sparring with earlier. He hadn't wanted to bring anything with him to the meeting that the council could use against him.

"Look," Silo gasped as a flock of Vulteron began to descend on them. They formed a spiraling tornado that was headed straight for the Headmaster. "Vulteron wind magic!" She shouted, pushing out of her chair.

The Headmaster didn't move. He continued to sit calmly in his chair. He met Dylan's gaze. "Go." He gestured at Silo, "Protect her and it at all costs."

"What?" Dylan refused to leave him, but the Headmaster didn't give him a choice.

The Headmaster pushed the air in front of him. A strong force of magic hit Dylan in his chest, sending him, Kai, and Silo flying back down the hallway behind him. Dylan screamed, seeing the flock of Vulteron crash into the Headmaster. Just before they did, the Headmaster blew into his hand, and all the bird's bodies began to expand before exploding.

Dylan slammed into the bookshelf at the end of the hall, as did Silo and Kai. A couple of the books from the upper shelves fell and toppled on them. The minute the books hit the floor, they vanished into thin air. Dylan looked around and saw other books doing the same, but some books remained not covered by the magic protection of the library. Dylan didn't have time to think about why, though.

"Come on!" Kai roared, helping them both up and leading them back the way they came.

They sped down the aisle, Dylan tried his best to tune out the screams of the Vulteron behind him. "We can't just leave him!" Dylan blurted out, feeling a sudden sense of responsibility.

"He looked like he could handle himself," Silo said, running beside him. "Plus, we have bi—" Kai pushed Silo back into Dylan, dropping his rapier for his two axes. Phagos appeared before them, his sword colliding with Kai's axes.

Kai growled, holding his ground under Phagos's strength, but Dylan could tell Phagos was holding back.

"Hello, Dylan." Phagos grinned. His eyes went to the amulet in Silo's fist. "I enjoy killing Fairies, so I'll be needing that."

Dylan stood frozen, unable to move under Phagos's red gaze. He felt his anger and hatred for the Demon rise inside him. Silo pulled his arm, trying to get him to move away. "Please, Dylan, please!" She begged.

"Snap out of it, Hybrid!" Kai roared; his wings extended from his back, jolting Dylan to his senses. "I got this. Just focus on getting my sister out of here!" He commanded.

Kai slid both axes down Phagos's sword and pushed back. Phagos's smile faded as his back leg began to slide. "Feel the heat!"

In one swift movement, Kai brought his axes up, overpowering Phagos. Phagos leaned back, unbalanced, with his sword lifted in the air. Kai swung his axes, gathering as much wind as he could. He spun around, and Dylan watched as the wind was set on fire. The axes slung through the air at Phagos, sending him flying back into the wall with his fur ablaze. Kai glanced over his shoulder and winked at Dylan arrogantly before running towards Phagos. Kai barely gave him time to look up before he attacked again.

Dylan picked up the rapier Kai left behind. For a moment, he hesitated, unsure if he could just walk away. Phagos had taken everything from him— Dylan's grip on the sword tightened— he couldn't just let him go. An explosion resounded through the air, causing Silo to cry out beside him. Without a second thought, he took Silo's hand and ran in the opposite direction. He gritted his teeth, hearing Phagos's laughter ring through the air.

"It'll be okay," Dylan said. He wasn't sure if he was trying to convince himself or reassure Silo. Silo squeezed his hand in response.

Dylan took them down another aisle, on either side of them, battles ensued. He'd planned to go around, circling back to where they had entered from the pocket dimension.

"This way!" Silo tugged him left as he was about to go right.

A bookcase toppled to the ground, blocking his original path. He followed behind her, letting her guide the way. They ran as fast as they could. Dylan could feel Silo's pulse in her hand as she held onto his. He squeezed her hand tighter, picking up his pace, forcing her to do the same. He refused to lose anyone else today.

A Vulteron flew overhead toward them. Dylan released Silo's hand only for a moment to jump up and slice right through the Demon in one motion. He landed, taking Silo's hand again. It felt good to hold a sword again, Dylan smiled to himself.

Another explosion suddenly shook the library, causing the ground to open up beneath them. Dylan lost his footing and tumbled into the deep hole, pulling Silo down with him. His rapier slipped from his hand and fell into the darkness. Silo grabbed hold of the ledge, stopping them from following the rapier's descent. Dylan breathed heavily. He looked beneath him, unable to see the bottom of the hole.

"Shit," he said. He tried to swing his legs over to the side to grab ahold of the rock wall the mouth of the pit gave way to. Silo's hand slipped, unable to hold the weight of his swinging.

"Hold onto my waist!" She cried, digging her fingers into the rock. The silver chain of the amulet was wrapped around her fingers. Dylan still held onto her hand, but his grip started to slip as well. "I can try to grab the ledge with both hands and hoist us up that way!"

Dylan contemplated what she said. She wouldn't have the strength to do it, not if he was weighing her down by her waist. Either way, he'd have to let go.

Silo squeezed his hand hard, her nails digging into his skin. "Don't you dare."

A dark shadow descended over them. Phagos stood at the edge, staring down at them with an arrogant grin. Dylan felt Silo's boot and pulled free the dagger she had hidden in its sole. "Be ready to fly," Dylan said slowly.

"What?" Silo squealed.

Phagos's grin widened. He snatched the Elemental from Silo's hand. She pulled against him but lost her grip on the ledge. In a panic, she let go of the chain, grabbing the ledge instead.

"No," She whispered.

"Now!" Dylan shouted, throwing the dagger at Phagos. It hit his hand, tossing the amulet into the air. "Grab it!"

"Wait, what?" Silo shouted, still holding onto the ledge.

Dylan kicked back, the momentum of his move forcing Silo's hand to slip off the ledge. He waited for her wings to expand and for her to grab the Elemental, but it never came.

"I can't!" She yelled as they both fell backward.

Dylan stared at her in shock. A Vulteron swooped in above them and caught the amulet in the air. The last thing Dylan saw was Phagos dropping a bomb on them. The building began to collapse, and the force of the bomb made them fall even faster. Dylan heard Silo call out his name as they fell deeper into darkness. He reached out his hand for hers but couldn't find it. The ground came faster than he thought possible as his face slammed into the cold ground, making everything go black.

Chapter Twenty-Two

The truck went over a bump in the road, tossing everyone in their seats as it did. Cryis kicked up his feet onto the middle console between Arthur and Ami.

"Sorry about that," Arthur apologized again.

Ami glanced back at Cryis. "Maybe I should have driven after all."

Cryis began to laugh as Arthur got defensive. "It's a lot harder driving off-road through the forest in snow."

"Don't worry," Cryis leaned forward and placed a hand on Arthur's shoulder. "We're almost to the city, then we can judge your driving skills for real." Cryis smiled.

"Very funny," Arthur mumbled.

Cryis stared out the window. They'd been driving for most of the morning. The sun was steadily creeping higher into the sky. Soon, the snow would melt, and spring would come. Cryis wondered if he would be around to see it. He smiled softly to himself; it was the first time he was experiencing such thoughts.

Cryis turned to stare out the window. They'd finally made it to Willamette Forest. The closer they got to the city, the denser the forest became. At one point, all Cryis could see were trees stacked closely together, but now he could see straight through them. Up ahead was a small pond not too far from a plowed path. Even from a distance, he could see the sparkling reflection of the sun glistening on the surface of the water.

"Finally, a road!" Arthur gleamed. The truck went over another couple of bumps before Arthur was able to get them on the correct path.

Cryis narrowed his gaze, watching as one of the tree branches towering around the pond began to rustle. Beady red eyes stared back at him through the window. The black jaded wings of a raven flapped hard, flying from the tree and towards the truck, disappearing into thin air. Cryis narrowed his gaze, suddenly on alert. He looked for others, but the raven was alone.

"Stop the truck," Cryis said quietly.

"What was that?" Arthur asked.

Every hair on Cryis's body stood up in alert, and he could feel a dark magic surging in the air. "Stop the truck!" Cryis shouted, leaning forward.

He felt the familiar pull of magic surround them as the truck passed through a pocket dimension. As it did, the world around them began to change. The season went from winter to fall. The fallen leaves were crimson red and orange and covered the path entirely. The raven from before had returned and was perched on one of the branches above them. The ice on the pond had melted, making it larger than it had appeared to be before. The sky's sun was replaced by a red-tinted fractured moon.

"What the—" Arthur slammed on the brakes, and the truck came to an abrupt stop.

Cryis followed his gaze to find a shrouded person standing in the middle of the road before them. A gleam of light came from beneath the person's cloak as Cryis caught a glimpse of a thick, silver sword. The sword was wide, long, and rusted. The hilt was wrapped by dirty, gray strips of leather. Cryis felt his heart skip a beat; he'd seen a similar sword like that before. He raised his gaze to the dark shadow covering the person's face. He gripped the back of both seats, digging his nails deep into the leather. The person's cloak slipped off, fell to the ground, and vanished in a pile of dust shards.

"No," Cryis and Ami both whispered at the same time in disbelief.

It was Riley.

A smile began to form on Ami's lips, but Cryis still felt cautious. What was he doing out here? The last time Cryis had seen him, he was strapped to the table in Aturdokht's hideout. Had he escaped?

Riley stood before them in the same clothing he wore the day he'd left. His shirt was in shreds, revealing his dark brown bruised skin, ripped abs, and shaven chest. His jeans and boots were caked in blood and mud, as if he'd recently been in a fight. Green and purple veins bulged from beneath his skin. The purple veins pulsed throughout his arms and chest, creeping up into his eyes. His gray eyes had become yellow and bloodshot. The scar that ran just above his left eye and cut into the tail of his eyebrow now had a pair. Another scar had been stitched up and went diagonally across his bald head and through his right cheek. Not an ounce of recognition reflected in his eyes as he stared at the truck.

"Riley..." Cryis said his name slowly. His breath hitched as he recognized the purple veins that had been the same ones Jay had.

The longer Cryis stared, the more Riley began to look more unrecognizable. He looked just as Taybeith had when he'd been possessed by a Demon but less present. Soul possessing had been the Demons' greatest strength during the first of the Aris Magica Wars. Cryis couldn't recall just how many humans and Magicians he'd found at the mercy of the Demons' magic. But it looked very different from what Cryis had seen now compared to back then. Now, it was as if Riley had been injected with a similar form of magic instead of possessed, much like he'd seen used on Jay and the body Kazimir had been in.

Cryis's eyes widened as if just now realizing it. He hadn't noticed it then, but with Kazimir, the human body had become a second skin, a shell, completely taking control of every aspect of the body. Or how Kanon had been, still in control of his body, but his mind and desires were being guided by a Demon's. That was true soul possession: when the Demon became the human, but what he saw now was something different: Riley had become a Demon.

Ami rolled down her window and stuck her head out. Cryis's eyes widened as he realized what Riley had become. He reached for Ami, but it was too late.

"Ami, no!"

"Professor Riley!" She shouted.

In an instant, Riley raised his sword to the sky and swiped it through the air. Cryis grabbed Ami's arm and yanked her back inside just as the sword came down towards her head. Ami's hand fluttered to her neck. Any second later, her head would have been rolling on the ground.

Arthur put the truck in reverse and tried to back up. He didn't get far before bouncing off an invisible wall. Arthur looked behind him. "What the—"

Cryis looked up at the raven, who was still watching them. He could feel Aturdokht's presence through it. She'd finally mastered shapeshifting after all these decades. As long as they were inside the pocket dimension she created, she had full reign.

Riley lifted his sword again, ready to strike. "Everyone out!" Cryis said, opening the door. Cryis rolled under the door just in time. Riley's sword went right through the metal, shaving a few inches off his door and Ami's.

"Guns are in the truck!" Arthur shouted, already at the truck's bed.

"No!" Ami shouted. Red mist extended from her arms, surrounding her body. "We can't kill him!"

Cryis called *Jevit* forward. It appeared on demand, falling into his hands. He raised it into the air, digging his heels into the pavement as Riley's sword came down. The two metals collided, their power creating a ringing sound that resounded in the air.

Cryis clenched his jaw and pushed against Riley's sword. He stared into his eyes, still seeing not an ounce of recognition. Cryis slid his left hand further down the staff, dragging his scythe as he went forward, forcing Riley off balance and from up under the sword. Riley's tip of his blade hit the ground where Cryis once stood.

"Arthur, no!" Ami shouted.

Cryis looked over at Arthur, who stood on the other side of the truck. He held a sniper rifle that rested on the closed hood of the truck. A bullet whizzed through the air towards Riley. A wall of black mist shot up, protecting him. The bullet melted as it phased through the wall, leaving particles of metal floating in the air. Riley and Cryis looked back at Ami. Her mist receded into her arms. Riley picked up his sword and dragged it across the ground, ruffling the fallen leaves around them as he did. He charged at Ami, who stood frozen, staring back at him.

Cryis brandished his scythe through the air. In one swift arc, his blade surrounded Riley, separating him from Ami. The act didn't faze Riley as he grabbed hold of the blade with his free hand. Blood spurted from the palm of his hand as Riley pushed his scythe down, Cryis felt the weight of his body following the direction of the scythe. When had Riley gotten so strong?

Cryis hit the ground face first, his scythe falling from his hands. Seconds later, Riley's sword pierced into Cryis's back, going straight through him and into the ground. Cryis let out a blood-curdling scream that blended in with Ami's pleas for Riley to stop. Riley yanked his sword free and kicked the scythe further away from Cryis's reach.

Cryis's vision began to blur, his hands fisting a pile of leaves beneath him. He coughed, and blood splattered the fall colors. Riley huffed, satisfied. He gave Cryis one last glance before he stalked towards Ami.

"Cryis!" Arthur shouted. He was at Cryis's side in a second, helping him to his feet. The diamond-shaped hole that was left behind in his chest was already closing. Cryis looked down at it to see the faint traces of blue and gold magic from the Elemental seeping out of his body.

"Arthur." Cryis coughed up more blood, a trail of it coming from his chin and dripping onto the ground. His eyes connected with Arthur's, seeing the fear evident in his gaze "My scythe," Cryis said. He had a hunch. The Elemental he had housed extraordinary magic, if Cryis could channel it with his scythe-reaping powers, maybe he could liberate Riley's soul from the Demon.

Arthur hesitated, looking worriedly at Cryis before his gaze flicked to the scythe. He huffed and let Cryis go, and quickly grabbed the scythe. Cryis staggered, trying to keep himself upright as Arthur left his side. He looked forward, seeing Ami doing her best to fend off Riley. Her mist kept switching shades between red, blue, and black, reflecting the anger, sadness, and fear she felt. Arthur handed Cryis his scythe. Cryis raised it and slammed the end of the staff into the ground. He heard the pavement crack as his scythe embedded within the road.

Ami's mist surrounded Riley, putting him in a hold. Riley's face seemed to distort for a second; a snout began to form from his lips, but then it quickly snapped back to normal. The quick transformation was enough to shock Ami. She lost control over her magic. The thick mist coming from her arms thinned just enough for Riley to drag his sword up and through it. As he did, he cut half of his own body, but he was unfazed by the blood coming from his chest.

He brought the sword around, slashing through Ami's mist and cutting through her left arm. The mist shot back into her as she screamed. She collapsed to her knees, holding half of her arm in her opposite hand, the other half was left in a pile of blood at her knees. As she looked at her lifeless forearm on the ground, her screams got louder. Ami called upon her mist with a shaky hand, it came out in small tendrils of white, wrapping itself around her stubbed arm to stop the bleeding. Above her, Riley raised his sword.

Cryis used his free hand to direct the magic pouring out of him and into his scythe. The magic wrapped itself around his staff, infusing with the blade. Arms of magic residue shot out from the staff's core and towards Riley. It collided with his back, creating a chain. Cryis could feel its hold on Riley's soul. Cryis grabbed his scythe with both hands and yanked Riley away from Ami.

Riley grunted, his body dragging along the ground and toward Cryis. He dug his sword into the road, trying to stop it, but Cryis's magic was stronger. Cryis swung his scythe around with one hand and grabbed the chain with the other, pulling Riley up as he did. His scythe wrapped around Riley's body, as did the chain. It was an unbreakable bind. Cryis pressed his hand to Riley's chest, finding his soul. He could feel it faintly beating beside his heart. Riley's face began to change again into a Demon with a long, wide snout and straight horns.

"Found it," Cryis whispered.

Cryis pulled his scythe back away from Riley. Its blade was bright, glowing blue trimmed with gold. He pierced the tip of his scythe into Riley's chest. The blade didn't cut through flesh but spirit, leaving Riley's body unharmed. Cryis could sense a crack forming within Riley's defenses. Cryis pressed harder, pushing his scythe deeper into Riley until it could go no more.

Moments later, the chains holding Riley shattered, and Cryis's scythe vanished from his hands. Cryis stumbled forward, losing his balance as Riley crashed to the ground. An unsettling silence surrounded the air. Even the wind had stopped moving. Cryis grabbed his chest and sank to his knees. Using the Elemental had temporarily stopped him from healing, he could feel the process slowly starting again, but it was painful.

Riley's face snapped back. His eyes lost their bloodshot yellow hue and began to clear, returning to their normal gray. The discolored veins protruding from his skin faded away. The pain came rushing into Riley's face. His expression was contorted as he struggled to speak. He gasped for air. His eyes met Cryis and then fell to Ami.

Cryis's small smile quickly faded, something was wrong. "Ugh," was all Riley managed to grunt out. His hand was over his heart, clawing away at his skin. "A...m...i..." Riley struggled to say, "Cr...y...is..." He continued to claw away at his skin, leaving scratch marks behind.

"Hey, hey, it's okay." Cryis grabbed both of Riley's wrists, stopping him. Cryis's eyes widened, seeing tears trickle down Riley's cheeks.

"G...et," he gasped for air, "out of here." Riley pleaded. His eyes kept shifting, not staying on one thing for too long, until they finally landed on Cryis's concerned gaze. He managed to hold his gaze for the longest and then smiled. In one breath, he said, "End it."

Cryis's breath hitched, seeing Riley's eyes quickly fall to the back of his head, exposing the white of his eyes.

Why didn't it work? Cryis thought, his hands shaking as he held Riley close to him.

Riley's veins began to swell again and take on a purple hue. Fangs grew from his teeth.

I failed again.

Cryis felt his eyes burn with tears.

Cryis sat frozen in shock. He watched helplessly as Riley suffered against the constraints of the magic. Cryis closed his eyes and cursed himself. He let go of

Riley's hands and pounded his fist into the ground until they started to turn red.

Arthur scrambled over to Cryis as Riley's transformation began to intensify. Fur started to appear on his skin in patches, and claws grew from his fingernails. Arthur grabbed Cryis's arm and tried to pull him to his feet away from Riley. Once on his feet, Cryis snapped back to reality and pushed Arthur out of harm's way. He raised his hand into the sky and called *Jevit* once more.

"Cryis, no!" Ami shouted through sobs.

Cryis gritted his teeth, refusing to look at her. "What choice do I have?" He shouted back, his voice breaking.

Jevit appeared, and Cryis spun it through the air, stabbing Riley in the heart. Riley's eyes widened, but there was peace to them. As quickly as the transformation materialized, it left him. Black clouds of smoke seeped from his pores and vanished into the air. Relief, happiness, and sadness transpired across Riley's face. He smiled as he looked up at the sky.

Cryis removed his scythe from Riley's chest and dropped it. Before Riley could sink to the ground, Cryis caught him, and they fell together. Cryis sank to his knees, cradling Riley's body close, his heart aching with each passing moment. As he gently laid Riley on the ground, tears that burned with the sting of failure began to fall, splashing onto Riley's face. The heat of his failure seemed to sear him from within.

He opened his eyes to see Riley gazing up at him, but instead of sorrow or pain, Riley's face was illuminated by a serene, almost reassuring smile. The light in Riley's eyes dimmed slowly, leaving behind a profound silence.

Cryis's heart felt heavier with the realization that, although he hadn't known Riley for long, this loss was a stark reminder of his constant failure to keep the promise he'd made to the first Ancient and Jay. He felt he had failed Jay again. Riley had been like a father to Jay and Dylan, and Cryis's grief was compounded by the crushing thought that he was once again falling short.

Cryis attempted to return the smile, but his tears blurred his vision. He leaned over Riley, holding him tightly against his chest, and wept. Each sob was a raw echo of the pain he couldn't contain, the profound loss settling heavily in his heart.

Chapter Twenty-Three

Cryis wasn't sure how much time had passed as he continued to stare at Riley's lifeless body at his knees. This wasn't the first time Cryis had lost someone, but it was the first time he'd killed an ally. Yet, in the reality of war, such moments were inevitable. Still, Cryis grimaced, it didn't make it any easier.

The wind blew around them, creating rainfall from the leaves. It was quiet. Riley's eyes were open, staring at the reddened sky. His body was covered in scars. But there was a sense of serenity left behind on Riley's face. The corners of his mouth turned up in a smile. Cryis had only known the man for a few days but still felt an overwhelming sadness toward him.

Ami crept slowly toward them, collapsing onto her knees. White mist was still flowing from her right hand, holding together what little left she had of her left arm. She leaned over Riley and let out a scream that turned into deep sobs. Arthur stood over her, his hand rubbing her back. He glanced at Cryis with sorrow in his eyes.

Cryis sighed, he knew what Arthur was trying to tell him, Arthur's pity was towards Cryis's blame on himself. Cryis couldn't help but think there was more he could have done. He held out his hands, glaring at his palms. With all this power the Elemental bestowed upon him, he still couldn't save Riley. Could he even save Jay?

Cryis took a deep, shaking breath. He reached across Riley's body and grabbed his scythe, using it to help himself stand. His knees threatened to buckle beneath his weight. Slowly, he raised his staff into the air with both hands. He felt power growing inside him as his eyes changed to a red hue and fangs grew from his teeth for the reaping ritual.

"Let your soul be purified..." His voice caught in his throat as Ami's cries began to grow louder. Cryis took in another difficult breath, but no matter how many he took, he couldn't calm his heart. Even so, Cryis continued in a faint whisper, "And the gates of the heavens open wide... as you travel to your next destination." He slammed his staff into the ground.

Blue streams of light rooted from under his staff, stretching across the ground like a network of tree branches. The blue light covered Riley's body, wrapping him in an embrace. His body began to glow the same soft blue before slowly fading away. A single blue wisp remained. His soul lingered for a moment before them.

Cryis could feel the essence of Riley shining through the light. The air around him felt warmer than before. He felt the corner of his mouth as it began to curl into a sad smile. Riley's soul seemed to glow brighter before shooting into the sky and vanishing.

Cryis leaned against his scythe as tears fell down his face. "The rest is up to him now."

Ami bowed her head into her lap, continuing to cry. Cryis took a long, deep breath as he felt his body return to normal after the reaping. The stillness that followed was heavy, marked only by the faint rustling of leaves.

As Cryis tried to steady himself, footsteps began to approach them from a distance, crunching the leaves in their path as they did, breaking through the silence.

"I thought he'd be the one." A deep voice sighed, disappointed.

Cryis spun around upon hearing the familiar voice. The footsteps had stopped. Taybeith leaned up against a tree not too far behind where Cryis and the others stood. He looked less like the shy, scrawny kid Cryis had initially met back at the Institute and more monstrous and further from his former self than ever. His skin was as pale as the moon, while his eyes were a wild, bloodshot yellow, much like Riley's had been. Horns sprouted from his temples, sticking straight up toward the sky. Black bat-like wings were folded against the center of his spine. He wore a dark suit that complimented his black hair. His hair was pulled back into a long ponytail at the nape of his neck, showcasing his sharp, angular chin. His face held a sinister gaze as he stared at them from afar.

"Taybeith!" Ami roared.

He smiled and then looked up into the sky. Cryis followed his gaze. He wasn't alone. Aturdokht sat on the branch of the tree Taybeith leaned on. The wings of a raven slowly disappeared into her dress.

Her white hair had nearly turned completely black, and her dark skin was pale like a ghost. The black dress she wore matched Taybeith's suit. The dress fell off her shoulders while the sleeves came down to her wrist in a diamond-like cut. The ends of the dress reminded Cryis of a raven's feathers, the way they flared around her knees, exposing her black leather boots beneath.

She paid no attention to them, staring at the sky where Riley's soul had vanished. Her eyes held a soft sadness to them. For a moment, she looked less like Aturdokht and more like her former self.

"Jay..." Ami said hesitantly.

Cryis gripped his scythe tighter, holding back his urge to run to her. As much as he wished for the girl before him to be the Princess, he knew, despite the look in her eyes, she was now Aturdokht. Cryis stuck out the end of his staff, blocking the others from approaching her.

Aturdokht returned as a wicked grin spread across Jay's face. The sadness in her eyes was replaced by disgust. She looked from the sky at them on the ground. "How touching," she said.

Ami stopped her mist from flowing from her hand and reached for the rifle in Arthur's hand. She took aim behind Cryis, resting the gun on her knee to steady it.

"Ami, don't," Cryis said, hearing the click of the gun. He glanced back at her with pleading eyes. A gun would be useless to them, and she'd only be wasting bullets.

Cryis turned back to Aturdokht and glared at her. His gaze shifted to Taybeith. The serum had been useless against the Demon that had taken over his soul. Thanks to Aturdokht's attack at the Institute, he'd never been fully purified.

Cryis's eyes widened. It had been Aturdokht's plan all along. She'd used Taybeith to get rid of the serum. The serum had been a knockoff version of the Ancient's seal used to bind Aturdokht's magic. It had been their fail-safe if something had gone wrong and Jay hadn't been able to fight Aturdokht. The serum would have bought them time, stripping Aturdokht of her powers until Jay could defeat her. But they'd wasted it on Taybeith instead.

Cryis gritted his teeth, finally understanding. With the blood moon passing, their chances of defeating Aturdokht were dwindling as her powers continued to grow. An Ancient was strongest under a blood moon, and there wouldn't be another one for years.

"Did you do that to Riley?" Ami shouted. She used the rifle to help herself stand.

Cryis's blood boiled. Aturdokht had managed to turn an Aris Magician into a Demon. She'd create chaos using free will. His eyes widened in defeat—that was her plan. If she could do that to a Magician, humans didn't stand a chance. His free hand balled into a fist while his other gripped *Jevit* tighter until his knuckles turned white.

Taybeith's grin widened in response before he spoke, "Yes, but we didn't do it alone." His gaze shifted from Ami's to Cryis. Cryis stared back in confusion. He could feel Ami's eyes on him as well. "If it hadn't been for the blood Kazimir collected from you back in that prison, we wouldn't have had such a breakthrough in Magicians being able to withstand the Demon transformation without ruining the shell. You see, a human was simple, but a Magician needed...well, more longevity."

Cryis stifled a gasp, it was his fault, and he'd have to live with that. He found Aturdokht's studying gaze and glared at her. She smiled in response.

"If you think about it, you contributed to Riley's death in more ways than one." Taybeith laughed, and above him, Aturdokht smirked.

Cryis couldn't see an ounce of regret in her eyes. This wasn't Jay, he reminded himself.

"No! From where I stand, that man's blood is on your hands."

Beside Cryis, Arthur took a step forward. Cryis instinctively grabbed his arm, stopping him from taking another step. He shot Arthur a warning glare. He peered out the corner of his eyes and saw Aturdokht's eyes narrow on Arthur. Cryis pulled Arthur behind him, removing him from her line of sight.

Ami staggered. "Why?" Her voice broke as she fought back more tears. "He was good to you!" She shook her head in disbelief, directing her anger towards Taybeith. "Fight this! Whatever sick thing this is, remember who you are! You're an Aris Magician, a Tekhne, good-hearted!"

"No," Taybeith said calmly. He crossed his arms. "You stole that from me, remember?" He pulled down the collar of his shirt, revealing a deep hole in his neck.

Ami gasped, covering her mouth with her hand. Cryis looked away as well. The serum had done that.

Aturdokht finally spoke, her voice the perfect example of calm, "You're still Aris Magician. No one can take that away from you, my dear boy. Powerless or not." Taybeith smiled, looking up at Jay with admiration. "The age of humans and Aris Magicians who side with them is over. Demons and Faeries shall return and take their place among us. And as for the Black Gates, darkness like no other will reign over Aris Magica, and everyone will know true sorrow."

"What!" Cryis shouted, baffled.

The Black Gates sealed away a great evil that once roamed free across Aris Magica. It had no form, and it knew no boundaries. It eventually infected the human world as well, causing humans to fight alongside Aris Magica in the first war. The armies during the war managed to push the darkness into a space separate from the human world and Aris Magica, locking it inside a one-way pocket dimension behind black gates. During these dark times, the split between Aris Magica, light and dark, became deafeningly clear.

When Aturdokht had first risen to power, while she was still Mirama, she'd brought out the Demons and Faeries in hiding and used them to attack humans.

Under the cover of the first revolution in the human world, Aturdokht and her followers attacked humans and any Aris Magician who stood in her way. But the first Ancient had sealed her before she was able to accomplish her goal. And those that followed her went into hiding until the day she should return, an endlessly repeating cycle.

Cryis never once thought she could have a bigger goal in mind. He always believed Aturdokht's goal was to rid the world of humans and to allow Aris Magicians to reign as the superior race. Perhaps it was once, but now she wanted anyone who opposed her to suffer. If she opened the Black Gates, then the darkness would easily eat away at every living soul, turning the world into a wasteland stripped of magic and souls. But the darkness behind those gates knew no sides, just destruction. Aturdokht couldn't possibly hope to control it, not even with the Elementals' magic.

Cryis had never realized it because every time Aturdokht awakened, a reincarnation of the Ancient was there to seal her immediately. But this time, it had been different, Phagos had tried to eliminate Jay as a child but failed. He knew if he had killed her, then, as the last reincarnation, there would be no one left to stop Aturdokht from completing her plan.

"You can't," Cryis mumbled, shocked. He was too speechless to say anything else. If that darkness got loose, there would be no world left for Aturdokht to conquer. "You can't control it."

Out of the corner of his eyes, Cryis saw Ami dart past him. A black mist followed by a pungent smell came out of both her arms. Cryis swung his scythe, picking up speed, and followed her, knowing he couldn't stop her. He knew the two of them wouldn't be enough to stop Taybeith or Aturdokht, but they couldn't let them get away.

"Wait! I thought you said—" Arthur began. He shook his head, picking up the rifle. He checked the loading case. "Never mind!" He shouted, following them.

A wall of fire pushed towards them. Cryis grabbed Ami by the waist and pulled her to him. It was beginning to be easier to call on his Elemental's magic. A sphere formed around them as the fire hit, turning the flames into smoke.

Aturdokht's smug yet fearful expression stared down at them. She was still afraid of Cryis's Elemental, even with her own. She disappeared in a cloud of smoke, leaving behind a singed raven's feather floating in the wind.

Ami broke away from Cryis, going straight for Taybeith. He didn't even try to dodge as Ami flung her mist in his direction. Instead, he held out his hand towards her. His sleeve busted as his arm grew exceedingly large. Bulges of black and purple veins appeared in his arm, and his fingers grew into claws. When he smiled, his teeth had grown fangs, and his eyes narrowed.

Ami's mist hit the palm of Taybeith's hand. He clamped his hand shut, crystalizing the mist up to her elbows. Ami pulled back, trying to free herself from Taybeith's hold, and screamed. Taybeith clenched tighter, breaking the mist into tiny shards.

"Careful before you lose another arm," he warned.

"You should worry about yourself!" Cryis shouted.

Cryis jumped into the air as Taybeith looked up to see him mid-spin. Taybeith released Ami's mist, and it returned to its natural form. He jumped back in the nick of time as Cryis brought his scythe to the ground. Cryis barely gave Taybeith time to breathe before he attacked again. The sound of a bullet whizzed past Cryis and hurled towards Taybeith. Taybeith dodged them all.

"I swear you'll pay!" Ami yelled, shooting her mist towards Taybeith again. The mist singed his side and arms, turning his skin into rough scales.

Cryis dragged his scythe against the ground, kicking up leaves, using them to blind Taybeith. He transformed his other arm, grabbing Cryis's blade as it came down on him. Cryis held onto his staff and kicked Taybeith in the chest. The blade cut through Taybeith's hand, and he also fell back to the ground. A mixture of black and red blood stained Cryis's scythe. Taybeith attempted to get up, but one of Arthur's bullets whizzed past Cryis and hit Taybeith in the shoulder.

"It's over," Cryis said.

Taybeith growled beneath him. The rest of his body began to transform. His wings sprouted from his back. Cryis took a deep breath, closing his eyes. He felt the power of his Elemental build inside of him. Cryis wanted to try to pull the Demon from Taybeith like he'd done with Riley. He slowly opened his eyes, releasing his breath. At least his soul would be saved.

The energy around him began to cackle as the Elemental revealed itself. Cryis held his scythe out towards Taybeith. The energy and power jumped from Cryis to his scythe. Suddenly, a wall of fire rose between Cryis and Taybeith, separating them. Cryis looked up to see Aturdokht had returned. She stood on the branch above them, holding out her hand. She stared at Cryis with wild eyes.

She pushed her hand forward, commanding the fire to do the same. The energy formed around Cryis in a protective spear as the Elementals clashed—neither one giving nor taking. A wave of fire washed over him, creating beautiful sparks and smoke as his Elemental's power fought back. The fire disappeared into smoke.

Cryis looked through the haze to see Aturdokht helping Taybeith to his feet. There was hatred in her eyes as she stared at him. She raised her hands again. Cryis prepared himself, feeling his power rising again. Instead, the fire Aturdokht summoned surrounded her and Taybeith. In a matter of seconds, the two were gone, leaving behind a pile of ash. The pocket dimension around them broke, returning them to the snowy forest.

Anger boiled within Cryis's veins, but so did relief. They had managed to fend her off. They'd won. Despite Aturdokht's control over Jay's body, she wasn't invincible. Cryis knew it was wrong to feel hopeful, but he couldn't erase the initial trepidation in Aturdokht's eyes. She feared him.

Cryis returned *Jevit* to its pocket dimension and tilted his head toward the sky, staring at the white clouds above. He let out a slow breath that the icy wind quickly swept away. Cryis shifted his gaze to Arthur and couldn't help but smile. Arthur was staring at the sky as well. He was breathing heavily, but there wasn't a scratch on him. When he blinked, his gaze met Cryis's, reflecting the small smile he shared.

Arthur held his gaze for a moment longer before slowly peeling it away. Cryis did the same, but he couldn't deny the sad feeling growing inside him as he did. Given the opportunity, he would have liked to stare longer at Arthur, taking in every aspect of the man before him. Instead, Cryis focused his gaze on Ami.

Ami sunk to the ground, falling face-first in the snow. "Ami!" Arthur shouted, running over to her. Cryis did as well, they both helped her to her feet.

Cryis looked down at the stub that remained on her left arm. Her mist had managed to stop the bleeding, closing the wound, but she had still lost a lot of blood. Cryis pulled her to him and lifted her in his arms, holding her bridal style. Her body felt cold in his embrace.

"She needs a hospital," Arthur said, coming up beside him as they walked back to the truck.

Cryis stopped and looked off into the distance in the opposite direction from where they were going. There was another pocket dimension nearby that he knew of that would take them to Aris Magica. The council's base wasn't too far from where they were now. They could easily provide Ami with the healing she would need without raising questions a hospital would. Cryis looked back at Ami; her face was pale. He wasn't sure what to do.

Ami grabbed the zipper of his jacket. "There's no time," she said gently. "I'll be fine."

Cryis sighed, looking down at her. He turned to Arthur, "We must hurry and get to the library. If it gets worse, we'll stop and figure something out," Cryis said weakly.

Arthur sighed but obliged without a fight, even though Cryis could see from his expression that he disagreed. Arthur opened the driver's seat of the truck and got in. Cryis opened the back door and gently laid Ami down across the back seats. He removed his coat, flipping it inside out to avoid the blood on it. He laid it over Ami's missing arm.

"Tell me if you start feeling worse, okay," Cryis said, he pushed a strand of her hair behind her ear. She smiled weakly. Cryis closed her door and opened the door to his seat, hopping in.

Cryis buckled his seatbelt and then looked over at Arthur. There was an eerie silence in the air between them. Judging from his gaze, Cryis could tell Arthur had many questions. He quickly assessed Arthur again to see if he was badly hurt, but he wasn't. He'd been smart enough to keep his distance from the battle, only firing his gun from afar. Cryis let out a breath he hadn't realized he'd been holding. He reached over and grabbed Arthur's hand, giving it a tight squeeze.

"Okay," Cryis said as he slowly let go of Arthur's hand.

"Okay," Arthur repeated. He shifted the truck into gear and began driving toward their destination.

Chapter Twenty-Four

"Dylan! Dylan?" Silo coughed. He slowly came to and found himself resting his head on her lap. A bright, green light emitted from her hand as she healed his injuries. "Oh, thank god." She sighed in relief, leaning her head back. Sweat beaded her brow, and her skin looked pale even in the darkness of the light.

Dylan quickly sat up, looking around. He could barely see anything from the smoke and debris, but from what he could make out, they were stuck in some cave. Jagged rocks stuck out from the wall, as well as pieces from the fallen library floor.

A sharp pain pinched the back of Dylan's head. His hand went immediately to the stinging area. He tried rubbing it, his fingers touching something wet. When he pulled back his hand, his fingers were sticky with blood.

"Not so fast." Silo inched closer to him, pressing her glowing hand to the spot on Dylan's head. He felt a soothing feeling before the pain ceased.

Dylan touched his face, feeling a wound that wasn't there before. It went straight through his right cheek and across the bridge of his nose. Silo dropped her hand. Dylan looked over at her. She was just as banged up as he was. She had a gash going down her left arm and a bruise forming on her chin. On top of it all, she looked exhausted. Dylan watched as the faint green glow from her hand changed to a white light. The use of her magic was draining her.

"We have to get out of here." Silo stood to her feet.

She raised her glowing hand above her, casting out the shadows and creating a small spotlight on them. From it, Dylan was able to see more clearly. On the ground with them were tattered books and pieces of wood from the bookshelves, along with the shattered remnants of the pocket dimension crystal Eradine had given them. Dylan cursed to himself, feeling the weight of defeat on his shoulders.

The pit they were in was one elongated tunnel going up. Above them, the hole gave way to a small opening too high for them to reach. The higher the walls went, the smoother the rock became, making it impossible to climb. They'd fallen into a pit created by Phagos's final attack, with no way out.

"What was that back there?" Dylan asked, staring up at Silo. Her back was to him. He could see the thin lines where her wings should have sprouted from. "Why didn't you fly?"

"Maybe if you hoist me up, I could jump a good way and reach that piece there," Silo muttered, avoiding the question. She pointed to a rock sticking out of the wall further up from them.

"Silo." Dylan huffed. She flinched.

Dylan sighed. He didn't want to pry, but he had to know. They'd lost both the Elemental and nearly their lives, the one thing the Headmaster had asked him to protect. Dylan continued to stare at her back. Fairy wings made Fairies' magic stronger when they were expanded. He couldn't imagine why a Fairy wouldn't want to use them. The more Dylan thought about it, the more confused he became. He noticed that Kai didn't have a problem using his wings. Dylan had seen them twice and had felt the power they'd given him.

Dylan squinted his eyes, examining her slits. He noticed the slits in her back were sealed instead of slightly open. He couldn't help but reach his hand out. Silo jumped at his touch but didn't move. He lightly brushed his fingers over the lines, feeling healed scar tissue.

"What happened?" Dylan asked with an unsettling darkness to his tone.

Dylan felt Silo relax beneath his touch. A long moment of silence passed between them. He started to wonder if he should repeat his question. He stopped running his fingers along her shoulder blades and rested his hand on the small of her back.

"They were cut off," She confessed, her voice barely above a whisper.

Dylan's hand dropped to his side. He stared at her, astonished. "Why?"

Who would do such a thing? The thought terrified him.

Fairy wings alone didn't have much magical value unless attached to their owner. He recalled learning how, in the past, humans would hunt Fairies—stripping them of their wings in hopes of obtaining magic of their own, but it never worked. He didn't realize that Fairy wings were still in danger.

Silo turned, facing him. She sank to her knees. When she looked up at Dylan, she smiled with shame in her eyes. Dylan suddenly regretted asking her.

"It's because I'm not a Fairy, but a Faery."

A pit began to form in Dylan's stomach as deep as the one they were in. He felt his world turn upside down. Faeries were exiled creatures. Evil beings that caused havoc in both the human world and Aris Magica. Dream walkers and dream weavers who could control the mind with a simple thought.

Dylan gulped, thinking back to when he had memories, he couldn't remember how they had pieced together, they hadn't been fabricated but put in a disorder. It had been her all along, that's why she had apologized a week ago for messing with his head. He'd allowed himself to get close to her, for her to get close to him—could he even trust her?

Silo stared at Dylan with despair. Her eyes heavy with a sadness he'd never seen from her. Dylan's heart skipped a beat, and he instantly regretted his thoughts. He looked away, ashamed, unable to hold her gaze. He knew it couldn't have been easy for her to tell him her identity, and instead, here he was, doubting the person he saw before him now.

Silo was none of those things. From what he'd seen in the short time he'd been with her, she was loyal, kind-hearted, trusting, and brave. He found the courage to look her in the eyes. She was doing her best to hold back her tears.

"Who did it?"

Silo peered at him through long lashes, "My parents. Faery wings are much larger than Fairy wings, so they were able to tell right away." Silo reached behind her back and rubbed the scars.

Faery wings were larger but much thinner than Fairies'. Dylan always thought they looked like whimsy tree branches with thick, ovate leaves hanging from them. Dylan bit the inside of his lip. His heart filled with sadness; he could only imagine the pain she'd suffered the day it happened. Wings were a part of both a Fairy's and Faery's identity.

"They did it to protect me from the scrutiny of others." Silo explained. Dylan reached out his hand and gently squeezed her thigh. She grabbed onto his hand, holding it. He returned the small smile she gave him. "I learned to heal and use Fairy-like nature magic, masking who I am." She laughed, shrugging nonchalantly as she gestured to her hand lit with magic, "It just takes more out of me."

"Does Kai know?" Dylan asked.

Silo nodded, her smile growing even bigger. "Of course, he's my brother." She chimed admirably, "He covers for me when he can, and the council knows as well." Silo clasped her hands together, letting go of Dylan's. "That's why I cannot fail. I must stop Aturdokht no matter what. Otherwise, Faeries will always be misjudged, and the council's efforts and my brothers towards me would be a waste."

"No, that's not true," Dylan said, leaning forward on his hands. "It doesn't matter what you are. You shouldn't have to prove that you're good, not to the council, me, or anyone," Dylan proclaimed.

Silo smiled, but it quickly faded. "But I lost the amulet to that Demon." Her voice trickled off as she spoke.

"Phagos." Dylan glared. "Leader of Aturdokht's army, a murderer that just won't die." Dylan was reminded of his vendetta against the beast. He'd almost let his anger get the best of him, nearly endangering his life and Silo's life. He glanced over at Silo, who looked lost in disappointment. She had bowed her head towards her lap, still clasping her hands together.

"We still have a chance. No one knows where the third Elemental is, and we still have the Hidden Library." Dylan said encouragingly.

And the Infinity Staff, he thought to himself.

He still hadn't given up hope in finding a way to use it to free Jay. He wasn't sure if its powers worked in that way, but the Headmaster had assured him that with great conviction, anything was possible. He rubbed the inside of his wrist. He could feel the staff deep inside him beckoning to be set free but remaining just out of reach.

Dylan met Silo's gaze again. She quickly wiped away the tears that had fallen, then offered him a hesitant smile. "So don't give up hope," Dylan reassured, also giving her a genuine smile in return.

Silo leaned her head back, staring at the hole above. Dylan followed her gaze, catching a glimpse of the starry sky peeking through the gap in the library's ceiling.

"Yeah, if we ever get out of here." Silo sighed.

Dylan scooted closer to her, the light still emitting from her hand felt warmer. He gently grabbed her free hand and pulled her into him. He heard a faint gasp escape from her lips as he did.

"We will," Dylan whispered into Silo's ear.

The two of them sat in silence for a long time. Silo had finally put out the light. She rested her head against Dylan's chest. He held her close to him. He could feel her shaking; the magic she'd used made her body weak. He rubbed her arms, trying to warm her. Dylan could also feel his body growing weaker as well. The air inside the cave became stuffier, making it harder to breathe as more dust clouded the air.

In the dark silence, Dylan thought about their next steps. Even if they managed to find the whereabouts of the third Elemental, would there be enough time to track its guardian down? If Aturdokht already found two of them, it wouldn't be long until she focused all her efforts on finding the third one. Dylan didn't want to think about how powerful she'd be with all three of them. Their only hope lay with him being able to summon the staff.

When he closed his eyes, he could see the staff as if it were already in his hands. But the more he swam through the darkness of his mind, the further the staff floated down. In the past, it was like Jay had been his anchor when he called it forth, keeping him one foot in the light as he pulled the staff free. The staff held immense magic but just as much darkness. However, when the time came, could Dylan truly face Jay as she was now?

This time apart from her was testing him. Especially since he'd come to terms with his feelings for her. He missed her. Dylan bit the inside of his lip, even thoughts of her were becoming painful. He was in love with her. and every second he spent away from her made that fact painstakingly clear. He could feel his heart pounding inside his chest and wondered if Silo could hear it too. He glanced down at her; her eyes were closed as well, and her breathing had finally slowed. He smiled to himself, thankful she was there with him.

"Hey," Silo said, breaking the silence. "You won't tell anyone, right?" She asked nervously.

Dylan smiled, resting his chin on top of her head. "Of course not."

The silence around them grew, but so did the peace within it. Dylan absent-mindedly ran his fingers through Silo's braids. Her eyes were closed, and her breathing was slow, as if she were sleeping, but Dylan knew she wasn't. The two of them had brainstormed every way possible to get out of the pit but came up empty-handed. Regardless, Dylan didn't think Silo was strong enough to climb out. He didn't even think they could with how slick the walls were. After a while, Dylan closed his eyes as well, succumbing to the peace of the silence around them.

"Sy! Dylan!" Kai's voice rang out above them, shocking them both. Dylan looked up and saw a blur of light passing over the hole, but as quickly as it came, it disappeared.

"Kai?" Dylan said to Silo, looking at her as she stared past him at the ceiling.

Silo's face lit up. She sat up, leaned forward, and began waving her hands like a maniac. "Kai! Kai! We're down here! The ground collapsed in!"

"I know!" Kai shouted.

Seconds later, his face appeared in the hole's opening. His face was covered in blood and dirt. Dylan couldn't tell if it was his or not. He noticed Kai glaring at him. Dylan cocked his head to the side, confused, he looked down, Silo was still sitting in his lap between his legs. Dylan suddenly felt embarrassed, but he couldn't move even if he wanted to.

"I'll come down and get you one at a time," Kai groaned.

Kai swooped down, his wings scraping the sides of the wall as he did. Sparks of magic dust flew from them. Silo stood up from Dylan's lap and stepped to the side, allowing him the space to stand as well. She reached out her hand as her brother drew closer. Kai grabbed Silo's hand and pulled her to him. They flew to the surface.

In a couple of seconds, he returned, landing in front of Dylan. His wings created a marvelous light that lit up the entire tunnel and cast leaf-like shadows on the walls from his wings. Dylan held out his hand for Kai to grab, but he didn't take it immediately.

"You know, don't you," Kai stated. Dylan knew immediately what he was referring to. Dylan stiffly nodded.

For once, Dylan was unable to read Kai's expression. He'd never seen Kai this serious. Dylan knew what he wanted to say to him before Kai said it. He could see the protection of his sister in the way Kai stared at him. Dylan was aware of the possible consequences of people finding out about Silo's true nature and the reason for concern Kai had for anyone finding out.

"I won't say anything," Dylan promised. He cared for Silo, and he would never jeopardize her safety like that.

Kai scoffed. "I barely know you, let alone trust you," Kai said protectively.

"Look, I know the two of us haven't seen eye to eye, but I would never do anything to betray Silo. I know better than anyone what being different does to a person I've se—"

"But she does." Kai cut Dylan off. "She trusts you, so I guess that's good enough for me." Dylan stared at Kai, shocked by how quickly Kai had accepted trusting him with the truth. "So, thank you," Kai grunted. Dylan stared at him in disbelief. He hadn't expected to ever hear those words from Kai.

"Please don't make this weird." Dylan grinned, trying to lighten the situation.

Kasi scoffed, "Just take the compliment deumage."

And there it is. Dylan thought with a smile. Kai was back to his original self.

Dylan held out his hand again, this time, Kai took it. He dragged Dylan behind him as he lifted them both into the air and toward the hole. Silo was there, peering over the edge, waiting for them both. She helped them through the hole, both boys falling to their knees beside her. Kai retracted his wings and doubled over, panting as he tried to catch his breath. Silo quickly glanced at Dylan making sure he was okay. Dylan smiled at her reassuringly in response. Silo nodded before going over to Kai and helping him to his feet.

Dylan looked around; the entire library was destroyed, and none of it was left standing. There was a sadness to it, knowing that one of the three great wonders of Aris Magica had been reduced to rubble. The sun barely broke through the clouds above as it began to set. They'd long overstayed the three hours Eradine had promised them, and there was no way back through the original pocket dimension they'd gone through, especially since the crystal they'd been given had been shattered by their fall.

Dylan stood to his feet, brushing off his clothes. He looked around the area in search of the Headmaster or Doctor Herron, but he didn't see any signs of either of them.

Kai placed a hand on Dylan's shoulder. "The doctor went through a portal earlier before the battle ensued. And the old man..." Kai's voice trailed off; he glanced the other way, staring off into the other direction. Dylan followed his gaze set on a broken clock smashed in by fallen pieces of the ceiling.

Dylan's entire body rattled with grief. He felt as if he would fall. Kai steadied him, pressing firmly against his back to keep him upright. Kai looked between the two. "Where's the Elemental?" Dylan looked back at him, speechless. Silo didn't say anything either, unable to meet Kai's gaze.

"Dammit!" Kai shouted. He released Dylan and kicked up some rocks. They tumbled into the pit they'd just escaped from.

"I'm sorry," Silo mumbled.

"No, it's fine. It wasn't your fault," Kai said with a sigh. He lifted his armor flap hanging from his waist. He pulled out a small clear pouch of sand. Dylan stared at it, confused, it looked a lot like the dust Arden had used. "We need to hurry to the next library."

"What's that?" Dylan asked, pointing to the pouch.

"Portal magic," Kai said. "It works like a pocket dimension, but it's transportable. You just build it." Kai began to untie the string, keeping the pouch closed. "Anyways, Aturdokht and her goons are already two steps ahead of us. But if we find the third Elemental, we still have a chance." Kai surprisingly looked at Dylan for support.

"Even if we find the third one, we won't have the time to track the keeper down. I think we should focus on trying to find a way to use the Infinity Staff instead," Dylan said, voicing his concerns out loud.

"Okay. You're right," Kai said. Silo and Dylan gaped at Kai, stunned. "But we can do both. Once there, we split our search and look for both answers."

"Yeah," Dylan said, unable to form other words. He was still in shock that Kai agreed with him again.

"Fine," Silo agreed. She walked up to Dylan. "But I know what you're thinking." She stopped before him, staring into his eyes. He could see the determination in them. "I don't want you to get your hopes up. Even if we figure out how to call the staff, my brother and I's mission is to stop Aturdokht no matter what. Once someone's become vassalized or soul possessed, it's nearly impossible to free them."

Dylan shook his head before she even finished her sentence. He had to believe there was still hope. They needed Jay, he needed her, and there was still something he wanted to tell her. So he would never give up on her.

"Okay," Kai said. "Step back." He tossed the ribbon aside and cleared away some space on the ground. He dumped the sand on the floor.

Dylan watched as the sand fizzed in place for a moment.

Kai held his hand over it and said, *"Skrytý librere."*

Silver beams shot from Kai's palm into the sand, giving it life. The particles began to move as one in a spiral on the ground before rising into the air and creating a storm. Dylan shielded his eyes, unable to see inside the storm. The sand began to harden, coming together in a solid form. When the storm cleared, a tall door remained.

The door was oval-shaped. On the face of the door was a woman with wings sitting on a single petal that had been engraved into the wood. The door was rimmed with fancy cursive designs that connected like roots reaching from the woman's hair and towards the doorknob. Although the door looked like it was made of wood, Dylan noticed the tiny beads of sand moving slowly within.

Dylan reached for the knob. He looked back at the others before he opened the door. Once he stepped through the door, he knew there would be no going back. Whatever information they found on the other side, Dylan prayed it would be useful. Both Kai and Silo nodded, giving Dylan permission to continue. He took in a deep breath before opening the door and stepping into a blinding white light.

Chapter Twenty-Five

Jay couldn't breathe, and neither could Aturdokht.

After the shock of Riley's death, Jay managed to gain a small amount of control back from Aturdokht by aiding her friends in their fight against her. It hadn't been much, but she'd made sure Aturdokht couldn't use the full power of the Heart Elemental. However, she hadn't expected Cryis to have full control over his Elemental as he did. It was a small victory, but she had relished in it.

Jay sunk against the wall in the main hall, where her throne was.

Riley was dead. The words echoed endlessly in her mind. And it had been her fault. It felt as though a piece of her had been taken away. Riley had been the closest thing she had to a father. The realization that he was gone and would never return sank in deeply. He'd never chastise her again. He'd never be there to guide her through her assignments or to help Dylan practice honing his magic as a Hybrid. She'd never hear his laughter or comforting words when things didn't go her way. Amid her grief, Aturdokht taunted her with this knowledge at every chance she got.

Hot tears ran down her face as her emotions overwhelmed Aturdokht's control. "I'm so sorry," Jay whispered. She dug her nails into her thighs, wishing she had the strength to hurt herself, to hurt Aturdokht, but every time she got close enough, Aturdokht would stop her.

Her grief had given birth to a third presence, lurking in the far reaches of the mind she shared with Aturdokht. Jay felt fear and rage overlapping her sadness, blurring the lines between herself and Aturdokht. She could no longer distinguish where she ended and Aturdokht began. But she did know that, deep within her mind, they were no longer alone.

"Ma'am?"

Jay jumped, looking across the room to find Phagos standing in the doorway. His hands were behind his back, and his voice was stern. Jay glared. She hated him.

Unwillingly, her body stood. She smoothed out her dress and then her hair, wiping the tears from her eyes with the back of her sleeve. "Phagos," Jay hated her voice because it was no longer hers alone. "Welcome back."

He stalked forward, and as he did, Jay noticed a mischievous glint in his eyes. He even had the gall to smile. Her stomach churched. She met him halfway, her heels clacking against the floor with every step.

"What news do you have to bring?" She asked, sounding exhausted.

Phagos pulled out a pendant that shimmered with a green stone. Jay's heart broke further.

No...

It was the Headmaster's.

In contrast to her emotions, a satisfied smile spread across her lips. "Yes."

Jay felt herself reach up and snatch the stone free from the pendant's clasp, melting the metal in the process. She turned the small stone in her hand, feeling the power of the Elemental housed inside it. She closed her fist around it. There was only one more to go now.

Chapter Twenty-Six

Dylan stepped through the door, finding himself at the start of four steps leading up to a podium. The portal had transported him to the center of the Hidden Library. At the top of the podium, there was a large open book with magic dust lines floating in the air above its pages. These lines continuously transformed into random patterns, never settling on one thing for too long before changing again.

Dylan averted his gaze, taking in the rest of the library. Surrounding the open space were thousands and thousands of bookshelves; some were grounded, while others were suspended in the air. Books soared across the room to and from the shelves, and the bookshelves on the ground led to the center of the room where he stood. The flooring beneath him resembled the pattern of the sun surrounded by star constellations.

Dylan noticed that the walls looked similar to the pit Silo and he had just escaped. He could see pieces of moss hanging from cracks within the rock, making it appear as if the library was underground.

Dylan walked the stairs to the podium overlooking the book. Shortly after he did, Silo came through the door, followed by Kai. Once all three were through, the sand burst into nothingness.

Kai shrugged, looking at the others. "Guess this was a one-way ticket."

Dylan stared at the pages of the open book before him. They were crisp and thin, filled with silver printed words. Some were written in an ancient text, while others were written in various languages. Dylan recognized English, Spanish, French, Latin, and Swahili. He traced his fingers over the words and lifted the page to turn it. He noticed the foreign words in the book began to change into English at his touch. He saw each page was titled with a number. The page he was on was 2047. Dylan looked up, and his eyes found another number, 157, engraved on the front wall of the nearest bookshelf. He looked back at the book, astounded.

"I think it's a guide," Dylan said.

"Omnes," Silo whispered. She stepped onto the podium beside him. She looked over his shoulder at the book inquisitively. "But how does the damn thing work?"

Dylan chuckled, flipping through a couple of pages. "Well, we can start by turning the pages like any other book." He teased.

Suddenly, a book flew over them, nearly whacking Dylan in the head. Another followed. Silo brandished her small spear, causing it to extend into the air and transform into the size of a javelin. She whacked the next book out of the sky.

"Haha," She sarcastically replied to Dylan. The book fell, its pages struggling to lift itself under the weight of her spear.

The Omnes's pages began to turn under Dylan's hands. He raised them, letting the book take control.

The book underneath Silo's spear continued to wriggle itself free. "Let it go," Dylan said. She frowned but removed her spear from its cover.

The small book flew at Dylan, knocking him back several steps. He caught it, holding it close to his chest. He looked up to see that the Omnes had settled as well. The magic lines above began to form the word *spear* before transforming into a spear of its own. The lines intertwined into a straight line with a pointed tip. Dylan looked down at the book in his hands, it read the *Inner Workings of Hasta Magic,* with the image of a hand-carved spear below it.

"What is it?" Silo asked, she didn't retract her spear just yet, keeping it at its full size.

Dylan didn't answer her. He wanted to try something first. He set the book he was holding on the ground. He went over to the Omnes and began to think of portals. The dust lines changed into a door that fell into a pile of sand. The guidebook flipped to page 47, and another book from the back of the room came flying at them.

Silo got her spear ready. "Again?" She mumbled.

"No, wait!" Dylan said, stopping her. Instead, he caught the book. He flipped it over, discovering it was about portals. "Ah hah!" He beamed. He held the book up, showing the others.

"'Ah hah, what? You can catch?" Kai mocked. He sat down on the top step leading up to the podium. "Good for you."

"No." Dylan ignored his mockery. "I know how to narrow our search." He explained his theory. The Omnes seemed to respond to the user's touch and thought, reflecting it as illusion magic before summoning the correct book. "I think the library and the Omnes are connected."

Silo came over and placed her hand on the book. Seconds later, the lines shifted into a winged pattern, and a book from behind them came soaring at them. She caught it with one hand and turned it over to show them. The book had a pair of Faery wings on its cover.

"I think you're right," she said.

Kai joined them on the podium. "So, these lines," he touched the dust with his fingers. The lines froze before fizzling into the book. His eyes grew wide. "Uh..."

Silo gasped, "What did you do?"

"I don't know!" Kai raised his hands. "All I did was touch it. Was I not supposed to?"

"Ugh!" Silo closed the Omnes and opened it again. Dylan had hoped it would work just like turning the computer off and on again when it stopped working, but nothing happened. "This is great! Just great, Kasid!" Silo snapped as she turned towards Kai.

"What? Is it broken?" Kai asked, alarmed.

Dylan ran a hand down his face, "I think so."

"What now?" Kai looked at Dylan, his face begging for an explanation.

Dylan let out a long-drawn sigh. He turned away from the book and stared at the endless shelves of books around them. "We do it the old-fashioned way."

Kai let out a slur of curses before stalking back down the stairs. Silo and Dylan returned to the book. She opened it, landing on page 23.

"There has to be some organization to this thing," Dylan said, glancing at Silo. He was highly aware of how close she was to him. The podium wasn't big, so the two stood right next to each other, her shoulder pressed up against his as they looked over the book.

He felt his face beginning to warm. He could smell the familiar scent of lemons and mint on her, which he'd come to enjoy. Dylan felt his face flush even further, and he quickly looked away before she could see it. He couldn't deny to himself the attraction he felt for Silo. Ever since the first time he'd met her, he'd undoubtedly been drawn to her. He admired her determination; when she set her mind to something, nothing could stop her, even if it took her on a different path than others.

The thought reminded Dylan of Silo and Kai's mission to kill Jay. That thought alone was enough to refocus his mind. He cleared his throat and honed in on the book.

Silo ran her hand down the page, reading the words under her breath. Her eyes lit up, "There it is." She pointed to the text.

Dylan's eyes tracked where Silo's finger was pointing to. It was in a language Dylan didn't understand—ancient text. He'd always struggled to learn the first language of Aris Magicians. To him, it only looked like a bunch of symbols thrown together in disarray.

Silo must have noticed his confusion because she further explained what she saw, "These here are titles and descriptions." She said as she tapped the page with her index finger.

Dylan leaned closer to the book. "Are they alphabetically aligned with the numbers?" He asked hopefully.

"No, descriptively synced, unfortunately." Silo said as she withdrew her finger from the page. "They're grouped by likeliness."

Dylan felt his stomach drop. A task that could have been accomplished in a second would now take the rest of their night. They'd never make it before Aturdokht figured out where the third Elemental was.

"Divide and conquer, remember?" Silo said, smiling at Dylan. He nodded, taking a deep breath. "Wait," she said, causing him to look at her again. "Perhaps," she turned to the page near the middle of the book. "The Elementals resemble the life cycle. Ignis, Život, Anim, and Chi. So maybe..." Silo rambled. She continued to flip through the pages. "Here, I found it!" She smiled as she rapidly tapped her finger on the page yet again.

Dylan looked at the titled number 363. He scanned the bookshelves from the podium but didn't see the bookcase in sight. He began to back away from the podium in an attempt to get a better look.

"Wait!" Silo grabbed Dylan's wrist before he could take off. "What about the staff?"

Dylan gently removed her hand and caught a flash of hurt in her gaze before she quickly masked her expression. His heart tightened; he hadn't meant to hurt her. "The Elemental first," he said, offering her a small smile, but she only nodded in response. "And then we'll look for more information on the staff."

No matter what, Aturdokht couldn't have all three, even if all they could do was send a warning to the keeper about the impending danger. Dylan glanced back at Silo, but she wouldn't meet his gaze. At first, he thought he saw her blush, but she turned away too quickly for him to be sure.

He descended the podium steps. "Spread out!" he shouted.

Suddenly, a group of books rained down on him, knocking him to the ground. Out of the corner of his eye, he saw Kai kicking a couple of the attacking books off him. Dylan pushed the rest aside and noticed that each book's cover bore a variation of the word *silence*.

Silo rushed to Dylan's side, helping him up. "Look quietly," she suggested with a small laugh. "The Hidden Library is known to have a sense of humor."

"I'll go this way," Kai said as he sulked off to the left.

"Come on," Silo whispered.

She led them down the hall straight ahead. The two went separate ways once they reached a fork in the road. Dylan thought the library was more like a maze, luring him deeper and deeper into its confusion.

As Dylan walked, he couldn't find a single pattern to how the shelves were organized. Some of the numbers were low, while higher numbers occasionally appeared, either floating above him or resting on the ground beside him. He scanned the books he passed for the words *staff* or *Ancient*, hoping to accomplish two things at once, but he had no luck.

Dylan began to wonder why it was called the Hidden Library. Most of the books he'd seen were common knowledge, so what purpose did the library serve?

Dylan sighed, coming to a stop. He leaned against the wall of a bookcase beside him, sinking to the ground. He needed a break. He closed his eyes, rested his head back, and took a deep breath. He could sense that they were near and on the verge of a breakthrough, but his mind was consumed with thoughts of doubt.

Dylan rubbed the inside of his wrist, where a throbbing pain had begun. At first faint, the sensation intensified the deeper he ventured into the library. The more he rubbed it, the more he felt as if he were holding the Infinity Staff. His hand felt incredibly heavy, but when he opened his eyes, nothing was there.

Dylan closed his left hand into a fist and willed himself to his feet. He needed to find Jay to prevent anyone else he loved from suffering. He had so much to share with her. The noose around his heart tightened again; he realized he loved Jay with all his heart. Being away from her, especially knowing the danger she faced, was the most heartbreaking feeling he'd ever experienced. It overshadowed the loss he'd felt in recent weeks.

Despite all those years spent with Jay, Dylan had only now been made aware of his feelings. He had Silo to thank for that. Spending the past couple of weeks with her reminded him of his time with Jay, bringing to light his faults and the things he wished he'd done differently. Once he got Jay back, Dylan hoped to make things right by being the partner she deserved, not the one who had held her back.

Dylan began to walk forward with a newly founded pep in his step, only to slide and nearly fall. He grabbed onto the shelf beside him, steadying himself. He looked down to find ice decorating the floor.

What in the world?

Dylan looked around; he hadn't heard the ice form, nor did the room feel cold enough for ice to begin with.

He peered around the corner and saw more ice forming on the ground, creating a trail for him to follow. Dylan took a step forward, keeping one hand on the bookcases as he walked. The ice continued to grow, covering the bookshelves and the walls around him.

Suddenly, the air changed, becoming as cold as the ice beneath his boots. The bookshelves no longer formed a maze but seemed to act as guards, as if they were hiding something. The ice continued between the shelves, and Dylan carefully followed, watching his step as frozen books lay strewn across the pathway.

When he reached the last of the bookcases, he stepped behind them. The ice stopped, disappearing into a wall. Dylan looked up and saw a door embedded in the same wall, untouched by the ice. It was made of dark ebony wood, trimmed with a royal blue lining that formed two vines crossing over the door like a seal.

Dylan touched the door and felt a small pinch under his finger. He withdrew his hand to find a small, thin line of blood trickling from his fingertip. The vines on the door pulled back, and the door opened wide. Inside was an extension of the cave they were in, with the ice continuing inside. In the center of the room was a single bookshelf. Dylan squinted his eyes and saw the number 363 scrawled at the top outer frame of the shelf facing him.

Dylan smiled wide, sliding inside towards the shelf. He nearly crashed into it. Unlike the other shelves outside, there were only about twenty books on the one before him. Dylan grabbed one of them and slipped, the book fell from his hands and hit the ground. He started to pick it up but stopped. Within the ice, the ground had pictures drawn into it. Each one poked out from beneath the shelf.

There were five pictures in all. One was of a grand clock, and the second was of four orbs stacked on top of each other, each one holding a different spiraled pattern inside. The third was a compass, and the fourth was a sword that looked oddly like Phagos's sword. Dylan recognized the thick hilt and wide-cut blade with vines wrapped around it. The fifth drawing was of the Infinity Staff. Dylan looked at the trident on the inside of his wrist. The staff would transform from the trident into a long rod where the two outer prongs curled inward into the shape of a heart. The center of it held an orb of magic at its core.

Dylan returned his gaze to the single bookshelf at the center of the ice. The library had led him to the right place. It was as if this section of the library had called him to it. Dylan grabbed as many books as he could and slid out of the room. Once on regular ground, he took off in a run back toward the center of the library. On the way, he ran into Kai, nearly crashing right into him.

"What the hell!" Kai said, dodging Dylan.

"I found it!" Dylan said breathlessly, showing Kai the books he'd grabbed. "Meet back at the podium." Dylan didn't take the time to look at any of the books he'd grabbed, but he knew they had to be of some use based on the drawings on the floor he'd seen. He shoved them into Kai's hands.

Before Kai could protest, Dylan had already taken off back to the room of ice. When he reached it, Silo was standing at its entrance in awe. "You found the Forbidden Library," she said, not bothering to turn around.

"Yeah," Dylan said. "Here, help me with the rest," he said, going back inside. There were still a handful of books left. Dylan was about to show Silo what he had found, but the drawings on the ice disappeared. Had he imagined them?

"What's wrong?" Silo asked, coming inside.

Before Dylan could respond, Silo slipped. He turned back, hearing her gasp, but before he could catch her, she caught herself, skidding to a stop in front of the bookshelf. Dylan's heart skipped a beat, relieved she hadn't fallen, but the concern he felt didn't immediately subside. As if nothing had happened, Silo began grabbing books and creating a small stack in her hands.

"As I was saying," she said, nervously chuckling, giving Dylan a lopsided grin.

"Um...nothing," Dylan said with uncertainty. He glared at the ice on the ground, shaking his head. There was nothing there.

They divided the rest of the books between the two of them and made their way back to Kai. For some reason, the Headmaster's words continued to resonate within Dylan, *unwavering conviction.*

When Silo and Dylan arrived at the podium, Kai was already looking through the books Dylan had given him. He had four of them spread out around him while the others were stacked near the podium. Silo and Dylan joined him, opening some of the books they had grabbed, adding the rest to Kai's pile. The covers were all blank, as well as the spine, making it impossible to know what each book was about without reading it.

Dylan opened the first book. The pages at first were blank, but words quickly rushed onto the page, turning into a language he could read. Dylan could feel his heart racing as he flipped through the book's pages.

Please be here, please, he begged as he turned the next page, diving deeper into the book.

The book he'd chosen was about a clock he'd never heard of. The clock that struck the end of life. He looked desperately at the pile they'd made. This was their last hope.

Chapter Twenty-Seven

Downtown looked much gloomier than usual. The truck that Arthur drove, with Cryis in the passenger seat and Ami in the back, finally crossed the river and arrived at the heart of the city. The clouds hung low over the sky, and a much colder breeze blew through the air. Even the buildings seemed to reflect the solemn mood this winter carried.

The people walking along the sidewalks and the cars whizzing past them seemed oblivious to the impending danger they could soon be in. If Aturdokht could turn Riley, a Hybrid, into a Demon, what chance did the humans stand? No matter how Cryis looked at it, he'd also been a part of Aturdokht's success in creating such an experiment. Just another failure he had to atone for.

Cryis looked out the window of the truck and into the sky. Even though the sun was out, the moon could already be seen. It was a faint white that he'd almost mistaken for a cloud. The blood moon had passed without Aturdokht causing an incident, but a war still loomed on the horizon. In fact, Cryis was currently in the middle of that war, holding back a battle he hoped the humans would never come to know of.

Cryis's thoughts wandered to Agent Kanon. He hadn't spoken to the agent since he and his friends had left the prison. Cryis had at least managed to free him from a Demon's clutches, but the trauma left behind would be a different experience. He hoped Kanon was okay. If he was, Cryis had no doubt Kanon was doing his best to prevent the secrecy of Aris Magica from being revealed. But it wasn't as if Aturdokht was in a rush to reveal Aris Magica's great magic to the world as she had been in the past.

She's changed, Cryis thought.

When he'd known her as Mirama, she wouldn't have hesitated to be the first to strike. But all of that could change soon enough if Aturdokht got her hands on all three Elementals. Cryis clenched his fist while he stared out the window. He couldn't figure out which was worse: Aturdokht using the Elementals or releasing her experiments on Aris Magicians and humans.

It was more important than ever that they got to the library quickly, Cryis had to find a way to pass the Elemental to Arthur without his immortality before he found a way to wake up Jay.

"Take a right on Southwest Avenue," Cryis said as Arthur approached the third light on the street.

The truck began to turn as Cryis glanced towards the backseat. Ami was sound asleep with her head resting on the window.

"She could use a hospital," Arthur mumbled.

He'd been quiet for the past hour until now. As they started to drive down another street, the buildings became taller as they neared closer to the heart of downtown.

"I know. But she stopped the bleeding," Cryis said in response.

He began to feel a small web of magic running through the streets as they came closer to the library's entrance. The quiet hum of magic steadily grew around them.

"Cryis," Arthur began. Out of the corner of his eyes, Cryis noticed Arthur gripping the wheel tight until his knuckles turned white. "Aris Magica can be dangerous."

Cryis looked over at Arthur and wondered what could be going through the boy's head. He suddenly felt a tinge of guilt. If the two of them had never met, would Arthur's fate still be the same?

Cryis didn't have to think long before he found an answer. If the two of them never met, Arthur wouldn't be ensnared in the problems of Aris Magica.

Despite this, a sadness began to overwhelm his heart. Cryis was glad he met Arthur, and part of him couldn't imagine a world where he hadn't.

"Yes, it can be," Cryis replied. "But it can also be beautiful."

As dangerous as magic was, there was also a beauty to it that no one could deny. Cryis would miss magic and Aris Magica. The day he would no longer be a part of it was nearing closer. And the closer they got to the library, Cryis had an inkling feeling that his time as an Immortal was coming to an end very soon.

Even if he managed to pass the Elemental on to Arthur without his immortality, the Elemental was still responsible for Cryis's immortality. He wasn't sure what would happen to himself once it was gone.

"Was the person you've been searching for her?" Arthur continued, there was a sadness to his voice.

Cryis let out a heavy sigh, something he noticed he'd become accustomed to doing. If Arthur was the one to replace him, he might as well know everything, just in case Cryis were to fail. Cryis clenched his jaw; he'd been failing a lot lately.

"Aturdokht is a Witch whose crimes run very deep within both Aris Magica and the human world. She's also now the keeper of the Heart Elemental." Cryis remarked bitterly. "I'm still unsure how or when it became in her possession, but she has it now, and that's all that matters."

A longing that Cryis couldn't control seeped into his voice as he continued to speak, "But when I first met her, she wasn't as corrupt as she is now." Cryis thought back to when he had first met Mirama before she became the daughter of fire. Her intentions had been good, but her heart was just lost. "She used to believe humans and Aris Magicians could co-exist."

Arthur frowned in disbelief. "What happened?"

"Human betrayal." Cryis said, unable to help the disgust he felt. "And the second Aris Magica War further proved that it wasn't possible." He sighed. "But things change with time...always. I mean, look at us now, fighting alongside each other," Cryis said with hope. Arthur smiled.

"About the guy back there..." Arthur hesitated, cleared his throat, and then continued, "Were you two close?" He asked.

Cryis quirked an eyebrow, thinking he heard jealousy in Arthur's voice. He smiled to himself; it was only wishful thinking. Arthur had given him no reason to think his question had meant anything more. Cryis wouldn't be foolish to think that Arthur's kindness to him had been anything but that.

"Riley? No," Cryis stated, his voice breaking at the end. "He was someone close to Jay, Dylan, and Ami." He added. As Cryis spoke her name, he couldn't help but turn in his seat to glance at her. Ami hadn't moved and was still soundlessly asleep.

"I'm sorry..." Arthur whispered.

Cryis's mouth twitched into a sad smile; he was sorry too.

"Being an Immortal isn't always easy." Cryis admitted. "On the upside, you get to see the world from a new perspective. But for most parts of history, we observe and stand by until our purpose calls for us to interfere."

Cryis tugged at his seatbelt absentmindedly, readjusting it so that it was no longer digging into his shoulder. "As you know, Immortals must guide souls to their next life, but we all have an agenda we must fulfill as well. A reason why we were chosen per se."

Cryis recalled the promise he had made to Emilia, the first Ancient. Sealing Aturdokht and her growing magic away had taken everything out of her—including her life. On her last breath, she asked Cryis to guide the rest to do the same, as if she knew it wasn't her nor Aturdokht's last life. She had asked him to promise until her seventh reincarnation; then, it would finally be over.

"And after that?" Arthur asked solemnly.

A long silence passed between them. Although it wasn't the path Cryis wanted for Arthur, he no longer feared it for him. Arthur was strong, and Cryis knew once his time came to an end as an Immortal and Arthur's to a beginning, he could rely on him to rise to the challenge. He'd already proven himself capable many times. Knowing this, though, still didn't make it any easier.

"I move on, and the next unlucky soul is chosen."

Arthur seemed to force a laugh as he rubbed the back of his head. "Unlucky for sure." Cryis noticed Arthur's grip on the steering wheel tighten. "Move on, how?"

Cryis glanced at Arthur out of the corner of his eyes. Cryis hadn't thought about what was next for himself. He'd be free. Free to grow old, free to love. The idea almost sounded ludicrous—it had been so long since he'd truly had a choice in life. He wasn't sure how to answer, so he didn't.

"Make a left at the next light. It'll be on your right at the bank."

"Cryis," Arthur said, the tone of his voice causing Cryis to pause and look at him. Arthur came to a stop just short of the light and pulled over, allowing the car behind him to pass. He switched on the hazard lights, then turned to face Cryis.

Cryis glanced over his shoulder at Ami, but her eyes were closed, and her head still leaned against the window. He turned back to Arthur, meeting his gaze.

Cryis braced himself, seeing determination burning in Arthur's eyes but also passion. Arthur took a deep breath, and Cryis prepared himself to listen.

"This might not be the right timing, but I've given it some thought, and considering what's at stake, I want to tell you this before..." Arthur's voice trailed off, and he shook his head, reconsidering his words. Arthur sucked in a breath.

"The reason why I joined you wasn't because of some righteousness I felt towards doing the right thing. That was part of it...but it was mostly because of you." He paused, holding Cryis's gaze.

Cryis stared back at Arthur, speechless, and Arthur continued. "I like you. And I'm not talking about like you as a person but like you...like you." Arthur's determination changed to embarrassment and uncertainty all at once.

Cryis slowly began to smile, but it quickly started to fade. "Arthur..."

Arthur held up a hand, "No, let me finish, please." He met Cryis's gaze, and Cryis couldn't help but smile because of it. "I'm not just saying this because we can die at any moment." He sighed. "This has been on my mind for a while, and the more time I've spent with you, the more these feelings have grown from you being a crush to wanting to, I don't know, find out more about you...about us."

Cryis's heart swelled with each word Arthur spoke. The smile he'd worn just seconds before vanished, replaced by a profound speechlessness. Everything inside him told him to run, to protect Arthur from his destiny. He set his jaw, feeling the weight of his heart overpowering the logic of his mind. Maybe this once, it was okay for him to be a little selfish. He could worry about the future tomorrow.

Cryis felt his hand twitch at his side. He wouldn't let this be another one of his failures. Before Cryis could let his guilt talk him out of it, he quickly leaned in toward Arthur and kissed him. He wouldn't make any promises he couldn't keep, but he hoped this would at least give Arthur an answer to what he'd been feeling too.

He cupped Arthur's face in his hands and kissed him with everything he had. Cryis knew it wasn't the best kiss; he hadn't kissed another person in years. But when Arthur didn't pull away, Cryis's body relaxed. Instead, Arthur kissed him back with just as much passion.

He felt one of Arthur's arms reach over the center console and wrap around his waist, pulling him closer to him while his other hand found its way to his hair.

The kiss was everything and more. It was the first person Cryis had been with in a long time. His hands dropped to Arthur's waist, Cryis didn't want to let go. The kiss had felt like it lasted a lifetime, and when the two pulled away from each other, they were both panting slightly.

"Wow…" Arthur whispered after the space between them had calmed. A huge grin spread across his face. The action was contagious as Cryis found himself smiling, too. "That was…" Arthur's voice trailed off again into a laugh.

Cryis eyes widened, realizing what he'd done. "I'm so sorry, I didn't even ask. Was that okay?" He hadn't even asked him if it was okay to kiss him. Cryis had been caught in the moment, in his own emotions.

"No," Arthur rushed out, seeing Cryis's worry. "It was great!" He said, his smile never faltering. Cryis took a deep breath, relieved.

"About time," Ami muttered, her voice sounded like sandpaper when she spoke.

Both Cryis and Arthur's faces flushed red at her words. They turned back to look at her. "How long have you been awake?" Arthur asked.

"Long enough, trust me," Ami said with an eye roll. She shifted in her seat, pulling herself from the window. "But," she exchanged glances with them both, holding Cryis's gaze the longest. "I'm happy for you."

Cryis and Arthur smiled at each other. Who knew what the future could hold for them in the next moments, but Cryis knew he wouldn't regret what happened between them. As if Arthur had read his mind, he reached over and squeezed Cryis's hand.

"How about we finish this conversation later?" Arthur asked, offering a small smile.

Cryis nodded his head in agreement. After all, they did have a lot to talk about.

Arthur turned back to the wheel. He turned the hazard lights off and put the car in drive, preceding down the route he'd been pursuing before. He approached the green light and took a left turn down the road. A few moments later, Arthur came to another stop.

He pulled the truck into a spot on the side of the road. Not many cars were parked along the street, even though it was midday. Cryis looked out the window and up at the skyscraper before them.

A lady in a business suit walked through the revolving glass doors. She walked down the numerous steps and past their truck, not giving them a second glance. Cryis's gaze shifted back toward the building.

Above the glass doors was a sign with bold red and blue lettering. Cryis looked over at Arthur, whose mouth hung wide open in shock.

"You're telling me the Hidden Library is *hidden* in a Chase Bank?" He asked, amused. "I thought it would be in—"

Cryis unclicked his seatbelt. Aris Magica could be found in the most unexpected, guarded, or overlooked places.

"A library," Cryis said, completing Arthur's sentence. "Why would we hide the Hidden Library in another library?" He chuckled. Cryis couldn't help himself, but he found what Arthur said to be cute. "We'd have stragglers accidentally stumbling in Aris all the time."

"Do you even know the vault number?" Ami said groggily from the back seat.

Cryis found himself looking back at her again. Her face was still drained, but she had successfully pushed herself up into an upright seated position.

She glanced down at her missing arm and rolled her eyes. "What an inconvenience."

Cryis smiled, it was refreshing to see her back to her old self. "I might have a friend behind the counter." He opened the door and got out of the truck. "Let's go."

Ami looked over at Arthur, who was still leaning over the wheel, staring at the Chase Bank sign. "A bank…" He mumbled again, still in shock.

Ami smirked, "Aren't you coming?"

Arthur shook his head and turned off the truck. He stepped out of the driver's side, followed by Ami. The two of them followed closely behind Cryis as they walked up the stairs leading to the door.

The sun was setting over the horizon, playing against the glass's reflective lights. The bank would be closing soon. Cryis felt a tug on his shirt sleeve before he reached the top step. He looked back, finding Ami a step lower. She handed him his coat back, gesturing to the blood on his shirt.

"We can't go inside like this." She pointed to them all.

Thanks to their battle earlier in the forest, the trio looked worse for wear. Dirt, blood, and bruises covered their bodies. Except for Cryis, his skin was flawless as he had taken the remainder of the drive to heal. Ami did a double take, her eyes widening as she looked at Cryis.

Cryis uncomfortably pushed his hair behind his ears and shifted his gaze to the sky, avoiding her piercing gaze. "What?"

"Your eyes…when did they?" Ami stopped herself and then pointed to the glass door ahead.

Cryis ran to the revolving doors and stared back at his reflection. He was afraid his eyes had returned to being red. Instead, he found his eyes were their normal blue, but a gold ring encased his irises. It reminded him of the Elemental he guarded.

"What's wrong with them?" Arthur asked, coming up beside Cryis.

He gently rested his hand on Cryis's shoulder, and Cryis shifted his gaze to him. "Oh. It suits you," Arthur said shyly. Cryis smiled, then leaned over and kissed Arthur on the cheek.

Ami rolled her eyes with a smile of her own and pushed past them. "Let's go, lovebirds."

They walked through the doors and inside the building. Immediately, once on the other side, they felt out of place. Everything inside the building was mundane and polished. They walked slowly through the wide lobby, trying to draw little attention but failing. Everyone they passed either gave them a quick disgusted glance or a worried gaze. Cryis looked elsewhere, unbothered by their stares. He was used to the attention since he normally got it because of his white hair.

Cryis focused on the five receptionists who sat behind a long beige desk. A plastic wall sat between them and the customers they helped. Off to the side were groups of individual desks stuck inside glass-boxed rooms. Behind each desk was an employee typing away on their keyboards. From the lobby, he could also see the offices on the floors above them. Each level was blocked off by a glass railing.

As they neared the desk, a small round of black couches was set up to the side as a waiting area. Before they could make their way to it, one of the spaces at the receptionist counter opened. Cryis's eyes lit up, recognizing her.

"This way." Cryis ushered, walking quickly down the blue carpet that led to the counter.

Once at the open window, Cryis tapped his knuckles against the countertop and cleared his throat.

A woman with long box braids and dark eyes was busy typing on her computer. She had yet to notice them. She wore a gray blouse and dark pants. The Chase Bank logo was pinned to her chest right above her nametag, which read Aireena.

"Rea," Cryis whispered after she didn't respond.

The woman slowly looked up, revealing a faint line of freckles under her eyes. Her eyes widened with shock, but when she smiled, her entire face lit up. Cryis couldn't help but return her smile. She looked around as if she'd committed a crime before returning to staring at him, but she failed to hide her excitement.

"What are you doing here!" She chuckled. "What the hell happened to you?" She asked, quickly assessing him.

Cryis laughed as well. It had been a while since he'd last seen her. The last time had been a couple of years ago when they both were at the council headquarters in Aris Magica.

Although she didn't look like it, Aireena was an Immortal and one of the few Immortal friends he had. But she chose to wear a wig and contacts to better blend with the human world in order to complete her purpose. Cryis understood why; most Immortals he'd met held no shame in the way they looked, but Aireena hadn't been immortal for long and was still getting used to it.

Cryis's smile slowly disappeared as he remembered what he was here for. "I need a favor."

Aireena's smile faded, "Oh, no." She looked around again. "You know I'm not supposed to let anyone inside this way unless the council deems it necessary."

"Since when?" Cryis asked, confused. He'd never heard of the council dictating passage into Aris Magica, not since the first war, and that was only to protect humans during the dark times.

Aireena's face softened, "That's right, you weren't at the last meeting a couple of weeks ago." She sighed, leaning forward on the counter. "Some great evil beings have made their way back into Aris. Demons and Fae have become restless both behind and outside of the gates. So, the council has been in distress these days, trying to get a hold of the situation before it got even more out of hand. Thank God the humans haven't noticed anything," she added, waving her hand in front of her face.

"Evil beings?" Ami whispered beside Cryis.

Cryis knew what she was thinking—he was thinking the same thing—Aturdokht. The council knew she had awoken and that Jay had failed, but they were keeping her presence a secret. Even in the past, every time she'd been reborn, the council never mentioned her by name. The only ones who knew of her were the council, a few Immortals who were still around from that time, and a few trusted Magicians who had passed the knowledge down from generation to generation.

Cryis couldn't blame them, at the beginning of Aturdokht's rise to power, she'd obtained quite the following among other Witches, Demons, Faeries, and other breeds before Emilia had sealed her away.

"Please, Rea, the world is at stake," Cryis begged.

Aireena rolled her eyes. "When is it not?" Cryis smirked at her response.

She pulled out a golden keycard from under her desk and slid it into the small window beneath the plastic. "Take the elevator to the basement. The vault you're looking for is B12. It'll be in the back of a room all on its own," she whispered. Then, louder, she said, "Thank you for banking with Chase Bank."

Cryis took the card, sliding it into his pocket. "Thank you," he whispered. Aireena smiled and then gestured her hand to the left, towards the elevators.

Cryis and the others walked quickly towards them, pressing the down button. There were two elevators, and both of them seemed to take forever before one finally made its way to their level. Once inside, Cryis finally felt like he could breathe. They were so close now.

They rode down to the basement in silence, so many thoughts raced through Cryis's mind, but not enough time to process them all. Cryis looked at the numbers ahead as they blinked across the screen as the elevator continued to descend two floors down. He needed to find a way to pass the Elemental safely to Arthur without his immortality attached to it, but before that, he needed to free Jay.

Cryis had a growing hunch. Perhaps he could use his Elemental to pull Aturdokht's soul free from Jay like he'd done with the Demon in Riley. Then, they could find a way to temporarily bind her soul with his Elemental until they got their hands on the Infinity Staff.

Every time he'd faced Aturdokht, he'd noticed the fear in her eyes whenever he showcased his Elemental, Cryis began to assume she was afraid of it for that reason. Still, Cryis didn't have full control over his Elemental; he killed Riley by attempting to free his soul, and he would have killed Taybeith if Aturdokht hadn't stopped him.

The elevator creaked as it came to a stop and slowly opened. The vault floor was a narrow room. It stretched underneath the building like a maze. Narrow paths led to small, enclosed rooms.

At the beginning of their walk, the rooms contained small lockers with numbers assigned to each one. The numbers then turned to letters as the lockers transformed into silver vault doors, two to each room. The further they went, the more spacious the rooms became as the vault doors grew larger. Huge metal circular plates with bars locked the doors into place. Each one had a magnetic slot for a keycard.

"She said B12, right?" Ami asked, pointing to a sign that hung from the ceiling. Off to the left was a white sign with the letter B, bolded with an arrow pointing straight ahead.

They followed the sign and found room 12. Inside was a silver vault identical to the others they had passed, but it was the only one in the room. Cryis went up to it and inserted the gold card Aireena had given him. The vault took it, and gears began to click in acceptance.

The vault's door changed from silver to gold. Carvings of ancient Aris Magician inscriptions began to form in the circumference of the door, creating a text that spiraled towards the center of the metal. The words faded, replaced by a carving of a tree whose branches stretched out across the vault's door and onto the walls of the small room.

"Wow," Cryis heard Arthur whisper.

Cryis smirked, *that wasn't even the best part.*

Cryis turned the wheel on the vault and opened the door. A wave of magic washed over them as Cryis pushed the door completely open. Inside was a plethora of books and a room bigger than what a normal vault could hold.

A set of spiral stairs along the wall led them deeper into the library. Above them, books were soaring through the air, and floating bookcases danced in response as the books found their way back to their shelves. The inside of the vault was like a cave, and the walls were rigid and rock-like, but the ceiling was like a black sea, speckled with tiny, white stars that seemed to glow.

On the ground, the bookcases were lined in long rows that led directly toward the center of the room, but from the stairs, it was difficult to see the center of the room over the tall bookshelves before them.

"So, this is magic," Arthur said, amazed. "It's beautiful."

Once they reached the ground, they stepped onto a patterned floor. It was a rippling blue rimmed with gold rays that led to the center. Tiny constellations lined the pattern, overlapping the gold lines. Cryis recognized it instantly as a star map as he noticed Orion's Belt ahead.

"At the heart of the library, there's a book. Essentially, it's a table of contents," Cryis explained as he began to walk along the gold lines, disappearing into the rows of bookshelves. "It'll be easier to navigate this." He gestured to the library around them. At first glance, there appeared to be no organization to any of the books because the books weren't organized by author but by content.

Cryis led the way down the aisle. He ducked, causing the others to do the same, as a book came hurtling from above them and into an empty slot on the bookshelf they'd just passed. Cryis noticed Arthur's look of amazement as he watched the book fit itself perfectly in place.

Although it hadn't appeared so on the staircase, the center was much further than Cryis had originally thought. Cryis took the time to scan the shelves they passed, hoping to get lucky and find what they needed, but nothing useful caught his eye.

As they neared closer to the center, Cryis heard the faint sounds of whispers but thought he was mistaken. Moments later, he came to an abrupt halt, causing Ami and Arthur to nearly collide with him.

"What is it?" Ami peeked from behind him.

Cryis put a finger to his mouth. "Do you hear that?" Hushed voices were coming from up ahead, from where the path slightly curved at the end.

Cryis motioned for his team to follow him quietly. He patted himself for a weapon smaller than his scythe, and when he came up empty, he wished he'd grabbed something from the duffel bag in the trunk before coming inside. He doubted the others had anything to offer either. His scythe would be hard to maneuver in a tight space.

Cryis was the first to round the corner. The center of the room was a wide circle with rays shaped like the sun in the middle. On top of the sun was a large podium with a weathered book lying on top of it. Sitting below the podium was a girl with dark skin and blue hair, sharpening a spearhead while overlooking a book in her lap.

On the other side of the podium was a muscular boy with red flaming hair. He was the first to notice them. He dropped the book he had been reading in exchange for the two curved axes that had been hanging from his hips.

"Who the hell are you?" The boy glowered.

Cryis looked past him and at the boy who stood over the closed book on top of the podium. His brown hair was a lot shorter than it had been the last time Cryis had seen him. He also had a few more cuts and scars to add to his collection, particularly one that went straight across his right cheek and into the bridge of his nose. The only thing that hadn't changed was the heavy look in his storm-gray eyes. Cryis let out a sigh of relief.

"Dylan."

Chapter Twenty-Eight

Cryis could barely believe his eyes. Dylan looked up from the book he was standing over, and Cryis recognized it as the Omnes—the very one he had intended to find upon reaching the center.

Why is it closed? Cryis thought, but he didn't have time to process it before Dylan finally spoke.

"Cryis," Dylan said, his eyes showing his relief and surprise to see them. Ami came from behind Cryis at the sound of Dylan's voice. "Ami!" His smile widened further.

Cryis felt his heart rise to his throat. He couldn't contain how happy he was to see him and unhurt as well. He walked to Dylan in large strides, unable to keep his distance any longer, Ami right on his heels.

Dylan moved from behind the podium and around the red-headed man. Cryis held out his arms, embracing Dylan once he reached him. He could feel both Ami and Dylan shaking with tears as they were pressed against his chest. Cryis couldn't help the tears that fell from his eyes, dropping on Dylan's shoulder.

"I thought you were dead," Ami said between sobs. "Or I thought Aturdokht had made you like..." She stopped herself and instead buried her head into Dylan's chest and cried more.

Cryis suddenly felt a wave of remorse in his chest. He let go of Dylan, taking a step back. Dylan smiled at him, but Cryis turned his head, unable to meet his gaze. He slowly looked back to see Dylan reaching for Ami's half-arm. His fingers grazed over the stub as concern riddled his face.

"What happened?" Dylan asked.

Ami shook her head against his chest and started to cry even harder. Dylan gently rubbed Ami's back, consoling her. He looked at Cryis, giving him a wary glance while looking for an explanation. Cryis shook his head in response, unable to give him one.

Cryis couldn't bring himself to tell Dylan the truth, so he said nothing. He knew how much Riley meant to Dylan, and knowing he'd lost him would destroy him. Especially once he found out how Jay was involved. Therefore, Cryis feared for when he would ask about it.

"You've seen Aturdokht?" The blue-haired girl from earlier stood to her feet. She leaned her spear against the podium, walking over to them.

Ami pulled away from Dylan and wiped her face with her sleeve. "Who are you?"

Cryis knew what she was without her having to say it. The two companions Dylan traveled with were Fairies. The two favored each other in the face but still had striking differences.

Cryis narrowed his eyes, staring at the girl a little harder. Her eyes held a dark shimmer to them, something he'd only ever seen in a Faery. The shimmer grew with the amount of times the Faery dream wove. Most knew nothing about the small trait, but Cryis had been around long enough to figure it out. He withheld his reservations; if Dylan had befriended her, then there was nothing to worry about. Cryis trusted his judgment.

"This is Silo and her brother Kasid," Dylan said, introducing the two. Cryis saw a glimmer of a smile on Silo's mouth as Dylan said her name.

"We're Hunters," Silo said proudly.

Cryis resisted the urge to roll his eyes. He'd met Hunters before. They were the council's way of meddling in affairs they couldn't directly handle because of Aris Law.

Ami pointed to herself. "I'm Ami, and this is Cryis and Arthur, um, he's a..." She looked back at him, hesitant. "A bodyguard," she said with a shrug in an attempt to pass it off as nonchalant.

"A human," Kai said angrily. He began walking in Arthur's direction, causing Arthur to flinch away.

Cryis stepped in between his path. "A friend," he corrected sternly.

Kai stood before Cryis, glaring up at him. Cryis was a head taller than he was. Kai's angered eyes narrowed, but Cryis didn't move, nor was he intimidated. He'd faced fiercer foes than a hot-tempered teenager.

"Careful," Cryis warned, already seeing a rebuttal building in Kai's eyes.

"How dare you bring a human into Aris Magica territory." Kai said.

Cryis unclenched his jaw; Kai was right. After the second war, humans and Aris Magicians created boundaries. One of the unsaid rules was that humans were no longer allowed into Aris Magica territory, hence the use of pocket dimensions that only Aris Magicians could see and hide in—unless a human was invited in.

Cryis had his reasons for ignoring the rules of Aris Magica, aside from trusting Arthur, he needed him to be here. He looked nervously back at Arthur. But he couldn't possibly tell Kai what those reasons were without telling Arthur, and he wasn't ready for that yet. Cryis sighed, pinching the bridge of his nose.

"He's important enough," Cryis said as he turned his gaze back to Kai. "Perhaps the key to putting us a step ahead of Aturdokht," Cryis admitted. Behind him, Cryis heard Arthur shift uneasily from one foot to the other. Cryis knew he couldn't continue hiding the truth from Arthur, but he didn't want to burden him.

Kai looked ready to argue, but Dylan was quick to step between the two of them. "So, you really have seen Jay?" He asked, diverting the conversation.

Cryis nodded sadly, but the hope in Dylan's eyes didn't fade. "Her spirit is trapped deep within herself."

"Meaning she can't be saved," Silo said. Dylan glared at her.

"No, we have a way," Cryis insisted. "But first, Dylan," he took a deep breath, slowly letting it out.

There was so much to tell him, but Cryis knew he had to tell Dylan about Riley sooner rather than later. No matter how much it would hurt, he owed him at least that.

"Dylan, there's something I need to—"

"Wait." Dylan looked lost in thought, finally looking up to meet Cryis's gaze. He hadn't been paying attention. "We met the council." Everyone in the room grew gravely silent.

Cryis looked at Dylan, shocked. It was rare that the council granted an audience with anyone, meaning they deemed Dylan a necessary solution to the problem at hand. Cryis held his breath, awaiting Dylan's response.

"They know about Aturdokht's awakening and about what happened to Jay. They'd been monitoring the situation long before any of us even knew of her fate," Dylan explained. "But they said they can't interfere with the works of an Ancient...not directly anyways. But we found a loophole..." He hesitated, glancing back at Silo and Kai for approval; both nodded. "They gave me...I mean us, a chance to save Jay, and if we can't..."

"Destroy her," Kai finished.

"But you can't do either. Not without the Infinity Staff," Ami said, even though her statement had sounded more like a question as she looked to Dylan for assurance.

"We know," Silo said.

"I might be able to raise the Infinity Staff without Jay. That's part of why we're here," Dylan further explained.

"What, how?" Cryis asked, taken aback.

He knew Dylan played an important role in calling forth the staff, but he never expected him to be able to master it alone. Cryis noticed Dylan rubbing the inside of his wrist. The trident did appear on him first before it had Jay.

In the past, the Ancient only ever bore the symbol. This new development was intriguing. If Dylan could call forth the staff by himself, then once Cryis extracted Aturdokht's soul from Jay, then there was a chance they could end this battle once and for all. Cryis thought about it longer and began to pace back and forth while Dylan explained.

"I feel it, but every time I try to call for it, it's just out of reach," Dylan confessed. He gestured to the nameless books behind him. "We thought we'd find something here, but—"

"It's been another dead end," Kai confessed.

Cryis stopped pacing and looked over at Dylan. "Great, so like I said, no Infinity Staff." Ami huffed. Dylan looked away, disappointed.

Cryis couldn't shake the feeling that Dylan was on to something. "Keep looking. There must be something."

"The Elementals," Silo said, causing Cryis, Arthur, and Ami to exchange glances. "Oh, so you've heard of them," Silo added, noticing their reactions. "Then you know there's three."

"Yes, and Aturdokht has one," Cryis added. "Aturdokht has Heart."

Silo and Kai looked at Cryis, but he was unable to read their expression.

Cryis still had no idea how Aturdokht had come to possess the Elemental or for how long she'd had it. Maybe she'd had it since the beginning but was waiting until the last Ancient reincarnation to pull her trump card.

Cryis felt Ami place a hand on his shoulder. She smiled, reassuringly. "It doesn't matter. There's still two she doesn't have."

"No," Silo said, guilty. "We lost the Life Elemental to Phagos." Ami gasped, looking at Dylan, but he stared at the ground, avoiding their gazes. Cryis saw his fist clench at his side.

Cryis's heart dropped again. The Headmaster had been the keeper of the Life Elemental. He looked nervously at Ami. If Phagos had it, then that could only mean the Headmaster died in the process of protecting it.

Cryis caught Arthur also looking at Ami; his gaze shifted, connecting with Cryis. Cryis watched as Arthur came to the same conclusion as he had. The two of them shared a sorrowful look before dropping their gazes back to Ami.

"That's just great..." Ami mumbled, not understanding the full weight of the situation.

Cryis looked at Dylan, waiting for him to tell her what he suspected, but Dylan couldn't bring himself to look at her.

Cryis sighed. "Then the Headmaster is...I assume dead?" Dylan looked slowly over at Cryis but still didn't say a word.

Ami's eyes widened, filling with tears, she bit her bottom lip before she bowed her head. Cryis hesitated to say more. His heart ached for her; she was trying her best to hide her pain.

"Dammit, not again," Ami whispered, barely loud enough for him to hear.

Cryis was about to lift his hand and put it on her back when she abruptly raised her head with a forced smile on her face, surprising him.

"But at least we still have one." Ami added.

"What?" Kai said, stepping forward.

Cryis turned towards him after giving Ami a worried glance. She refused to look at him, but he could see her fist shaking at her side as she fought to keep herself together.

"You have the Soul Elemental?" Kai asked, slightly bewildered. He looked back at Silo and then Dylan. "We've been searching this damn library for hours for info on that thing, so how did you three find it first?"

Ami slapped Cryis across the arm. "Well, it turns out it was a walking, talking one."

Cryis laughed shyly as everyone turned to stare at him. "Turns out I had one sleeping inside of me," Cryis admitted.

"Okay, this is good," Silo said energetically. She grabbed Dylan's hand and squeezed it. "The Soul Elemental is a powerful one; we can still use it to take down Aturdokht."

"Are you crazy!" Arthur nearly shouted. He'd been silent for a long time, leaning against the bookshelf and watching the others. "One Elemental against two! We barely stood a chance against her when she only had one!"

Cryis put a finger to his lip. The library didn't take kindly to loud voices. As if on cue, a book came hurtling at them.

Kai knocked it out of the sky angrily. "What do you even know?" Kai hissed.

"He's right," Ami confessed. "She pretty much wiped the floor with us without even using the full power of her Elemental. But at least we nearly finished off Taybeith."

"That bastard is still alive?" Dylan asked.

"And mostly Demon too," Ami confirmed. "Aturdokht is planning to turn everyone into these half-human, half-Demon experiments."

"Even more reason to try to use the Elemental to kill her!" Kai whispered harshly. He gave Dylan a sideways glance, "Since there's not much hope on the Infinity Staff."

"No! There's another way!" Ami rushed out. Cryis attempted to warn her with a gaze, but she didn't notice. "We fought two of her experiments, and Cryis was able to pull the soul out of—" Tears began to rush down Ami's face as she suddenly stopped.

Kai looked at his sister and Dylan in a panic, stumbling over his words. "I didn't mean to make you cry," he mumbled, rubbing his head and looking anywhere but at her.

Dylan frowned, "Ami, what is it?" He looked to Cryis, but Cryis couldn't hold his gaze for long, if he did, he knew Dylan would be able to see the guilt he carried.

Dylan sighed, "Look, our main priority should be to figure out how to free Jay's spirit and to find Riley. Maybe he'll know what to do. He's a Weapon Master like me, and the staff is just another weapon. I'm not giving up on it." Dylan looked wistfully at Cryis and then Ami. "I was hoping he would've been with you; the two of us got separated."

Cryis flinched at Riley's name. He glanced at Dylan, afraid he would notice, but he didn't since his gaze was now on Ami.

"Fine. We find Aturdokht, but I'm going to stop her no matter what because that's what the council trusted us to do," Silo affirmed.

"We talked about this," Dylan said harshly.

"What choice do we have? We're clearly out of time!" Silo challenged. "Once she perfects that experiment of hers, then both the human world and Aris Magica are in danger. And if she gets her hands on the last Elemental, who knows what will happen." She searched Dylan's eyes with a pleading expression, "I thought you understood that."

"And how do you plan to do that? No one other than an Ancient can take her down," Cryis said darkly. "Even if Dylan manages to get the Infinity Staff, he won't be able to destroy her. Its full power only works for the Ancient."

"And we're just supposed to believe that because history has said so," Ami said surprisingly, taking Silo's side. "It's not like anyone other than an Ancient has tried to stop her before. And why not? Because of some law Aris set a long time ago?"

Cryis applauded their optimism but hated their naivety as they discussed the situation. Of course, others had tried to destroy Aturdokht, but only an Ancient held that absolute magic because of the bond Mirama and Emilia held before becoming enemies. A bond that strong no one could break, despite how much time had passed.

If they tried to attack Aturdokht with the Soul Elemental, even together with their magic combined, all they would do is injure her temporarily, if that. To destroy her, the responsibility lay with Jay. Otherwise, the cycle would continue to repeat itself.

"We have a plan. It'll take two steps, but it'll put us ahead of her," Cryis began. "We use the Soul Elemental to pull Aturdokht's spirit from Jay, and hopefully, that awakens her own." He confessed. "And then I pass the Elemental on to someone else, someone she wouldn't expect," Cryis looked back at Arthur.

"Can you do that?" Silo asked at the same time her brother said, "Him?"

"Me?" Arthur said, astounded, pointing to himself.

Cryis nodded with a sad smile, keeping his eyes fixed on Arthur. He saw the hurt, sadness, and confusion in Arthur's eyes and wanted to tell him how sorry he was for keeping the truth from him.

"He can do it," Ami confirmed. "We came here to find a way, but it hasn't worked the way we thought it would the last two times..." Her voice trailed off again as she looked at Dylan. Cryis held Arthur's gaze for a moment longer before finding the courage to look at Dylan.

Dylan frowned again, but this time, he didn't let it go. "First, Cryis, then you, and now this boy," he gestured to Arthur, "is looking at me strange." Dylan mumbled.

Cryis sucked in a shaky breath. He had to tell him.

He walked over to Dylan, placed both of his hands on his shoulders, and pulled him into a hug. "We saw Riley," Cryis said in a whisper. Upon hearing his name, Dylan's body went rigid up against Cryis.

"She'd used him as an experiment." The heaviness in Cryis's heart continued to grow, "I tried to use the Elemental to free him, but it was too late. Maybe if I was earlier then..." Cryis stopped himself, unable to make an excuse for why he'd failed. "I'm sorry," was all he could say.

Cryis felt a tear fall onto his shirt and then another until they kept coming. Cryis squeezed Dylan tighter, heartbroken. Dylan pulled away from Cryis with his head bowed. He stormed from the center of the room and into the maze of bookshelves, disappearing.

Ami began to go after him, but Silo stopped her. "I'll go." Ami looked slightly annoyed, but she stepped back, allowing Silo to go past her.

Cryis could feel his tears starting to rise as well. He bowed his head and stared at the floor, trying to focus on the gold lines instead of the empty pit in his heart.

"I'm sorry," he whispered again.

Arthur came up beside him and gently patted Cryis on the shoulder. "Let's just look for what we came for," he said to both Cryis and Ami. "Give him some time. Okay?"

Cryis sniffed and whipped his face with the back of his sleeve. He let Arthur guide him to the Omnes, lying closed on top of the podium. Before Cryis had a chance to start, Arthur stopped him. "We should talk," he said, quietly enough for the others to not hear.

Cryis tensed. He'd just accomplished one battle only to walk right into another. He knew what Arthur wanted to know. But, like with Riley, he wasn't ready to talk to him about it yet.

"Why me?" Arthur asked. "I mean, I get the element of surprise. But anyone else's hand would make for a better protection detail for that much magic."

"Because you were chosen."

Cryis took a deep breath, taking in the glory of the book before him. It was bound by an old brown, tattered leather with gold string woven into the outer binding. The pages were thick, with a gold lining on each one. Cryis held out his hand over the book's blank cover. He felt the magic from the book tremble and reached up to touch his fingertips as the book answered his desire for knowledge. The pages of the book rapidly turned as magic streams shot into the air above it. Kai gawked at him, looking at the book and then back to Cryis as he easily controlled its contents.

"And no one can escape their destiny," Cryis stated.

Chapter Twenty-Nine

Dylan heaved in another strained breath. He clenched his shirt in his fist around his heart. His chest was bursting with pain, and the tears wouldn't stop falling. He leaned against the side of the bookshelf. He wasn't exactly sure how far he'd gone from the others. Everything had been a blur as he'd run from them.

Riley...

Dylan punched the ground. Another piece of him was gone while another piece returned. As overjoyed as he was to see the others alive after believing them to be dead, he just couldn't believe that Riley was gone.

Dylan punched the ground again and again until his knuckles were bruised. After everything Riley had done for them, how could Taybeith and Aturdokht treat his life so recklessly?

Dylan punched the ground a final time, and his skin broke as blood smeared across his knuckles.

Riley had died a monster. He hadn't even been himself, which made the pain of losing him even worse. Dylan thought back to the first time he'd met the man. He'd been so open and kind to him, the first adult Dylan had been able to trust in a long time.

After his parents died, no one wanted anything to do with him or Jay, even his own family. Riley had been there. Dylan cherished Riley like his own father.

Dylan hugged himself, letting his tears flow freely. He couldn't fight them anymore. He screamed, not caring about the books that came hurtling toward him. He let them hit his body and roll to the floor. Feeling their pain was better than facing his own.

"How could you?" Dylan whispered.

How could Jay sit by and do nothing while Aturdokht used her—Dylan stopped himself. It wasn't her fault; Jay was as much of a victim as Riley had been to this cruel fate.

"Wow, what did the carpet ever do to you?" Silo asked, appearing in front of him.

Dylan didn't have the energy to look up. His eyes met the dirt caked on the tip of her boots. "Not in the mood, Sy," Dylan whispered, using her nickname for the first time.

"That's too bad."

She sat down beside him and rested her hand on his shoulder. She wrapped her arm around his, resting her other hand on his shin. Dylan leaned into her body, resting his head on her chest.

"I'm sorry about your professor."

Dylan bit down hard on the inside of his lip to stop it from quivering, but it was no use. Aside from Riley, he'd also noticed Lyid hadn't been with them either. He'd lost so much already, and the list was only growing.

Silo gently ran her fingers through his hair with her free hand. In a coaxing voice, she whispered comforting words, "It's okay. Cry all you want. I'm here."

"Shit," Dylan said as his body released itself, and his tears turned to sobs once more.

Silo continued to whisper into his ear, she turned her body into his and hugged him. Dylan clung to her, crying into her shoulder. He squeezed her tight, afraid if he didn't, she'd disappear too. He wasn't sure how much more he could take.

"It'll be okay," Silo said. "Maybe not now, but one day. This won't all be for nothing. I promise."

He felt her plant a kiss on his temple and embrace his body with her arms. He clung to her as sobs racked his entire body. He buried his head into her chest, letting go of the feeling he'd been fighting, the sadness, the torment. He let it all fall out with every tear.

Dylan closed his eyes, letting himself fall into the darkness of his mind. He let Silo's gentle words coax over him like a blanket. He felt hopeless and lost—unable to fight the pain that threatened to swallow him. Instead, he let it consume him, let it push him deeper into his mind. It felt like a sea of black water overtook his body, pulling his consciousness down into the depths of his soul.

When Dylan opened his eyes, he found himself in his Soul World. He felt his body take a deep breath; he could still feel the warmth of Silo's arms around him, as well as her voice echoing off the walls of his mind.

Dylan's Soul World was empty like everyone's should be. Beside the small light that came from his depleted soul, it was entirely black. He moved as one with his soul, exploring the depth of where the darkness had taken him. He came across another light.

At first, it was faint before a gold light trickled on the ground and then expanded. Between him and the darkness stood the Infinity Staff. He felt its power resonating with his soul.

I've lost everything, Dylan said to the staff.

It was strange speaking inside of himself. He was highly aware of his voice bouncing off the walls, overshadowing the echoes of Silo's voice that still managed to reach him.

He'd gone deep inside himself, deeper than he'd ever been before. He recalled Jay telling him she'd visited her Soul World before and how at peace she felt inside herself. She explained it as an out-of-body experience. But Dylan just felt emptiness as he explored his.

The staff pulsated its magic, beckoning Dylan as it had done before when he first held it. He heard faint voices coming from it that he could barely understand, yet he knew they were calling for him to reach out.

Dylan had tried before, but every time, the staff had moved further away. Perhaps now he could reach it since he no longer cared enough to fight the darkness the power held. If that's what it took for him to reach Jay, he'd do anything.

His soul glided closer to the staff until he was right beside it. He could finally do it. His soul extended an arm; it was white and blue, almost flame-like, as it branched from his soul and towards the staff.

The moment Dylan touched it, a calm, unwavering sense of conviction flooded through his soul. He felt his insides burning, and a white light sounded from inside his soul.

The Infinity Staff emitted the same bright light. As the two lights met, Dylan watched as the staff turned into tiny beads of light as it flowed into his soul. The magic was overtaking his mind and body. He could feel the darkness tugging at the corners of the light. The voices he'd heard before screamed at him, but Dylan fought back. He wouldn't let them get in the way of stopping him from taking the staff's power.

Dylan had never possessed magic. Even though he was a Hybrid, his magic came in the form of skill. He couldn't do grand tricks like Ami or Jay. Before his first encounter with the staff, he never knew what holding magic felt like until now. It felt nice.

Dylan wasn't sure how much time had passed before he'd managed to settle down and pull himself free from his Soul World. It was almost like waking up from a dream. However, the inside of his wrist burned. The scar on his wrist tingled and hummed with the familiar sound of magic. Dylan was sure of it, that something inside of him had changed.

He slowly pulled away from Silo, but she held him tighter, stopping him. His face was only inches away from hers. She gently wiped the last of his tears away with her thumb.

"Better," she smiled.

Dylan blushed, embarrassed. The last time he'd cried this much was after losing his parents, and even then, he wouldn't let Jay see him like this. He noticed her eyes drop; he did the same, mimicking her gaze. His eyes fell to her lips. They were round and slightly red, and Dylan couldn't help but wonder if they were as soft as they looked.

"Yes...thanks," Dylan said, clearing his throat. He forced his eyes to look away, staring at the books on the shelf behind her.

Silo moved closer, "Of course," she whispered.

Dylan could feel her breath blow on his face. He wanted to pull away, but he didn't. He'd seen the way she looked at him when she thought nobody was looking, and he'd found himself doing the same. But Dylan had convinced himself that he didn't feel the same way, and he didn't want her in the same way, but his body stayed exactly where it was.

Dylan looked back at her, ashamed. He saw in her eyes that she wanted more. Did he? Was it possible to want someone else but also be interested in exploring what was right in front of him? Dylan already knew the answer to that.

He gently began to pull away again, but Silo made her move, her lips gently brushed over his, pausing there for a brief moment. Dylan froze, instinctively closing his eyes. Dylan felt the warmth of her lips against his, the air igniting with electricity between them. He caught a brief whiff of the familiar scent of lemons and mint that he had come to adore.

Against his lips, he felt Silo's voice fall into a soft chuckle. Instead, she placed a kiss on his cheek. He slowly opened his eyes, looking at her. Her lips lingered on his face for a moment longer before she slowly pulled away.

"Don't worry, I know you belong to another," she said, looking down at her lap.

She carefully raised her eyes, meeting him, "But I just want you to know that you're not as alone as you think you are," she said. "And..." Her voice trailed off. She shook her head and smiled instead. "Never mind. I'll tell you some other time."

Dylan smiled sadly. His hand went to his face, covering the spot she had kissed him. He was grateful to Silo, and part of him was happy she'd been the one to come after him, but he also couldn't deny the heartache he felt lingering between them. He knew his heart belonged to Jay, and Silo knew that she could never replace her. But Dylan still cared for Silo deeply, and that would never change.

"What are the others up to?" Dylan asked, changing the topic.

Silo stretched her arms up into the air and looked at the sky. "Your Immortal friend is looking for a way to break free Jay's soul by using the Soul Elemental without killing anyone this time."

Dylan thought for a moment, looking at the ground. Using the Elemental would be much safer than the Infinity Staff to save Jay.

It could work.

Dylan's gaze shifted to the trident scar on his wrist. Instead of it being black like a burn, it had turned gold. He stared at it in confusion. Had it happened when he'd touched the staff while in his Soul World?

Come to think...

Dylan pondered. It was almost as if Dylan could feel the staff in his hand. He felt confident that he could call forth the power when he needed it. It no longer seemed to be floating away from him but a part of him, coursing from his left wrist and into his hand.

Silo grabbed Dylan's chin, forcing him to look up, "Wait a minute," she moved her face closer to his, staring deeply into his eyes. "Have your eyes always had a gold ring around them?"

Dylan scrunched his nose in confusion. He knew his eyes were a stormy gray. Was it another trait of the staff?

"Weird," Silo said, letting go and not waiting for a response. She stood to her feet, brushing off her clothes. "Let's go," she held out her hand for him to take.

Dylan grabbed it, letting her help him to his feet. He thought back to what Silo had said. It was a solid plan. Once Cryis freed Jay, then he'd call upon the staff and use it to hold off Aturdokht until Jay could finish her off. He wasn't sure how far his limitations were when using the staff, but he knew he'd be able to use enough of its power, if anything, to stall Aturdokht. The long-lasting battle between the Ancient and a Witch would finally be over.

"Do you think it'll work?" Dylan asked Silo.

She grinned, "It has to." She stood to her feet, and Dylan did the same.

Silo led the way back to the others. Dylan kept close behind her. He kept the knowledge of the staff to himself. As much as he trusted Silo, he knew she and her brother had a different agenda. He didn't want to take any chances of them trying to use the staff once he did call it.

He only had one shot, and he knew Aturdokht would come at them with everything she had. At least from what Cryis had said during his fight with her, she hadn't used the full power of the Elemental against them, which assured Dylan. It meant that somewhere deep inside her, Jay was still fighting. They just had to do their part on the outside.

Dylan and Silo arrived at the center of the library. More books had accumulated since he'd been away. The others were knee-deep in them, looking for information. They'd even managed to get Kai to help. He laid on his stomach lazily across the bottom step of the podium, flipping through a book. Above him, Cryis read through the Omnes, the magic lines had returned, floating over his hair.

Dylan caught a glimpse of Ami. She peered at him over the rim of the book she held. When he locked eyes with her, she quickly looked away, blushing. Dylan smiled and walked over to her. He crouched down and pulled the book down, exposing the rest of her face. The book fell into her lap.

He stared at her; she looked the same as she always had. Her hair had gotten much longer, but her face was still bright, and her cheeks were rosy. Dylan smiled again. In the past, she had openly liked him and hated Jay; it was funny to see her trying so hard to save Jay now. His eyes fell on her missing arm.

"What happened?" He said gravely.

"Oh, this thing?" She lifted her shoulder, and the remaining part of her arm wiggled. "It's fine," she squeaked with a wry grin.

Dylan chuckled, glad to see she hadn't lost her humor. He glanced behind her at Cryis. Arthur was now at his side, pointing to something on the Omnes.

"Those two seem very close," Dylan observed. He could see an unspoken thing between the two. The same thing others had seen between him and Jay before he came to realize it on his own.

"Yeah." Ami's voice fell. "It's like watching you and Jay," she said, rolling her eyes with a smile. Dylan laughed as well, reminiscing on old times. "But," her voice suddenly became serious. "It's because Cryis believes Arthur is going to replace him as an Immortal soon," she said. "No more secrets," she mumbled, looking at Dylan out of the corner of her eyes.

"What?" Dylan whispered, alarmed. He nearly fell back on his butt. He felt the pain in his heart return. He wasn't sure how much more bad news he could take. "When?"

"I don't know," Ami said softly. "If it wasn't for that Elemental awakening, I don't think Cryis would be in this position," she said bitterly.

Dylan clenched his fist. "I can't lose another friend."

Ami gave him a hopeful but sad look. "You might not have to. I'm hoping once Cryis finds a way to transfer the Elemental to Arthur, then it'll stop eating away at what little immortality he has left." She picked up the book in her lap and opened it. "Who knows, Cryis might still live longer than us," she chuckled.

Dylan smirked. "He is resilient."

Dylan smiled again; if only Jay could see them now, taking a page from her book. Who would've thought he would reunite with everyone in a library?

Dylan looked off into the distance at the floating bookcases above. Soon, he would be reunited with the person he cared for most in the world. Dylan smiled to himself.

Just wait for me a little longer.

Across the room, the podium and the Omnes toppled over, barely avoiding hitting Kai. The book fell off the platform, crashing into the ground. Arthur began shouting, pulling Dylan from his daydream. Dylan looked over to find Arthur and Cryis engaged in a heated argument.

Chapter Thirty

"There has to be another way!" Arthur shouted.

Cryis sighed, picking up the podium and the book Arthur knocked over, setting everything upright. The Omnes had shown them the truth, and the library had sent them a book with the answers he sought. The Elemental decided the time it would be passed to another. Therefore, Cryis was stuck with it until his immortality left him.

"There isn't," Cryis said.

He turned to Arthur; the passion he'd seen earlier that day in his eyes was gone, replaced by anger. Cryis also noticed his teary, glazed eyes. He reached up, cupping Arthur's face in his hand. He'd just finished telling Arthur what would happen once he'd completed his purpose. The minute he had stepped foot in the library, he knew his time was nearing an end.

The book the Omnes had given them had shown him that he could use the Elemental to free another soul without killing them as long as the keeper had enough conviction to convince the Elemental to do so. However, the Elemental's magic also had a mind of its own, and until it was ready to leave its keeper, Cryis was powerless to go against it.

"Once my immortality is gone, you'll be immortal and a guardian. There's no changing this kind of destiny," Cryis confessed.

Arthur rested his cheek in Cryis's hand and closed his eyes. He lifted a single hand to cover Cryis's hand, which was cradling his face. Cryis felt the warmth of Arthur's hand seep into his.

"I wish there were another way," Arthur whispered.

Cryis softly smiled. He knew Arthur was looking for hope, but Cryis couldn't give it to him. There were only two ways to become immortal: to either be chosen or the gift passed down to you from another. Cryis had finally come to terms with the fact that there would be no way to resist the change from happening. Gradually, he was beginning to accept it.

Cryis slowly lowered his hand from Arthur's cheek to his neck, pulling his head forward until their foreheads touched. They were only a breath away now. Despite Cryis accepting his fate, he wasn't ready to let go of everything that would come with it. Cryis squeezed the back of Arthur's neck tighter. He wasn't ready to let go of all that he had found.

"We still have time," Cryis lied.

"Lots of it," Arthur smiled back.

Once Arthur was immortal, time would be endless for him but limited with the ones he loved. Cryis knew that better than anyone.

I'm sorry.

Cryis slowly pulled away, letting his hands drop to his side. He took a slight step back from Arthur. Hurt flashed across Arthur's eyes, a brief glimpse of vulnerability that tugged at Cryis's heart. For a moment, the weight of unspoken emotions hung heavy in the air. But just as quickly as it appeared, that hurt was replaced by a flicker of understanding as Cryis picked up the book that had delivered him the truth.

The book was warm to the touch. The binding was frail but well-kept. The cover sported a twisted blue flame with gold butterfly wings. It didn't need a title, for Cryis knew what it was the moment he'd seen it. The only words that decorated the front were written in small print at the very bottom: *Written by Aris, the first and last.* The very first Magician who founded Aris Magica and had found a way to harness Old Magic. Cryis smiled to himself. He hadn't been around that long to have met Aris, but of course, he would be involved with the Elemental's power.

"Is there a problem?" Kai said, sitting up on the step he'd been sprawled on. Ami looked up from across the room as well, just as curious. Kai tossed his book to the side.

Cryis had recalled when they first entered, Kai, Silo, and Dylan had been doing research on their own about the Elemental, although none of them had managed to find the book Cryis had called forth, Dylan had been able to find something quite interesting. Kai had explained that Dylan had found a room covered in ice.

The books they had found were all cold to the touch, but according to Kai, none of them had been useful to what they were looking for, but Cryis had reminded him that it didn't mean they didn't hold useful information. The library had shown them to Dylan, after all, for a reason.

Arthur grumbled something under his breath. Cryis caught the words Immortal and Elemental at the end of his sentence. Cryis glanced over at him and couldn't help but give him a stern glare. The others didn't need to know the extent of what the two had discussed. Arthur looked away, but Cryis could see the sorrow lingering in his eyes before he did.

Cryis sighed before he turned back to Kai, who was still awaiting an answer. Cryis decided to share what he had discovered about the Elemental, but nothing more. Everything else he had told Arthur was meant only for him, and Cryis wanted to honor that trust until Arthur had accepted his fate.

Cryis opened his mouth to explain, but before he had the chance to, the lights above them began to flicker, darkening the room. Cryis searched for Arthur, finding him with one foot on the platform and one foot on the step below it. Their gazes connected, and a heat of emotions raced through Cryis's heart. But as quickly as it came, Cryis averted his gaze, his eyes catching a glimpse of a flash of light.

In the center of the room, sand appeared, sifting between their shoes and creating a sandstorm in the air. A loud whistling wind broke through the silence as it lifted the sand from the ground and into a spiraling twister, separating Cryis and Arthur from Kai and Ami. Pages from the nearest books started to detach from their bindings and spin, following the same path as the sand.

"A sandstorm, seriously?" Silo shouted over the wind.

She was shielding her face with the back of her arm as she approached from behind one of the rows of shelves off to Cryis's left.

"Sometimes I hate magic!" Silo yelled to no one in particular. Still, Dylan nodded in agreement he was standing next to Ami, whose mouth was agape with what seemed to be surprise. Through the hazy sand, Cryis could see from Dylan's slightly swollen eyes that he had been crying.

"But how?" Arthur said, amazed, pulling Cryis's attention to him. He shielded his eyes with his arm from the sand and paper.

"Sometimes the library has a mind of its own," Cryis said barely above a whisper.

"What?" Ami shouted from the other side of the sandstorm.

Cryis shook his head, catching a glimpse of her through the cloud of thinning sand. "It's the library's way of telling you it's closing!" He shouted over the sound of the howling wind. "Upon that time, a door leading you to your heart's desire will appear as the library sends you on your way!"

"How could you forget to mention that!" Ami yelled.

Cryis shrugged, he'd thought it was common knowledge. He glanced over at Dylan, who looked less surprised to see the erratic magic. The wind began to calm as the pages and sand formed together, becoming a solid object. A single door stood between them. The words on the page aligned to form a doorknob framed against an array of colors.

"Just like the Wizard said, huh," Silo said to Dylan.

Cryis.

Cryis looked beside him, hearing the voice he knew again, but no one was there. Behind him, Cryis heard Arthur's hesitant voice as he stared at him, confused.

"Cryis?" Arthur's eyes searched his face, a mix of worry and rejection flashing across them.

But Cryis ignored him, his eyes landing on the door. The voice in his head grew louder, echoing around him, drowning out Arthur's call.

"Should we...touch it?" Ami whispered.

"No, don't." Kai said curtly.

It's time.

"It's calling to me." Cryis whispered, almost in a trance. He made a move toward the door.

Ami gasped. She left Dylan's side and ran over to Cryis, blocking his path to the door. "Not this again."

Dylan walked over to her side. "Why, what's wrong?"

Dylan stared at Cryis, but Cryis's gaze was fixed on the door behind him, his mind distant and his words barely registering. It was as if he were looking straight through Dylan.

Ami held her ground as she placed a hand on Cryis's chest. Cryis didn't move, but he looked down at her hand with unfocused eyes.

"It's this voice. Cryis thinks it's Jay, and she's been calling out to him, but I swear to you it's a trap." Ami explained.

"Are you sure?" Dylan challenged. Ami stared at Dylan, her mouth gaping, stumbling for words.

Cryis, there is little time. Hurry.

"Move," Cryis said, pushing past them both. He knocked Ami off balance, causing her to fall.

Dylan hastily caught her before she hit the ground. "Cryis, wait!"

The door opened as Cryis approached, a black empty void awaited him on the other side. Cryis could feel the voice rising inside of him, pulling him through. He closed his eyes, letting the darkness wash over him.

"Cryis, wait!" Dylan shouted again. In the distance, Cryis could hear footsteps rushing to catch him. But it was too late. "Arthur, no!"

"Cryis, please do—"

Cryis became swallowed by darkness as he stepped into nothingness while the door slammed shut behind him, swallowing up the last of Arthur's words.

The first thing Cryis felt was a cold draft biting away at his face. He opened his eyes to find himself in a vast field that had been transformed into a construction site. He recognized the bare trees, covered in ice, that surrounded a frozen graveled ground. Once upon a time, Cryis knew it as a meadow outside his village, but now the grass and dirt had been replaced by pavement and gravel from the off-beaten road to his right.

Mounds of gravel had been pushed into a pile to create a separation between him and the surrounding trees. Off to the side, nestled between two piles of gravel, there was a serene creek with floating chunks of ice that meandered deeper into the woods. Cryis knew if he were to follow it, he would find himself at the nearest city, Kansas City.

Cryis looked around, unable to see the moon as it hid behind the clouds in the sky. The air felt thicker in Missouri than it did in Portland and less salty. Cryis already missed the ocean breeze that would flow in from the mountains. He kneeled to the ground, sifting his hands through the frozen gravel. He could almost feel the forgotten grass beneath it. He was reminded of the memory Tarquin had shown him as he had been dying. Cryis knew it had happened exactly where he stood when the area had looked significantly different, barely touched by the advancements of man.

Everything around him seemed frozen in time, and although there was a wind, the trees didn't blow, nor did the gravel shift. Even though the creek's water was calm, Cryis could still feel the pocket dimension surrounding him, its magic sifting with the wind.

"You came," a familiar yet weary voice before him said.

Cryis slowly raised his head, looking up from the spot where he kneeled. He half expected to see Aturdokht standing before him, but instead, it was another. A young woman, her body as transparent as the moon's light. She stood before him, barefoot in a white dress that matched her hair and seemed to make her dark skin glow bright. Her hand was outstretched to him with a smile of gratitude on her face that lit up her blue eyes.

Cryis nearly fell back onto his hands. Everything began to make sense, the voice he'd been hearing but unable to place had neither been Jay's nor Aturdokht's but had belonged to her, his first.

"Princess!" Cryis said breathlessly.

Every fiber in his body came alive, tingling with excitement but also an immense amount of guilt as he started face-to-face with Emilia, the first Ancient.

He looked away from her, ashamed. He wanted so badly to apologize for failing her last wish to him. He'd failed to keep her last reincarnation safe, to keep the Ancient bloodline safe.

Emilia let her hand fall to her side and knelt so that she was even with Cryis's gaze. Her smile never faltered. She pulled him into a tight embrace, her spirit's body becoming tangible for only a moment. Cryis sunk further into the ground, feeling the warmth of her spirit against his, overwhelming him.

"Shhhh," she whispered soothingly, patting his head. "Rest now."

"No," Cryis squeezed harder. He'd been waiting a lifetime to say this. "I'm sorry, I'm so sorry. I failed," he confessed, heaving in a heavy, shaking breath. His body filled with an anguish of emotions he'd been holding back, falling down his face in warm tears.

Emilia hushed him, saying kind words in response, "You've done beautifully. You did not fail me nor yourself. Everything that has happened was meant to happen to my last reincarnation," she assured him. "All is right." Emilia pulled away. She cupped Cryis's face in her hand.

He pushed his cheek up against her palm, staring at her. He could easily get lost in her blue eyes. He'd always admired how much strength she possessed, even when knowing she was destined to die.

Cryis closed his eyes, taking in a calming breath before opening them. She was still smiling at him.

"I am most proud to have enjoyed this life with you," she said while she rubbed her thumb across his chin and lips. Cryis could feel the Elemental rise and calm inside him at her touch.

The Elemental's power began to consume his body as magic coursed through his fingertips, Cryis felt connected to every soul around him. He felt the ones in the ground who had passed, and he felt the ones outside the pocket dimension and further into the city. All of them called out to him as the Elemental's reach grew. This was its true power.

When Cryis opened his eyes, Emilia was gone, but straight ahead of him was Aturdokht.

The world around him had changed. Cryis could feel the cool grass beneath his legs as the meadow he remembered replaced the gravel. The trees were full of green, and the small creek had transformed into a rushing lake. Not a single trace of winter remained—only the vibrant essence of spring. Emilia's last parting gift to him: time had been turned back inside the pocket dimension.

After death comes life, Cryis thought as he rose to face Aturodokht.

She held a green orb of pure magic in her outstretched hand. Bits of magic residue seeped from the orb and fell onto the ground in a trail of liquid. The Life Elemental. Cryis knew it well. The Life Elemental could call forth the cycle of life: creation, death, and the most forbidden form of magic that no one other than the Elemental possessed, rebirth. It had the power to bring someone back from the dead with their soul still intact. The Elemental could only be used three times before it found another user.

Cryis noticed how much the Elemental was leaking, judging from the amount of magic seeping out, Cryis could tell it only had one use left. Without being told, he could guess what she'd used it on. Without Jay's body, Aturdokht was merely a soul, if he were to succeed, then she would need a new body. But Cryis knew she wouldn't want just any kind of body; she'd want her rebirth. The only thing left for the Elemental to give was death. Cryis sighed, his own Elemental allowing him to feel Aturdokht's desperation. Her red eyes glazed piercingly at him.

Aturdokht wore a red and black dress that fanned out in a train behind her as if she were attending an elaborate funeral. The end of the dress was tattered in flame-cut designs that were burning the grass beneath her. The collar of the dress went up to her neck, and the sleeves were sparkling sheer. In a way, she looked like a raven without its wings. Her hair was nearly entirely black, the only thing that remained white were the ends. Her eyes were lined with a dark liner that intensified her gaze.

Cryis closed his eyes, taking a deep breath. He searched for the sound of Jay's soul hidden deep within herself. He listened carefully, catching the soft thrum of her soul. It was faint, but she was still there. She was still fighting.

I found you.

Cryis released his breath and opened his eyes.

"Mirama," Cryis said, calling out to her lost soul. As she lowered her hand, the Life Elemental disappeared into her palm. "You've been busy." Cryis gestured to the Elemental as it vanished.

Aturdokht smirked, "You came." Then she laughed. "I didn't think it would work. Wonders, these Elementals."

Cryis knew she had summoned him alone so that she could strip him of his Elemental. *"Jevit."* His scythe appeared in his hands. Although she underestimated his power now that she had two Elementals, he would not do the same to her.

"Come at me with everything you've got," Cryis said calmly.

Rage flushed in her eyes. She didn't hesitate to call forth her magic. It was the first time Cryis saw her use the full power of the Elemental inside of her. Her chest seemed to glow as a storm of fire hotter than he'd ever felt began to surround her. The white flames licked the sky like the tails of a giant lizard. Cryis stared at her, amazed by the beauty of the flames. The flames were white, the hottest they could be, but traces of red swirled within them as if the Elemental's magic was mixing with her fire magic.

Cryis felt his power rise and reveal itself before him. He glanced over his shoulder, two transparent butterfly wings sprouted from between his shoulder blades, leaking with magic. Lightning bolts shocked the air around him, encircling his body in a field. Tendrils of gold strings made of magic flowed from the ends and corners of his wings, coming to his aid as he advanced toward Aturdokht.

Their powers clashed in fierce sparks and smoke as Cryis tried to break through the flames protecting Aturdokht. Waves of magic pulsed between them, flowing over the trees and grass and sucking the life from everything around them.

Fireballs tore away from the wall, shooting at Cryis and sending him hurling back into the ground. The other embers deflected off the magic tendrils that flicked them away. Cryis rolled in the ash-colored grass, dirt caking his clothes. He shed his coat before standing to his feet.

Cryis dug his scythe into the dirt. He directed his magic into it. The wings disappeared, but everything else remained as a portion of the Soul Elemental's power dived into *Jevit's* blade. Cryis swung his scythe with a significant amount of force as Aturdokht ran to him. The fire swarming her transformed into a whip. She grabbed ahold of both ends just as Cryis's scythe swiped the air where she stood, she blocked the blade with the whip, stopping it from touching her.

Cryis narrowed his gaze and gritted his teeth, putting everything he had into pushing down on his blade and breaking through her hold. The fear he'd seen in the past in Aturdokht's eyes was no more. She looked at him with eerie confidence as the corners of her mouth turned up in a smile as if she had a secret to hide.

Cryis could feel the Elemental taking the bait, begging to attack directly. The lightning whipped the ground beside them, igniting the grass in flames. While the tendrils of magic swarmed around him in a chaotic frenzy, Cryis withheld the power from disobeying him; he needed to wait for the right time if he wanted to pull Aturdokht's spirit free from Jay. Cryis couldn't explain it, but he had a feeling it would work this time. He felt more in sync with his Elemental than he had ever been.

Cryis's body began to warm from the stress of holding off his power. Beads of sweat fell from his forehead and onto his nose. Cryis took a deep breath, continuing to hold the string. He wasn't alone; he could feel Emilia's spirit deep within himself. She'd been the one there all along, guiding him. She would help him reach Jay.

Cryis kicked out his foot, knocking Aturdokht off balance. She stumbled back, her whip slacking. Cryis hooked his blade around the whip, pulling her forward. He twisted the whip around his weapon as he continued to yank her forward. He snatched it free from her hands and, with the butt of his staff, slammed it into her chest. Cryis could see the wind knocked out of her. He pulled back his scythe and flung the whip across the lake. It sank into the water, creating a cloud of steam as it did. Aturdokht grabbed her chest, doubling over.

Now, Cryis heard Emilia's soft voice whisper to him.

Cryis dug his scythe into the ground once more. He extended his hands out on either side. The power field around him did the same, the tendrils of magic and lightning becoming one, following his movements. Cryis pushed the rest of his magic into his scythe. Energy and magic cracked at the tips of his fingertips, shooting into the weapon's blade until *Jevit* glowed brightly. Cryis could feel his immortality slipping away as the Elemental's magic completely left his body, leaving him vulnerable.

"ENOUGH!" Aturdokht roared, standing straighter.

Beneath her, the grass became scorched as fire began to spread from underneath her feet, growing from the ground, the trees, and the lake shooting into the air. Cryis could hardly breathe as the smoke from her flames filled his lungs. Aturdokht rose into the air, taking the fire around them with her. She lifted her hands, mimicking the movements of a huge wave.

The flames towered above Cryis, casting a dark shadow over his body. He gasped, taking in what little breath he could from the pungent air the fire created. He grabbed hold of his scythe. A small field extended around his body, the magic anchoring him in place. He only had one shot at this.

Behind the wave, Aturdokht wickedly grinned, her hands still high in the air. A dark green line of magic trickled from her body. The Life Elemental revealed itself again.

"Burn." She let her hands fall, and the wave of fire came crashing down, collapsing in on itself.

Cryis lowered his stance, spread his legs, and planted his feet. *Jevit* cut right through the fire, parting around him and creating a narrow path. Cryis lifted his scythe and charged at Aturdokht. Fire singed the hairs on his arm as he ran towards her.

Cryis swung his scythe, using the force to shoot him into the air. The wings from before returned, helping lift him higher. In one swift arc, his scythe's curved blade wrapped around her body, cutting through her in a diagonal arc. The blade passed through her skin, leaving her body unharmed and reaching deep into her soul as the full force of his Elemental's magic sped into her.

Aturdokht screamed in agony, but her screams changed to despicable laughter. She knew something he didn't. Out of the corner of his eyes, the Life Elemental's magic struck Cryis in the chest just as a dark mass was pulled free from Jay's body. Cryis screamed, feeling as if his body was burning up from the inside. He hadn't seen where the attack had come from.

Above him, Aturdokht's dark soul became trapped in a cage created by the Soul Elemental. The cage sparked with lightning as Aturdokht's soul struggled to break free. Within her soul, Cryis could see two orbs, one green and the other red. For a moment, the three Elementals were reunited.

Cryis could feel his body growing weaker. His scythe fell from his hands, crashing to the ground. He grabbed Jay's body from the air. Her body went slack against his chest. His vision began to darken as he could no longer hold himself up in the air. He began to fall, the wings of a butterfly folding over him to cushion his landing.

Above them, the Life Elemental grew brighter as the pain continued to elevate inside Cryis. It shot free from the cage and vanished into thin air. Its magic was enough to overtake the Soul Elemental. Aturdokht's soul erupted in flames before vanishing, leaving behind the faint sound of laughter that lingered in the air at her escape. The Heart Elemental departed alongside her, leaving the Soul Elemental alone.

The wings surrounding Cryis and Jay disappeared, returning to the Soul Elemental. Cryis felt his body shrivel as his soul could no longer take the magic that coursed through his body without the protection of the Elemental. Dark clouds filled his irises. The Soul Elemental returned to its true form, the ball of light fizzed in the air in a frenzy, sensing that Cryis's body was too weak for it to return to. It began to go haywire, flying around in the air without a sense of direction.

Cryis looked down at his body. A hole had formed in his chest from the piece of the Life Elemental's magic that had attacked him, that was destroying his body. Cryis wondered who it ran off to. Whoever it was, he hoped the others would find its new keeper before Aturdokht did. Cryis looked down at his arms wrapped around Jay's body. One of his hands had already begun to disappear, tearing into the wind like paper. Cryis gently patted Jay's cheek.

"Princess," he weakly croaked. He barely had the strength to talk.

Before them, the door from earlier began to form. The Soul Elemental transformed into the form of a small blue butterfly, bursting through the partially created door and disappearing on the other side. Cryis smiled, he could feel himself fading faster as the power completely transferred to its next host.

In his arms, Jay began to stir. Her eyes slowly fluttered open, revealing their natural blue color. She tried to speak, but her words came out in a slur. Cryis watched as her eyes widened with fear upon seeing him.

Cryis smiled sadly, knowing she saw what he felt. His body was slowly being poisoned from the inside out. The Life Elemental's last form—death.

"It's okay," Cryis lied. "It's how it should be." Each word came out harder than the next as his throat burned with pain.

He looked down, seeing his remaining hand dissolving into nothingness. But he wasn't afraid. His affairs were in order, and his purpose was finally fulfilled. He didn't fear death, and just like before, he wouldn't die alone.

Jay struggled to sit up and lift her arms, but her body was still too weak. He smiled down at her. He gestured to the door, "He's waiting for you."

Jay managed to lift her hand, cradling what was left of his body. She grazed his cheek, holding it in her palm. Cryis pressed his face against the warmth of her hand. She let out a loud cry. His lip began to tremble as tears glazed in his eyes.

He'd waited for this moment ever since he'd become an Immortal, but there were people he'd miss. Everyone he'd met up until now and everyone he'd spent his last days with. Arthur's face was the last to flash across Cryis's mind. He wondered what life could have been like if he had met Arthur under different circumstances. Would things have been different?

The tears he'd been holding back finally fell, dissolving into nothing before they could hit the ground. A bright white light began to illuminate the space behind Jay before it became the only thing Cryis could see. Emilia had returned.

It was finally over, Cryis thought. She smiled at Cryis before holding out a hand towards him. Through his tears, Cryis managed to smile. He was finally at peace. Everything would be okay.

Arthur's fuchsia eyes rose from the corner of Cryis's memory. His bright smile and passionate heart as he'd kissed him in the truck... the thought left Cryis with one regret.

Although he could no longer see Jay, he could still feel her. She'd found the strength to cradle what was left of his disappearing body.

"Tell Arthur I love him."

Chapter Thirty-One

Jay stood frozen, the weight of her guilt anchoring her to the spot as the door of light began to form before her. The echo of Aturdokht's laughter still clung to the corners of her mind, a haunting reminder that the battle was not truly over. Cryis had torn her soul free from Aturdokht's grasp, but the separation had left scars—deep, invisible wounds that throbbed with every thought, every breath.

She wanted to scream, to cry out against the unfairness of it all, but the words died in her throat, swallowed by the overwhelming tide of emotions that crashed over her.

Cryis had been her friend, her ally, someone who had believed in her when she barely believed in herself. And now, because of her, he was slipping away. The light that had once been so bright within him was fading, dimming like the last embers of a dying fire. Jay felt that light extinguish something in her as well—a piece of her soul fractured and lost.

But it was more than just the loss of Cryis that weighed on her. It was the shadow of Aturdokht that still lingered, a phantom presence that clung to her mind. Jay could feel it in the corners of her thoughts, a dark echo of the battle that had almost consumed her. Cryis had saved her, had ripped her free, and even though Aturdokht had escaped, using the last of the Life Elemental's magic to retreat to the body she had created for herself, the trauma of that connection still pulsed within Jay, a constant reminder that she had not been entirely in control.

Prior to arriving at the battle, Jay had discovered the addition to the experiments Aturdokht had been conducting. It had been a secret even to her, somehow, Aturdokht had found a way to hide it from Jay, without her realizing. Aturdokht had created a new body for herself in case things didn't go according to plan. Thanks to Cryis, she hadn't. He'd prevented a convergence between the Elementals. But in this moment, Jay didn't feel victorious. Cryis had put his life on the line, and although he'd won, he was now dying, and it was her fault.

Jay barely noticed the reappearance of the door, Cryis had come through, materializing a few feet before her. It wasn't until a stream of light touched the edges of her dress that she finally was able to avert her gaze, for only a moment, from the last bits of Cryis's body.

As the door of light continued to open wider, Jay's breath caught in her throat. She wondered if Dylan would be waiting on the other side of that blinding glow. She closed her eyes for a moment, and there, silhouetted against the brilliance, she imagined him, tense and filled with anger. Though she couldn't see his features clearly yet, she could almost sense the storm brewing in his eyes. The air between them crackled with unspoken tension.

She opened her eyes, letting the imagination of him slip away. If he was waiting for her on the other side of the door's light, she couldn't bring herself to move, torn between running to him or fleeing away. How could she face him, knowing that her actions had led to this moment? That her struggle with Aturdokht had cost Cryis his life? In this moment, she felt truly alone. Jay's heart ached under the weight of that truth, a pain that felt almost too much to bear.

And then, as if her thoughts had conjured it, she felt a presence beside her. *Emilia...*

For a moment, Jay thought she was imagining it—a cruel trick of her mind, born from grief and guilt. But when she turned her head, Emilia was there, kneeling beside Cryis with tears in her eyes and a gentle smile on her face. It was the first time Jay had seen Emilia since she'd been gone, and the sight of her sent a wave of sorrow crashing over her.

Emilia's hand hovered over Cryis's heart, and though Jay could see the pain in her, there was also a deep, abiding peace. Jay couldn't understand it, couldn't reconcile Emilia's calm acceptance with the storm raging inside her chest as the last part of Cryis disappeared.

The laughter in her mind grew louder, mocking her, reminding her that no matter what she did, no matter how much she fought, there would always be a part of her that was not entirely her own. She wanted to fight, to push Aturdokht's presence out of her mind, out of her soul, but she knew it wasn't that simple. This wasn't a battle that could be won with magic or strength—it was a battle within herself, one that she would have to face every day, every moment, until the end.

As the door continued to open, bathing everything in blinding light, Jay knew that this was just the beginning. The real fight was still ahead, and it was a fight she wasn't sure she could win. But for Cryis, for Emilia, for herself, she had to try.

Chapter Thirty-Two

Dylan and the others threw everything they had into opening the door. He pushed against it with Kai and Silo while Ami and Arthur went to the other side and threw books at it. Nothing worked, the door remained shut.

Dylan backed away, breathless.

Why won't it open?

He could feel the panic rising in his heart, and he couldn't shake the feeling that Cryis had walked into a trap.

"Give him back!" Dylan heard Arthur shout, followed by a loud thump against the door.

Dylan peered around the corner to find Arthur pushing the door with all his might from the other side. His face was beginning to turn red.

Silo pushed Dylan aside and pulled Arthur away from the door. He resisted her, elbowing her out of the way. Kai came around from the other side, pulled Arthur's arms behind his back, and yanked him from the door. Both boys toppled back onto each other.

"Let go!" Arthur shouted.

"Enough!" Kai said. "He's gone. We can't do anything for him."

Silo crouched down so that she was level with Arthur. "I don't know why the door only took him, but this library is filled with some of the oldest magic. It knows what it's doing."

Ami wiped away her tears. "Yeah," she sniffled. Arthur's gaze lazily shifted to her. She forced herself to smile, "Plus, he's immortal, he'll be fine." Arthur grimaced, looking away from her. Dylan noticed her hand shook at her side.

"We don't know that," Dylan whispered. He sighed and went back to the door. Dylan glared at the palms of his hands. "I won't sit by and do nothing, not this time," Dylan said louder. He turned to face the door on the other side of Arthur, Kai, and Silo.

"What?" Silo said. She got up and walked to the other side of the door, meeting him there.

Dylan closed his eyes. He concentrated his mind on the Infinity Staff, unlike before, it came easily into focus, rising from the darkness of his mind and into his reach. He grabbed it. His wrist burned as the trident pulled free. Dylan opened his eyes to see the trident glowing.

A bright light came from it, causing Silo to gasp and shield her eyes. Once the light cleared, the Infinity Staff was in Dylan's hand. It felt cold to the touch as the darkness it had been trapped in lingered.

He followed the staff with his gaze, looking up. It was taller than he was. The rod extended above his head as the three prongs of the trident finished their final transformation. The two prongs curled over the red gem in the center, while the third flattened for the orb of magic to sit on.

Dylan blinked, feeling his eyes emitting the same burning sensation his wrist was. He wondered if his eyes were glowing as well. He felt incredibly powerful, but physically, his body felt drained and weak. He was shaking, just holding the staff for this long was proving to be too much for his body to handle. The voices from before became clear, whispering in and out of his ears. Before, they had been in a language he couldn't understand, but now their words rang clearly in union.

Kill.

Power.

Destroy.

Dylan flinched, shaking his head. The voices continued to attack his mind, repeating the same three words over and over again.

"Dylan?" Silo hesitantly approached him. "You did it." She said in awe.

Her voice was enough to pull him free of the voice's sinister tune. Dylan breathlessly looked at her.

"Uh-huh," he nodded, the movement taking everything out of him.

He hadn't planned to use the staff yet, but he was no longer going to allow fate to toy with his friends the way it had. However, he wasn't sure how long he could use its power. Dylan gripped the staff tighter as a trickle of sweat ran down the side of his face.

"Wow," Kai said, coming around the corner.

Kai was followed by both Arthur and Ami. Ami held Arthur's hand, her eyes puffy and swollen from crying.

"How?" Ami asked.

"Everyone stand behind me," Dylan commanded.

Once they were in the clear, he lifted the staff in the air and aimed it at the door. At first, he wasn't sure what to do, but it was like the words came to him as naturally as breathing did.

"*Flatus.*" The staff became warm in his hands.

The red orb at the tip began to glow a dark black before a stream of light shot out from the staff and blasted the door. The pages parted but never fully lost their shape. Dylan widened his legs, holding onto the staff with both hands. The force of the magic manifested and threatened to push him back. The voices returned, growing louder. He blocked them out, focusing on opening the door.

The blast of power from the staff began to narrow, becoming a laser drill. The paper beneath began to shift and turn as the door started to shake under the pressure of magic. Dylan could see a hole beginning to form in the door. A green leaf sifted through the crack. It floated towards him, landing on the ground at his feet.

"He's doing it!" He heard Kai say from behind him.

The hole steadily grew bigger. Dylan grinned, unable to hold back the joy he felt. Soon, they could see a branch followed by another until the whole tree was visible.

A dark cloud began to cover Dylan's mind. He gritted his teeth. His insides felt like they would explode. The staff grew heavy in his hands. He fell to one knee but kept his grip on the staff holding the magic up. Silo gasped, coming to his side. He felt her arm slip around his, and she guided him back to his feet using her body as his support.

"Look!" Ami shouted. She came on the other side of Dylan and pointed past the tree. Cryis's back was to him. He looked to be talking to someone, but all they could see was a faint cloud of light before him.

"Cryis!" Arthur yelled. But he didn't hear him.

Dylan was at his breaking point. The light stopped and rebounded back into the staff, sending both Dylan and Silo to the ground. The staff vanished, disappearing back into Dylan's wrist. Silo wrapped her arms around his chest, pulling him into her lap. Dylan clung to her hand, doing his best to stay conscious.

The hole began to close. Arthur ran toward it, putting his hands through the space and trying to push against the sides, but the pages formed together regardless.

"Dammit." Arthur cursed under his breath. He pounded his fist against the door.

Dylan watched as Arthur's shoulders rose and then fell as he took a deep breath. Arthur slowly turned around. The pain in his expression was unbearable for Dylan to witness.

Dylan gave him a pained expression. "I'm...sorry..." Dylan struggled to say.

Arthur sunk to the ground. Ami came behind him and gently rubbed his back. "He's okay. We saw that much," She said reassuringly.

Dylan tried to catch his breath, relaxing against Silo's chest.

Kai came up to them, sitting on the floor. He patted Dylan on the chest. "Well done, Dylan." He laughed. "You pulled the damn thing out of thin air."

For a moment, Dylan only stared up at Kai, unsure how to react. It was the first time Kai had called him by his name. Then, Dylan began to laugh, a burst of joy erupting from within him. He'd done it. Even though the door hadn't stayed open, he'd finally managed to call the Infinity Staff on his own. But that elation was short-lived as his laughter twisted into a grimace and the weight of his exertion settled in.

"Are you okay?" Silo asked gently, rubbing his arm. "You scared me."

Dylan looked up at her. Her braids were hanging in her face and falling on his shoulders. He reached up, and his hand touched the side of her face. She pressed her cheek into his palm.

"I'm okay," he said, gaining some of his strength back.

Kai looked between the two. "Please stop," he said, gaging.

Silo rolled her eyes and then pulled her arms free, allowing Dylan a chance to sit up. He still felt sick to his stomach.

"Here, let me," Silo said. Her hand was glowing a soft green. She placed her hand on his chest. Instantly, his body cooled, and his heart slowed to its regular beat.

"Thank you."

Dylan stood to his feet. Silo and Kai both followed. Dylan sighed, seeing Arthur still on the ground. He walked over to him and Ami. He gently touched the boy's back. Arthur stiffened and rose to his feet. He locked eyes with Dylan, and Dylan could see the pain in his gaze. He opened his mouth to say something but stopped. Arthur looked away, almost disappointed. He brushed past Dylan and Ami, heading to stand at the back of the circular space they were in. Dylan let him go, unable to find the words to comfort him.

Suddenly, a grinding sound broke the silence, causing Dylan to turn back. He realized he wasn't alone; everyone had frozen, their eyes strained on the door. A flicker of wariness crossed each face, mirroring his own. The door was finally opening—but how?

Out of the corner of his eyes, he saw Kai and Silo brandishing their weapons. Dylan instinctively held his arm out in front of Ami, who had already summoned her mist. A red trail trickled from her hand, lingering at their feet. Every hair on Dylan's body stood on end as the tension in the air grew; the door slowly came to a halt.

The door fully opened, sending a ball of restless magic whirling in their direction. Dylan ducked as the magic came whizzing at him. He looked behind him, everyone except for Arthur had managed to move out of the way.

Suddenly, Arthur's fuchsia eyes began to glow as the magic was absorbed into his body. His orange hair became a snow-kissed white, and his eyes changed to a deep blue.

"Wait, was that the—" Silo began as she looked back at Arthur.

Ami interrupted, finishing her sentence. "The Soul Elemental." She gasped and looked behind her at the door. "No." She sobbed. Her mist disappeared as she sank to the floor.

Dylan looked back at the door just in time to see the rest of Cryis's body dissolve into nothing in the arms of Aturdokht. Cryis was gone.

The world seemed to stop around Dylan. He turned behind him and grabbed the dagger Silo had hooked to her hip. He blindly ran through the door, and as he did, he barely heard Silo's voice calling after him. All he could see was Aturdokht staring straight ahead, frozen in shock, and it infuriated him.

This was his first time seeing her. She looked a lot like Jay, but he knew it wasn't her. Her hair was black at the roots, most of her natural white gone. She wore a red and black dress that cascaded around her like flames. She was a mixture of beauty and desire, just as she had always been. Even with Aturdokht's hold on her, that hadn't changed.

Jay was here. For weeks, he had longed to be reunited with her. He wanted to hold her and tell her how he felt, but Dylan pushed the thought away. This wasn't the Jay he knew.

He tried to call the staff but was too weak to grab onto it. He gripped the dagger; it would have to be enough. He was tired of Aturdokht taking people from him.

First Jay, then the Headmaster, Riley, Lyid, and now—Dylan choked back his tears—*no more.*

Aturdokht hugged herself, crying into her lap, she wasn't even paying attention to him.

How dare you cry.

Dylan's hands balled to fists at his side.

What could she possibly know about loss?

Aturdokht's eyes met Dylan's, a look of daze clouding her expression. She created the perfect opening. Dylan lunged at her, knocking her flat on her back. She didn't struggle beneath him. He slammed her arms above her head, holding them down in the dirt by her wrists. He placed his knee into her thigh so she couldn't escape. The familiarity of the move caused a pang of sadness to swirl inside his chest. He shoved it aside as he raised his dagger into the air. He wanted to see the life leave her eyes.

Dylan felt his breath catch as his gaze locked with hers. Eyes he knew well—eyes he had been longing to gaze into once more. As Dylan stared into her blue eyes, all his anger washed away.

"Jay," He gasped.

She opened her mouth to speak, but no sound came out. She kept nodding and crying. The dagger fell from Dylan's hand, clattering into the scorched dirt. He pulled Jay from the ground and embraced her. He caressed her face, continuing to pull her back and look at her through his tears. Even without words, their feelings were clear. He kissed her, pouring every ounce of longing and need into the moment. She kissed him back, her lips fitting perfectly against his. Dylan hugged her tighter, determined this time not to let her go.

"What the hell are you doing?" Kai shouted, his voice carrying across the distance between them.

Dylan and Jay's lips slowly parted from each other. He leaned his head forward, touching her forehead with his. She smiled at him, but her smile didn't light up her eyes like it normally did.

"Wait, I think…I think that's Jay!" Dylan heard Ami shout behind him.

It took all of Dylan's strength to take his eyes off Jay. He was afraid if he did that, she would vanish before his eyes. Finally, Dylan glanced over his shoulder. Kai had one foot through the door while Ami stood in front of him with her arm stretched out. He noticed the door had begun to shake.

Silo yelled from behind Kai, "The door's closing! Get your ass back here!"

Dylan turned to Jay, "Can you stand?" She nodded. He helped her to her feet. "Hold on to me." She leaned most of her weight against him.

Dylan and Jay half ran, half stumbled back to the door. It was closing fast. Kai and Ami braced against the walls, holding the door open to slow its process. As Dylan and Jay neared, Kai extended his hand. Dylan pulled Jay closer with one arm and stretched the other toward Kai. Their hands clasped. Kai yanked hard, only releasing Dylan once he and Jay were safely through the door.

The door shut, and the pages collapsed, returning to individual pieces of paper strewn across the floor. Warmth enveloped them once they were on the other side of the door. Before either one of them could catch their breath, Ami threw herself into Jay and pulled her into a hug. Dylan stepped out of the way just in time but kept one arm wrapped around Jay's waist.

"It's really you, right?" Ami pleaded. Out of the corner of Dylan's eye, he saw Jay nod into her shoulder.

"She can't talk right now," Dylan said. He wasn't sure why, but he suspected it was a lingering effect of regaining control over her body.

Jay waved her hand through the air where the rest of Ami's arm should be. Ami pulled back, "Oh, this," she awkwardly laughed. Jay looked at her with remorse. "Don't worry about it," Ami said. "It's not your fault."

"How can we be sure it's her?" Kai asked, still holding onto his weapons, ready to attack.

Dylan didn't have the energy to glare at him, although he understood his concern. But Dylan had no doubts that it was her, no matter how much Aturdokht tried, she could never emit the sadness Dylan saw in Jay's eyes.

"It's her. Cryis gave his life to make sure of that," Arthur said, walking up to where Dylan and Jay stood.

Arthur looked so much like Cryis had that Dylan had to do a double-take. Every cut and bruise he had before was healed. His skin was flawless and pale, his hair was as white as snow, and his eyes were a deep electric blue.

Dylan saw Jay's eyes brimming with sadness. Her hand went to her heart and made a fist. She bit the inside of her lip. She stayed like that for a moment before finding it in herself to walk the rest of the way to Arthur. Dylan watched as she half walked, half stumbled to Arthur. He caught her in the end, steadying her.

Jay peered up at Arthur with tears falling from her eyes. She mouthed the words, "I'm sorry." Arthur shook his head; Dylan could tell he was doing his best to smile. Jay started to mouth more words, "Cryis said," she stopped and instead used her hands to explain. She pressed a hand to his heart.

"That idiot," Arthur whispered.

Dylan wondered if they shared the same connection Cryis had with Jay. He knew at one point that Cryis and Jay could communicate telepathically.

Dylan looked to see Arthur's eyes swell with tears. His arms were trembling with sobs. Jay pulled him into a hug. Dylan tore his eyes from them, feeling himself growing sad at the thought of Cryis. Arthur and Cryis shared a connection that had ended in sacrifice. Dylan wondered how many more of his friends would have to die before Aturdokht was finally laid to rest.

Dylan's eyes landed on Silo; she was glaring at him. He walked over to her. He knew what she was thinking before she even said it because he was thinking the same thing. What now? They'd gotten Jay back, but what happens now?

Dylan hoped, with Jay's return, she could implore the council for help. Maybe learning about Aturdokht's experiments would motivate them to act against the law after she returned what the first Ancient took from them. The world couldn't afford another war.

"Did you kill her?" Silo asked, coming up beside Dylan.

He had known the question was coming. She held Dylan's gaze for a moment longer before shifting to look at Jay. Everyone in the room looked at Jay. Suddenly, the air in the room seemed to thicken. Jay shook her head no. A look of defeat reflected in her eyes as she stared at the ground.

"But she was right there!" Kai said, stunned.

Kai swung his axe in frustration, slamming it into the side of the podium. The library's walls shook in anger, sending books flying in the air. Soon after, it calmed once Kai removed his axe.

"You saw exactly what I did. Aturdokht was already gone," Dylan said.

"What's the point of some savior if she doesn't save anything," Silo stated, glaring at Jay.

Jay held her ground, returning Silo's glare. She stepped towards her, but Arthur grabbed Jay's arm, holding her back. Dylan could tell that Arthur was able to read Jay like a book. Even though Arthur had stopped her, Dylan still noticed the familiar irritation flare in her eyes.

"Look," Dylan stepped in between Silo and Jay. "We'll figure it out once we get back to the council." He knew there had to be a reason why Jay and Cryis had failed to stop Aturdokht, but at the moment, he didn't care. He was just glad that Cryis had managed to bring her back to him.

Ami perched up, "The Aris council?"

Kai grunted, "Yeah, they'll want to know she's back." He pointed his axe towards Jay. "And our next move since we blew this one."

"Okay, but how are we getting there?" Ami asked. "That place isn't easily accessible...right?"

Kai smirked, "Sis, would you like to do the honors?"

Silo reached for the pocket dimension crystal she had stored beneath her flap, but she came back empty-handed. She shared a look with Dylan before rolling her head to the side as she let out a defeated sigh. The crystal Eradine had given them had shattered when they'd nearly fell to their deaths.

Kai looked back at her expectant, "That was your cue for the crystal?" He whispered harshly. Ami rolled her eyes, overhearing him.

"What are the chances that you still have some of that portal magic left?"

"It broke," Dylan explained, seeing the confusion on Kai's face. "Back at the Record Hall." Kai's eyes widened in understanding.

"We have a truck." Everyone looked over at Arthur. Dylan didn't hold his gaze for long before he found Jay's. She was still at Arthur's side. She was hugging herself, clearly uncomfortable in the dress she was wearing. Her gaze shifted to his but didn't stay for long before she quickly looked away.

"Great," Kai mused.

Ami led them out of the library, following the path she, Cryis, and Arthur had used to enter. Dylan was surprised to find that it led to a bank; he was even more surprised to see a young African American woman waiting for them on the other side. She was wearing a Chase Bank uniform, with her white hair braided firmly to her scalp in rows of cornrows folded on top of each other. She carried a bag in one hand and a hairnet in the other. She quickly stuffed the hairnet in her pants pocket upon seeing them.

She didn't say much, but Dylan saw sadness in her eyes when her gaze met Arthur's. She placed a hand on his shoulder and offered a small smile. It was at that moment that Dylan recognized the woman as an Immortal. He wondered if she knew Cryis. The thought of his name brought upon a swell of emotions. Dylan quickly blinked the tears in his eyes away as the woman passed by him.

Kai was the last one to follow up the party, after he'd exited the tunnel, the stranger closed the vault, sealing it shut.

Ami led the way to the elevators at the end of the hall, followed by Arthur, then Jay. Silo paused, causing Dylan to do the same, as well as Kai. She turned back to the woman who was still lingering by the vault.

"You don't happen to have a crystal, do you?" she asked.

"No, not on me," the woman said.

Silo's shoulders slumped. "Okay."

She gave Dylan a defeated look before walking out the door after the others. Dylan and Kai exchanged a glance before following her. Once through the door, Dylan heard locks sliding into place, but he didn't bother looking back.

The elevator ride that followed was silent, as was their walk to the bank's front entrance. Dylan noted the emptiness of the bank, and when they reached the main level, he could see darkness outside, illuminated by street lamps.

When they exited the bank, they were met with the deafening chill of winter. Dylan stopped at the top step and stared up at the sky. The clouds were dark and heavy with snow. He let out a slow breath, seeing it materialize in front of him.

Dylan looked ahead, down the steps, to find the others already piled into the truck. Arthur had taken the driver's seat, while Ami took the passenger one. Jay was seated in the back behind Ami. She stared out the opposite window, her elbow propped up, with her hand covering her mouth. When Dylan approached and pulled open the door, Jay didn't even spare a glance his way. He grimaced but said nothing.

Beside him, Kai groaned. He pulled out his axes and tapped the side of the truck with one of its hilts. "I'll ride in the back. Stop anything that tries to pursue us."

Dylan gave him a nod, even though he doubted anything would be coming for them, and watched as Kai hopped over the side and into the truck bed.

Dylan turned to Silo. "After you," she said.

Dylan slid in beside Jay, and Silo followed, closing the door behind her. He glanced over at Jay, but she didn't move.

Just look at me, please.

He kept his gaze strained on her for a moment longer before looking away.

"W-what in the, how do you work this thing?" Silo grumbled beside him.

Both Arthur and Ami turned in their seat to see the problem, and even Jay glanced her way. Dylan looked as well to see Silo yanking on the seatbelt, but it was stuck. He bit his lip to stop the smile from coming; he'd almost forgotten that this might be Silo's first time in a human vehicle.

"Here, let me," Dylan said, reaching over.

His hand brushed over Silo's. When he turned his face toward her, they were only a breath away. She froze. He could tell she was trying her best to stare at anything but him, but it was difficult since he blocked her view of anything else.

Dylan released a slow breath and gently pulled the seatbelt across Silo's chest before clicking it into place. "There," he said, smiling at her. He lingered there for a moment longer before pulling away. Beside him, Jay bristled.

"Thanks." Silo mumbled, her embarrassment only causing Dylan's grin to grow.

The ride back to the council building, or as close as they could get to it, had been mostly somber except for Silo's guiding voice. The others didn't talk much aside from exchanging information about their journeys before reuniting.

Dylan had shared with his friends his discoveries about the council and what the Ancient had stolen from them. It was the first time Jay had looked his way. Her hand had dropped from her mouth, and her gaze went wide with guilt but also surprise. He also shared with her, specifically, how he'd managed to call the Infinity Staff by himself. She looked as if she wanted to say something in response, but no words followed. His disappointment was palpable.

Ami and Arthur took turns telling them about Agent Kanon and the prison he had built for Aris Magicians. As much distaste as Dylan held for the man, he still hoped he was okay after suffering from a soul possession. After what the others told him about Riley, Agent Kanon was lucky to still be alive. Dylan knew their paths would eventually cross again.

While Arthur and Ami continued revealing what Cryis had seen about the experiments Aturdokht had been conducting, they looked to Jay for answers, but she didn't meet their gaze.

Their knowledge of the Elementals was on equal standing, but Dylan couldn't help but look over at Jay and wonder if she knew more about them. He sighed; he couldn't begin to imagine what she had gone through. His hand found its way to her thigh and squeezed. Out of the corner of his eye, he saw her wipe away a fallen tear in a quick haste.

"Lyid died from his injuries," Ami said, answering the question Dylan had just asked about their friend. "Kanon tried everything he could to save him, but his injuries were just too great." She wiped tears away from her own eyes.

Dylan took in a shaking breath. Silence once again claimed the inside of the truck. They were traveling off-road through a forest now. It had changed from an icy barren to a flourishing green the moment they slipped back into a pocket dimension. Everyone was itching to know what Jay had been through, but her voice had yet to return. Even if it had, Dylan wasn't sure if she was ready to talk to anyone, even him.

Silo leaned toward the window before tapping on the glass. "Make a right there and stop on the top of that hill. We'll go the rest of the way on foot."

Dylan gripped the edge of his seat as the truck jerked up over the hill to prevent his butt from lifting in the air. Once up the hill, Arthur parked the truck horizontally so that they had space to get out without risking plummeting downhill. Kai was the first one to get out. Through the window, Dylan watched as he threw his arms in the air and stretched. The rest of them slowly unloaded from the truck.

Dylan looked down the hill and saw the lights illuminating Fairy District come into view. They'd driven through most of the night, but the town below still looked fully alive and busy. From this angle, he could even see the shadow of Nivea towering over the buildings from the market street. Dylan looked over at Arthur, Ami, and Jay, recognizing their familiar looks of astonishment. He'd had the same reaction once before.

"The council building is through there." Kai pointed past Fairy District to where Dylan knew Wizard and Witches City resided. "We'll have to cross through another city before we hit it, so it'll be a hike unless we find another crystal or stumble upon some portal magic." He looked over at the others. "Everyone ready?"

Dylan's heart was suddenly filled with excitement and nervousness at the thought of Jay and her mother reuniting. He hadn't yet had the chance to tell her about it, but he also hadn't wanted to talk about it with an audience. He glanced at Jay with a slight nervousness. She surprised him by meeting his gaze with confusion but also concern. He apologetically smiled.

"Um, no," Ami said, throwing her hand on her hip. "There's no way we can go in dressed like this." She gestured to herself, Jay, and Arthur.

Except for Arthur, whose body had healed, Ami and Jay both had blood and dirt caked in their hair, and Ami's clothes were torn in various places. The dress that had suited Aturdokht clung awkwardly now to Jay's small frame.

"Even you three look bad." Ami said, pointing to the others. Dylan looked at Silo and Kai and noticed the dirt and lingering sand that clung to their clothes.

"She has a point," Dylan said.

Kai groaned. "Fine, we'll make a quick pit stop first." He grumbled, already starting down the hill to Fairy District.

"Guess we're going home," Silo smiled at Dylan as she passed by him following her brother. Dylan chuckled, knowing she'd use this opportunity as another excuse to show the others the rest of the district.

"Save me some cake," Dylan called after her.

Before Jay could pass by Dylan, he grabbed her hand. She looked over at him questionably.

Dylan turned to Arthur and Ami, "Go, we'll catch up in a bit."

The two continued down the hill without saying a word. Ami looked back at the two of them, fighting a smile.

Dylan waited until the others were further down the hill before he gently tugged Jay in the direction of the forest entrance to the right, in the same direction the truck was facing. He wasn't sure exactly where he was leading them, but he just wanted time alone with her. When he glanced back at her, he noticed the familiar glint of mischief in her eyes as they entered the dark canopy of the forest.

Dylan stared up at the sky, catching a glimpse of the moon in between the trees' leaves. He grinned, unable to hide his reaction and reassurance. She was still herself. It reminded him of the many times they used to sneak off together and ditch class. In the past, their spot had been the rooftop.

The thought brought Dylan to nostalgically think about their home. Dylan wondered what would become of the Institute. Once this was all over, would another professor take on the mantle of Headmaster and rebuild it? Would he even want to go back if they did?

Dylan wasn't sure how long they walked before he heard rushing water. He slowed his pace. Jay heard it, too. She came to a stop and let go of Dylan's hand. He looked over at her to find her smiling. She was hopping on one leg, struggling to take off her boots. Dylan arched an eyebrow but started to follow her. Once she had hers off, she ran ahead of him toward the sound.

Dylan quickly removed his shoes, running after her. The grass was extremely soft beneath his feet. With every step, his body felt rejuvenated, as if the grass had healing powers. Moments later, a small creek that led into a pond revealed itself between two hills. Across from the creek at the base of the pond was a stronghold of rocks with a small waterfall trickling between its cracks.

Jay jumped into the water, the ends of her dress becoming soaked. Dylan followed her in. His eyes lit in awe at the small oasis they'd found. The water glistened in the sunlight, creating a sparkling effect across the ripples. The water felt nice against his skin, washing away the dirt.

Dylan looked at the rock structure ahead of them. He grabbed her hand. "Come on."

He led them to the base of the rock and let go of her hand. The top wasn't far, and it didn't take him long to climb it. He looked down at Jay and patted the space beside him. She scrunched up her nose as she stared at him. He noticed the heavy dress she was wearing, now weighed down by water. But it didn't stop her. Jay tore the bottom of the dress, creating a deep slip. She tied the rest of it behind her legs and began to climb.

"Wow," Jay whispered in a hoarse voice as she reached the top. Her voice was finally starting to return.

She swung her dress under her in one swoop, sitting down. She pulled her knees to her chest, overlooking the water.

Dylan closed the space between them by reaching over and grabbing her hand, holding it close to his lap. Jay leaned her head on his shoulder. He leaned over and kissed her temple.

They stared at the water in silence. The peaceful sounds of nature filled his ears. There was so much he wanted to tell her, so much he had left unsaid. But all he could think about at this moment was Jay and how he'd felt once he found out that he'd lost her to Aturdokht. He'd lost a piece of himself, only to get her back and find it again.

Now, his thoughts were entirely consumed by her. He had to tell her how he felt, but the words that left his mouth were the complete opposite. "I fought Phagos," Dylan whispered, "and I lost."

Jay glanced up at him but didn't say anything. She gave his hand a comforting squeeze. Dylan looked down at her. He knew he'd have another chance to fight

Phagos, but first, he had to get stronger so that when the time came, he could finally move on.

"Jay," Dylan began.

He saw a tear fall down her cheek. He let go of her hand and cupped her face in his hands, turning her face to his. His voice became filled with worry.

In the gentlest voice, he asked, "Jay, what's wrong?'

"How do I come back from this?" She whispered.

Dylan wished he had an answer.

"I've done too many horrible things. Riley..." Her voice cracked in anguish as her tears fell harder at the mention of his name. "Cryis..."

Dylan pulled her closer to him as she cried into his chest. Jay had been there watching, unable to do anything like the rest of them. He understood her feelings of powerlessness.

"None of it is your fault," he assured her.

"But it is," Jay softly spoke. "I failed everyone. Not just my friends but the whole world. I let myself become her vessel, and then I was too weak to even fight back."

Dylan pulled her away just enough to look into her eyes.

"Look," Dylan searched for the right words to say, he couldn't begin to imagine how it must have felt for her, "I don't want to pretend to understand what you went through, but no one can blame you for what Aturdokht has done. We all underestimated her, but next time, we'll be together, and we will destroy her."

"No," Jay said, shocking him. "I don't think we should."

Dylan stared at her in disbelief.

Jay wiped her tears. "When our minds were one. I felt her agony, her sadness, and regret. But I also felt something else, a controlling darkness that didn't belong. She's been crying for help this whole time, and no one's realized it."

Dylan pinched the bridge of his nose. "Jay...see reason, that dark presence you felt was just in her nature. She's evil."

Jay shook her head, continuing to stay firm in her stance, "She wasn't always that way." Dylan wasn't sure what she had meant by that. Jay groaned, "But she does need to be stopped."

Dylan nodded, at least they could agree on that. "I'm just happy you're back."

Jay fell forward, resting her head against his chest. He wrapped his arms around her. "As am I."

Dylan could only imagine what Jay had suffered through. He could see the immense amount of guilt she felt weighing in her gaze, and he knew it couldn't be erased by a few simple words. But Dylan had decided that he would stand by her side no matter what she decided to do.

He glanced down at her; Jay's eyes were closed as she rested her head against his chest. Her comment about Aturdokht still lingered in Dylan's mind. How could Jay believe that Aturdokht deserved a second chance?

Dylan gently moved a strand of hair behind her ear. Her eyes fluttered open, but only for a second before she closed them again. Although Dylan partially saw what happened to Jay when Aturdokht took her as a vessel, he knew being bound with another could have a lingering effect. He knew the battle ahead of her wouldn't be easy. But right now, he was thankful to have her back in his arms.

Dylan watched as Jay opened her eyes. He pulled her away so that he now faced her. Dylan took a deep breath; he had finally mustered up the courage to say the words he'd been wanting to tell her. He lifted his hands and placed them on either side of her face. Her brows furrowed as her cheeks were squished between his hands.

Dylan pulled her face closer to his. "Jay." Dylan took a deep breath again. Jay's eyes grew wide as he came closer to her. "I—"

Jay's hands covered his mouth, causing Dylan to stop. She gently lowered his hands down away from her face. She turned away from him, hugging herself tightly.

Jay sighed. "I know what you're going to say," she hesitated, "but I need time." She glanced over at him, tucking her chin into her shoulder.

Dylan smiled sadly to himself, unable to say the three words he had been longing to tell her. But the sadness he felt wasn't for him instead, it was for her. The past couple of weeks had been a nightmare for them both. He nodded his head.

He understood that she needed time to heal, so instead, he pulled her into a tight embrace. She buried her head into his shoulder. Dylan felt her body relax in his arms once more.

He let out a deep breath that he'd been holding since the day he'd left the cabin. He was just glad to have her back.

For now, that was enough.

Epilogue

Jay stared at herself in the mirror of the bathroom in the council's headquarters. Silo had lent her some new clothes, and Ami had helped her with her hair. Jay pulled at the collar of her shirt. It was a jaded blue color and slightly too tight for her. The outfit was uncomfortable but suited her way better than the dresses Aturdokht had paraded in.

Jay barely recognized herself anymore. Although her eyes were back to their normal blue, her hair wasn't. Ami had cut away the remaining pieces of white from her curls. She had said once Jay's hair started to grow, it should grow back to white, but for now, Jay was stuck with black hair. She hated it.

Even being back in control of her own body, she still looked like Aturdokht. On top of it all, Jay could still feel her lingering in the back of her thoughts. It terrified her.

Jay took a deep breath and held out a single hand toward the mirror. She could see the trident on the inside of her wrist glow slightly. She no longer needed harnessing words to call upon her magic. She willed for the mirror to crack, but instead, the bathroom lights flickered as the magic built up in her hand but didn't reveal itself.

After Aturdokht left her body, her powers were taking a lot longer to return. Jay could still feel them, but it was like her magic was trapped deep inside herself, barely out of reach. Jay let her hand fall. She gripped the edge of the porcelain sink before remembering her time under Aturdokht's thumb.

She rubbed at the trident on the inside of her wrist. She couldn't shake the feeling that Aturdokht was a puppet while the strings were being pulled by the dark force she had felt enter her mind after Riley's death, also fighting for control in the back of her mind. Jay could no longer hear Emilia's voice either. She hoped it was just another lingering side effect from being joined with Aturdokht.

An immense amount of regret formed within her, causing bile to rush into her throat as flashbacks of the horrific things she'd done came to mind. Jay rushed to the stall behind her and leaned over the toilet. She sank to the ground, letting everything she had come up. Across the room, she heard the door open.

"Jaynie."

She froze, gripping the two metal bars on the side walls of the stall. Footsteps came further into the restroom. Jay flushed the toilet and left the stall, making her way back to the sink. She glanced at the woman standing at the door. She seemed to be middle-aged, Jay could tell that much by the wrinkles around her eyes. The woman was dressed in a pink gown with a veil hanging from her shoulders. She looked at Jay with a concerned stare. Jay turned on the sink water and flushed out her mouth.

"What is it?" Jay said, speaking coldly to the woman.

Jay glanced at her again, trying to place a name to the face. So many people had already come up to her, knowing who she was, but she knew none of them. Jay noticed the woman had soft, round brown eyes, and her hair was twisted back away from her face. The way the woman looked at her with a nervous worry to her expression, but also a familiarity, scared Jay.

"If you've come to get me," Jay began, "tell the council and the others I'm almost ready. I just need a little more time."

"This couldn't wait," the woman said nervously.

Jay turned off the water and leaned against the sink. The woman continued to stare at her while remaining by the door. Jay stared back. The woman was familiar, and the more Jay looked at her, the more she seemed to resemble someone she once knew. Jay's heart stopped as she came to the shocking truth.

Jay grabbed hold of the sink's ledge, steadying herself. The lights above them flickered. Still, the woman was unable to keep her eyes off Jay.

"Mom," Jay cynically stated.

The woman began to weep as she walked towards Jay, nodding her head. "Yes." She didn't wait for Jay to respond and pulled her into a warm embrace. Jay stood frozen, unable to push her away. "We have so much to talk about."

Jay felt tears rise in her eyes, but instead of tears of joy, they were tears of anger. She'd imagined this moment over and over in her head a thousand times. But she had never expected to find her mother here in Aris Magica. Jay found herself lost in resentment, but she found the strength to fight through it and lift her arms. She wrapped them around her mother.

"Yes, we do."

A Guide to Aris Magica

Name Pronunciation

Ami: *Ah-mee*

Aturdokht: *Ah-tour-duct*

Cryis: *Cry-is*

Emilia: *Ee-mill-yah*

Kasid: *Kai-sid*

Kazimir: *Kah-zee-meer*

Mirama: *Mee-raw-mah*

Nivea: *Nih-vee-uh*

Phagos: *Fae-goes*

Silo: *Sigh-low*

Taybeith: *Tay-bee-ith*

Vastille: *Vah-steal*

Vulteron: *Vull-tear-ron*

Word Terminology

Anim (*Ah-neem*): The Soul Elemental that strengthens with the user's conviction. It's highly protective and connects deeply with the user's soul, often manifesting in times of great need.

Aris Magica: The world of magic hidden parallel to the human world.

Aris Magica Council: The governing power in Aris Magica is composed of three women acting as one. This council is one of the most closely guarded secrets of Aris Magica.

Black Gates: Doors hidden deep within the realm of Aris Magica, sealed to keep the darkness of the world from escaping.

***Chi* (*Chee*):** The Energy Elemental, the most powerful of the Elementals, formed by combining Ignis, Život, and Anim. It represents the ultimate balance and power.

Deumage (*Day-oo-mahj*): A derogatory term used by Aris Magicians to refer to Hybrids or those with lesser or no magic abilities.

Elementals: The oldest and purest form of magic, incredibly difficult to control. There are four known Elementals: Heart, Life, Soul, and Energy. Together, they form the ultimate power.

Ignis: The Heart Elemental, which enhances all forms of magic. It represents fire and passion.

Infinity Staff: A powerful magical staff that requires immense conviction to wield. Its full power can only be harnessed by the Ancient.

Magicians: The racial name for those who belong to Aris Magica.

New Magic: Magic that is controlled, created through spells or nature, and comes without a cost.

Old Magic: Unpredictable magic that demands a steep price: if drawn from a souled source, a piece of that soul is used; if not, the user must sacrifice part of their soul.

Omnes (*Ohm-nes*): A magical guide that helps users navigate the Hidden Library. Its magic operates based on the user's thoughts.

Pocket Dimension Crystals: Small, transportable versions of a pocket dimension that originate from a pocket dimension's true form. These can only be obtained from the Aris Magica Council.

Pocket Dimensions: A type of magic used to make it possible for two places to exist in the same time frame without disturbing the other.

Portal Magic: A transportable form of pocket dimension magic, often unstable and resembling sand. The user must build the door they seek to enter.

Serum: A drug that can permanently strip the powers from a Pure breed Aris Magician.

Soul World: The essence of a person's soul. Beings can visit their soul world through dreams, although humans may not remember it for long after waking up.

The Institute: The Institute for Aris Magicians and the Gifted, once a haven for Magicians practicing magic, was destroyed by Aturdokht and her army of Demons.

The Symbol of Eternity: An S with a diagonal slash through it.

Život (*Zhee-voht*): The Life Elemental, representing the three cycles of creation, death, and rebirth. It can only be used three times by its wielder, once for each cycle.

Harnessing Words / Spells

Words that are used to anchor powerful magic.

Flatus: Creates a beam of magic that is used to blast objects or people.

Anima ligature: A spell used to bind a spirit.

Ex vita revirescit, potestate iuro uti fide. Teipsum revela: A spell used to reveal what is hidden.

Vitrum pulvis: A spell used to turn something into dust made of glass.

Thank you for reading

I hope you enjoyed the book. Please leave a review wherever you purchased the book and check out my website: www.autumn-green.com. Until next time!

Acknowledgements

I'd like to first thank God for giving me the dream that inspired the start of this entire series. Without Him, I don't think this series would have ever come to fruition. This story has held a special place in my heart for many years. I'd like to take the time to give a special thanks to my loving partner, Noah Falcón, who has always kept encouraging me to continue pursuing the end of this novel, even when I didn't have the heart to do so. Without you, my love, a lot of this would not have happened the way it did. You have been one of my biggest fans, thank you for always offering to help me in any way to continue making my dream a reality. My mom and dad have always said it takes a village. You always know exactly what to say for me to get the job done. Thank you, Stacie Green, Verdis Green, Alexandra Green, and Aliyah Green, for being the first ones to believe in me. I'd like to thank Jill and Andy Falcón for their unwavering support and express my gratitude to Andy for his enthusiasm in reading and editing my manuscript. I'd like to give a special thanks to my nana, Mary Allen, my grandma, Romaine Green, my auntie, Chantal, my aunt Phyllis, who always sends me sweet cards that encourage my writing, my uncle Dominic, my extended family, my English and Animation Professors at Drury University who have helped me along the way, and finally my church family, coworkers, and friends who have given me advice and continuously supported my journey. Thank you to my dogs, Jack and Diamond, for all the cuddles you gave me while writing this story. Thank you, Johnny Brown, for helping me with workshopping titles by always letting me bounce ideas off you and not being afraid to tell me, "Yeah, that's not it." Thank you so much, Micayla King, who has let me talk her ears off about story ideas and who gave me the ending of my previous book that led to the outcome of this novel. Thank you, Samantha Gallasch, for providing the developmental edit, your feedback was a tremendous help. Thank you, Claire Plaster, my unofficial agent and editor, who has helped me tremendously get to where I am today. Thank you to the greatest friends a girl could have, Dianel Paran and Megan Makabali even though we live so far apart, you guys always support my clownery and let me truly be myself; your uplifting words and laughter have carried me through this journey. Thank you, Louis Bailon, for always making me laugh. Thank you so much to Britt and Sarah at Spoonbridge Press for guiding me through the publishing process and making this journey so much fun to be on. Lastly, thank you to the readers. You are the reason why I write. I hope everyone found something they've loved throughout this story, and I can't wait to share more with you soon.

About the Author

Autumn Green is the author of *The Keepers of Aris* and *Elemental Convergence*. After graduating from Drury University with a degree in animation and writing, Autumn has spent the last few years writing YA novels. In her writings, Autumn enjoys crafting characters with a tangible spark and designing an escape for readers. Autumn lives in Kansas City, Missouri, and spends her summers exploring the world with her family and friends.

Follow her online at www.autumn-green.com.

www.ingramcontent.com/pod-product-compliance
Lightning Source LLC
Chambersburg PA
CBHW071357300726
48976CB00006B/1910